SUN TOUCHED

DIAMARA
BOOK I

ISBN-13: 978-0-473-33352-2

DEDICATION

This one is for Lauren and Natalie, who gave me the idea for
this novel through a combination of sleep deprivation and
crazy pregnancy dreams.
It's also for Ivy, who may not have kept me up at night but
always has something creative to add to life.

Thanks, little ones, for always inspiring me.

ACKNOWLEDGMENTS

This book has been a very long time in the making, so it's with great pleasure that I'm releasing it into the world. Special thanks to all my writer friends (and the few non writer friends) who read the book before it was published, for helping me knock it into shape and do the story justice. It's a blessing to know that Madea has some fans already.

As always, massive thanks to my designer, Kate from Dwell Design & Press, and to my editor, Meryl Stenhouse—you both help my work shine.

CHAPTER ONE

Madea passed the case containing the jinweed injection from one hand to the other while the technician finished setting up the Hollowing machine. Nerves swam in her belly, the same as they always did, but this seemed worse somehow. The shape of this girl's face, the shimmer in her eyes—deep blue, like Madea's—the size, the shape, the age of her. Well, it wasn't a stretch to imagine herself strapped to the chair, waiting to be stripped bare of her personality, emptied of her memories. Hollowed.

The muted white walls trapped the sound inside the building, while the skylight lit the space with filtered orange sunbeams. Madea stood with Sullivan, her boss, in the waiting area off the concrete platform the chair was mounted on, and despite the heat of the day she shivered as the girl muttered and writhed against her restraints.

"What is she saying?" Madea whispered into Sullivan's ear.

"Who knows?" Sullivan shook his head. "It doesn't matter. Better we don't know." His face was blank, this being just another Hollowing for him. He'd begun to bring her along, let her give the injections, which made her hope he was finally beginning to trust her, to allow her to do the more important work he normally kept to himself.

The technician nodded to her, so she left Sullivan's side and stopped before the girl in the chair. "What's your name?"

"Janae," the girl whispered, her voice rough and low. "Help me." Her lips were cracked, her breath bitter.

Madea shook her head. "I'm sorry. I'm just here to administer the injection. It will help."

"I have a son. Jaxon, in Dome Four. Help him, if you won't help me." The girl's voice dug into Madea's head and her hand went to her stomach, the mention of a child worming under her skin.

Madea paused, then took a breath, steeling herself. "I can't. After I give you this, you won't feel anything, okay?"

Janae nodded, though tears slipped from her eyes as the technician placed the gag over her mouth. Madea resisted the urge to reach out, to drag the cloth away and let the girl speak. Those eyes, they begged her to do more. Instead, she slipped the needle into Janae's arm and injected the local anaesthetic. Then she put the needle back into the case and put her hand into Janae's, interlocking their fingers. The other girl squeezed back and the hard lines on her face relaxed a little, even as the technician pulled the machine over her head and placed the cables.

"Come, Madea. We're done here," Sullivan called. He was already part way out the door, his fingers tapping against his thigh in agitation, his handsome face marred by a frown.

"I'll catch up," she said, keeping her eyes from his. She couldn't leave this girl. She reminded Madea too much of herself.

"We've done our duty," he insisted. "Come." His command was blunt. He was used to being obeyed, by her at least.

"I'll catch up," she repeated, an edge of steel to her tone. She wouldn't leave, no matter what the cost might be.

"She won't remember, Madea." His tone softened slightly. "It doesn't matter whether you're here or not."

"It matters to me. I'll work late tonight, if that makes a difference." Madea faced Janae again, giving her a small smile.

Behind her Sullivan muttered as the door swung shut and the latch clicked.

The technician moved soundlessly. Two Enforcers guarded the door in their distinctive black and red uniforms, and another stood behind Janae's chair. The girl had no one who cared enough to be there for her last lucid moments. Or perhaps she'd killed them all. Madea should have asked before she chose to stay. But would it have made a difference? She squeezed Janae's hand harder, pushing away those niggling thoughts.

"Where will she go, afterwards?" The question surged out her lips. She'd never needed to know the specifics before— knowing that the Hollowed would still be useful citizens had been enough—but this girl made her want to know. It seemed bad enough that the manual labourers on the planet had a higher chance of being exposed to the harmful rays of the sun on Diamara, and thus a higher chance of being Sun-Touched, but to have their family, their friends caused such grief through Hollowings? It wasn't right, or fair.

"She'll be sent to one of the food farms. The good thing about the Hollowed is that they can't get Sun-Touched again. Eases the workload of everyone else, you know, having them out there for longer."

Madea wanted to ask about Janae's son. If Janae was asking a stranger to help the boy, there must be no one to care for him. She tried to imagine what his life would be like; with his mother dead, he'd be tainted by her affliction in the minds of others, if not in reality.

"Are you sure you want to stay?" The technician paused, waiting until she looked him in the eyes.

"Yes," Madea said firmly, giving a sharp nod. Janae's hand had become heavy in her grasp. The girl's eyes were white, her head lolling against the high back of the chair.

"Alright. She's ready. You need to step back, we don't know whether any of the process transfers through contact."

"No one's ever tried?"

"And I'm not going to start now." The technician shook his head. "Step back, please."

"I'm sorry," Madea whispered to Janae. Her eyes were closed and her body relaxed; the jinweed had done its work. The girl didn't seem to notice when Madea released her fingers.

Madea took a deep breath and pushed her shoulders back. She didn't want to show the technician any sign of weakness, despite her unease. She shouldn't have stayed, she should have left with Sullivan, the same as always. And yet here she was, watching a woman much like herself be Hollowed.

The machine clicked a few times and then a buzz filled the room. Madea stepped back a little further, crossing her arms over her chest when she was unable to find something to occupy her hands. A pulse of energy blasted through the room and Janae's body jerked, despite the restraints around her. White hands flailed in the air before dangling limply beside her body.

Madea couldn't turn away. She could feel the energy washing through the girl, could see the whites of her eyes as her lids flew open and they rolled back in her head. They were as full as the moon, as white, as luminescent, and Madea knew she would never forget the sight of them. She closed her own eyes in response, wishing that she was somewhere else. Safe in her apartment. At work. Anywhere that wasn't here.

Janae gasped. Madea's eyes shot open and she stared at Janae. The girl sucked air into her lungs and then let out the most awful, soul-crushing scream. Madea's eardrums vibrated as her hands flew to cover her ears. The gag did nothing to dampen the noise, her fingers were useless too, pressed as hard as they could be against her skull.

Madea fled. Her sweat-damp fingers slipped on the door handle, but she eventually managed to open it and force herself through, dragging it closed behind her. A sob tore free and she slumped against the wall of the building, pulling her knees to her chest and burying her face.

She could still hear the scream, it was echoing in her brain, bouncing off the soft edges of everything she thought she knew. That girl might not remember what was done to her, but Madea would. How could the technician do that? How could their government maintain that this was a fitting treatment? Surely there was something less painful, less intrusive and destructive?

As tears continued to flow down her cheeks, she wished that it would rain, would wash away her tears. But of course, here in the domes, it never rained, and the only wind was generated by the air pumps. She pushed herself up from the ground and headed home, desperate to wash today's events from her body, even if she couldn't eliminate them from her mind.

Perhaps that was something good about Hollowing. She wished she could forget.

CHAPTER TWO

Madea stood, dripping, in her bedroom with the door closed. She could still hear her father's muffled prattling. He shouldn't even be here—she had moved out years ago—and yet there he was, listing a million reasons why she should attend his latest function in just a few hours. She didn't have a thing to wear, let alone the desire to go. Janae's tortured face was still clearly visible in her mind, the scream of agony rattled in her ears. It just wasn't a good time.

"I don't want to hear your reasons. Go away."

"I've got a dress, and shoes. Rickard will be there, and he's promised to help keep away any men you're not interested in."

Madea felt her heart beat faster, not at the mention of Rickard, but at the realization that once again, this whole upcoming debacle flowed from her father's desire to see her married off to someone of influence. Someone like him. Someone who held important connections for him.

She pulled the door open, clutching her towel closed with one hand. "I'm not getting married. I'm not going to your function, and I am not going to date a single one of the men you deem acceptable."

"Madea Linae." The use of her full name took her straight back to childhood and the many dressing-downs her father had given her. Some things never changed. "You have a duty to your family, and you almost never socialize. Now get dressed. I put your things in the wardrobe. We've got people to wine and dine, and you know how much better it looks when my children are there for events."

Madea ground her teeth together and resisted the urge to slam the door in his face, like she'd done so many times over the years. Instead she set her shoulders and took a deep breath. "I'm not coming." She swung the door closed, gently.

"Your sister is announcing her engagement," her father said.

The words made her freeze. Sarai getting married? Already? It had been months since Madea had seen her baby sister in person, and their phone conversations were always short and to the point. But surely this was one of those things you told your sister.

"Why didn't you say that to begin with?" she asked, resting her head on the door. A blend of emotions swam in her belly, but the desire to cry overwhelmed them all. Why couldn't any of this be easy? Their family was so dysfunctional, had been for years.

"I don't know," her father admitted. "Perhaps I wanted to see if just once you'd come because I asked you." He paused for a moment and took a deep breath. "I'll see you at home then?"

"Okay." She leaned against the door, listening to his steps shuffling down the hallway and out of the house. After the front door clicked shut she went to the wardrobe to see what he'd bought for her this time. He had good taste, if you liked to be fashionable. Madea preferred comfort over style though, and his choices were never comfortable.

She pulled the rack out and frowned. This wasn't the current style at all. It hit her then where she'd seen this dress before; a photo of her mother, from back on Earth, before they had left for Diamara. It was made of silk, or something, a royal blue in a Grecian style, drawn in beneath the breast and pooling to the floor in ripples.

7

It was stunning, possibly the most beautiful thing she had ever worn. She paused for a moment, trying to fathom what subtle message her father could be sending with this choice of dress—if only she knew the occasion her mother had been wearing it in the photo—and then pulled it over her head. The dress fit perfectly, snugging against her body in all the right places, hiding the slight roundness of her tummy.

She swung the wardrobe door shut and looked in the mirror. Madea had never realized how much she looked like her mother. But then, her mother had been dead for years now, so it wasn't as though it was an easy comparison to make. Maybe now her father was finally coming to terms with her death. Why else would he gift this to her?

The shoes her father had left were in a more modern style, though still practical, like everything on this planet. Madea slipped her feet into them and rummaged through her jewellery box, trying to find something to match the dress. She settled on a simple black cord with a silver drop pendant that sat above the swell of her breasts.

She looked like such a girl. Rickard would give her grief for it all night, but she at least she would get to laugh at him, busy fending off her suitors.

They had known each other since childhood, and were among the youngest Earth-born currently living on Diamara. Between them they had hoarded all their memories of that distant, blue planet, speaking only in whispers as if sharing those moments with others would weaken them.

Now that she thought about it, it'd been months since she'd really spent time with Rickard, either. As much as it pained her to admit it, her father had been right when he'd said she had no life. What he hadn't understood was that the man who held her interest was her boss. For all of his brusque nature and huffy moods, Sullivan was an incredible man. His obsession with making Diamara a better place by experimenting with their local plants to improve medicine and health had drawn her in and fuelled her crush.

Not that he was really that interested. The few times she'd convinced him to sleep with her were pure luck. He was taking advantage of her desire, and for right now, she didn't mind—even a smidgen of his intensity was enough.

And maybe soon he'd give her more attention. Her hands moved to her belly, which she was sure was bigger than it had been this morning, though knew it was only be her imagination. It was probably too early to test, but she was fairly convinced she was carrying Sullivan's child. She hadn't bled in months now. It hadn't been in her plan, but maybe...

So tonight, she would reject the advances of all the handsome men at her father's gathering, avoid alcohol, be grateful for the opportunity to catch up with her childhood friend, and most importantly celebrate her sister's engagement.

It was settled.

Tomorrow she'd be brave enough to take a pregnancy test.

The room was filled with the noise of important people—Madea could tell they were important by the airs in their voices, and the way their hands drifted in space as they gave examples of the progress they were making in their areas of expertise. Even the plushness of her father's décor couldn't absorb the pompous buzz.

Madea had to restrain herself from rolling her eyes every time someone attempted to engage her in conversation, and the distance between the entrance and where she could see Sarai and Rickard standing across the room was mired with pitfalls, the largest of which was turning towards her now, the young woman tucked against his side grinning insipidly. How had they managed to colonize new planets, and yet still have room for vapid women? Madea would never know.

"Father," she said curtly.

"So pleased you could make it, Madea." His eyes twinkled as he smiled. He stroked the hand of the woman next to him. "Have you met Gwen?"

"No, I don't think I've had the pleasure." Madea plastered on her fake smile and shook Gwen's hand briefly, unable to ignore the woman's smooth skin next to the more worn lines of her own. "You have so many...friends. It's hard to keep track."

Gwen's eyes flashed wider and her grip on Madea's fathers arm tightened.

"You should go and see your sister. She's been waiting for you." Her father's voice was terse and Madea's smile slipped from fake into genuine.

"I was just heading that way." And she was off, keeping her eye on her destination, ignoring everyone in the way, and snatching a glass of juice from one of the circulating waiters before arriving.

"Hello, strangers." She smiled and gave them each a lingering hug. "It's been too long. Forgive me?"

"I do," Sarai said, her voice soft, her smile coy. "You've been working too hard and having no fun at all."

"You sound like Dad, Sarai." Madea rolled her eyes. "What about you?" she asked Rickard. She felt a warmth in her belly that wasn't tied to the thing she was sure she was growing there. He was still a handsome man. She'd always thought that maybe, when they were both ready, they'd settle down together. But before now he'd never managed to stick with one girl for long, and she didn't want to be one of a string of lovers.

"I've been well, thanks. And," he said in a serious tone, though his lips curled up in a smile, "we've devised a way to prevent so long from passing between visits, haven't we Sarai?" He slipped a hand into Sarai's and the two of them smiled at each other.

Madea couldn't breathe. Her muscles went stiff and her brain struggled to process the information quite clearly displayed. "You two? You got engaged?" she managed to squeak out.

"Don't look so surprised!" Sarai laughed. "I'm just pleased I got in before you did." Her sister gave her an over-the-top wink.

"I just...I mean...I guess I never expected it. When did this happen?" Madea asked, trying to sound happy for them.

"While you had your nose buried in the workings of the lab." Rickard smiled. "You didn't expect us to put our lives on hold until you decided we were worthy of your attention, did you?" He quirked an eyebrow.

"Well, no. I guess I didn't realize just how much might change while I was busy." She took a long sip of her juice, and then another, wishing it was alcoholic, or at least able to ease her suddenly dry throat.

Madea couldn't bring herself to be angry—it's not like she'd shared her private thoughts with either of them—but that didn't stop the ache she felt. She took another sip of her drink and forced a smile. "It's quite a surprise. How amazing."

They were both looking at her intently, unconvinced by her act. Who was she kidding? She'd never been great at lying. Why start now?

"I'm sorry, I just never expected it. I mean, I had never imagined the two of you...I'm struggling to get my head around...none of my words are coming out right. I'm sorry." Madea shook her head, pushing back through the crowd before either of them could see the tears welling in her eyes.

CHAPTER THREE

Rickard found her first.

She had known he would look for her there, on the terrace of her old bedroom. They'd spent many hours dangling their legs over the edge, talking about what life might have been like for their families if they had stayed on Earth and what their futures might hold here on Diamara.

"We've got ten minutes, and then your sister's coming to talk to you," he said as he sat down, his leg brushing against hers. He put an arm around her and she leaned her head against his shoulder.

"She won't get mad if she sees us like this?" Madea sniffed back tears.

"She's your sister, and I'm your friend. We love you."

Those words set her off again, she let the tears stream down her face while Rickard pulled her closer. He smelled so good, so manly.

"I just...I..." She swallowed back the words.

"You thought that maybe it would be us one day. I know. Me too," he admitted. "But we're not kids any more, and one day might never come. While you were off studying, and working and doing all the important things you do, we were left here, missing you. She's pretty amazing, your sister. I'd do anything for her." He paused. "Do you think you can be happy for us?"

"No. Not tonight. Ask me again tomorrow?" Madea smiled at him. He laughed and she felt a little less sick. "I can't hate you for this. I can't hate her. It's not your fault."

"It's no one's fault. This is a good thing. Wait and see— there's someone else out there for you, someone who fits, who will make you feel the way Sarai makes me feel."

"Do you really mean that?" She knew how clichéd that was, how needy and pathetic she sounded, but she couldn't help it. It had been so long since anyone had reassured her about anything.

"Of course. Any man would be lucky to have you, you just have to stop working so hard. You're not going to meet someone when you spend all your time at the lab."

Madea bit her lip, feeling another bout of tears approach. If only he knew—anyone knew—about Sullivan.

"Madea?" Rickard nudged her. "What's wrong?"

She closed her eyes and kept biting her lip, willing his question to disappear.

"You know I'm not going away. You either tell me now, or you tell your sister and she'll tell me later. It's your call."

Madea dwelled on that for a moment. Then, seeing as they would both know eventually she buried her head in his chest. "I think I might be pregnant. My boss..."

"You what?" The surprise in Rickard's voice was priceless. "Sullivan? I thought he was as celibate as they came. How did you tempt him?"

Madea punched Rickard's arm. "Don't you tell me I'm at fault for this."

"Ow! No, I meant that I thought he was immune to the charms of the opposite sex. Though, I guess if anyone could persuade a man it would be you." He laughed and she punched him again.

"Stop that. None of this is funny! What if I am—" She placed a hand on her belly and cringed.

"Well, you don't know that you are." Rickard shrugged.

"Take a test? Maybe you should talk to your sister about this one..."

"Men, so useless."

"Hey, it wasn't me! Does he know?"

"I don't even know for sure, why would he?" She shook her head. "You are so frustrating. We'd never have made it as husband and wife, Sarai can have you."

"So gracious of you," Sarai said as she stepped through the door and onto the terrace. The humour in her voice was undeniable. Sarai sat down beside Rickard, their hands intertwining easily, each surface of their body drawn to the other like a magnet. The perfect reminder of what she didn't have with Sullivan.

Madea sighed.

"Are you going to tell me what's up? Or will I have to drag it out of Rickard later?"

"She thinks she's pregnant with Sullivan's baby," Rickard whispered loudly. "Don't tell your father."

"That's really going to put a dent in his marriage plans for you," Sarai quipped.

"You two are made for each other," Madea grumbled. "I shouldn't have said anything." She pushed herself up and away from them, but Rickard caught hold of her hand.

"Take the test, then call us, okay? We'll come and have dinner with you tomorrow night—if you can drag yourself away from work for that long."

"Work is the last place I want to be right now." Madea pressed the palms of her hands into her eyes, wishing that some of the tension in her head would disappear. "I'll see you tomorrow night, and if you breathe so much as a word of this to anyone..."

"Like we would." Sarai placed her hands on Madea's shoulders. "You're my big sister, but that doesn't mean I can't help you. You were always there for me, after Mum...let me be here for you. Please? A baby is a wonderful thing. Every baby on Diamara."

Madea pulled her into an embrace, though it wasn't as comforting as it should have been. Logically she knew that the colony needed children to thrive, but she'd always thought her value was in the work she did, not in bearing babies. "Thank you," she whispered.

"I would do anything for you. Anything. Now sneak out before Dad starts parading men in front of you. You don't need that tonight." Sarai kissed her on the cheek then gently pushed her towards the steps. "Love you."

"Love you, too. See you tomorrow." Madea slipped her shoes off and headed down the steps and into the shadow of the house, hoping no one would notice that she was missing.

Halfway home, Madea changed her mind and headed for the lab, knowing that Sullivan would be there. He almost never bothered going home, the fold out bed in his office useful for naps as well as other things.

She didn't want to face her own empty rooms, the cold sheets of her bed. She couldn't think of anything worse right now. Well, one thing—rejection—but that was worth risking on the chance that Sullivan would let her in, wrap his arms around her and obliterate the night's losses.

As she drew closer to the lab she felt a pang of grief. It wasn't often that she remembered life on Earth, but living in a domed city where the air was always the same temperature and there was never any wind or rain, it sometimes felt stagnant, lifeless. During the night the vents would open and fresh air would be pushed through, and occasionally Madea would stay up for that moment, relishing in the cool, crisp air as it invaded the domes.

Right now she could have done with a gust of wind to dry her tears, or a shower of rain to refresh her mind. She'd have to face Sullivan like this. Madea smoothed her dress out, only then remembering that she was wearing the one her father had gifted her. Sullivan wouldn't refuse her when she looked like this.

She pressed her palm to the sensor at the door and it slid

open for her. The lab was cool and the combined fragrances of the chemical compounds and organics they kept comforted her with their familiarity.

"Sully?" she called. She couldn't hear him moving around, but that didn't mean he wasn't here.

"Maddy." The warmth in his voice surprised her, but as he popped his head around the office door she could see that his cheeks were flushed with the tell-tale signs of his drug use. "Didn't expect to see you back tonight."

He had the decency to look apologetic, but Madea couldn't hold it against him. He worked hard, and sometimes he needed something to help him stop. He'd crafted the perfect drug for it too, along with a secondary component to flush it from his system as soon as he needed to be clear-headed. "Do you want some?" He offered her small pink pill, but she refused. She didn't like to lose control, and while the dosage was probably fairly low, it wasn't worth the risk if she were pregnant.

"Do you want some company?" she asked.

His smile spread as he took in her attire. "Like any man would turn you down looking like that." He chuckled. "No luck for Daddy finding you the right man tonight, huh?"

"Not you, too." She rolled her eyes to blink away the tears that threatened to return. "I came here to escape that kind of talk." Madea walked towards him, slipping off her shoes and letting her hair loose to fall down her back. She placed her hands on his chest and felt his muscles through the roughness of his shirt, inhaling the scent of him. He was enough to make her forget, and this might be her last chance to take comfort in Sullivan if they were having a baby. Who knew how he would respond to it.

"Don't worry. I'm probably the man least likely to talk of marriage and all the stuff that goes along with it." He pulled her towards him and Madea did her best to ignore his words, focusing instead on the taste of his skin, salty with sweat from his days work, and the feel of his slightly greasy hair through her fingers.

CHAPTER FOUR

The first thing Madea noticed the next morning was the overwhelming desire to puke. She'd unravelled herself from Sullivan's embrace and left as soon as he was snoring, but hadn't had the energy to shower once she'd got home.

It was part of their unspoken agreement that she never spent the whole night with him, though last night would have been the perfect time to make an exception to the rule. Last chances...she was so sure he would cut her off once she told him about the baby. Anything that took him away from his job was considered a waste of his precious time.

A coppery tang rose in the back of her throat. She sat up and dangled her legs over the edge of the bed, scuffing her feet across the rough rug as she tried to decide whether she was actually going to throw up or not. She grabbed the glass of water beside her bed and finished it off, even though it was lukewarm and stale.

A shower would improve things. Running water always did. It didn't matter that today she intended to head outside the domes where the dust would infiltrate every crease of her body. Right now she needed to feel fresher.

And before the shower...well, she would take that test. She already felt awful, the result wasn't going to make her feel any worse. Madea felt the tell-tale tingle in her nostrils and crinkled her face, squeezing her nose to try and prevent the tears that threatened. Life sucked right now, it did, but things could be worse. She wasn't Janae, whose whole life had been stripped away in a few moments of terror. And she wasn't Janae's son, who was left without a mother, or anyone to really care for him. Where was he now?

Her baby, at least, would have a mother, a family who would care for it, even if the father chose not to be a part of its life. It would have an education, hope, a future lined up for it, serving their colony and making life on the planet better than it was now. A purpose.

Despite these thoughts the tears spilled out. Madea brushed them away and pushed up from the bed. She crossed to the bathroom and opened the cupboard, pulling down a test and driving the needle into her thumb before she had time to stop and think about it.

The sting was bad enough to make her grimace. She put the test on the counter and switched the shower on. She waited for the temperature to be perfect, her eyes on the test strip, and before long the double yellow lines appeared. Her wet hand dropped to her stomach, resting below her belly button.

A baby.

She barely made it to the toilet before last night's dinner reappeared.

A baby.

Her baby. Sullivan's baby. Gorgeous Sullivan, who didn't want a real relationship. Who most certainly didn't want a family. Oh God.

Sarai's words rang in her head. Her father was going to be angry. As much as babies were a welcome thing, those old Earth hangovers were still around and there weren't that many men willing to shack up with a pregnant woman. Not that she wanted a husband. She didn't even know if she wanted a baby. And yet, here she was.

She submitted to the pressure and heat of the shower, letting her tears mingle with the water.

Madea's skin was a vibrant red when she stepped from the shower; thoroughly clean, wrung out, washed free of emotions. She pulled on her clothes, laced her boots, grabbed her pack from the end of the bed and strapped on her timer. She needed to be out, to get away from everything which troubled her inside these glass walls, but she wasn't foolish enough, or depressed enough, to go out without the timer.

Her street was quiet at this hour of the morning, only a few others were making their way to work, and no one would be heading outside the domes yet. Madea didn't mind; she didn't want company right now, although being left alone with her thoughts probably wasn't a good thing either. She paused, looking across her dome, the housing units stacked on each other, only slightly more spacious than those in the poorer sectors; the streets only wide enough for the city transports to pass through. It was all so mundane, but it felt alien to her in that moment. What was she going to do?

Have a baby, that's what. Tell Sullivan and her father so that they could get their respective rants over with. Though she didn't think she could face her father. He was going to give her that disappointed look, the one he'd mastered.

She hated to admit it, but she had never wanted to rebel to this extent. This was possibly the worst thing she could have done. She would be worthless in his eyes now, of no use as a pawn in the game of power that took place behind the scenes. He might be high up in the Council, but that didn't mean there weren't still useful alliances to be gained. And while that should have made her happy—hadn't she always longed to be free of his machinations?—she couldn't find an ounce of glee.

She had never wanted to be the perfect daughter, but at least she'd never done anything obvious to get in the way of his plans. Master politician that he was, no doubt he'd find some way to spin this in his favour. His wonderful daughter was pregnant; not only was she helping the colony with her scientific endeavours, but she was boosting the population as well. Smart women have smart babies. She could hear it now. Her baby would be a pawn, just like Madea was.

Would it be a boy or a girl? Could she wait the months to find out, or would she succumb to the curiosity and take a test in the next few weeks?

Janae had a boy. The woman had called him Jaxon, had begged for Madea's help. But what could she do? She had managed to avoid thinking about him last night, but the confirmation of a child within her womb only added to her guilt. She could go to Dome Four. Just to see him, make sure that he was being looked after, and then she wouldn't feel so bad about what had happened to Janae.

In fact, the fields could wait. Right now, this was more important.

Madea ducked back into her house and shoved some jars of food, some fresh fruit and bread into her bag, hoping that would help.

CHAPTER FIVE

Madea had to nudge the sliding door between Three and Four to make it open. Obviously maintenance didn't come by here often enough. The smell of the working class hit her unsettled stomach hard, sending bile up the back of her throat. Water was a precious resource on Diamara, but here that became more apparent. Fourth was dominated by those who weren't skilled enough to work within the domes. It was really no surprise when one of them got Sun-Touched, but it hadn't been until Madea met Janae that she'd really thought about that. It wasn't fair that they should suffer losses when the richer, more skilled, could go largely un-Touched.

Blinds twitched open as she passed. People in safety overalls to protect them from the sun headed for exits. They looked tired and overworked, despite it being morning, and she felt out of place in her reasonably new clothing.

It had been many months since she had ventured down this way, and it seemed worse to her now than it had back then— but perhaps that was because this time she was actually looking rather than passing through to wherever she'd been going. It wasn't like she thought she was better than anyone else, but everything looked different after meeting Janae.

Lost in thought, she bumped into a man, his skin well

browned from time spent outside the dome and his face lined with age. She couldn't see his eyes, hidden behind the dark glasses worn by workers.

"Sorry," she said, catching his elbow to steady him. "I wasn't looking where I was going."

He laughed for a moment, shaking his head. "I'm blind, lass. But it's nice of you to take the blame."

"I didn't realize..."

He sniffed at her, his mouth hardening. "You're not from this sector, are you? What are you doing here?" There was an accusation in his voice, tempered by curiosity.

"I'm looking for someone. A boy."

"There are a lot of boys down here, and we'd prefer it if you left them alone. Don't you have enough young men calling on you back where you come from?"

"We are all part of the domes—" she began to recite the doctrine taught in school.

"We might be, but you know as well as I do that doesn't always count for much."

Madea took a deep breath, biting back a retort. "This boy, Jaxon. His mother was Janae, she was Sun-Touched." Madea spoke quickly, trying to get the words out before the old man cut her off again.

"Oh. Well, that's a different story entirely. What do you want with him?"

"I was there when she was...when she was Hollowed. I held her hand until they wouldn't let me anymore." Madea swallowed the lump in her throat, trying not to let the vivid memories of that occasion gain a hold in her mind. "She asked me to help him. Jaxon."

"And who says he needs help?"

"He's just a boy. I think her family are dead. No one came." She struggled to get the right words out. "I want to help."

The man sighed and shook his head. "Hate to admit it, but the boy could use a hand. What are you going to do with him?"

"I...I don't know. I hadn't thought about it." Madea frowned. She hadn't thought about anything beyond coming here and seeing that he was okay. "I brought some food, I thought maybe he could use that."

"Food won't do him much good. He needs someone to take care of him and if you've come all this way, you might as well take him home with you. Follow me." The old man shuffled off, his cane clacking in front of him, pausing for a moment. "Are you coming, or what?"

"Okay, but I can't take him, you have to understand." Madea followed, trying her best to be patient as he paused at each corner, listening for who knew what.

Eventually, he led them to a prefab unit with a blue door. The paint was peeling, exposing the metal beneath. "Give me some of that food you brought down."

"You didn't tell me your name," Madea said as she fished into her pack, handing him a loaf of bread and some fruit.

"Better you don't know my name. Don't want you coming back down to find me." He bit into the fruit, smiling as the juice flowed over his chin. "God, this is good. You must be pretty well off." He took another bite before banging on the door with his elbow. "Hurry up. I've got someone you'll want to see."

After a moment, the door rattled and then opened. A small woman peered out, squinting at the light. She was only a decade or so older than Janae, but their noses had the same small bump in them. "What do you want, Dad?"

"Janae sent this lady, she's taking Jaxon."

"Janae didn't tell me she was going to send anyone." The woman shook her head and strands of red hair fell free of its binding. She pushed the door closed, but Madea stepped forward.

"I don't want to take him, I just—I wanted to see how he is."

"No, you're taking him," the old man said firmly. "Go get him." He stared in the approximate direction of the other woman, who scurried off, leaving the door open. "Now put your food inside, for their troubles."

"I'm not going to take the boy. He should be with his

family."

"He doesn't have a family now, does he? And do you really think it's safe for him here? You were one of them that Hollowed her, you can pay the price." His words trailed off to a mumble, though Madea was sure she heard him say she was a fool for coming down here.

Perhaps he was right. Woodenly, she opened her pack and removed the food items, stacking them neatly inside the door. It was the least she could do for these folk, who obviously weren't doing too well, but that didn't mean she would take Jaxon. She had work to do, and enough problems of her own already.

A young boy, no more than six, shuffled towards her. He kept his eyes on the floor, only glancing up quickly as he stopped in front of her. He had the same blue eyes as his mother, the same puff of golden hair, though his was shorter and cleaner than Janae's.

"Are you Jaxon?" Madea asked. She squatted in front him and tilted his chin up with her hand, trying to get a good look at his face.

His eyes slid away from hers, as if by looking at her he would expose himself to more hurt. He nodded.

"She's taking you to a new home. You'll be better off, boy." The old man reached out a hand and fumbled until he found the boys shoulder, which he patted roughly. "Did you get his things?" he asked of the woman, who had returned to the door.

"Not that he has much." The woman handed over a small pack which Jaxon shrugged on.

"He belongs with you lot," the old man said. "You might not see it, but we know. One of your Misters up in the rich domes knocked up our Janae. It was his fault she got Touched. Left us to deal with his bastard. No offence, Jaxon."

The boy sniffed, keeping his eyes on the ground and chewing the side of his mouth.

Madea didn't know what to make of the scene. They seemed intent that she take the child, but what was she going to do with him? She didn't know the first thing about children, and it wasn't like she could pass him off as her own. No, it was too much, too risky. This wasn't the help she was willing to offer.

"I can't take him. I can bring you food. I can help you with credit, but I can't take him with me."

"You don't really have a choice, is how I see it." There was a threat in the old man's voice which confused her. What could one blind old man do?

He coughed and Madea felt a prickle at her neck. She scanned around to see three men step out from the nearest alley, and she could feel the presence of another slip behind her, ready to enforce the old man's word. "So are you going to take the boy, or...?"

"Do you care nothing for him?" Madea asked. She took a few deep breaths, attempting to calm the pounding in her head.

"Like I said, he's one of yours. Better he's with you. At least they won't Hollow you to keep you quiet." He laughed, an unpleasant smile on his face. "Help the lady find her way back where she belongs, boys. Gently, now." He walked away without another word.

Madea wanted to protest, but the man behind her grabbed her arm and twisted her, nodded back down the street to the direction she'd come from. He had his other hand on the hilt of a knife at his waist and Madea's stomach tightened in fear. What length would they go to? What had she walked into?

She swung her pack on, and then slipped a hand into Jaxon's. "Come on, then. I better get you...home."

Her place was only just big enough for herself, and now she had a young boy to look after and a baby on the way. If only someone had invented a time travel machine, she could go back a few months and prevent herself from getting into any of this mess.

Jaxon's small fingers clasped hers the whole way home, as though she could be the anchor he needed in the turbulent sea of his life. It felt strange to walk this way, hands linked, his so much smaller than hers. But maybe she could offer something more than what he had come from. The blind old man had said enough to make her curious, but she had no idea whether he was just spouting conspiracies or whether there was truth to his words. The suggestion that Janae had been Touched because of the circumstances of his birth? That was ridiculous. Wasn't it? Madea couldn't help but wonder who the old man had been referring to when he said that Jaxon's father was one of hers. It wasn't unknown for the classes to mix, but why would it be such a problem that Janae got pregnant and had the child? She was a consenting adult, and Jaxon looked healthy. *All children are a blessing*, she reminded herself.

She thumbed open the door of her unit and let out the breath that she felt like she'd been holding for the entire journey. The men had left them at the entrance to Fourth, but she felt like other eyes had been observing their passage since then.

"Well, this is home." Madea shrugged. "It's not much, but it's all I've got for now." All she'd had since she moved out of home, but she was going to have to ask for an upgrade into a bigger unit soon. Jaxon stared at the floor, still gripping her hand. "Are you hungry?" she asked.

He gave the briefest of nods. She could see the hunger in his eyes—lucky she hadn't taken all of her supplies down to Fourth with her.

"Alright, let's see what I can find then." She pried her fingers free and headed for the kitchen. "You can come with me, if you want. Do you talk at all?"

He nodded slowly, a small smile slipping across his face.

"Come on then, why don't you tell me what you like to eat?"

"Have you got more fruit? Like the one you gave to Grandfather?" The look of hope in his eyes made her stomach cramp. She wouldn't have imagined anyone could look that way over a piece of fruit. Things were obviously worse than she'd realized. There should have been ample food on the plantations, and the council provided the essentials for everyone. Perhaps fruit wasn't on that list anymore. She would have to talk to her father.

"Of course." She beckoned him into the kitchen and helped him onto a stool at the bench before handing him a piece. "So that man was your grandfather?"

The boy nodded, not speaking with his mouth full—someone had taught him manners, at least. Madea pondered the oddness of the situation. A Touched and Hollowed mother, a grandfather willing to farm him off to the first person who came snooping, accusations of a rich father from one of the well-off domes, and pure, unadulterated pleasure over a simple piece of fruit.

"I don't know if you can stay here for long." She regretted the words as soon as they were out. Jaxon stopped eating. His mouth fell open and his eyes welled up. "I mean, it's not a very big unit, and I work a lot. I don't know if it's the best place for you to be."

"I don't have anywhere else to go." Jaxon sniffed.

"What about your father?"

"I'm not meant to talk about him," Jaxon said softly. "I don't know his name."

Madea pushed a hand through her hair and sighed. This wasn't how this was supposed to go down. "Look, I have to go out for a bit. I've got work to do. You need to stay inside, do you understand? Don't answer any calls, don't open the door or even peek out the windows. In fact..." She grabbed a bottle of water from her cooler and some more food from the pantry before scooping Jaxon from the stool and plonking him on the ground. "Follow me."

"Am I coming with you?" he asked.

"No, I can't have anyone else see you. Not until I figure this out. You can stay in my room, it's the safest option." She pushed open the door and placed everything on the bed. "You can have a sleep if you want, or...I don't know. What do you like?"

Jaxon shrugged.

This was not going to be easy.

"You might be a bit bored today, then. I can't really do much about that. I didn't think I'd be coming home with a child." Madea felt a pang of guilt as Jaxon slumped down on the floor by the bed and began to cry. "I'm sorry. I didn't mean it like that. I...well, I don't know what I thought was going to happen. Your mum asked me to help you, and so I came to find you. I do want to help you. I didn't expect that they would give you to me."

"You were with my mum?"

"I was. She was really worried about you," Madea said. She thought back, trying to think of what Janae had said. It wasn't much, but a little embellishment couldn't do any harm right now. "She wanted you to know that she loves you very much. She's sorry she had to go. She didn't mean for it to happen."

"I know. Granddad told me. The bad men made her get Touched so that they could take her away."

"He said that, did he?" Madea rolled her eyes at his grandfather's conspiracy theories. People would tell themselves whatever made life easier. "I'm really sorry to leave you like this, I am, but I've got to get out to the fields and get my work done or I'm going to get in trouble. Do you think you'll be okay here for a bit?"

Jaxon nodded. "I'm used to being quiet. I promise, no one will know I'm here."

Madea smiled at him. "You're a good kid. I'll see you soon, okay?" She looked around the room, wishing she had something, anything, that a child might enjoy playing with. She didn't have a single toy in the house, even though some of her friends had started families. No one visited here. But she was the only one to blame for that.

Jaxon was fiddling with his shoe laces, avoiding eye contact again. What was she going to do with him?

CHAPTER SIX

Madea pressed her thumb to the console and exited the dome, pausing for a moment as the doors slid closed behind her. A shimmery haze hung on the horizon; she could almost feel the heat from here. It wouldn't be long before the sun was at its peak. She shouldn't really be out now, she should have been back at the lab, but there was no way she could have predicted this morning's detour.

Had it been only yesterday that she'd witnessed Janae's Hollowing? It seemed like a lifetime of things had happened since then; things lost, things taken away—things confirmed to be growing, invited or not. She reset her timer for three hours, plenty of time to get out and back without any danger to herself. It wasn't like she could leave Jaxon alone for much longer than that—who knew what trouble the boy might get himself into while she was gone?

She couldn't think of that now though, she had work to do.

She kicked black dust up from the arid ground as she walked, black rocks dotted the roadside, and large trees loomed ahead—the shelterbelt that protected their medicinal crops. She should have taken a transport, but the exercise helped clear her head. It had been too long since she'd stretched her muscles like this.

She pushed through the rickety gate—only there to keep the native rodents out, not for security—and scanned the field. Only one other person was there. He wore simple clothing, like herself, his pack rested on the ground and he was bent low over a bush of jinweed—the same plant she'd come to harvest.

These fields were communal, used to provide supplies to the medical and scientific services. And yet she had never seen this man here before. There was something about him which made her hang back and tend to the capsulim. She pulled some weeds from around the plants before taking some leaves and pressing them into a sealable bag for later. Madea worked her way closer to the jinweed, though it was apparent that the man had no intention of moving on.

He had his hands in the yellow dirt, loosening it and ridding the ground of even the tiniest of weeds. After twenty minutes she crossed to him, unable to put it off any longer. She placed her pack on the ground and knelt next to a plant, carefully stripping off the leaves—only as much as she needed—and placing them in her container.

She couldn't help but flick her eyes in his direction. He was darker than most of the people she knew—perhaps he spent more time outside than others—but he didn't seem Touched.

A shadow moved across the sun and she glanced up to find the man standing above her. He seemed very tall from this angle and well-muscled, his face shadowed so she couldn't make out his expression. He may not have intended to be threatening, but she couldn't help but shudder as a ripple of fear swept through her body.

"I don't normally see others out at this time of day," the man said. "I'm Garrett." He held a hand out. She paused for a moment before taking it and was surprised at the ease with which he pulled her to her feet.

There was a sting in her wrist, so she swept her hands down her pants, trying to shake off the bug that bit her, and brushing the dirt free. "Madea. I haven't seen you here before." His pitch-black hair was cropped close to his skull, and the stubble lining his cheeks and chin only enhanced his good looks. He was rougher, rawer, than the other men she knew.

"I'm a...transfer, I guess you'd say. Used to live in the new set of domes but they needed my skills here. Not sure how long I'll be around." His eyes glinted in the sunlight. There was a sheen to them, a hint of something which Madea found unsettling. "What about you?"

"I work in the labs. We needed to stock up on a few things, so I thought I'd come...and I guess I needed to get outside. Like you said, people don't normally come here at this time of the day." She shrugged and gave him a half smile. "So who are you working for?"

"I'm afraid that's confidential, but I think we might cross paths again, soon enough." He nodded. "You take care, Madea."

"You too." She frowned, watching Garrett as he retrieved his pack and headed away from the field. Madea rolled her shoulders, trying to free herself of the traces of his smile, which lurked in her mind's eye. There was something about him, unsettling, yet appealing, something in the way he had looked at her, his deep blue eyes full of mirth and knowledge. And certainty, something she'd never really felt herself. She and returned to her knees and the jinweed.

A bug crawled over her face and she swatted it off without opening her eyes. A moment later she became aware of the brightness outside her lids and they flew open. The sky looked strange from this angle, with the plants waving above her in a slight breeze. She was lying on the ground, and the vibrant orange sun was much further across the sky than she remembered it being.

She sat up and glanced at her timer but it said she still had an hour before she risked exposure.

That couldn't be right.

Madea glanced around, but the fields were empty. Had anyone come while she'd been asleep? Surely if she'd been seen lying on the ground, someone would have come to help her. She got to her knees and reached for her pack, pulling it on as she rose. Her skin was flushed with the sun's heat, but a chill to balance that warmth took root in her veins.

She had fallen asleep. For some reason her timer had stopped working and hadn't set off an alarm. A chill ran down her spine as she sat, her stomach clenched. Until she got back to the domes, she wouldn't know for certain, but she was sure she'd been exposed. It was only a matter of time before madness set in.

Only a matter of time before she became one of the Sun-Touched.

CHAPTER SEVEN

It wasn't until she pushed through her bedroom door, already half undressed, that she remembered there was someone else in her house. Jaxon looked up at her from the floor. She squealed and tried to get her top back on, then gave up, resorting to covering her chest with it.

"Sorry. I forgot..." She didn't want to say the wrong thing. "I forgot that I'd asked you to stay in my room. I need to have a shower... Are you okay?" She paused, frowning. Jaxon nodded. He must have been so bored. And she still didn't know how long she'd been gone for. "Do you like to draw?" she asked.

He nodded again and she left the room, dragging her top over her head and crossing to her desk. She pulled out her tablet and selected a drawing programme, then went back to the bedroom and handed it to the boy, chastising herself for not thinking of it before. "Here. I won't be long. I need to get clean."

"Thank you," Jaxon said. He chewed on his bottom lip, as if deciding whether to speak again. "What's your name?"

Madea's mouth fell open. She raised a hand to cover it, stunned at her stupidity. "Madea. My name is Madea." She sat down beside him and placed a hand on his. "I'm really sorry. I didn't think to...Well, I think you can see that I'm not very good at this. I'm sorry."

Jaxon grinned and a laugh slipped free. "You're funny."

Madea snorted. "Well, I'm glad you think so!" She found she was laughing too. "Do some drawing. I'll be back in a couple of minutes." She stood again and grabbed a change of clothes from the wardrobe before shutting herself in the bathroom.

As she stripped, she checked her timer again. It still said she had an hour. Still said she was safe. Something had gone wrong, but she had no idea what. It had been serviced recently.

She pulled the useless piece of equipment off and threw it to the ground, stomping it with the heel of her foot. It was pointless—it would take much more force to damage it—but she felt better for it. She would find a way to wreck it, to hide the evidence that she had been over-exposed, before turning it in for a new one.

For the second time that day she stepped into the shower, waiting for the heat to wash away her worries. Her brain felt a little fuzzy—was that madness, or the fact that she'd not eaten in a while?—and her limbs ached. She needed to eat.

Crap.

Sarai and Rickard were coming for dinner. Could her day get any worse? At least they knew about the baby, they could help her resolve one problem, even if she had added an extra few to her life since the night before. What was she going to do with Jaxon? Was that also a burden she could share?

No, he would have to stay in her room. Tomorrow she would take him out, let him get some fresh air, but for tonight she just wanted to pretend that everything was normal.

Madea flicked the water off her body before stepping from the shower. She should have chosen her clothes more wisely, as the pants and t-shirt she'd grabbed weren't really tidy enough for company, but at least she would be comfortable, and hopefully she had enough food in the house to conjure up a halfway decent meal.

Jaxon perched at one of the stools in the kitchen while she

cooked, passing comment on the smells and playing at taste tester. Madea was surprised by how intelligent he was, considering...considering what? That he had been raised in Dome Four and his mother had been Touched? Madea snorted. She was going to have to stop passing judgement so readily.

"What's funny?" Jaxon asked.

"Nothing, really," Madea said with a smile. "I never thought my day would turn out like this."

"I'm sorry." His lip quivered.

She stopped slicing vegetables and caught his gaze. "Don't be. I might not have expected it, I might not have been ready for this, but it's okay. Really. You're a cool kid."

"I am?" His eyebrows shot up and he leaned forward a little.

"I think so. But then what would I know?" She shrugged, her lips quirking in a grin. "I'm not very motherly, but I want to help you. Be patient with me while I figure it out. Okay?"

"Don't worry," he assured her. "Nothing could be worse than living with my Aunt Lucinda."

"Were you there for long?" Madea went back to slicing, only glancing up at Jaxon occasionally. She desperately wanted to know his story, but she didn't want to make him feel like he was being questioned.

"A few days. They took Mum...They took her away, after what she did..." He stopped talking and dropped his gaze to the bench.

"I'm sorry. Jaxon. I'm really sorry." Madea moved behind him so that she could place an arm around his shoulder. "I know it's hard. I didn't mean to make you upset."

He shrugged.

"If you want to talk to me about it, then I want to hear. But I'm not going to make you, okay?"

Jaxon nodded, then finally looked up at her and gave her a half smile.

"Now, I better finish up here. Then we can get you some food sorted, and I think I might have something to keep you busy. I'll try to keep dinner short. Okay?"

He nodded again, and went back to his drawing.

She had barely managed to settle Jaxon into the bedroom when Sarai and Rickard showed up. She opened the door, a smile on her face, heat in her cheeks

"Hey, Sis." Sarai leaned in and hugged her. "You're looking less distressed than last night."

"I am?" Madea laughed. "I guess that's a good thing. Come in." She stepped aside to let them pass. Rickard stopped and gave her a quick squeeze before following Sarai into the kitchen.

"Smells good in here. I wasn't sure whether you could cook," Rickard quipped. He managed to duck out of the way of Madea's fist, grinning. "Well, you're always at work..."

"You guys need to lay off with the whole workaholic thing. It's getting old."

"You can't say it's not true, though. All I really want to know is whether you work so hard because you're in love with the work, or with Sullivan." Sarai's gaze was glued to Madea's, but she couldn't quite fathom the emotion that filled them.

Madea glanced away. "That's a bit harsh. I thought maybe we'd have something to eat before you started the interrogation."

"We're here to help you, Maddy." Sarai reached out and grabbed her hands. "We can't help if you won't tell us what's going on."

"I know, I..." Her shoulders slumped and she leaned against the doorframe to the kitchen.

"Do you love him?"

It was pity, Madea realized. That was the look in her sister's eyes.

"No, I don't love him. I admire him, I think he's great, but...I'm not deluded enough to love him. There would be no point." Madea shrugged away from Sarai and moved into the kitchen, pouring glasses of juice for each of them and pushing the tray of nibbles closer to Rickard.

"The way I see it, it's really none of our business how you got knocked up," Rickard said. Sarai hit him in the arm. "Ouch! It's not. Madea is a grown up, she makes her own choices—what we can do is support her with those." He took a cracker and bit into it. "So you took the test, right?"

"Yes, I'm definitely pregnant," Madea said. Her voice was quiet, but firm. She knew that she would raise this baby, not give it to someone else to look after. Having Jaxon here, imagining how it might be to have a child of her own...she felt a connection to this being inside her, even if she'd only found out about it yesterday. She wanted to have that fierce love she had seen in Janae's eyes when she'd pleaded with Madea to help her son. She could imagine herself in the same position. Except that if she was Touched, if anyone found out—if she was Hollowed—her baby would still be growing in her womb. As far as she knew, it wasn't known what affect being Touched, or Hollowed, might have on an unborn child because those pregnant were given jobs within the domes. Madea wasn't prepared to find out. She would fake sanity for as long as possible, for the sake of herself, and her child.

"When are you going to tell Sullivan?" Sarai asked. She was chewing on her bottom lip, a trait that Rickard obviously found endearing from the way he was gazing at her. Sickening.

"I don't know. When I have to? It's still early."

"If you tell him now, maybe he can help?"

"And what kind of help do you think I need, huh?" Her back stiffened and she turned away, pulling out plates and cutlery and thumping them onto the bench.

"I didn't mean it like that." Sarai's voice was soft as she came into the kitchen and placed her arms around Madea's shoulders. "I think that maybe he'd like to be there for you, too."

Madea closed her eyes, rigid in Sarai's arms. She tilted her face up towards the kitchen light, wishing for a moment that she could believe in some higher power that could help her out. "I need a few days to get my head around it. To figure out what this means for me." She relaxed into her sister's embrace.

"I'm still getting used to the idea."

"You're not the only one who has to adjust," Rickard said. "I'm going to be an uncle!"

"Had to find a way to make it all about you," Madea said with a snort, though she smiled. He always knew how to lighten the mood. "Let's eat."

Sarai helped her serve the meal and they sat at the small table in the kitchen.

"So tell me, other than falling in love, what have you two been doing?"

Sarai and Rickard clasped hands across the table and grinned at each other. Stupid, happy grins. "Rickard has been overseeing the new construction in Dome Eight. They're thinking about shutting down Dome Four because the building was a bit shoddy."

"What kind of shoddy? Putting the people in danger shoddy?" Madea raised an eyebrow, her thoughts going back to what Jaxon's grandfather had said.

"Not enough to cause over-exposure," Rickard said quickly. "The layout is all wrong though, and with the new work fields being developed they want to move some of the labourers over, and then re-develop Four with some better housing and infrastructure."

"They're going to put him in charge of that too," Sarai added. "Father—"

"Father has great connections. I know. Sounds like things are going really well for you Rickard. What about you, Sis?" Madea forced herself to eat more salad, though her stomach was beginning to churn.

"I've been doing some work for Father. He's been very busy. You know he's running for Elect Chairman on the Council."

"I'd seen something about it. I'm sure he'll breeze in, with your assistance of course." Madea smiled, though she didn't really mean it. Sarai was smart enough, but the primary benefit of having Sarai with him was that it made him look good. Caring father, dutiful servant of the people. Bleck.

They argued over her father's ambitions until the plates were cleared and stacked in the kitchen. She yawned and stretched her neck, surprised by how many pops she could hear. "I'm going to have to kick you out," she said. "Hope you had enough to eat."

"Definitely," Rickard said with a smile. He patted his belly. "I feel better knowing you'll be well fed."

"It sounds like you're hoping to fatten me up like a prized pig."

"Just keeping my niece or nephew in mind." Rickard winked. "No, really, we just want you to look after yourself."

"I know. I'll take it easy, I promise. Besides, if I tell Sullivan, maybe he'll fire me and I won't have any work to do." Madea rolled her eyes.

"If? Don't you mean when?" Sarai asked, a frown creasing her brow.

"When, if, whatever." Madea sucked her bottom lip in. "I don't know how to broach the topic. I can't see him being happy about it."

"Who knows, maybe he'll surprise you." Sarai smiled as she stood from the table. "You'll find the right way, I know you will." She kissed Madea on her forehead. "I love you. You know where I am if you need me, okay?"

"Yeah, I know. Love you too." Madea smiled.

"Same goes with me," said Rickard.

"I know, I know!" Madea laughed. "You're going to kill me with your kindnesses before this baby arrives."

"Who knows, maybe we'll have a baby soon, and we can raise our wee ones together." Sarai beamed at Madea, who felt like she'd had a bucket of cold vomit poured down her back. She couldn't play happy families with her sister, not when she didn't have one of her own.

"Who knows?" She did her best to smile, but avoided her sister's gaze, knowing it wouldn't reach her eyes. "Thanks for coming. I'll see you soon."

"As soon as you want. Remember, you're the workaholic here, not us." Sarai's eyes filled with what could be sadness, and Madea couldn't help but wonder if Sarai was actually jealous. She swallowed a laugh as she ushered her guests out the door and closed it behind her. Wouldn't that be funny— she was jealous of her sister, who was marrying Madea's best friend, and her sister was jealous of the baby Madea had conceived without knowing. The laugh erupted from her chest then, harsh and humourless. It echoed down the hallway as she walked to her room.

She opened the door to find Jaxon curled up in a ball on the floor, tears streaming down his face. All her self-absorbed thoughts vanished when she heard the sorrow in his sobs.

"Jaxon, honey, what's wrong?" She rushed to his side, dropping to her knees and placing a hand on his arm.

"You-you-you're having a baby. I heard." He sniffed and wiped at his face.

"I am." Madea nodded, not sure why this was so upsetting for him.

"That's why you don't want me. Isn't it?"

"I didn't...I never..." She struggled to find the right words. "It's not that I don't want you. I...I've never looked after a kid before, and I don't know what I'm doing. Wouldn't you be happier with your family?"

Jaxon cried harder, his thin shoulders heaving. She scooped him into her arms, feeling his grief wash over her. He'd lost everything in the last few days. What did he have left, but her?

"I'm sorry, Jaxon, I'm so sorry. I do want you, I do. I didn't think you'd want me." He was so small, so lean, his ribs poked into her and his scraggly hair tickled her nose.

"Please don't send me away. Please. I promise I'll be good. I promise. I'll do whatever you want."

"Oh, honey." Madea held him as tightly as she could, rocking on her knees until his sobbing ceased and his breathing evened out. She could feel his heart beating against her chest, slowing into a steady rhythm until eventually he became a dead weight in her arms and she realized he was asleep.

So much had changed. Everything, in fact. She had made a pact with this boy, now she would find a way to make this work. There was no way that she would abandon him like the others had. She didn't think he would survive if she did.

Madea managed to get to her feet. Jaxon dangled in her arms and she tugged the covers of her bed back before gently placing him down. Even in sleep he didn't want to release her from his grasp so she folded herself in beside him, listening as his gentle snores filled the room.

He was so young and already his life was a mess. If there was a God then he was cruel, because what kind of deity would drag a boy from one Sun-Touched mother to another? It didn't seem fair—and not just because she didn't want to go mad, didn't want to be Hollowed—but because he deserved better than this. He hadn't done anything wrong.

Neither had Janae, unless there was something to her father's words and Jaxon's father had been trying to keep her quiet. It seemed too strange to be true, but she would do some digging and see what she could find out. Maybe the father wasn't as bad as Jaxon's grandfather had made out, maybe he could help provide for this young boy who so desperately needed someone to take care of him.

Madea sighed and tried, unsuccessfully, to drag her arm out from beneath Jaxon. She was well and truly trapped, and her inability to get up and move around meant that her mind was free to think about the future, something she would rather avoid at the moment. There was too much going on. Yes, she was strong, and yes, she was an independent woman, but how much was one person expected to handle?

Tears trickled down her cheek, across her nose, making her sneeze. Jaxon twitched in his sleep but didn't wake. She couldn't even move to wipe them from her face, but she didn't want to. They felt good, like they were washing away some of the angst that had gotten wound so tightly in her stomach. She needed the relief they brought, needed to accept the hurts for what they were. And maybe, after sleep, she would wake refreshed.

CHAPTER EIGHT

For a moment, she could pretend that the weight on the other side of the bed was a man, not a boy, and that the baby growing within her was welcomed by this man. Muted morning light washed in through the slats in the blinds and she could picture what would happen in her perfect life: she would get up and make tea for the two of them, then they would eat breakfast together, talking about science and the state of things, politics even—that would make her father happy—because those things were more important now that they were bringing a new life into the colony. She'd want to change the systems in place to spread benefits more widely, make sure that food was shared more evenly between the skilled and working classes, that healthcare was freely available, because it was obvious now that not everyone was getting the same opportunities. The ideals of everyone having a role, everyone being nurtured, hell, of life on Diamara being better for even the least important was far from accurate. And this man of her imaginings would agree with her, because they valued the same things, had the same goals and vision.

Madea took a deep breath and exhaled the dream, pushing it as far from her body as she could. Things could be worse.

Really, they could be. She could be homeless, jobless, without a family who cared about her.

The only thing that was unrecoverable from was the potential over-exposure yesterday. And even then, it might be days before she knew for sure if she had been Touched. Today, she couldn't think about it because she had bigger things to deal with.

Like telling Sullivan about the baby.

The best thing to do was get it over with as soon as possible so that they could work out whatever kinks they needed to in their 'relationship' and get on with being coworkers, and coparents. He was the father, and he could deal with whatever feelings that brought up, but the bottom line was that he didn't have to be involved if he didn't want to. She didn't need him for that, she didn't want him for that.

She pushed herself up from the bed, feeling grotty from sleeping in her clothes. Jaxon was still snoring softly, oblivious to the fact that she was awake and moving around the room, so she grabbed some clean clothes and headed for the shower.

Maybe it was the fact that she was pregnant that was making her need to be immersed in water on such a regular basis. Whatever it was, her skin felt prickly and her clothes irritated her. She stripped off and washed as quickly as she could so that she could maximise the time spent just standing there, letting the water flow over her body.

Once she had dried off she pulled a simple dress over her head. The fabric was soft—the most comfortable thing she owned—and felt amazing next to her skin. She glanced in the mirror and for once felt vaguely pleased with her gently rounded belly. At least now she could feel good about it, knowing it was nurturing something.

Madea went into the kitchen and put water on to boil. She would make tea, she would make breakfast and then she would wake Jaxon so that they could talk over the meal—he wasn't the man of her dreams, but he was part of her family now and for once, she had the opportunity to be the adult in the situation.

Before she had got everything ready, the boy shuffled into the kitchen, rubbing his eyes. "Morning," he said with a yawn.

"Hey." She bit her lip, watching as he pulled himself onto a stool. "You feeling okay this morning?"

He nodded, giving her a brief smile. She pushed a cup of tea towards him, and watched as he took a sip. His nose crinkled up, but he took another sip anyway.

"Thanks."

"Do you want something else? I could make you a hot chocolate instead."

"Yes please." He pushed the mug back towards her, and waited patiently as she made him a new drink.

"Hungry?" She held up a box of cereal after she'd served his drink.

"Starving." He grinned as she poured some into a bowl and then sloshed milk after it. "Thanks."

"Jaxon." She waited until he was looking at her again before speaking, and reached a hand across to place on one of his. "I want you to know that I meant what I said last night. I want you to stay with me for as long as you want to."

"I do want to. I really do." He was so earnest, eyes damp with hope and vulnerability that she could have cried.

"That's great!" She smiled at him. "Bear with me while I figure a few things out, okay? I've got to head into work today, talk to my boss, and...we might need a bigger place sometime, but don't worry about that. It's my problem, and I'm sure if I put a request in with Housing they can sort us something out soon enough." She breathed deep, her shoulders relaxing a little, feeling like maybe she would be able to handle this after all.

She could ask her sister for help. She could find a school for Jaxon and make up some story about why he was living with her. Her father would ask a million uncomfortable questions, of course, but maybe Sarai was right and he would want to feel needed. She could ask for help, and if he rejected her now, it wouldn't be any worse than the other times he had disagreed with her, or been disappointed that she wouldn't live up to his expectations. She poured her cereal and gulped it down, feeling eager to get on with the list of things she had in her mind. It was a new day, one that held the kernel of hope, and she was going to have to make the most of it while it lasted.

"Do you think you'll be okay here? I hate leaving you alone, but I don't really have another choice right now."

"I'll be fine. You've got food, and I like to draw."

"Excellent." Madea laughed. He was so easy to please. This wasn't going to be as hard as she'd imagined.

She let herself into the lab, locking the door behind her. She didn't want anybody interrupting what she had to do, or she might lose her nerve entirely.

"Sully?" Madea called out then waited for a response. It brought back a sense of déjà vu from a few nights before—only this time she didn't expect to find comfort in his arms.

"Maddy." Sullivan came through the office door. He was wearing his glasses today and his lab coat was stark white and wrinkle free. "You're late, and you didn't check in yesterday."

"Sorry, something came up. Something I need to talk to you about." She walked towards him, but his eyes were still on the chart in his hands, and he moved toward one of the benches, fiddling with some tubes before turning toward her, his eyebrow raised.

"Do you want to do this in my office, or out here?"

"Office." She pushed past him, through the door and perched on a chair, torn between feeling sad he was being so brusque, and pleased that he was keeping this professional.

"Okay." He entered and closed the door behind him. "What's up?"

"I just need to tell you that I'm pregnant, and..." A wave of nausea swept over her, whether in response to the words she had spoken, or to the hormones, she didn't know. She swallowed hard and continued, "And, as my boss, and the father, I thought you should know." She nodded, released the breath she'd been holding and finally looked up to see his reaction.

He was noticeably paler. "Pregnant?" Both of his eyebrows were raised now. "Pregnant." He took a deep breath and let it out slowly. "Pregnant...right. Well. Are you sure?"

"Am I sure?" Madea's laugh was shrill. "I took a test. The test confirmed what I already knew. Yes, I'm bloody well pregnant. Why would I tell you if I wasn't sure?"

His shoulders slumped. "It's mine, isn't it." He scratched his chin. "How far along are you? Let's run some more tests."

"What?" Madea narrowed her eyes. "That's all you have to say?"

"Well, no. But if I do the tests, then it will tell me what I need—"

"I'm not a science experiment! I can tell you what you need to know: Yes, you are the father, and I've been suspicious for weeks now, months even, I only took the test yesterday. What more do you want?"

"I could find out the gender, and exact date of conception, whether everything is okay—"

Those last words sent icicles through her veins. What if he could tell that she'd been Touched? What if it showed that the baby was damaged? "No. I'm not a pin cushion. You can't make me take any tests."

"But I'm the father." Confusion clouded his eyes.

"Biologically, yes—but do you have any intention of playing a major role in this kid's life? You were saying a few days ago that you weren't the kind of guy to settle down and have a family." She took a deep breath then said, "And that's okay with me."

"Oh." He seemed to deflate, as though he had expected she would want something more. But did she? Wasn't it kinder to tell him from the start that he didn't have to play a role? It was her choice to have this baby, not his.

"I'm not trying to hurt you, Sully." She softened her voice and leaned towards him. "You mean a lot to me. You're my friend, my boss, my lover. But you didn't ask to be a sperm donor, and it's not something we planned or thought would happen. I'm not blaming you. I just..."

"You don't want me to be involved."

"I didn't say that!"

"Actually, you did."

"I meant that you didn't have to feel like you owed me anything. Like you were responsible for this." She gestured to her stomach. "It's my burden."

"You don't have to carry it if you don't want to."

"I do want to," she replied, her words as firm as her resolve.

"Well, then you don't have to carry it alone."

"But—"

"Just shut up for a minute, would you?" He scowled and shook his head. "See, this is why we would never work—you get these ideas in your head and nothing I say can move you. But that's not what I wanted to say." He rubbed his temples for a minute. "You're right. I don't want to be a dad, or a husband. As great as you are. You said it though, you're my friend and as your friend I want to support you in any way that I can."

"Oh." It was her turn to be stunned into silence. He wanted to be there for her. Not as the father, but as her friend—that was more than she'd hoped for. While she might have joked last night about him firing her, it had been one of the possibilities that flitted through her mind. Or running from her, screaming, never to be seen again...

"Not often you go quiet." Sullivan smiled. "What's going on in there?" He tapped her forehead gently and she burst into tears. He gathered her in his arms, drawing her into his lap and holding her while she wept.

"I really don't know what I'm doing," she confessed.

"Who does? If it helps, I'm sure you'll be a great mother. You have compassion, which is more than a lot of people these days. That's a good start."

"Thanks." She sniffed and climbed off his lap, placing herself back in her chair. "I'm sorry about this. I know it wasn't in your plan."

"Ah, well. Life's unexpected at times. We all know that the colony needs more babies, new life. The children born on Diamara are going to help forge the future we've begun here, and now I can say I've contributed my genetic material, and if I'm to father a child, I'm pleased it's with you."

She leaned back, trying to decipher the look on his face. He was taking this a lot better than she had expected. Almost too well.

"What?" he asked.

"This wasn't the response I expected. I still don't know how I feel about it."

"Relieved? At least, I hope so. I don't want to make this difficult, and I certainly don't want it to get in the way of our work."

"Yeah, relieved. I didn't expect it to go down so well."

"This is your idea of well? I didn't get down on my knees and beg you to marry me. Wouldn't that have been more fitting?" He laughed, the grin had returned and he seemed relaxed. At ease. Which meant he was doing better than her, or perhaps he was simply better at acting.

"If you had done that then I'd have started thinking you'd been Touched." The old, judgemental words came out without thought. Madea stiffened and then forced herself to relax.

"Ha! Well, you might have been right, if I had." He laughed and she made sure to join in, though hers was slightly more hysterical than his.

She didn't know for sure that she had been Touched. Maybe the time she'd spent outside the domes before now would mean she could be exposed for longer without her brain being affected. What would he say if she confessed that to him? Would he retract his offer of help and force her into custody?

Madea wasn't going to breathe a word about it to anyone. Not until she knew for sure, and even then she would hold onto whatever shreds of sanity she could, for as long as possible. There was more than just her life at stake now.

She'd been working for several hours when her back began to ache. Madea pressed her fingers against the curve of her spine and her vision swam, the air seeming to shimmer. She shut her eyes tight, and when she opened them again the blur was gone. Had she been getting enough sleep? This pregnancy thing was taking it out of her—first she fell asleep in the fields, and now she was seeing spots?

"Sullivan," she called. "I'm not feeling so great. Is there any chance I can take the rest of the day off?"

"Sure, in fact, that works well. I've got some testing to do on capsulim variant A." Sullivan didn't turn from his work, though she didn't expect him to.

"Variant A? What's that?" She crossed to his bench, but he flicked the screen of his tablet dark and pushed away the microscope.

"Something I've been working on for your father on the side. You'll be let in the loop when it's been approved."

"By Father." She wanted to know more, but it didn't seem like the time to press. Why her father had anything to do with their work, she had no idea.

"Yes." He fidgeted, glancing over her shoulder at the door. "I shouldn't have told you."

"Well don't worry, I won't tell anyone." Madea rolled her eyes. "I'll see you tomorrow, then."

"Call in if you need another day to rest." He waited until she'd thumbed the door open and crossed the threshold before turning back to his work.

Weird. She had known he worked on things that he didn't share with her, but for her father? That was news.

Sunlight filtered down through the dome, warming her back. At least the morning sickness was keeping at bay, though as she walked blurs streaked her vision occasionally, making her pause.

"Jaxon," she called out as she entered the house. "Jaxon, where are you?"

"Here." He poked his head around the doorway of the living room. "I'm hungry."

"Right." She smiled. "Come on then, let's get something to eat." He followed her into the kitchen, reminding her of the puppy she'd had when she had lived on Earth—it wasn't often that she thought back to those days, now, but they were all tinged with a little sadness. Earth had been pretty wonderful, and while life here on Diamara wasn't horrible, it was something that had taken a few years to adjust to, what with living under the cover of the domes, and the vibrant orange of the sun, darker than the earth's, a constant reminder of the threat of being Touched. Even now it seemed alien, and she'd been here for years.

She quickly fixed some sandwiches, shoving a plate towards Jaxon as she picked one up and took a bite. The sweetness of jam hit her tongue and she gagged, spitting the chunk of soggy bread onto the plate before covering her mouth and swallowing hard, trying not to vomit.

"They said my mum was really sick when she was pregnant with me," Jaxon said. "She puked all the time."

"Bet you're glad you weren't around to see that." Madea took a deep breath, then grabbed a glass and got herself some water. It didn't take away the taste, but at least it made her mouth feel fresher, for a moment. Her eyes felt a little funny and she blinked, trying to clear the blotches from her vision. It only made it worse, because now she felt lightheaded and she could hear faint sounds that didn't seem to be coming from anything in the room. "I think I need to lie down for a bit. Are you going to be okay?"

"I'm used to being by myself." Jaxon nodded, still eating his sandwich.

Even with his mouth closed Madea could smell it in the air and this time she couldn't hold back the vomit. She turned and retched into the sink. "Oh God. Go in the other room, please. I don't want you to see this."

"I won't watch. Promise."

He climbed down from his seat, and his soft footsteps crossed the kitchen. His small hand was gentle on her back as he rubbed circles across her spine. Something about the gesture broke through her self-pity and she sat on the floor, bringing her cup with her. "Thank you," she said.

"It's okay. It's not fun being sick. I don't like it."

"Me either." She smiled at him. "You're a good kid. Has anyone ever told you that?"

"Only Mum, but I think she had to. It's a mum's job to say that kind of thing."

Madea laughed softly. He was so sincere, so sweet. "I'm sure she meant it, every single time she said it."

"Thanks."

Every time she said something kind, he looked like he might burst into tears. She felt the same way these days. They were an odd pair. Perhaps they could prop each other up. Having someone else who needed her right now was keeping her from spending all day moping about her life.

"Give me a hand up," she said, extending her arm. Jaxon leaned backwards, helping to pull her off the floor. "You might need to put on some more muscle. By the time I'm at the end of this pregnancy I'll need lots of help." She smiled at him as he flexed his muscles, showing off his thin arms. "If you get too bored, come and get me. Okay?" She reached for the bench, using it to steady herself as her vision blurred again.

"Okay!" He left her to it, and she made her way slowly to the bedroom where she promptly fell asleep.

CHAPTER NINE

Nausea woke her. She rolled from the bed and knelt on the floor, trying to orient herself. This pregnancy thing wasn't very glamorous. The stories about a healthy glow and shining beauty had to be wrong because she had never felt more unattractive—and it was only going to get worse. There was a coppery tang in her throat so she reached for her glass of water, slugging it back as fast as she could.

It didn't make a difference.

Madea groaned, closing her eyes in the hope that it might stop the room from spinning. It did help, but she could hardly go through the rest of the day blind.

With her eyes closed, she could hear people talking. Jaxon and...who was he speaking to? A bolt of fear pushed Madea to her feet and she groaned, reaching for the bedside table. She forced herself into the hallway, bracing herself for the worst.

"And this one, that's a picture of my mum. Her name is Janae."

"Where's your mum now, kid?"

Rickard. It was Rickard. Madea sighed with relief.

"She's—"

Madea cut him off as she stepped into the lounge. "She's had to go away for a bit, hasn't she, Jaxon?"

"Yeah." He nodded, eyes wide.

"What are you doing here, Rickard? I wasn't expecting you."

"Obviously." He raised an eyebrow and cocked his head towards Jaxon.

"Why don't you come and help me make some tea. You'll be okay for a bit, won't you, Jaxon?"

"Sure." He nodded again, gaze flicking back and forth between Madea and Rickard.

"Great." Her broad smile felt fake. She headed for the kitchen and Rickard fell into step behind her, grabbing her elbow as soon as they were out of earshot.

"What's going on, Maddy? One day you tell us you're pregnant and the next there's a strange boy in your house."

"Why don't you tell me what you're doing here?" Madea asked. "How the hell did you get into my house? Because I know for a fact that Jaxon wouldn't have answered the door."

"Sarai gave me a key. She asked me to check on you." Rickard ran a hand through his hair and sighed. "I guess I should have called ahead. But still, that doesn't explain what he's doing here. What's going on?"

"I can't explain—"

"You better try," he demanded.

"I'm going to make a cup of tea," Madea said with a sniff.

"I'll make it. You start talking." Rickard let her go and moved to the sink to fill the jug.

Madea perched on a stool, relieved she didn't have to move around. "I provided the jinweed at a Hollowing a few days ago, and the woman spoke to me. She told me about her son, asked me to help him out."

"You mean that boy? His mother was Touched?" Rickard frowned.

"She was, and now she's Hollowed."

The words hung in the air for a moment. A flicker of grief flashed across Rickard's eyes. He visibly shook it off before responding, his voice more subdued. "Well, that sucks."

"No kidding." She rolled her eyes. "I needed to make sure

he was okay, so I went to find him and...well, they pretty much ordered me to take him. They couldn't give him the life he deserved." She decided it was better to keep the grandfather's conspiracy theories to herself until she knew whether there was any truth in them.

"So you brought him home?"

"What else was I meant to do? It wasn't like I had a choice." Her shoulders slumped. "I was going to try and find another place for him but...he needs me." She glanced up at Rickard, who was staring back at her.

"I guess that makes sense. But really, Maddy. You work full time, you're having a baby. Do you need this right now? As if your life isn't busy enough."

"It's not about me. It's about him. Can you honestly tell me you'd abandon him if you were in my place?"

"No, I guess I wouldn't." Rickard let out a long breath. "You sure know how to make a mess of your life, you know that?"

"I don't think it's a mess, thank you very much." She poked her tongue out at him and he smiled. "Just because you and Sarai have a perfect little life lined up, doesn't mean that's what everyone wants."

"And this is what you want?" He frowned in confusion.

Madea thought about it for a moment and then nodded. Apart from the whole 'probably going to go crazy and kill someone' thing, she didn't want to change her life now. It might not have been her first choice, but considering she hadn't really had a plan to begin with, she was okay with it now. "Don't tell Sarai about Jaxon, though. Can you keep your mouth shut?"

"I don't know about that." Rickard shook his head. "She's pretty good at getting things out of me."

"The way I see it, you owe me. Big time."

"Huh?"

"You went off and fell in love with my sister, without even telling me you might be interested. You were my best friend, you were...we were...you know what you were, and still you went behind my back and now you're getting married. To her!"

Rickard eyes widened in shock. In fact, she was quite stunned herself. She'd wanted to keep those emotions close to her chest. He knew how she felt, and she shouldn't have had to tell him.

"I'm sorry, Maddy. Really, I am." His eyes were full of sorrow as he reached out to grab her hand. "I didn't think anything was ever going to happen with you and I missed you. Sarai...she filled that void, and then she carved out a new space in my heart. I love her, Maddy. More than I thought I could love anyone."

He was being so careful with his words, dodging around her like he always had. She should have known he would fall for someone else—she wasn't easy to love and she had never made room for him in her life. It didn't change the fact that it stung, the way they had each other now and she was left alone.

Well, not so alone. Maybe that's why she wanted to keep Jaxon, to take care of him. Not to mention the baby. She didn't know what to say, so she said nothing.

"Are you ever going to forgive me?" Rickard asked. His voice was soft, and he was still holding her hand.

She glanced away, unable to hold his gaze. "Like I said the other night, I can't hold it against you. It hurts, more than it should."

"I'm sorry."

There was a loud bang at the door and Madea jumped from her seat, letting go of Rickard's hand. "Go keep Jaxon quiet." She waited for him to disappear back into the lounge, and then took a breath and went to the door.

Night had fallen, and before her stood an Enforcer. Her heart thumped in her chest.

"How can I help?" she asked cautiously. She held her breath, waiting for his response.

"We can't find Sullivan and we need you to medicate the Touched. There was an incident." He seemed to have no intention of giving her more information.

"Right, give me a minute. I need my jacket, and the lab

keys." She closed the door and let her breath out. At least they hadn't come about the boy, or her.

Madea grabbed her things, then went into the lounge. "Rickard, can you stay with Jaxon? Something's come up."

"Is everything okay?"

"Just a work thing. Don't worry about it." She glared at him, hoping that he would hold any questions until later, then knelt down next to Jaxon. "I'll be as quick as I can, okay? Make sure Rickard makes you something good for dinner." She winked at the boy, then gave him a quick hug.

After a quick stop at the lab for the medication, where there was no sign of Sullivan, it was barely twenty minutes later that they got to the Hollowing facility. The Enforcer would only say that the degree of the crime committed had been so severe that an instant Hollowing was necessary, nothing more.

Madea got out of the transport and was escorted inside. There were more guards on duty tonight than she had ever seen before, and they weren't just armed, they had their weapons at the ready. That was a first.

She was led to the same chamber where Janae had been kept and was surprised to see Jaxon's grandfather strapped to the chair so tightly that the bindings cut into his skin. He was gagged, though that didn't stop him from shrieking.

"What did he do?" she whispered to the Enforcer. The old man's eyes were wide, pupils dilated and the lines on his face carved deeper than they had been the other day.

"It doesn't matter." The Enforcer's tone was clipped as he crossed to the man. "You'll need to dose him quickly."

"Can you tell me, please?" Madea tugged on the enforcer's sleeve. "I've never seen a Hollowing go through this fast, I—"

"If you must know, he went nuts and killed his family. The madness must have come on quick. There were twelve dead when we got there, four injured. It's the worst case we've seen, and we're not about to wait and see how much more dangerous the man will get." He raised his eyebrows at Madea. "Satisfied?"

"I guess." She nodded, and chewed her lip. Just a few days ago he hadn't seemed mad at all. Well, unless you counted his ravings about Jaxon's dad being the reason why Janae had been Hollowed. Madea remembered how that thought had made her feel, how it had been like tiny claws digging into her belief that the system worked.

The fact that he was here, now, about to be Hollowed, certainly lent some weight to his conspiracy theories—unless those theories had been born of madness too. But he had seemed so coherent...

It was too confusing. She had never been good at head games, never been good at political intrigue, and here she was, possibly right in the middle of one. When it came down to it though, she couldn't bring herself to believe that the State was responsible for even a portion of the Sun-Touched in the colony. How could they possibly resort to exposing people, just to get them out of the way? Surely if that was the case, she would have heard rumours of it by now?

"Are you ready, Miss Linae?"

"Huh? Oh, yes." Madea shook her head, trying to clear her thoughts. She hadn't realized that they were waiting for her. She got the injection from its case and slid the needle into his vein. He tried to pull away, huffing out his nose, his breath faintly tinged with capsulim. Madea swallowed hard. Sullivan had talked about a new capsulim variant he was working on for her father, but surely he couldn't be involved in this?

"Did you want to stay this time?" The technician asked her; the same one who had Hollowed Janae. She'd barely noticed him there.

"No, I'm fine. Thanks." She shook her head fiercely and backed away. The old man's eyes rolled in his head, but she turned away. She hadn't seen madness there, only indignation, rage.

The Enforcer followed her out and closed the door behind him.

"Did you know that man?" he asked, stepping close to her and grabbing her arm.

"I think I might have seen him once in the street or something. I don't know his name though." She twisted away from him, aiming for an indignant expression. "Can I go now?"

"Yeah, you can." He looked her up and down, and she hoped he couldn't see any falsehood in her. "The transport is waiting outside to take you home. You have a good night."

"I'll try..." How could anyone have a good night after being called to a Hollowing? And where had Sullivan been that he couldn't make it?

CHAPTER TEN

Madea slipped into the transport and closed the door behind her. It wasn't until she had settled herself on a seat that she realised she wasn't alone.

"Hello again." A vaguely familiar face smiled at her. Garrett's skin was darker than the last time she had seen him, but he still had that aura of intrigue about him. She brushed her fingers across her skin where she'd felt that sting when they shook hands.

"It's you, from the herb field...Garrett, wasn't it?" She braced herself as the transport began to move. He half bowed, his lips twitched into an even wider grin. "What are you doing here?"

"I have a message for you, and I thought this was the best place to pass it on."

"A message? For me?" Madea frowned. "I think maybe you have mistaken me for someone else."

"Trust me, I'm not wrong. Your father is Carson Linae, isn't he?"

"Yes...but what does my father have to do with this?" She raised an eyebrow.

"I need you to give him something from me. From us."

"Look, I don't know who you think I am, or what you

want, but I'm too tired for this. I feel terrible. I've just come from a Hollowing—"

"I know."

Garrett slid along the seat until he was opposite her. Their knees were almost touching. "You're in a unique position right now."

"What do you mean?" A chill ran down her back. This man knew something, but what?

"I saw you in the fields yesterday. And I noted that you were gone for an awfully long time. Are you feeling okay?" He raised an eyebrow, his face serious, but not accusing.

"I feel fine. Thanks. I don't know what you're talking about." She hunched her shoulders, tension filled her body. He knows, he knows, he knows.

"You don't have to admit it, that's okay." He dismissed her body language with the wave of a hand. "My point is that your life is going to change pretty soon, and I know some people who want to help you—if you give them a little help in return."

"What help?" She leaned against the seat, trying to give herself some space from him, trying to feign a lack of interest. She didn't know what was going on here, but she didn't like it. Not one bit. Was this to do with her? Her father? Or was it all tied up with Jaxon and Janae? Did it really matter, if it meant that someone could help her?

"You might find yourself going through certain...changes, and we can help you with those. Give you some guidance."

"And if I find that I don't need that help?"

"There are things you don't know yet, things I'm not at liberty to tell you. I can assure you that sometime soon you are going to start seeing a whole new side of this world though, and when that happens, I want you to contact me."

"What do you mean?"

He shook his head, a smile playing on his lips. "No point telling you now, you wouldn't believe me anyway. Trust me."

"I don't know why you think I would." It was her turn to shake her head. "Either you tell me what you want, or leave. I don't have the energy for this."

"Here." He reached into his pocket and pulled out a slim phone. "This is how you can get in touch with me. Mine is the only number you can call, and only once. I'll be keeping an eye on you, from a distance, but if you need me, call."

"Wait, you mentioned my father. You had something you wanted me to give him?"

"Ah, yes." He smiled at her, his teeth white and clean. They seemed at odds with the tan of his face. He reached into another pocket and drew out a small box. "The contents won't make any sense to you, but he'll know how to interpret it."

Madea took it and shoved it into her pocket. There would be plenty of time to open it later. "Is that all?"

"For now," Garrett said. "Be assured that I'll be in touch, if you don't contact me first."

"Don't hold your breath."

He reached a hand out and placed it gently on her knee. She could feel heat radiating off him, more than was normal. "I know it might be hard to believe, but I genuinely want to help you. I hope you'll let me."

"I don't need your—"

"This is my stop." Garrett winked, opened the door and jumped down from the transport, despite the fact that it was still moving.

Madea was left wondering what had occurred as the door slammed shut behind him. The transport felt empty, cool. His presence did something to the air, but she couldn't put her finger on what exactly. She patted her pocket, making sure the box was still there, then drew it out, not wanting to wait until she got home to see what was inside it.

It was made of wood, and the lid slid free easily. The inside was lined in dark blue fabric and the only thing it contained was a seal with an emblem on it that she couldn't identify. What could it possibly mean? Madea chewed her lip, half tempted to ask the transport to take her straight to her father, to demand answers. But would he give them to her? Or was she better to hold on to this for a few days and ask around? Surely someone must know what it meant.

She pushed the lid closed again and slipped it back into her pocket.

She had the unsettling feeling that whatever she was involved in was bigger than the problems that seemed to be cropping up for her left, right and centre. In time, she would find out, but right now all she wanted to do was go to bed.

Jaxon was asleep on the couch when Madea got home, his gentle snores forced the tension from her shoulders and she leaned against the door, watching him snooze until Rickard came up behind her.

"He's a good kid," he said. "Do you want to tell me what's going on?"

"What do you mean?" Madea turned towards the kitchen and Rickard followed. Half of her was pleased he was there, the other half wished he would leave her be. She was so very tired.

"Since when do you get called out in the evenings for a Hollowing? Since when do they start doing them after hours?"

"It was a special case," Madea said, choosing her words carefully. She started to heat some coffee, but stopped, opting for cold water instead. "Since when do you care?"

"You know I care about you."

"That's not what I meant." Madea sighed and rolled her shoulders. "Since when do you care about how and when they do Hollowings?" She was too tired for this conversation. And when, when would she be able to let her hurt go and stop picking fights with Rickard?

"I don't, except when they have something to do with you."

"They couldn't find Sullivan. I'm the next person on the list, and it's my job to medicate them. That's as involved as it gets."

"But you don't think it's weird?"

"Rickard, drop it. Okay?" She wasn't ready to fill him in on the suspicions nagging at her brain, as if speaking them might make them true. "It was a special case, that's all. It's nothing to worry about."

"If you say so." He shrugged. "It's getting late. I should get home."

"You should," Madea said. She huffed out a breath and then added, "Thank you for sticking around and taking care of Jaxon for me. I'm still getting used to the idea of it. It's probably good for him to have a guy around from time to time."

"So you're not kicking me out for good?" Rickard smiled. "I knew you couldn't stay mad."

"Get out of here before I change my mind," Madea said, though she was smiling now. "I'm in a weird place at the moment, so bear with me, okay?"

"You know where I am if you need me. And you know where Sarai is. Don't forget that you have people who care." Rickard strode to the door.

"I won't. Oh, I forgot to mention that I told Sullivan about the baby."

He swivelled back. "How did that go?"

"Better than I expected. He's supportive of whatever I want to do. He made sure I knew he was my friend, even if he couldn't be my partner."

"Couldn't? It's a choice, Maddy. He could, he just won't."

"Do you think that's how I want to catch a man? By getting pregnant with a child he doesn't want and forcing him to agree to a relationship he had no intention of having?" She spat the words at Rickard, who recoiled.

"That's not what I meant—"

"Then why don't you say what you mean? I don't need your charity, and I don't need you to get angry at him for me. He gave me more than I had hoped, and for that, I'm grateful."

"You...you deserve better. You should have a husband who dotes on you, and a beautiful family home where you can bring up your baby in comfort. I wish you could have those things."

"My baby will have everything it needs. Jaxon will have everything he needs, too. It might not look like the perfect situation to you, but it's going to work for me. I'll make it work."

"If anyone can, it'll be you." He grinned at her suddenly and she felt the tension in the room dissipate.

"I'm sorry for snapping at you. Can we put it down to hormones?"

"Sure, that works for me. I...I care, I need you to know that."

"I never doubted. I think you need to know that I can do this, on my own. Don't feel sorry for me, or my situation. I can handle it."

"You shouldn't—"

"Stop talking. Now." She smiled. "Before you say more stupid things."

"Good plan." Rickard stepped closer and folded her into a hug. "Sleep well. I'll catch up with you soon." He pulled away.

What had that look been? A flash of regret, sorrow? Was he grieving the loss of their potential relationship as well?

There was no doubt in her mind after the last few days' events that he was more suited to Sarai than her, but that didn't stop the twinge. She wasn't sure if she was comforted, or uncomfortable, that he seemed to share those emotions with her. He was out of bounds now, no matter what, so there was little point dwelling on it.

Madea walked back into the lounge to check on Jaxon. He was still asleep, his mouth moving slightly, but she couldn't make out what he was saying. She grabbed a blanket from the chair and placed it over him, hoping that he wouldn't fall off in the night and hurt himself.

She'd have to find somewhere else to live soon, or change the furniture around to make room for a bed. He couldn't sleep with her, and he couldn't sleep on the couch every night, though at least it would do for now.

There was something about knowing he was safe that made the rest of the day bearable. She couldn't tell him about his grandfather. He'd lost too much already. No, she would find ways to build up his life, and together, they could welcome her baby. And things would be good.

Unless of course there was something wrong with it. Something mad. Something Touched.

CHAPTER ELEVEN

The buzz at her door woke Madea. She raised her head slightly to check the time. Pre-dawn. Who in their right mind would be at her house this early? She shook the webs of sleep free and pulled herself out of bed, shuffling through her bedroom door and down the hallway.

She thumbed the console and the door slid open. Sarai stood there, looking like she'd been awake for hours and was simply out for a morning stroll. The sunny smile plastered on her face was a good façade, but Madea could tell that it had been painted on.

Madea frowned. "Let me guess. Rickard couldn't keep his mouth shut about Jaxon, and you had to come and see for yourself?"

"Jaxon?" Sarai's surprise was genuine. "Who is Jaxon? Are you living with a man now?" She cocked her head, eyebrows pushed together as she tried to put the pieces in place. It was so comical that Madea couldn't help but laugh.

"So he didn't tell you...okay, second time lucky. He hinted that there was something you didn't know, and he was worried, so you rushed over here to see what you could do?"

"Exactly. I don't like mysteries. Now, who is Jaxon?" Sarai pushed her way past Madea and swept into the lounge. Her sister froze as she laid eyes on the boy, still fast asleep on the couch. Sarai backed out of the room. "A boy? Why is there a boy in your lounge?" she whispered.

Madea grabbed her by the elbow and led her into the kitchen. "That's Jaxon. The short version is that his mother was Hollowed, and I'm looking after him now." Madea shrugged, as if it were nothing major.

"But—"

"No buts. You either accept it, or you stay away. What's it going to be?" She had always needed to take a firm stance with her sister, who had often fallen into line with her father's decisions.

"Of course I'll accept it, if it means that much to you—"

"It does. You and Rickard are going to have to trust me. I need supportive people around me. I don't have time for people who won't be."

"I think you should talk to Dad." Sarai's gaze slid away from Madea's as she said the words.

"Okay," Madea said with a huff. She tried to pitch her voice right, tried to make it sound like she was caving in. She needed to see her father anyway, so she may as well let Sarai think she was winning a battle.

"Really?" Sarai shoulders shot back and her eyes lit up. "You'll talk to him about all of this?" She waved her arms in the air.

"Well, maybe not everything, but I will talk to him. He should know that he's going to be a grandfather. Right?"

"Oh, Maddy." Sarai threw her arms around Madea and squeezed. "He might be surprised, but he'll come around. I know he will," Sarai gushed as she pulled away. "Thank you for doing this, it means a lot. When can we go? Now?"

Madea shook her head, though she had to supress a grin at her sister's glee. "He'll be at work, remember? And I have work, too. Why don't you see if you can arrange dinner tonight? Just us, and Dad." She stared at her sister who scrunched up her nose, but eventually nodded.

"Okay. I'm sure I can do that. He'll be so pleased to see

you."

"You act like he misses me or something. Like I'm the one causing the problems."

"Well...I mean, it's not just your fault. You're as stubborn as each other. I guess that's something you got from him." Sarai grinned. It did nothing to alleviate the ache in Madea's stomach. In fact, the whole room seemed to be spinning, enough to make her feel uneasy.

She was the problem? Or at least a part of it? "Well, let me know what you've organised. I should get ready for work." Madea only made two steps before Sarai grabbed her arm.

"What about Jaxon?"

"What about him?" Madea frowned.

"You can't leave him here by himself."

"No. No, I guess I can't. He's used to being alone, but I need to make some arrangements..." She trailed off. Last night, she thought she had been doing well, but really she'd been deluding herself. How did other people do this? Who looked after children when their parents went back to work? It wasn't something she'd ever concerned herself with.

"I can stay for a bit, if that would help?" Sarai offered.

"Really?"

"Of course. I said I'd support you, Maddy. Didn't you believe me?"

"I...thanks. Let me get dressed, and then I'll wake him and you guys can get to know each other before I leave."

"Sounds perfect. I'll go make some tea," Sarai called as she headed into the kitchen.

Confusion and dizziness swamped Madea, making her feet so heavy that she struggled to make it to her room, where she flopped onto the bed. She wasn't sure what was real and what wasn't. Was she really the one to blame for the rift with her father? Did she not trust her sister, whose only betrayal—falling for Rickard—had been no real betrayal at all? And what made her think she could parent anyone, even a six year old who seemed fairly self-sufficient, let alone a baby?

By the time she left her house, she was running late, again, but she didn't think Sullivan would hold it against her. At least this morning she wasn't throwing up. She almost felt okay with the world. Jaxon was cared for, and the small wooden box that was like a stone in her jacket pocket would be delivered to her father that night, if all went to plan. Hopefully she could get some time alone with him, get him to explain what was going on. Sarai had no place in whatever mess Madea had managed to get involved in, that was for sure. And Garrett, whatever role he had to play in it all, well, she wouldn't give him the satisfaction of contact. He could come to her if it was really that important. She didn't need him.

Madea swiped her thumb against the pad and entered the lab, pausing as she always did to hear where Sullivan was. There was no noise in the building though, other than the hum of the lights and the slight buzz of equipment. By now he should be hard at work, there should be music flooding the room and he should be so caught up in whatever he was doing that he wouldn't notice her arrival until he needed something from her.

"Sullivan?" His name hung in the air and her brain shuffled through all the potential causes for the strangeness she felt. She thumbed the door closed and headed for his office. The door was locked, so she entered the pin code and pushed against it. There was weight behind it, more than the door, and there wasn't much give.

"Sullivan!" she called, her voice frantic. It had to be him pressed against the door. She grabbed a chair and shoved again, wedging it in before the door slammed shut.

"What have you done," she muttered as she forced the chair further into the gap and tried to jam the door open. After a few minutes of giving it her best, the door moved enough that she could get the seat of the chair in. She stepped over it, squeezing into the office. The muscles in her groin ached, but she ignored that as she knelt beside Sullivan, fingers reaching to press against his neck.

He still had a pulse, that was the main thing, though his

skin was pale and his hair damp with sweat.

"Sullivan." She pushed against his chest, trying to get a response out of him, but he didn't move. Madea crossed to the desk, grabbing the comm from under the mess of screens and vials, and those damn tablets, and speed dialling the special medical team. She wasn't equipped to deal with an overdose, and that was the only explanation she could think of.

"I need some help at the lab in Dome Three. My boss seems to have overdosed. No, I don't know what, exactly, I have some of the pills, but I don't know what he's put in them. No, he's not conscious, just hurry up! He needs help." She ended the call, not waiting for a response, and dropped to the floor at Sullivan's side. "Come on, come around, you idiot. What were you thinking?" She shook him again, but he still didn't respond.

At least he was breathing.

Madea glanced around the office, trying to figure out what might be in the pills. She'd never wanted to know—never really wanted anything to do with it before. What had he taken? She leaned in and took a sniff of his breath. There was something there, a tang she wasn't familiar with. Perhaps he'd mixed something new?

"Come on," she said again, grabbing him by the shoulders and shaking him. His head banged against the door and she swore.

"Wazz appening?" He slurred the words, and his eyes fluttered open.

Relief flooded through her. "You overdosed, you idiot. I was so worried." She dug her nails into her palms, resisting the urge to slap him. Her heart still hammered and she took a deep breath, collapsing on the floor beside him.

"Nahhhh. Dint." His hand twitched in her direction, but he couldn't seem to get it to work properly.

"Shut up, Sullivan. Don't die on me. Okay?"

"Kay." He went silent, his breathing evened out and his body slumped further, but she was done worrying. He would make it.

The muscles in her abdomen tightened, cramping worse than before. She'd had to push hard to get through the door, and now she was paying the price. She didn't have long to contemplate that before the medical team burst through the door.

"Over here," she called, waving to them. Sullivan's head was cushioned in her lap. He hadn't said anything more. Whether that was because he was obeying her or because he couldn't speak, she didn't know. She didn't have the energy to find out.

Madea waited while they lifted him onto a stretcher, then pulled herself upright. She folded her arms across her stomach, hoping the pressure would ease the cramps. "The tablets on the table are what he must have taken. He said something though, said he didn't overdose."

"We'll take it from here, Miss. Thanks." One of the men nodded, scanning her face before his eyes flicked to her tense arms. "Are you okay?"

"I'm fine." She waved him away with a hand. "Just pulled a muscle trying to get through the door."

"I can take a look if you'd like."

"No, it's fine. Really." She softened her too harsh tone with a smile. "Take care of him for me, will you? I'll come and check on him as soon as I get a chance." They carted him away and she watched, anxiety gnawing at her. He would be okay. There was nothing to worry about, she reassured herself.

The mess in the office was worse than normal. Who knew what he had done, and if he would even remember when he came out of the state he was currently in. She went back to looking around the room for clues about what had happened.

Because despite the slur, he'd been clear about one thing— he hadn't overdosed.

By the time she got home, Madea felt drained. Unfortunately, she still had to pull herself together enough to have dinner with her father. The box was still in her pocket, her cramps seemed to have faded, and Sullivan had been coherent when she'd checked in on him, though unwilling to elaborate on what had happened. Stubborn man.

Jaxon and Sarai were curled up on the couch with some children's books when she came into the lounge. It hit her that there was always someone else present in the house now, always noise, always space being occupied by someone other than herself. Madea had never thought she was a loner, but perhaps that was the case. Her nerves felt scattered and frayed and she wished, for just a moment, that shutting herself in her room meant she could feel alone. She would always know though, always be aware of the other presence in the house.

"How was your day?" Sarai scooted off the couch and came over to give her a quick hug. Madea felt a little like a husband then, returning from work to the family. Right now she wished she was still at work. It was a happier thought than dinner at the family home.

"It was...eventful. I'll tell you about it later. Where did you get those?" She pointed at the books.

"Oh, we went for a walk, got a few bits and pieces. I thought—well, you needed some stuff." Sarai shrugged apologetically. "I hope that's okay?"

"Of course it is." Madea crossed to Jaxon and sat down beside him. "Did you have fun with Sarai?"

"Yup." He nodded, then leaned in and whispered in her ear, "She's really nice."

"I know," Madea whispered back with a smile. "Are you okay to hang here for a little bit? I think I need to lie down."

"Sure." Sarai's brows knitted together in concern. "You don't want to talk about what happened today?"

"Not right now." Madea's eyes flashed towards Jaxon, and Sarai nodded. "Is dinner organized?"

"We're eating at seven, and Rickard will come hang out with Jaxon."

"Great." Madea smiled, and pushed herself up from the couch. "I'll be back soon, I— I just need to lie down for a few minutes."

Sarai flashed her a sympathetic smile, then took her place

on the couch and picked up Jaxon's discarded book. Madea felt a twinge of guilt, like she should be doing more, but the pull of solitude was too strong to resist.

She closed her bedroom door and threw herself down on the crumpled and twisted sheets. She hadn't made her bed that morning, hadn't even thought about it. So quickly her life had changed, her routine usurped. It seemed like not a single day went by where something didn't happen to make things more complicated.

A sob wracked her body. She dragged a pillow to her stomach, fingers clenched tight around it and released the wave of sadness that crashed down on her. Nothing was going right. She wasn't strong enough for this, wasn't equipped to deal with a kid, a baby, potential madness, conspiracy theories and a recovering boss/ex-lover. Was he her ex now? Could they ever enjoy each other's bodies again, knowing that their child was growing inside her? It was a mess. More than a mess, it was total chaos. What had she done to deserve any of this? Even one of these things, just one, would be enough for someone to deal with. Not all of it, not all at once.

Her sob became a giggle, slightly hysterical, as pictures played out in her head. It wasn't chaos. It was comedy. Back on Earth, they'd have a TV show about someone like her and all the crazy things that went wrong in her life. The audience would laugh and realize how trivial their own difficulties were. She would laugh with them, because somewhere in the middle of it all, something good would happen and she'd realize it wasn't so bad.

Taking Jaxon in was good. She may not be the best mother, but she could learn, and it had to be better than him growing up unwanted, passed around between family members because his father was someone to fear.

And Sullivan was a grown man. He could take responsibility for his actions, like everyone else did—like she was. This baby wasn't expected, but unless she'd managed to dislodge it when she tried to help him today, it was going to come into this world eventually, and she would love it, the way her mother had loved her.

If she managed not to go mad before then, anyway.

Garrett sprang into her mind, with his smarmy smile and that glint in his eye. He knew something, but he wasn't willing to tell her what, instead handing her a box and forcing her to speak to her father before she was ready. When would she ever really be ready to speak to him?

Madea took a breath, holding it in until she thought she'd burst. She brushed the tears off her face and sat up. She'd had a cry, allowed herself a moment to wallow in self-pity, and now she needed to get on with things. She had a dinner to prepare for.

CHAPTER TWELVE

She wore the blue dress again. The way it flowed over her body made her smile, even if she didn't have fond memories from the last time she wore it. Well, they weren't all bad, but she didn't want to dwell on the night she'd found out that Sarai and Rickard were engaged.

"You're wearing that?" Sarai asked when Madea stepped out of her bedroom. "You know it's just dinner at Dad's, right?"

"I wanted to make an impression." Madea chose her words carefully. It was going to be hard enough to get their father alone tonight, without Sarai getting curious. She should have thought about that before she put on the dress. For some reason though, it just felt right. The blue of the fabric mimicked the blue of Garrett's eyes, now that she thought about it.

Why was that man intruding on her thoughts, again?

"How long until Rickard gets here?" she asked.

"I'm already here." His voice came from the kitchen. "Did you want some tea?"

"No, thanks," Madea called back. "I didn't even hear him come in," she said to Sarai.

"He's sneaky when he wants to be." Her sister winked and Madea smiled.

"Are you going to be okay, Jaxon?" She crossed to where he sat, still on the couch, still with the books. "I'll try not to be gone long."

"I'm okay." He grinned at her. "I like Rickard, he's nice."

She felt a stab of pain in her chest at those words, realizing that in the grand scheme of things she was probably no more, or less, important than any of the people in this house now. With Sullivan under medical care for a few days, perhaps Jaxon could come to work with her and they could spend some more time bonding.

"Okay." She let out her breath. "I'll see you soon then." She reached out and fluffed his hair with one hand, giving him a smile. She stood, setting her shoulders. "Let's do this then."

"It won't be that bad," Sarai said. She looped an arm with Madea's and led her to the door.

"You would say that, you're his favourite." She couldn't keep the pout out of her voice.

"Look, I don't know what happened between the two of you. I don't know why you act like this, or why he gets all defensive when I try to talk about you, but I do know that he loves you. And you love him too, right?"

"I guess, yes." Why was it that whenever they talked about him, she felt like a twelve year old girl again? She wasn't a child any more, but she sure knew how to act the part. "I'll try to behave like an adult. Happy?"

"Yes." Sarai grinned and pulled her into the transport that waited. "He'll be happy too."

When they pulled up at their father's house a few minutes later, there was a servant waiting on the steps. He tried to take Madea's bag, but she waved him off. The box hadn't left her person since Garrett had given it to her, and she wasn't going to lose track of it now.

"Sarai, Madea!" Their father beamed, taking them into his embrace one at a time. When it was Madea's turn she tried to relax into it. He was getting old. She could see lines on his face that she hadn't noticed the other night, and his body felt frailer than the last time they had hugged. Her nose stung, but she wouldn't spill a tear. It wasn't only her fault that they weren't close.

"Father," she said, keeping the hitch from her voice. "What's for dinner?" *Keep it even, Madea, keep it neutral.*

"Lasagne. I remembered it was your favourite when you were little." His eyes scanned her face.

"I still like it," she said with a smile. A genuine one.

"Come on, I'm starving. You need more food at your place, Maddy." Sarai led them towards the dining room.

"What were you doing there?" her father asked.

Madea tried to catch Sarai's gaze, before she said too much.

Sarai frowned. "Sullivan had an accident at work, and I was checking that Madea was okay. Right, Sis?"

"And is he okay?" Carson's eye twitched, just a little.

"Don't you know?" Madea asked. "I heard he was doing some work for you."

"Be that as it may, I don't keep tabs on everyone in the colony, you know." His lips twisted into an awkward smile, though she could see a sliver of uncertainty behind his eyes.

Madea took the seat to the right of her father, the same seat she had sat in for years. Sarai sat opposite and their father waited until they were both seated before slipping into his.

"This is nice. It's been awhile since we've all had dinner together."

"Too long." Sarai's look was pointed.

"Well, we'll have to make sure it happens more often. I've missed having both my girls under one roof."

"It has been some time," Madea said. A servant brought in bowls of steaming soup. Hers sat untouched for a few minutes while she decided if it smelled like something she could stomach. She let their talk about the last few days wash over her, only commenting on their lives, not offering anything of her own. What could she say? *Daddy, I'm pregnant and the father may or may not have tried to kill himself last night. Daddy, I was outside too long. I think I'm Touched. Daddy, there is a boy at my house. No, not a man-boy, an actual boy, someone else's son who I'm taking care of, but I'm not very good at it. Daddy, what the hell did I do to deserve all of this?*

What had gotten into her? She took a deep breath, trying to focus on what was being said and push down all the crazy thoughts swirling in her mind. Sometimes, life sucked. She had to remind herself of that. Sometimes, bad things happen to good people. That was important to remember too.

"Madea?"

"Huh?" She frowned at Sarai.

"Daddy was asking what else you've been up to." Sarai was giving her the smallest of nods, as if prompting her to speak.

"I...well, I have some news." Her throat felt dry. She grabbed her glass of water and swallowed the rest of it. Her stomach heaved, but she was sure it wasn't morning sickness this time. Did she really want to tell him? Was Sarai going to give her a choice?

"Come on, spit it out." Her father smiled at her and reached across the table to grasp her hand. It felt awkward.

"I'm having a baby." She smiled, but her lips felt like jelly, their quivering betrayed her nerves. Her father pulled his hand back a little, then grasped her fingers firmer. His lips were tight, and his eyes bored into her. He opened his mouth to speak, then closed it again.

"Isn't that exciting, Daddy?" Sarai prompted. "I'm going to be an aunty, and you'll be a grandfather!"

"It's...wonderful." There was warmth in his voice, and shock. Madea clung to the sliver of tenderness.

"I know it's a bit of a surprise, but I wanted you to know." What she really felt like saying was 'I'm sorry, I know you wanted more than this from me,' but she was damned if she'd admit it.

"I...I don't really know what to say. When is my grandchild going to be born?" A smile cracked through the tightness of his face, like dry earth splitting from a drought.

"I'm not sure exactly. Maybe six months? I only found out for sure a few days ago."

"And the father?" He raised an eyebrow. "Is he in the picture?"

Madea took a deep breath, trying to swallow the anger that threatened to pour out of her like lava. She should have known he would ask. "He's supportive. Still getting his head around it."

"I see." He nodded briefly, eyes still boring into hers.

"You see what?" She pursed her lips. "What is it that you see? Why can't you be happy for me?" She pushed her seat back so hard that it tipped over and clattered on the floor as she stormed away from the table.

"Madea," he called after her. "I didn't mean it like that!"

She waved a hand behind her, dismissing him and anything else he might have to say.

Once she had locked the bathroom door she splashed cold water on her face. She had been holding it together so well, but he just had to ask. She should have told him it was fine, should have lied. It would have made life a whole lot easier. She let out a pent up growl, trying to push her rage out with it. There was a knock at the door, which made her snarl again.

"What do you want?"

"I just..." She could hear her father sigh on the other side of the door. "I wish we didn't have to do this. So many of our conversations are through closed doors. Have you ever thought about that? You know I wasn't trying to judge you. I'm worried about you. I'm your father. I'm allowed to worry."

"And I'm an adult, I'm allowed to..." She wanted to say 'make mistakes', but then this baby would be permanently labelled as one, and she didn't want that. "I don't want to fight about this. It's my baby, and I want it."

"I've always wanted to be a granddad, but I thought it would be Sarai having babies first."

A smile slipped across her lips. "Me too," she confessed.

"Come out and let's finish dinner. For her. You know how much she hates it when we argue."

"I'll come out, but after dinner, you and I need to have a talk. In private." She opened the door.

"Should I be worried?" His brow was furrowed, as if he were trying to figure out what else she might reveal to him, something that needed privacy.

"I don't know."

Her father closed the door behind them and sat down behind his desk. She hadn't been in his study for close to five years now, not since she had moved out of home. It was unusual enough to be here, but to be alone with him, well, that was almost unheard of.

"So, what did you want to talk about? Sit, please. You're making me nervous." He gestured to the chair at the other side of the desk.

"No. Thanks. I think it's better that I stand."

"If this is about the baby—"

"It's not." She let out the breath she'd been holding and then reached into her bag. Her fingers found the box, still cool despite the warmth of the evening. She drew it from the bag and placed it on the desk between them. "A man gave this to me, and he told me that I needed to give it to you."

Her father's eyes flicked between her and the box. It was a full minute before he reached out and pulled it closer, nonchalantly turning it so that its catch faced him. He flicked it undone with one finger and then lifted the lid and pushed it back. It hit the desk, the thud seeming louder than it should for the small size of it. He opened his mouth, then closed it again, his eyes fixed on the seal within.

"What does it mean?" she asked.

He looked up at her, shock making the whites of his eyes stand out more. "You've been Touched."

"What?" The blood rushed from her face and she grasped the edge of the desk. "No, I haven't."

"You don't understand, Maddy."

He never called her by her nickname. Never.

"This seal...I... They wanted me to stop the Hollowings, and they said that they would...I didn't. I couldn't."

She had never seen him struggle so hard to form a sentence. "I don't get it." She shook her head. "I'm not Touched. You don't need to worry." She tried to reach for his hand but he drew back.

"Don't touch me." He was shaking his head now too. "You're tainted. And my grandchild. You can't have this baby. We have to call the doctor. Now." He reached for the phone but she snatched it from his hand and pulled it from the wall.

"This is my baby. And I'm keeping it." She frowned. Anger, confusion and hurt welled inside her, fighting for supremacy. He couldn't mean she had to abort it. Could he?

"You are my daughter, and I won't let you. You will not bring a mad baby into this world. You will not taint our family name further." He stood, planting his hands on the desk. His face had gone from white to red in a matter of seconds.

Madea backed up a step. "Father, think about what you're saying. I'm your daughter. You don't want to do this."

"You've given me no choice. Consorting with people you shouldn't, bringing shame to our family. You're just like your mother." He all but bellowed the words, his body trembling with fury. "I can't let this affect our family, Maddy. You must see that. Surely." His features softened, his shoulders sagged. "You're not well. You're not thinking straight."

"I'm thinking fine, Father." Her voice was firm but her heart wavered. Was he right about her state of mind? And what had he meant about Mother? "Whether I'm Touched, or not, this is my baby and I'm going to have it."

"You can't bring an abomination into the world." He shook his head, disgust in his eyes.

She pressed back against the door, feeling for the handle. The metal of it felt slick under the sweat of her palms and she twisted it, pulling it open.

He lunged out of his chair toward her but she slipped through the door and pulled it closed. She glanced both ways then ran towards the back door, hoping it was the less obvious option.

"Maddy?" Sarai's confused call came from behind her but couldn't stop to answer it. Their father wasn't in the hallway yet, which meant one thing—he'd called Enforcers in to stop her. There was no time to waste.

When she had lived here, she had always found ways to escape her father's notice. Now those old paths came in handy. She slipped out the back door and pushed down the side of the house between the wall and the bushes that hugged it until she came to an old tank. Once wedged behind it she sank to the ground, hugged her knees and waited for the inevitable rush of bodies out the door as they went searching for her.

It didn't take long before footsteps pounded on the gravel. She closed her eyes, willing them to avoid the spot she was lurking in. No one had discovered this hidey-hole before, so she should be safe for now. She grabbed her phone from her pocket and put it on silent; it would be just like her sister to call her now and give away her location.

This was not how she'd planned for things to go. If only she'd known what that seal had meant, she wouldn't have given it to him. Though, that wouldn't have tied in with Garrett's plans, whatever those were. Had he known how her father would react?

Despite the fact that this predicament was very much his fault, Garrett was the only one who could help her out of this situation. He'd told her that things would get difficult—hell, he'd made sure they would—and that he would be there for her when that happened. Unfortunately for her, that was a lot sooner than she would have liked.

Madea drew in a shaky breath. She'd thought tonight would have gone some way to reconciling her differences with her father, but now he was determined to have her baby aborted and probably have her Hollowed. He should want to protect her, protect his grandchild. Tears stung her eyes and she rubbed them away with the back of her hand.

Madea pushed her way through the hedge and made her way from tree to tree, sticking to the shadows until she was well out of the property.

It took a good hour before she felt safe enough to pull out the slim phone Garrett had given her in the transport. Her hands shook as she made the call.

"Hello?" he answered on the third ring. His voice was full of sleep and she took a deep breath before daring to speak.

"It's Madea. I need you. Father turned on me and he said...he said..." She let out a sob, hating herself for showing weakness to him, of all people.

"Where are you?" His voice was alert now. She could picture him sitting up, leaning forward as though she were across a table from him.

"In an alley, Dome Five. I don't know if he's still looking for me."

"He will be, I'm sure."

"I don't know what to do."

"You did, you called me." He gave a soft laugh. "I'll come and get you. Do you think you can make it to Dome Four? In the communal area, there is a fountain. Wait within earshot of that, and I'll see you soon."

"Okay." She felt numb, unable to process what he was saying to her.

"Madea?"

"Yes?"

"You did the right thing. I can help."

"Thanks." It did little to make her feel better, but she nodded.

"And get rid of your phone. They can trace it, even if you have it off. We don't want to risk you getting caught."

"Right. Okay then." She ended the call and gripped her phone. It was just plastic and metal and computer components, but she felt a wash of anxiety at the thought of discarding it. Jaxon was at her house, Rickard was there too. How would she get in touch with them? Would her sister look after the boy until she could find a way to get him? She felt bile rise in the back of her throat and spat it onto the dusty ground, grimacing as she wiped her lips clean.

She couldn't leave Jaxon for long. She would have to appeal to Garrett's kindness, if he had any, and get Jaxon back. He needed her.

Or maybe, she needed him. Because, now that her father knew, the boy would be safer with Rickard and Sarai. Wouldn't he? He would have a stable, secure life. Sarai was motherly, and he knew them as well as he knew her.

No. No one knew his past, and if he was the son of a man who was out to get him then he wouldn't be safe anywhere. She turned off the phone and dropped it on the ground, crushing it beneath her shoe.

CHAPTER THIRTEEN

A chill leached through her coat, her dress, and into her skin. She lurked in the shadows, trying to be still as she waited for Garrett to show. Paranoid thoughts raced through her mind. What if he didn't come? What if he had wanted to cut her communications with others? What if this was all a trap? After all, he knew she was Touched, knew she would be going mad. Maybe he wanted to get her Hollowed for his own purposes.

She clenched her fists again, only stopping when her nails dug into the flesh of her palm. Where was he? She had no choice but to trust him, as annoying as he was, and she wouldn't handle it if he was out to get her.

"Madea." The whisper came from across the square. She could make out a shadow, dark black against the grey units. "Are you here?"

She paused for a moment, her reply catching on her lips before spilling out into the darkness. "Garrett?"

"Who else would be sneaking around at this time of night?"

She could hear the humour in his voice, and for the first time in hours, she smiled. She stepped out of the shadows and they met halfway across the square.

"So you're saying you do this thing all the time?" The

fountain burbled quietly beside them, and maybe, on any other night, it might have been a nice place to be. He took her by the elbow and led her down a short alley.

"I'm trying not to make a habit of it." He placed a bag in her hands. "Here, get changed. I'll keep an eye out, and don't worry, I won't peek."

"Right." She rolled her eyes. Whether he took the chance to sneak a look was the least of her worries right now. Still, she waited for him to get to the end of the alley and once he'd taken his place, she pulled pants and a hooded top from the bag. She stripped her dress off, and shoved it in, cringing as she thought of the wrinkles she was creating. At least it wouldn't get dirty. She dragged her new clothes on, pulling the belt tight to keep the pants from falling down. "I'm done," she called as she slung the bag over her shoulder.

"Great. Let's get out of here." He reached a hand towards her and she frowned. "What?"

"Nothing." She grabbed hold of it, unable to avoid thinking about the roughness of his fingers against hers.

"Once we're safe, you can ask questions. For now, follow my lead." He pulled her out into the street and they headed away from Dome Four and into the busier streets of Dome Three.

"What are we doing here?" she asked, her voice hushed.

He squeezed her hand and drew her body closer to his. "Blending in. It's far easier to lose someone in a crowd than in solitude."

"No one followed me—"

"We don't want to take any risks now. Or did you want to be Hollowed?"

Madea froze. "What did you say?"

"I know what happened, Madea. And if you're running from your father it means he didn't offer to keep you safe. Did he?"

The question forced tears into her eyes. She still couldn't believe that he would turn her, or her baby, over so easily. Their relationship had been difficult, but deep down she had always believed she was more important than his reputation. And it was his fault, he who ignored the threat and caused her to be Touched.

"I'm sorry," Garrett said. He squeezed her hand a little firmer. "I know this is a hard time for you, but we need to be careful."

"Yeah." She sniffed and shook herself free of sorrow. The crowd was moving around her, people coming from bars, or entering them. She felt out of place in this world, the one in which people had a life outside of work, outside of their homes.

"We have company." Garrett tugged on her hand and they were off, winding through the throng of humanity. They had only gone a hundred metres when he pressed her against a wall and leaned into her. "Follow my lead," he said again, a glint in his eyes.

She frowned, uncertain what he meant, but uncomfortably aware of the proximity of his body. He smelled like dust, like sweat, and then his lips were pressing against hers, his hands tangling in her hair. She pushed against his chest, but he moved his lips to her neck, then the lobe of her ear. She couldn't help but arch her body into him as he found her sweet spot and nipped it.

"We have an audience," he murmured. "Go with it."

Recklessness swelled in her. She brought a hand to his face and moved his mouth back to hers. His chin was rough with stubble but the scratch against her skin made the moment more real. This was nothing like kissing Sullivan. The fire she'd seen in Garrett's eyes the first time they met was present in the scorch of his lips, in each touch of his hands on her body.

Madea didn't have time to be outraged at the liberties he was taking; she was too caught in the moment.

And if this was how he kissed a stranger...

Well, he must really want to keep her safe.

After a few minutes he drew back from her lips and nuzzled her neck. "Can you see anyone looking at us? There were two burly men, black pants, red vests."

Madea took a shuddery breath and glanced around as she exhaled. The oxygen did nothing to slow her racing heart. "No, I don't think I can see them...are you sure we were being watched?"

"As much fun as it was making out with you, I usually try to get to know someone a little better before sticking my tongue in their mouth." She could feel him smile against her neck and the tingle it sent through her body made her shiver. "If you think we're clear, we'll make a move."

She contemplated for a moment whether to lie, whether to drag out this interlude a little. She deserved some fun, didn't she? She bit her lip. "I think we're okay."

He moved away from her. The heat of his touch drained from her skin and she shook her head to free herself from the desire he'd drawn out of her. Garrett pulled her close to his side, wrapping an arm around her shoulder and leaning into her again. "Do you think you can keep the act up? Lovers for the night?" A smile played on his lips and it was all she could do to stop herself from kissing him again. She put her arm around his waist and slipped a hand into the back pocket of his pants.

"How's that for familiar?"

His smile cracked wider and she could see that he swallowed a laugh. "It's a good start. Come on, let's get you somewhere safe." Before they moved off he leaned down and kissed her again.

"So tell me, do you do this with all the women who call on you for help?" She braced herself for the answer, sure that it couldn't just be her.

"Only in special cases." He winked, then led her down the street.

There was a scuffle behind them and Garrett pulled away from her. "Stay in the shadows."

She leaned away from the wall to watch him as he moved towards the sound, and then there was a hand around her mouth and an arm around her chest, tugging her back. She tried to cry out but the sound was muffled.

"Be quiet, Madea." The voice was gruff, but unmistakably Sullivan. "It's not like I'm enjoying this, but it has to be done."

The feel of a needle sliding into her arm made her try to scream louder, but the drugs flooded her system too quickly and she blacked out.

CHAPTER FOURTEEN

When she came to, she was strapped to the Hollowing chair. The cables and tubes stretched out above her and she screamed into the gag in her mouth, straining against her bonds. She couldn't see who was doing this to her, unable to believe it could be Sullivan. Her vision swam and she could hear voices, but couldn't seem to separate any into one she knew.

Sarai's face came into focus in front of her, and she ran a hand across Madea forehead. "It's okay, Madea. We're going to help. Stay calm. I'm going to remove the gag."

Madea stilled, waiting for the release. When the band holding the gag loosened she spat the wad from her mouth and inhaled deeply. "Why am I here? I shouldn't be here Sarai, I shouldn't. This isn't right."

"Daddy said that you're Touched, Maddy. He said your baby—" Sarai averted her gaze, tears spilling down her cheeks. "I can't believe this is happening. I didn't want to believe it, but it's for the best. I'm sorry."

"How could you do this to me?" Madea strained against the bonds again, felt them cutting into her skin but didn't care. She had to get out of here. She couldn't let them Hollow her, because what would happen to her baby? What would happen to Jaxon?

What would happen to her? She didn't want to be nothing, a drone, only able to do repetitive tasks.

She lowered her voice and tried to sound calmer. "You have to help me get out, Sarai. Please?" The pitch of her voice made her think of Janae. She was a mirror image of the other woman right now.

Sarai leaned down and brushed her lips against Madea's cheek in a soft kiss. "I wish I could. I really do." Sarai squeezed her hand and walked away, but Madea could hear her sob as she left the room.

Her father stepped into view then, his expression flat. "I wish it didn't have to be this way."

"You don't even know if I'm Touched," she spat at him. "You think I am and this is the most convenient thing for you." She writhed in the chair, not caring if she looked insane. Nothing she did would change his mind anyway.

"Sullivan," her father called.

Sullivan stepped forward, tightening all the straps. He gazed into her eyes, holding a jinweed injection up. "It will make it easier."

"What if I don't want it to be easier? What if I want you to know that I'm suffering, that you are the one doing this to me? To your baby?"

He swallowed, measuring his words. "If the baby survives, if it's not damaged, I'll make sure it's looked after. Okay?" He raised an eyebrow as she ground her teeth together. He pressed the needle to her arm, and she spat at him, the thick globule landing on his hand.

"Maddy. I'm only trying to help." He shook it off.

"No, you're trying to destroy me." She sucked in a breath, trying to calm the beating of her heart. This couldn't be happening. She needed to get out of here. Her father stepped forward and clamped the gag over her mouth. The smell was vile, like they didn't even bother changing it between Hollowings, and bile hit the back of her throat. Tears trickled down her face as hopelessness set in. It was over. There was no point fighting.

And did she really want to be aware of the Hollowing? Did she want to be conscious as her memories, her personality were stripped from her? The whine of the machinery began to fill the room as the device warmed up, and Sullivan slipped the needle into her arm.

This was it. It was happening.

The door banged open. Multiple people, by the sound of it, boots thudding against the cold concrete floor.

"Turn off the machine and step away from her," a man demanded. He came into view. Garrett. Madea sighed with relief for a moment, as Carson bolted for the other exit, but then Sullivan flipped the switch. The room hummed and the air vibrated and she wanted to puke. She could feel the energy travelling up her arms, radiating out from the pads against her skin, her scream added to the intensity in the room. She pressed her eyes shut, just as Garrett swung at Sullivan. And then the tension dissipated and the pain stopped. Her skin itched, but the machine was off. She was safe.

Madea burst into tears, unable to form a single word. Garrett moved swiftly to her side, undid the clasps which held her bonds in place and helped her from the seat. Her body shook uncontrollably and she couldn't stand on her own, so he scooped her up, his arms gentle but firm.

"Let's move out before they send reinforcements," he said, giving a nod to the others in the room. Madea rested her head against his shoulder, unable to focus on anything but the fact that she was safe. At least for now.

CHAPTER FIFTEEN

When he closed the door behind them, Madea found herself staring at a dome within the domes. Lamp light filtered down through the tinted glass ceiling, casting a rainbow of colours on the floor. She felt her mouth open in awe as Garrett placed her on a bench seat. "Where are we?"

"Back when Diamara was first colonized, they built churches, like back on Earth. They've fallen out of use, for the most part, so we use them when we can—salvation for the Touched."

She turned towards him at those words. "Speaking of the Touched. How did you know?"

"How did I know that you were?" He raised an eyebrow, lips quirking into that ever ready smile.

"Yes, that."

"What did your father say when he saw the seal?" He plonked himself down, leaving a foot of space between them.

"He said that he'd been asked to do something. That someone threatened to— You did this to me." She thought her heart might stop beating. She sat still but she could feel the blood rushing through her body, her heart pounding in her ears. "You..." She rubbed her wrist. There had been that sting she'd thought was an insect.

"I had a part in it, yes." Garrett stood, moving away from her. It was lucky for him, because she felt the urge to hit someone. "But there's more to this than you know."

"So tell me!" She stood too, her hands curling into fists which she pressed against her thighs. Her legs were still weak, so she plonked back onto the seat. "Tell me. You made me Touched, and then you send me into the lion's den and reveal it to my father. Give me a reason not to walk right back out that door."

"It's not my place—"

"What the hell do you mean it's not your place! You either know something, or you don't."

"Fine. Fine." He held his hands in front of his chest, palms facing her as though he could calm her with his gentle pushing motions. "Being Sun-Touched isn't what you think it is, Madea."

"What do you mean? It makes you crazy. Everyone knows that. People who are Touched eventually lose it, and they end up hurting other people, usually their loved ones." The pitch of her voice rose as she spoke.

"Sometimes they do hurt people, but that's only if no one is there to help them. What people who aren't Touched don't know is that it's not really madness."

"What do you mean? Stop talking in riddles and tell me what you're on about!" Madea pulled her fingers through her hair, tugging strands as she did to try and wrangle in her growing rage.

"There are things on this planet, things that regular people can't see. We call them ether creatures." Garrett stopped talking, as though he were waiting for the words to sink in.

"What?"

"The Touched aren't mad, they just see things that the un-Touched can't."

Madea closed her eyes and let her head rest on her knees. "I don't get it. If I'm not going mad, what's with the dizziness, the blurred vision, the whispering in my head?"

"If you've been told you're going to go mad, don't you think you'll over analyse everything that goes on up here?" She assumed he was tapping his head, but she didn't want to look. Couldn't bring herself to. He'd done this to her.

"You're not mad, Madea." He spoke softly as he stepped closer to her. "You're not going crazy. It takes some time for your body, your mind, to adjust to this new way of seeing the world."

"If it's not madness, then why are people dying? Why do we—why do the Touched—get violent?"

He stood before her, his face relaxed, as though he'd said this all a million times before. As though he actually believed it. "The creatures, they move right through us." Garrett dropped to his knees. "If you saw things moving in and out of people, strange creatures, sometimes frightening to look upon, might you not feel like you're in danger? Like your loved ones are at risk? Is it not possible you'd take a weapon, try to slay these creatures, protect your family, yourself, but end up hurting the ones you love?"

Madea took a deep breath, trying to decide whether she could buy into this or not. What reason did he have for lying to her though? "I haven't seen these creatures."

"It's still early. You mentioned that you'd been hearing things. The blurred vision?"

"Sometimes. I thought it was stress, or the madness."

"It's the change. It won't be long and you'll start to see them." Garrett had a gleam in his eyes, like maybe he was remembering his first sighting with fervour. "They are strange, beautiful but so very different from us. Just wait. It won't be long." He smiled and placed a hand on hers. "Knowing this makes it easier. When it happens, you'll know what it is. We try our hardest to get to those who've been Touched before the Council does, before they start seeing things, before they get Hollowed."

She shuddered.

"There's something else you need to know," Garrett said.

"No, I don't want to know anything else. Not right now. I

don't think I can handle it." She kept her eyes tightly shut. Garrett placed a hand on her shoulder and squeezed until she had to open them, had to look at him.

"You want to know this. Trust me." He nodded, the ghost of a smile on his lips.

"I don't, I really don't." Tears slipped free and tumbled down her cheeks. "I can't."

"Your mother sent me. She was the one who set this whole thing in motion."

For the second time, she thought her heart might stop. She pushed aside the flutter of hope, drowning it with all the stories her father had told her of her mother's death—she'd died outside the domes, on an excursion. There was an accident and her body was beyond recognition. They'd driven past the crash site, seen the twisted metal shell of the transport, the scraps of fabric swaying in the mild western wind, the blood peppering the ground.

"You're a liar. My mother is dead." Madea pushed herself up from the seat and stepped away from Garrett. His presence gave her no warmth now, and there was no comfort in his smile.

"Madea, I'm not lying." He stepped forward, one hand reaching toward her.

"She's dead! How dare you try to tell me otherwise? Did you think you'd fool me with your lies? I can't believe anything you've said." She took a few more wobbly steps, backed into one of the benches and barely stopped herself from tumbling. The wood scraped through her pants but she couldn't think of the pain. She had to get out, get air, get away from him and the lies he told, lies which made the hollow place in her heart burn with sorrow.

The air outside was only mildly cooler. It wasn't fresh, wasn't new, but at least she wasn't confined within that building, that building which gave false hope. Like Garrett. Tears streamed down her face as she ran. She didn't know where she was, didn't know where she was going, only knew that she had to move and move now.

Madea had barely made it ten metres before she could hear Garrett giving chase. What did he want with her? What game was he playing? She couldn't fathom what he could gain by telling her that her mother was still alive. She was dead, Father had said. He was many things—power hungry, manipulative, controlling—but he'd never lie to her about something like that.

"I can prove it!" Garrett shouted at her, his words muffled by the sound of her feet against the pavement. "Give me a chance! Don't you want to see her?"

Madea's feet thudded against the concrete road, unable to process where she was going. Her breath came in shallow gasps and then she doubled over as a cramp gripped her. Garrett caught her before she fell the ground.

"The baby," she gasped.

"What baby?" Garrett shook his head in confusion.

"I'm pregnant." She cringed, pressing down on her side with both hands. "It hurts."

"We have to get you to a medic." He scooped her up in his arms and she had no will to fight as unconsciousness pulled her under.

CHAPTER SIXTEEN

A chill seeped through her skin, bringing her back to consciousness. She struggled up before she'd even opened her eyes, the sensation too similar to that of the Hollowing chair, but firm hands pushed her back.

"Just lie there, darling."

She opened her eyes, her vision swam for a moment. A woman, familiar and yet changed, hovered above her, that voice one from her past. The stark light of the room made her blink, but for a few moments more her brain couldn't make sense of what she could see.

"Mum?" Madea whispered the word, her brow furrowing. Tahra was bending over her, older, but still so familiar. Her cheekbones, her full lips, her blue eyes and that smile, the same smile she'd given Madea whenever she'd been a good girl.

Garrett hadn't been lying after all.

"Oh, Madea." Tahra's words caught in her throat as she grasped Madea's hands. "It's been too long."

"But you died. Father said."

Tahra chewed her lip before speaking. "He lied. He couldn't have his wife Touched. Couldn't have her Hollowed. It would look bad for his career, he said. So he faked my death and sent me out of the domes. I consider myself lucky. If he'd had no love for me, he'd have actually had me killed." While the words said she had been lucky, the bitterness in her voice told a different story.

"You were Touched?" Madea sat up, pulling her hands back from her mother and tucking her legs beneath her. "I can't believe he lied to us. I can't believe that you had me Touched knowing what he might do to me."

"I—" Tahra stroked her hair, tucking it behind her ear before chewing on a nail. She'd always been so composed in the past that Madea wasn't sure what to make of her actions. "We didn't know for sure what he would do, but I would never have let you be Hollowed. Never. If you believe nothing else today, believe that."

Madea crossed her arms over her chest. "I can't believe you're here, alive. I went to your funeral. I cried. Do you know how hard that was? Growing up in a house with him and being so like you? Do you have any idea?"

"I'm sorry. I've always been there, keeping an eye on you. I couldn't find a way to get in touch with you and still keep you safe. You have to believe your safety has always come first."

"So why now? Why after years of silence? What's changed?" Madea demanded. "What was so important that you had to ruin my life too?"

"I..."

Madea pushed herself off the table, scanning the room for an exit. "Maybe you should have thought of that before you decided to expose me."

"Maddy," her mother said, her voice soft, pained. "I thought it was better to leave you with your father, to have the life you were used to. It's not been easy these last years, finding a way to survive, missing you and your sister. But I did it because I had no other choice—it wouldn't have been fair to take you with me. Besides, he never would have let me."

"You are my mother! And more than anything, I needed you." Madea tried to hold back her tears. "I'm going to ask you again, and I want you to think carefully before you answer. What has changed, what was so important that you felt you needed to get in touch with me now?" She took a shaky breath and faced her mother.

"I've learned things about these ether creatures. They are amazing, Maddy. I wanted to share that with you. I want to share it with everyone, eventually, but you, first."

"And what about Sarai?" Madea raised an eyebrow and crossed her arms over her chest again. There was a flutter of something—satisfaction? Joy?—that their mother had thought of her first. She'd always thought she was her mother's daughter, whereas Sarai was definitely Daddy's girl, and this confirmation sent a surge of warmth through her body, brief and soon swallowed by renewed anger, at both Sarai and their mother.

"We'll get Sarai soon, as soon as we can." Her mother crossed the room and placed a hand on Madea's folded arms. "When you can see what I see, when you know what I know, you will want her to be exposed too, you'll want to share this with everyone." Her eyes were lit up with that very same look Garrett had back in the church. Until that point Madea hadn't given a thought to how long she had been unconscious, or the fact that the pain in her abdomen was gone.

"My baby. Is everything okay?"

"The baby is fine. Congratulations, by the way. I have always dreamed of being a grandmother, though I had hoped it wouldn't be like this..."

"Like what?" Madea spat the words out, then wished she could take them back. She took a deep breath. "I'm sorry. I...I guess a lot of people aren't thrilled for me, and I feel like I'm the only one that wants this baby." She moved a hand to her belly and rubbed it. "It wasn't even that long ago that I found out. I'm still getting my head around it, but I know I want this child. That's all that matters. I don't want it to ever think it wasn't loved."

"Is that how you feel now?"

"I...I don't know how I feel." Her shoulders sagged and she let her head flop back though the muscles of her neck were bunched so tightly that it wasn't relaxing. Firm arms wrapped around her and a hand guided her head forward, onto her Tahra's shoulder. A sob tore free and she brought her arms up, wrapping them around the familiar shape of the mother she hadn't seen in so long.

"I never stopped thinking about you. Never stopped hoping that someday I would find a way to bring us together. I know you probably don't believe me right now, but it's the truth and I will work my hardest to prove it to you." Her mother was crying, fat tears that soaked through the fabric of Madea's top.

Madea pulled back and wiped her own tears away. "Don't worry about it for now, okay? I'll try to understand all of this, if you'll promise to forgive me my outbursts. There is way too much going on in my brain right now, and I don't even know how to start processing it."

Her mother smiled sadly. "I'm sorry. I really am. I never wanted to use you like this."

"I thought you said you wanted to share things. What do you mean, use me?"

"Your father is an important man, Maddy." Her mother stepped away and began to pace, not looking at Madea as she spoke. "He doesn't know what I know, he thinks all these people are mad, thinks being Sun-Touched is a bad thing. He strips them of their hopes, their dreams, their personalities. It's not okay, not when I know what I know. I've tried to send him messages, to get him to listen to me. But he won't hear a word of it. He's so stuck in his ways, so determined not to hear the truth that I had to find another way to get to him." The bitterness in her mother's voice surprised her, but it wasn't enough to distract Madea from what she had said.

"Me." The word echoed around the room and the meagre warmth she had stored from her mother's embrace fled.

"Yes. You. I'm sorry. But you have to believe that wasn't the only reason. I wanted you here with me." She turned back, eyes wet with tears.

Her mother had never been able to hide her emotions, so Madea closed the space between them. This time it was she who initiated the embrace, pulling her mother in, trying to squeeze away the distance of years between them.

A knock on the door drew them apart. Garrett entered, bearing a tray of food and drink. "I thought it was time you have something substantial to eat. It's been a while since your last meal."

"How long?" Madea sat down on the bed again and reached for the tray. The scent of fresh, warm bread hit her nostrils and she had to swallow the saliva that instantly filled her mouth.

"Almost a whole day." He smiled as she bit into the bread, her eyes rolling back in pleasure.

"This is really good. Where did you get it?" She took a second bite, then a third.

"Garrett makes it himself," Tahra said. "He's quite handy to have around."

Madea shoved more bread into her mouth and reached for another piece, but Garrett grabbed her hand and pushed it down. "Pace yourself," he said gently. He scanned her face, for what, Madea wasn't sure. "Are you feeling okay now? Is the pain gone?"

"I told you she was fine, Garrett," Tahra huffed. "Stop fussing over her. That's my job."

"I don't need fussing over, by anyone," Madea said, her voice firm. "But thank you for asking." She reached out and squeezed Garrett's hand. His skin was warm and the connection sent a jolt up her arm. She could forgive him his part in this; after all, it had been Tahra's orders he'd acted on, and without him she would be Hollowed by now and she wouldn't know her mother was still alive. And maybe, as they said, being Sun-Touched wasn't such a bad thing after all. Madea faced her mother. "So you're sure the baby is fine?"

"Perfectly healthy. You're almost into the second trimester, your initial symptoms should start clearing up soon."

"Really? That would be great." She smiled, one hand tracing the edge of her bump. "What about the exposure? Has anyone pregnant become Sun-Touched before?"

"Not that we know of, but there should be no danger. The creatures mean no harm."

"How can you be sure?" Madea chewed at the inside of her lip.

"It's hard to explain." Tahra smiled that blissful smile again, though it was beginning to give Madea the creeps instead of reassurance. "You'll understand when it happens to you."

"And when will that be?"

"It's different for everyone." Tahra nodded sagely.

"Speaking of everyone...we should take you to meet the others," Garrett said. He held a hand out to Madea and she grabbed it, letting him help her down from the table. "There are more of us than you might think."

"But where are they?"

"In our secret city." Garrett winked as he led her to the door and she couldn't help but giggle. He had a way of drawing her focus and for a moment she forgot that they were sharing this space with her not-dead mother. "After the first explorers discovered the madness, they tunnelled beneath the ground, hoping to avoid exposure. No one wants to live like a rat though, so they built the domes so the colonists could reside on the surface."

"I guess that makes sense. Does no one use the tunnels now, though? Surely the council knows about them."

"The entrances were all locked, though the tunnels were left in place in case of emergency," Tahra pitched in. "I had seen something about it in your father's files, and thought it was the best place to go. I've never seen anyone else use them since I found them, and we have good security in place. We've made some extensions, over the years."

"Your mother has done amazing things. Without her, none of us would have been saved." Garrett flicked his gaze to her mother, and Madea turned away, not wanting to see the reverent look in his eyes. "It might not seem like much, but its home to us."

"It's your home too, if you want it," Tahra said. Madea could hear the emotion in her voice and was torn between wanting to forgive her mother's absence, and wanting to keep her at arms-length. The mention of home sparked a wave of grief. No matter what happened, she would never be able to live in hers again. But she had to go back, she was missing something important.

"I need to get Jaxon." She really was the worst wannabe mother in the world. She had all but forgotten him in the last few hours. Madea scanned the room for the door again, spotting it along the left hand wall and heading for it.

"Who is Jaxon?" her mother asked.

"The boy I'm looking after. I asked Sarai and Rickard to take care of him until I could come, but I should go. He's already been through enough."

"It might be better for him to stay in the domes, Maddy," Tahra suggested. "He's in no danger there."

"I don't know if that's true." Madea stopped at the door, turning back to the others. "Jaxon's mother was Hollowed, and her father told me it was a set up. That she was Hollowed so that no one would know who the father was. Would they do that? Could he have been right?"

It was Garrett's turn to take a deep breath. "I don't know who exactly you're talking about, but if you're asking whether sometimes the people who are Hollowed are made that way to keep them quiet, then the answer is yes."

Bile rose in the back of her throat as she jumped to the next thought. "Her father...They said he was Touched and that it came on quickly." She scanned the room, looking for somewhere to vomit but there was nothing. She dropped to her knees, letting everything she'd eaten at dinner leave her body in one foul heave. "I need water." She wiped her mouth with the back of her hand and sobbed, fighting down the nausea that still threatened. "I...I... I gave him the jinweed. I was there to drug him. I was part of this, with him, with Janae. How many people? How many people have been Hollowed for no good reason?" Great sobs erupted from her chest making it hard to breathe. "I might as well have killed them!"

She felt a cool flask against her hand and groped for the lid, flipping it back and swallowing as much as she could, enough to stop the wail that threatened to tear free.

"You didn't know," Garrett said, his voice soft and calm. He smoothed the hair back from her face, ignoring the mess on the floor.

Madea took a deep breath, and then another. "But I know now." As she exhaled she closed her eyes and did her best to remember what it was like not to know the truth.

"Maddy, I want you to listen to me." Her mother's voice was the same tone she had used when Madea was a child, like the time Tahra had been explaining why another girl in her class picked on her. "If your father had listened, no one would ever be Hollowed. None of this is your fault. You were doing your job, and no one can hold that against you." Tahra tilted Madea's chin up and held her gaze. "Do you hear me?"

She nodded, fighting to hold back another wave of tears. "I'll try to think of it like that." But she knew she wouldn't be able to ignore it for long. How would she face Jaxon, knowing that she had played a part in destroying his mother, and his grandfather? "I need to get Jaxon. If what his grandfather said was true, then he's not safe."

"What did he say?" Tahra asked.

"That Jaxon is the son of some highborn, that they were trying to keep Janae quiet by having her Hollowed. If they could do that to her, they might do it to Jaxon, right?"

"Children aren't usually Hollowed," Garrett said. "It's not common, but it's not unheard of."

"I don't care how uncommon it is. He's not safe as long as he's up there, alone, with no one to look out for him."

"You said that Sarai would take care of him."

"She'll probably take him to father, and I can't trust him, can't trust her. Not anymore." Madea took another swig of water and then handed the flask back to Garrett. "I need to get Jaxon and if you won't help me, I'll do it on my own."

Tahra folded her arms. "You can't go back so soon, they will be looking for you. If anything, they will use this boy as a lure. You'd be walking right into their trap—"

"I'll help you," Garrett said, cutting off Tahra. "If it's important, if you think he's in danger, then we'll find a way." He shot Tahra a pointed look.

"It's not—"

"It's not up for discussion," Madea said. "I will find a way, with or without you."

"With," Garrett asserted. He held a hand up to Tahra when she opened her mouth. "First, let's get you familiar with our home, and then we can talk about Jaxon."

"Okay." Madea nodded. She had thought her mother would support her in this, would do anything she could to get back on side with the daughter she'd left behind. Apparently Madea's safety was more important than her peace of mind. "Lead on."

Tahra and Garrett led her through rooms and tunnels, sparse in their fittings, but comfortable enough. They introduced her to a range of people, whose names she instantly forgot: the guy who oversaw the armoury, the woman in charge of distributing supplies, the folks who organized and worked in the crews outside to make sure enough food was harvested, the men and women who monitored the cameras and made sure their facility was secure.

"Many of us are outdoors, finding food, keeping an eye on who is coming and going— anyone who might have been exposed."

"How do you get out of the city? I'm assuming you stay out of the domes as much as possible."

"We've got exits straight to the outside." Garrett grinned. "Saves worrying about being spotted, and because of the fear of exposure, not many spend time out of the domes unless it's necessary."

"That said, not everyone wants to go outside," Tahra pitched in. "The creatures are only on the surface, they don't seem to like coming into the tunnels, and there are those of us who aren't comfortable yet with their new knowledge. We don't push anyone above ground until they are ready to face their new reality."

"What about me?" Madea asked.

"What do you mean?" Tahra looked confused.

"I haven't seen these creatures yet. Aren't you worried about how I might react when I do see one? What if that happens when I'm getting Jaxon back?" She was worried now. She'd been catching glimpses of things at the edges of her vision back in the domes, but never anything solid enough to put a name to. "Is there any way to speed up the process?"

Tahra and Garrett exchanged a long look before Garrett spoke again. "There is a way, well, we think it works. We haven't had a chance to test it thoroughly, but more often than not..."

"And?"

"I can take you out of the domes to one of the places they congregate. The extra exposure to light, plus the density of them seems to push the person's vision to the point where they can see them. It's intense though, we've only had a few people experience it."

Madea had moved in front of Garrett. She grabbed his shirt in her hands. "Take me. The sooner we do this the better."

He glanced back at Tahra who nodded reluctantly. "Be careful out there. They probably aren't looking outside the domes, but you never know."

"I'll take the utmost care." Garrett nodded back at her and then grasped one of Madea's hands. "Do you need anything before we leave? I'll grab some basic supplies on our way out, but we shouldn't be gone more than a few hours."

"I'm ready." Madea swallowed. "I'll see you later?"

"Of course." Tahra smiled. "I've just got you back, I'm not planning on losing you again so soon."

Madea wanted to hug her, but Garrett tightened his grip on her hand and she let him lead her down another tunnel.

CHAPTER SEVENTEEN

The natural light hurt Madea's eyes when they pushed through the hatch. She stumbled into the clearing, trying to figure out where they were in relation to the city. She found it to the north, the multiple domes sloping above the treeline, sunlight reflecting off their surfaces. She revelled in the feeling of wind against her skin, out here, free from covering. Now that she was already Touched, she felt like she could endure the heat of the sun without fear for the first time since coming to Diamara.

Garrett concealed the entrance. He'd done such a good job that if she hadn't just come through it, she wouldn't have been able to spot it.

"How do you live like that? Under there?" she asked.

"How do you live in the domes? That's just as restrictive." He shrugged. "Besides, I don't spend nearly as much time down there as others. I like to watch, and help."

"How long have you been watching me?"

"A few weeks. Your mother was eager to bring you in with us, but she thought she'd give your father one last chance to help create change."

"And if he had? What then?"

Garrett shrugged. "To be honest, she probably would have exposed you anyway." Madea went to speak but he held a hand up. "Don't take that the wrong way. Once you've seen what we can see, you'll understand everything better. It's very hard to put into words, but hopefully it won't be long and you'll know, too."

"Right then. What do we do?" She glanced around the clearing. "Do we stay here, or...what?"

Garrett scanned the cleaning, then shook his head. "No, there aren't many here today. There's a good spot nearby though. Come on." He held his hand out and Madea paused before she took it.

"Is there a reason you keep holding my hand?" It seemed so innocent, the way he did it, and yet when she remembered the scorch of his lips against her body she couldn't help but wonder if there was more to it than kindness.

"Your mother would kill me if I lost you." He winked. "Humour me."

She let him lead the way to the trees and then through a twisting path that was barely there at all. "So where are we going?"

"It's a place I like to go when I need some space. I'm trying to encourage more of us to be out here, but years of living under the domes has affected people. It's like they don't remember what it was like back on Earth."

"The fear of being Touched is a real one. No one wants to get Hollowed."

"But you'd think that the Touched would lose that fear. At least, the ones we save." He shook his head. "We humans are strange creatures."

"How long has it been for you?" She stepped over a log and ducked under the branch he was holding up for her. They'd had to drop hands in order to traverse the path.

"A year, I think. Sometimes it seems as though it was only yesterday, and other times it's like the rest of my life, everything before I was exposed, was a dream."

"A good one, or a bad one?"

"Bit of both." Garrett chuckled. "I wouldn't go back though. I couldn't. So many people here cling to Earth and what we had, but this has shown me that we can have something new, something unique."

Madea stiffened. He could have been speaking about her. Perhaps he was—had he been watching her for long enough to know that she was one of them? One of the ones who wished that things were more like they had been on Earth?

"What's so wrong about wanting to bring some of Earth to Diamara? It was our home, the place where we were born."

"It won't be long until we've been here for half our lives, Madea. There is no going back, even if we wanted to." He shook his head. "We are not the same as we were then. We travelled through space, we colonized a new planet. That changes a person."

"Not to mention being Touched," she said wryly.

Garrett grinned. "And that." He pushed through a thick hedge and led her into another clearing. There was a small lake here, something she hadn't seen in quite some time. "And we're here. What do you think?" He spread his arms wide, like a child showing off his latest piece of art.

"It's beautiful." She exhaled, letting some of the tension in her body go. "Can we swim?" The words slipped out before she could stop them.

"If that's what you want."

"Wait. Are they here?" She glanced around, trying to spot one of the creatures. The air felt thick with possibility, and if the buzz in her ears was anything to go by, there had to be some around.

Garrett nodded. "They are. That was the point." He grinned wryly. "Let's get in the lake. The more relaxed you are, the better."

"I thought Mother said there hadn't been enough experimenting done with this."

"There hasn't." He reached down to grab the hem of his shirt, pulling it over his head and tossing it onto the grass.

Madea had to force her jaw to stay shut—she didn't need him to know how much of a distraction his body was right now. Garrett unbuttoned his pants, letting them drop to his ankles before he kicked them off, leaving him only in boxers.

"Coming? Or are you chicken?" The dare in his voice was impossible to resist.

Madea stripped off her outer garments, throwing them next to his, then took off at a run, hoping to beat him to the lake. She could hear his melodic laugh behind her as he gave chase.

It was impossible to try and keep her reasons for being here at the front of her mind when he was right behind her, more than half naked. She made it to the shore before he did and splashed into the water, gasping at the unexpected chill. She forced herself deeper, throwing herself under the surface of the lake before she really did chicken out.

The water was slick against her body, seeping into her skin and clutching at her hair, her limbs. It had been years since she'd swum in an open body of water—not since leaving Earth—and she could have cried at the release she felt, if she hadn't been so thrilled by the sensations in her body. Her muscles felt good to be used again, like this, and it brought home for her how much of her life since coming here had been tied up in work and responsibilities. And how little in play.

She looked through the clear violet tinged water behind her, taking in the sight of Garrett's lean body streaking towards her. She smiled, then pushed towards the surface, breaking through and taking a great gasp of air into her lungs. She kicked her feet, keeping herself in place as Garrett's head popped up beside her.

"This is perfect," she said. "I never imagined that at a time like this I would be swimming with some guy in a lake in the middle of nowhere."

"There is never a bad time for something like this." He grinned. "Now, what's this about some guy? Is that all I am to you?" He winked and she had no idea whether he was playing, or whether there was something more to his question.

"Well, I guess you're really my hero, saving me from my evil father." She grinned back, then slapped the surface of the lake, splashing water into his face. His shocked expression made her laugh so hard that she bobbed down, catching a mouthful of water herself.

"Oh, so that's how it is?" He shook his head, still smiling. "You shouldn't have done that."

"What are you going to do about it?" She raised an eyebrow and bit her lip. The rest of the world could wait, every worry in her life could be damned for now.

Garrett launched forward, grabbing her arms and pushing her into the water. Heat surged through her body and an ache she hadn't felt in a long time ripped through her core. She reached around him, drew him in and found his lips with hers, water seeping into their mouths between their lips, their teeth. They broke the surface, gasping, barely losing contact in the process. His hands caught in her hair and she moved hers to his hips, pulling him closer.

The kiss blew every thought from her mind, every thought but the one that said she wanted more. She slid her fingers down the back of his boxers, but Garrett grabbed her hand and moved it to his chest, breaking the kiss as he did.

"What?" she asked, confusion pushing her lust aside.

"We came here for a reason." He said the words gently, but they weren't making any sense to her.

She frowned. "What?"

"The creatures. We came here so that you could see the creatures," Garret said, his voice husky. He pushed a strand of hair back from her face, tracing the curve of her cheek before dropping his hand to her hip.

"Oh." Her cheeks flushed red, a different heat filling her. "Right. That was obviously what this was about. You must bring every recently Sun-Touched girl out to the middle of nowhere and swim half naked with them. Part of the process I guess. Silly me." She pushed his hands off her body, diving back under the water and swimming away from him as quickly as she could. She waited to hear the splash of his body as he came after her, but it didn't come. She fought back the urge to cry, tears of embarrassment, shame, guilt. She swallowed them down and pushed her body as hard as she could until she reached the shallows.

Madea flopped down on the grass by the edge of the lake, her feet still immersed in the water. She flung an arm over eyes that were closed tight, a double layer of protection against anything that she might see. To think that she thought he was interested in her—to think that she had blown off all her responsibilities on the off chance he would make love to her and eradicate her worries.

No, she was in this alone, she knew that now more than ever. She had to look after herself, and Jaxon, and this unborn baby. Look after Sarai and Rickard if she could, though they were grown-ups, they could take care of themselves. No one else really mattered. Not her father, not her mother, and certainly not Garrett.

She felt the press of his body on the grass beside her. He tried to pull her arm from her eyes but she wouldn't let him.

"Madea, I didn't mean to hurt you." She could hear him swallow, feel his breath across her skin.

"It's the baby. Isn't it?" She let out the breath she had been holding since he arrived. "You can't deny it. It's too much."

"What?"

She flung her arm away and sat up, glaring at him. "You can't handle the fact that I'm pregnant, it makes me unattractive. I get it. Don't worry about me, I'll be fine." Her jaw locked in anger. She wanted to scream at him, wanted to cry.

"No, Madea. No," he said, his words firm. He gripped her arm and pulled her towards him. "I...I owe your mother so much, and I can't repay her like this. I was meant to bring you here to show you the creatures and...I got distracted. You're quite the distraction..."

"So, where are they then? Or was this a complete waste of your time?" She knew he was trying to be kind, but she couldn't stop herself. She was so mad at him, so mad at him for stirring this desire in her, for making her think that he wanted her too. She should have known he was trouble from the moment she met him out in the herb fields. The fact that he worked for her mother was a huge mark against him as well. The air was positively vibrating around her, the buzz in her head externalized.

"Madea. Maddy, look at me." He reached out and placed a hand on each side of her face, forcing her to look at him. "You're thinking too much. Can you push those thoughts away? Push everything away and just be here, now."

"No! I can't!" She pushed his hands away and scowled. "You have no idea, no idea at all what is going on up here." She tapped her head and leaned towards him. "Don't you tell me to—"

He pulled her towards him, pushed his lips against her and kissed her complaints away. She fought back for a moment before she forgot what she was fighting against and had to give up, give in to his lips, his tongue and the press of his hand against her head.

When he let her go, she flopped back to the ground, taking deep breaths to try and stop her head from spinning.

"I don't—"

"Shh, don't speak. Don't open your eyes yet, just listen to me. Okay?"

She swallowed her irritation at being told to shush. "Okay."

"I want you to take three long, slow breaths, and then open your eyes. Don't look at me, relax as best you can and look up."

"Fine." She rolled her eyes behind her lids. She could humour him. She could do this one small thing, and then maybe he could explain what was going on between them. She inhaled, exhaled, the requisite number of times, letting her arms go limp on the ground beside her. When she had pushed aside all the thoughts she could, she opened her eyes and stared into the sky above.

The deep orange sun had turned red and sunk below the treeline, and the trees seemed to loom above her, dark shapes in the dusk light. She could hear the beat of her heart, could feel the blood rushing through her veins, but she didn't see anything different, anything new.

Madea sighed, shaking her head slightly, vision swimming as she tried to squash her disappointment. She turned to Garrett and it was only then that she saw it, hovering, tendrils of...something, stretched out toward him, into him. She stifled a scream, pressed her hands to her stomach in an attempt to quell the nausea that threatened to overcome her.

"Shh, shh. It's okay," Garrett said, his words soft. He stretched his hand out to her, placing it on her thigh and letting his warmth seep into her. "You can see it, can't you? It's not hurting me, it's curious. About me, and about you."

Madea didn't trust herself to speak. She opened her mouth, closed it. Swallowed. Licked her lips. There didn't seem to be an appropriate response—her body didn't know what to do, and her brain didn't know what to think.

"I...I can see it," she whispered. It looked like some kind of eel, if eels were made of light and swam through the air instead of water. One minute it was compact, and the next it stretched tendrils out in all directions, touching not only Garrett, but herself, the lake, the trees, connecting them all. She could feel a thrum in her chest where it touched her. Then it was smaller again, swimming through Garrett, extending out the back of him and then gone in a flash. "What...?"

"It's okay," Garrett said. He smiled at her. "I'm okay. See?" He twisted his torso to prove that there was no gaping wound where the creature had gone through him. She could see it now, behind him, hovering. If it had a face, she couldn't perceive it in the mass of glowing tendrils. Her initial shock was wearing off now and she could see the beauty in this creature, its ethereal nature as it floated in space, visible but translucent.

Madea swallowed the last of her fear and reached a hand towards it, as she might for an unfamiliar animal. It floated through the air, nudging closer and then pulling back as though getting a taste of her energy. Uncertainty sated, it moved forward more confidently, breaching her skin and entering her body, her being. Madea gasped, restrained herself from fleeing and was flooded with stimulation. She could hear a vague whispering in her ears, undecipherable words, fleeting thoughts, stronger than before. Emotions blazed through her brain; sorrow, anger, confusion, pure joy. Exhilaration. She couldn't determine which feelings were her own, and which were emanating from the thing within her.

Every inhalation seemed tinged with some essence of this creature. Her vision swam but this time with tears which poured down her face. She wrapped her arms across her chest, trying to hold herself together, trying to keep the bits of her that she knew were her separate from these other thoughts, other visions and feelings which invaded her body.

And then, when she thought that she was going to shake apart with everything that was happening inside her, a sense of peace swept over her and she found herself lying back on the grass, staring up at the stars, her muscles more relaxed than they had been in weeks.

"Is it always like that?" she asked, after a few minutes had passed and the intensity of the experience had faded away.

"No, not always. The first time you connect with one is the hardest, and then every time you connect with a new one, it's similar, like they need to search through your being, and once they know who you are, they can relax. That's probably not a very good way to explain it, but it's the best I can manage."

"It makes sense, I guess..." She let out a long breath and brought her hands to her face, rubbing at her eyes, suddenly exhausted. "Do you think we could sleep here? I don't know if I have the energy to get back."

"I could carry you, if you wanted?"

"You could cuddle me, if you wanted," she replied, rolling onto her side and crossing her arms over her chest. The smell of the grass was divine, fresh, as if she were smelling it anew. Garrett slid his arm around her.

CHAPTER EIGHTEEN

Madea woke to the smell of grass, struggling to remember why she was outside. The last time she had fallen asleep out of the domes was the time she had been exposed. That had been Garrett's doing, in part, and this time, it was his fault as well. Apparently he had decided that cuddling her was easier than carrying her.

She levered his arm off her waist and wriggled away, placing it gently beside him. He looked peaceful, for a crazy man. She smiled to herself, then pushed up from the ground, surveying the clearing from her knees.

There were creatures here, half a dozen of them floating lazily through the morning haze. Madea wondered if they had a consciousness, a purpose, or whether they were simply existing. She got to her feet and moved towards one, thinking that she might forge another connection. She wanted to experience that again, and yet...maybe it wasn't such a good idea. Who really knew what this was all about?

The lake beckoned to her, sunlight glinting off the surface, the breeze carrying the scent of water to her nose. She headed to it, ignoring the chill of the water on her feet, but unable to stop a shiver when it hit her thighs. It seemed less fun now, more full of potential danger, but she couldn't resist the lure.

She dove under, then surfaced, lying back, content to float where the water would take her.

Madea breathed deeply, exhaled, listened to the sound of it with the water in her ears. How was it that doing the starfish on another planet was the same as doing it on Earth?

Something nudged at her and she startled, swinging upright and looking around. She was still alone in the water, but there beneath the surface, she could see one of the creatures. She hadn't felt it yesterday when it reached for her, she had been too caught up in the new sensations flooding through her body and mind. It nudged at her again, more of a mental nudge she realized, and she frowned, unsure of how to proceed.

"Are you asking my permission?" The words sounded ridiculous, but she continued anyway. "It's okay, if you want to...you know."

The creature hesitated for a moment before entering her body. It broached the skin of her chest, half disappearing. She felt sick, watching it, so she closed her eyes. The same sensations as yesterday crashed over her and she lost the ability to tread water. She began to sink, catching a mouthful of liquid before finding herself buoyed by the creature. It wasn't doing anything that she could see, and yet it was the only explanation Madea could think of. She felt lighter, stable, despite the emotions that were overwhelming her.

Slowly, the feelings abated, leaving behind one thought, one image—Janae, cuddling Jaxon.

Madea tried to push the image aside but the creature was insistent on showing it to her. She had to watch as it played out. Janae, singing him a lullaby and tucking him into bed. Janae, watching from the doorway as he slipped into slumber. Love coursed through her veins, her whole body warmed by the intensity of the emotion. Tears pricked at her eyes as she thought of him at home, waiting for her to return—and yet here in this memory, he was happy, secure. She wished more than anything that she could give that back to him. Give him the love that she felt thrumming through her whole being.

The image flashed, jumped backwards in time to show a younger Janae—much younger—she was lying naked on a bed, beckoning to someone who moved swiftly to her side, climbed onto the bed and began laying ardent kisses on her breasts, her neck, her mouth. A different heat sparked in Madea's body despite the chill of the water, and then Janae's lover glanced up at her and Madea couldn't breathe for shock.

It was Rickard. Rickard's beautiful, youthful face, his lean body and his boyish grin. He was devouring Janae with his eyes, pressing as much of his body against hers as though he couldn't get enough.

"Stop!" Madea cried, wishing that she could push this creature from her being, expel it from her body, make it take these images away. Make it erase them from her mind, Hollow them out of her if that was what it took.

The pictures faded and the sense of relaxation she felt yesterday overtook her body. She went limp, exhausted from the connection, drained from the new knowledge she had been given. It made her sick to her core to think of the repercussions, but now, more than ever, it was important for her to get back, to get Jaxon and keep him safe. She didn't want to believe Rickard was capable of sending someone to be Hollowed to hide that he had a child, but what other explanation was there?

The ether creature withdrew and she had to summon the strength to swim back to shallower water. The beast swam around her, its tendrils expanding to reach out to her, each strand sending a tiny stream of calm into her body. By the time Madea could place her feet on the ground, her head was clear enough to start processing what she'd learned.

"Thank you," she said. On some level, this being understood her. Perhaps it could feel her emotions, respond to the chemicals coursing through her brain. Something. She probably didn't need to say the words, but she felt better for it, all the same.

Somehow, this creature had reached inside her, had pulled the images of Janae, of Jaxon, of Rickard and given her connecting memories. Madea's mind raced, trying to put the pieces together. If these creatures made connections, if they could touch human memories, human thoughts, if they fed off...

Maybe this creature, this one in particular, had touched Janae...Maybe it had fed off her memories, absorbed them somehow. And then, on reaching inside Madea, had seen some of the same faces and transferred those images to her—

"Madea!" Garrett's voice shook her out of her thoughts and she spun to the shoreline to see him standing ankle deep in the water, waving his arms at her. "We should go."

"Okay," she called back. She glanced around her but the creature was gone.

Garrett held out her clothes and she pulled them on with difficulty, the fabric clinging to her wet body.

"Right, then. Guess we go back and find a plan to get this boy of yours," Garrett said.

"Jaxon," Madea corrected. "The sooner I can go and get him, the better."

"We, the sooner we get him," Garrett said, his tone firm.

"We'll talk about that when we get back," Madea said. This time she reached for his hand. She wanted to feel his steadiness, to soak a little of that up before she decided whether to tell him about what she had seen, what she'd felt, from the creature in the water. Garrett's grip was strong as he pulled her away from the lake.

"Are you okay?" he asked with a glance backwards.

"I'm trying to get my head around all of this." It wasn't a lie. There was a lot to take in, a lot to learn, and she didn't have all the information. What she did know was that her mother was alive, that her father could not be trusted, that Rickard was Jaxon's father—and that there was more to these creatures than anyone was telling her.

They walked in near silence back to the hatch in the ground. Madea wouldn't have been able to find it had not it been for Garrett, though she made a point of memorising the rocks and trees closest to it. Just in case. The trip back through the grey-walled tunnels was quicker than she thought it should be, and when they began coming across people bustling down corridors, Madea spoke.

"I need food. I don't think I can face Mother on an empty stomach. Or do we have to report in?" She dropped his hand, feeling the chill of the tunnels instantly steal the heat his hand had generated.

Garrett frowned. "You're not being held hostage here, if that's what you think."

"Not exactly, but we haven't really discussed the finer details."

"That's a conversation you'll need to have with Tahra, but she's your mother and she loves you. If you want to eat first, then we can do that."

"I'm ravenous." She smiled at him, hoping that he would take it in part as an apology. There was something about being back under the earth, away from the sky—even if it was filtered through the domes—that made her feel as though she might be crushed at any moment. It was more obvious now, after spending time outside with nothing to impede her.

"Come on then," he said with a nod. "I know where you can get a top notch breakfast."

Ten minutes later, Madea watched as Garrett mixed together pancake batter.

"I never would have picked you for a cook," she said with a grin.

"Well, I used to do a lot of the cooking for our family, back on Earth." He moved fluidly in his tiny kitchen, putting the pan on to heat and adding a little butter before giving the batter another stir.

"How did you end up coming here?" She leaned forward, over the little kitchen bench, watching as he poured some into the pan. The smell was amazing and her mouth watered in response.

"My Dad was pretty high up in agriculture. They figured he'd be able to help establish crops and other things. And he did, he worked his ass off. Died a couple years ago now, accident out of the domes. No one's fault, really, but it meant that my mother and I lost the little prestige we had. She works in the fields still, so did I, that's how I got exposed. Out too long." He flipped the pancake over, nodding in satisfaction at the golden brown of it.

"So I guess we have that in common." She took a deep breath. "I've been meaning to ask you, how did you do it?"

"Do what?"

"Expose me." She scanned his face, seeing a smidgen of remorse there.

"As I've said, we've been watching you for a while. Me, mostly. We knew you would be out at your father's that night, so someone snuck into your home and tampered with your timer so that it wouldn't alert you. And then, when we had confirmation you'd left the domes, I was there. I injected you with a light sleep serum, enough to make sure you were exposed. Team effort." He grinned sheepishly.

"Right." Madea pursed her lips. She couldn't fault the plan, she wasn't even sure she was still mad at him—or Tahra—now that she'd seen the creatures. But still, it spoke of the measures they were willing to go to. "And you're confident it's the right 'team'?"

"I'm sure that it is. This is our home now, we need to adjust to life here and the creatures are part of that. Don't you think?"

"I don't know yet. I'm still trying to get my head around it. I can't deny that they are here, or that they are impressive, but I'm yet to see that your tactics are really the best way of going about things."

The stack of pancakes was growing, and Garrett gave the pan his full attention. Madea could see his shoulders stiffen.

"How much do you know about the creatures?" she asked, as much to change the subject as to gather information.

"As much as anyone else, I guess." He shrugged. "They seem to be drawn to something in us; a chemical, our thoughts, energy. We're not really sure. There doesn't seem to be any negative impact from the connection, but in reality, it's only been since your mother that we've known that there was more to it than madness. The fear of being Touched, the harsh reality of being Hollowed, is ingrained in all of us."

"And you think that we can change that perception?"

"We have some ideas. Don't you think everyone has a right to know? Wasn't it amazing? Don't you want to share that experience with those you love?" That fanatical gleam lit his eyes as he spoke.

"I think that, as we've seen, it's quite a lot to take on board for anyone. Even with having some idea of what to expect it was overwhelming. You can't expect people to trust you, just because you say it's a worthwhile experience."

"But it is worthwhile. Isn't it?"

Madea sighed. "That's not the point! The point is that people should have the right to make decisions about how they live their life."

Garrett placed his hands flat on the bench between them and leaned towards her. "But what if they won't let themselves see that there is an option?"

Madea leaned back, creating some space to breathe. "I don't know." She shrugged. "I guess that's something that needs more thinking about," she said, hoping to placate him enough to switch topics again.

"You'll get your head around it soon, I'm sure," he said confidently. He grabbed the plate of pancakes and placed it between them. "Butter?"

"Sure." She laughed. "Now, about Jaxon..."

"We've got maps that we can take a look at. Figure out the best route to get him."

"I think I should go alone."

"Tahra won't let that happen, so you might as well discard that idea now." Garrett shook his head. "Why would you want to go alone anyway?" He raised an eyebrow.

"Jaxon doesn't know you, and he's already been through enough. I don't want to frighten him."

"You'll be there. But I'm serious when I say that you're not going alone."

"When I was swimming this morning I had an encounter with one of the creatures." She took a deep breath. She still wasn't sure that she wanted to divulge this information, but she hadn't been able to think of a good reason to keep it secret. "I saw some things, like the creature was showing me memories and thoughts that it had collected from someone else. Someone I knew."

"Really?" He practically lunged across the bench, grasping her wrists. "Tell me more, what was it like?"

"So I'm guessing you haven't experienced this?" She quirked an eyebrow.

"No, at least I don't think so. I wish I had, that would be amazing. What did you see?"

"I learned something that I think puts Jaxon at risk. I learned who his father is."

"And?" Garrett was getting impatient now. She could tell that he wanted to know more about the experience, and was less concerned with what she had learned.

"He's a friend of mine, and I don't know whether he knows that Jaxon is his son."

"Does it really matter?"

"It matters to me," Madea stated. "Now butter me some pancakes. I'm starving." She gave him a pointed stare and he shook his head, affecting his regular grin and getting back to the task at hand. She grabbed one and took a bite. "Hey, these are actually pretty good," Madea said, swallowing her mouthful.

"I told you I'm a good cook." Garrett swiped one from the plate. His phone buzzed and he glanced at it with a frown. "Tahra needs to see us. Grab some for the road."

She loaded one hand with pancakes, shoving another into her mouth before following him out.

CHAPTER NINETEEN

"Well?" Tahra asked as soon as Garrett closed the door behind them. "Did it work? What took you so long?"

"It did work. Madea fell asleep afterwards, and I thought she needed the rest, so we stayed—"

"Don't you realize how dangerous that was? Anyone could have found you." Tahra planted her hands on the desk and stood, a vein in her neck pulsing.

"It was perfectly safe. We were well away from the domes and you know none of the city folk venture out that far." Garrett's shoulders tensed.

"And what about wild animals?"

"I was with her the whole time. You know I would never jeopardise her safety." He took a step forward, the intensity on his face matching Tahra's.

"I'm right here, you know, and I'm perfectly capable of looking out for myself." Madea slid herself between them, cutting her mother's gaze off from Garrett. "I know I'm new to this whole 'Touched' thing, but I'm not an innocent little girl who needs protecting."

Tahra's wrath melted somewhat and she sighed. "I didn't mean it like that. It's just that I've only had you back a few days. I couldn't bear it if anything happened to you."

Madea didn't say anything for a moment. The tension in the room was palpable, but she forcibly relaxed her shoulders and held out her hand to her mother. "Do you want a pancake? Garrett made them."

Tahra shifted her glare back to him. "You stopped to make—"

"They're really good. Here, try one." Madea pried one of Tahra's hands from the desk and placed a pancake in it. Her mother grudgingly took a bite, and a slow smile spread across her face. "Thanks, I guess I am a bit hungry. Still, you should have checked in first."

"She's pregnant, Tahra, in case you'd forgotten. Pregnant women need to eat, you remember that, don't you?"

"Again, I'm right here..." Madea bit her lip. "Is there any chance you could give me a moment with my mother?"

"Sure." He frowned, flicking his gaze to Tahra and back again before heading for the door. Once he was gone Madea let out the breath she was holding.

"I don't remember you being this..." She pursed her lips, struggling to find the right word.

"This what?" Tahra asked.

"This bitchy! I remember you as loving and kind. You were my rock, the one who made sure I settled in once we got here, made sure I had friends. You were my favourite parent." Her shoulders sagged.

"And now?" Sadness tinged Tahra's voice.

"Now I don't know." Madea shrugged. "I don't know what to think, or feel, but those things I thought I knew about you? There are only echoes of them now."

"Things change, Madea. And yes, I've changed too. I had to let that woman go. You think I would have survived if I had clung to my past? It would have killed me, and there was no way I would give Carson that satisfaction." The sneer on Tahra's face transformed her into someone entirely different. In that moment there wasn't an ounce of the mother Madea had known, the mother she had hoped to regain. And then it fell away and there was loss in Tahra's eyes again. She gave a harsh bark of a laugh. "I guess I'm still bitter about that. I'm sorry. I know he's your father, but..."

Madea shrugged. "It's okay. Sometimes I feel like that about him, too." She flicked her eyes around the room, taking in the books, the pictures. Her eyes fell on an old photo, crinkled at the edges. It was from back on Earth, back when they had all been a happy family. It was at the end of a canoeing trip, down some big old river a million miles from home. This photo had been taken by their guide once they'd pulled their canoe up on shore at the final destination. Their hair was knotted and sticking out all over the place, their eyes shadowed by fatigue. She could remember the way her skin had felt; grimy, despite having fallen into the water several times that day—or perhaps because of that—and yet she could see in her teenaged face a gleam of pride, of joy, which was mirrored in the faces of the rest of the family.

What had happened between then and now? Everything was different. Her father power hungry and uncompromising in his desire to obtain whatever rank he was after, her mother transformed into something else entirely. Betrayal by her husband, discovery of the ether creatures and who knew what else shaping her into someone Madea was struggling to relate to. And yet there, in that photo, she could see that once they had been so happy, despite the difficulties of their trip.

Apparently colonizing a new planet was a little harder than canoeing down a river.

"Do you think we'll find a way to be mother and daughter again?" She said it softly, almost hoping that Tahra wouldn't hear, wouldn't have to try and find an answer.

"Is that what you want?" Tahra bit her lip, reminding Madea of herself. Was it a trait she had picked up from her mother?

"I want— I want for us to be something. I thought you were dead, and it's hard to get my head around the fact that you're not. Because you're alive, but you're not the same, and I'm not saying that's a bad thing, or a thing you need to change, it's just something I've got to get my head around."

"The same is true for you, Maddy. If you could see how different you are now...not bad different, but when I saw you last you were still in your teens, finding your path, following the way that had been set out for you. And now you're here, cast out like me." She moved from behind the desk and reached toward Madea who allowed herself to be pulled into an embrace. "And you're pregnant." The words were a whisper, so fragile, yet holding such hope, such loss. "I can't imagine how it would have felt to have known you were having a child and yet not be able to be there with you. To be able to hold my grandchild."

"You could have contacted me. You could have said something," Madea said, a sob wracking her body. As much as she wanted to believe her mother's reasons for staying absent, she couldn't help but feel the pain of the knowledge that her mother had been out of reach from her own free will.

"I'm sorry, Maddy, I'm so sorry. I wish I had been brave enough to break the silence. I wish I'd been more selfish." Tahra was crying too, tears making Madea's shoulder wet. "I hope that someday you can forgive me. I know it's going to take time, but I'm willing to do what it takes, if you want me to."

Madea pulled back a little, wiping her eyes and sniffing back the last of her tears. "I do, but I need time."

"I understand." Her mother nodded, giving her a warm smile. "I'm grateful for even that much."

Madea smiled back. "Now, we need to talk about Jaxon. I need to get him back."

"I know you think he's in danger—"

"I do, and I need you to trust me on this one. If his mother and grandfather were Hollowed to protect his father, that means there is no one left to look out for him. And I don't know that he's safe with Rickard."

"That doesn't mean it's your responsibility."

"But it does. I brought him to my home and I made a promise to him. I told him I would be there for him and right now I'm not. I can't abandon him— I'm sorry." Madea's face flushed and she covered her mouth with her hands. "I wasn't trying to be cruel, and I'm not judging you. I'm not. He's already suffered enough, and I can't leave him just because you don't think it's safe to go get him."

"I understand." Tahra nodded. Her voice was subdued, her gaze on the floor. "Why don't you and Garrett organize it, and he can let me know what your plan is. Okay?"

"That's fine." Madea bit her lip, trying to figure out the right thing to say. "Mum? I mean it. I wasn't having a dig at you. I know it wasn't your choice to leave me, I know you stayed away for what you thought were the right reasons."

"Thanks." She nodded again, still not meeting Madea's gaze. "Go on, you better get organized."

"Okay, sure. I'll...um...I'll see you later." Madea stepped forward and gave her mother a quick kiss on the cheek before retreating. She closed the door behind her and leaned against it, letting out all the air in her lungs. Why couldn't anything be simple?

"Are you okay?" Garrett asked. She hadn't noticed that he was sitting on the floor to the right of the door.

"I'll be fine." She gave him a small smile. "We've got work to do. Where to?"

"Do you want to rest first? You look tired." He got up and moved towards her, gently grabbing her elbow in support.

"No, I want to figure this out."

"Alright." He shrugged. "Come on then." He led her down the tunnel. She wasn't sure where to, but she trusted him.

"I think we should go tonight," Madea said.

"Tonight? You don't think that's a bit soon? I doubt Tahra is going to agree."

"I think we do it, and then tell her about it when we get back." Madea flashed him a grin.

"And get another dressing down? No thanks. I'll have you know that she isn't done yelling at me for the last one."

Madea stopped walking. "Is she always like that?"

"Not always, no." He shook his head. "Unless it's something to do with you, then yes. She's been on edge ever since she decided she wanted to bring you in. I've never seen her this antsy before."

"I guess that means she really does care." Madea bit her lip, still trying to figure out how she felt.

"Of course she cares. I don't think she knows how to show it any more. You can understand that, right? I mean, when you see your family again, what are you going to say to them? How much will you tell them?"

"I don't know..." Her stomach roiled thinking about it. Would Sarai and Rickard give her Jaxon if they thought she was crazy? She would have to take him even if they did. She couldn't leave him there with the chance that Rickard might do something to him. But would he? She had told him Jaxon's story and he'd given nothing away. If anything, he seemed to take a liking to the boy.

Madea took a deep breath and glanced up at Garrett, only to find that he was watching her intently. "What?" she asked.

"Wondering what's going on up here." He tapped his head with a finger. "Care to share?"

"Thanks, but not right now. Sorry, I..."

"You want to get Jaxon. I get it. So, do you have a plan?" Garrett resumed walking, and she trailed along behind him.

"We have to check my place first, and if he's not there, we'll have to look at Dad's place, or Rickard's. I'm not sure where they would have taken him, but chances are high they aren't at mine anymore."

"I'll go by there, alone. You've only been gone a few days and your father probably has people keeping an eye on it."

"I guess." Impatience built inside her. "So what do we need?"

"Glad you asked. This is the Armoury." He swung the door open with a flourish. The walls were lined with shelving and a large man at the back was rifling through boxes. "We'll need things to override security, or break into houses, maybe some communications devices. You have no phone, remember. Can you recall your friend's number, or your sister's?"

"Not really, no." Damn her pregnancy brain. "I say we take a bunch of different stuff with us and wing it."

"Wing it?" Garrett laughed. "From my observations, you're not the kind of girl who wings it'."

"Correction. I never used to be the kind of girl to who just 'wings it'. I spent years doing things the right way, following the rules, doing everything that was wanted of me. And sure, ever since I started bending those rules life has gotten pretty chaotic, but for once in my life I feel like maybe I can decide what I want, instead of doing the things I know I should."

"Sounds like a good enough reason to wing it to me." Garrett grinned. "Hey Sturm," he called to the guy at the back of the room. "Come over here and meet Madea. Tahra's daughter."

Sturm grunted as he got up from his knees, dusting his palms off on his thighs as he approached. He held out a hand, which Madea grasped, his rough fingers enclosing hers.

"Nice to meet you Miss Linae. Glad to have you with us." Sturm bowed his head at her before turning to Garrett. "What are you two here for?"

"Just a few bits and bobs. Need to go and pick someone up from the domes."

"Alright, well, you know where everything is." He gave Madea another nod and then went back to work.

"Not much for small talk huh?" Madea whispered.

Garrett shrugged. "No. He's a man of few words, but he's as loyal to your mother as they come."

"Look, why don't you load up a bag for me, and I'll get out of your hair." She shrugged, hoping that maybe she could do this on her own. She had something with Garrett, or could have something with Garrett, but there wasn't enough there for her to want to introduce him to her family yet. And not like this.

"You couldn't get out of this place if you tried." He shook his head, a smug look on his face, though he grabbed a backpack and started loading it up. "And you need to rest.

Sometimes it seems like you're ignoring the fact that you're pregnant."

"Sometimes it seems like you're obsessing about the fact that I'm pregnant. For the record, I only found out a week ago. Between that and other things...well, I can't say that it's the most pressing issue right this minute. Does that bother you?"

"No. I get it. I just think someone should be looking out for you, and that someone seems to be me."

"I don't need looking after," she asserted. "Really. I'm a big girl and I can look out for myself."

"Fine. I still think we should have a rest before we go. Your head must be overflowing with information, and you've done a lot of running around. It could take hours to find Jaxon and extract him, so we might as well be fresh for it. I'll send someone to monitor your place, see if there are any Enforcers hanging about."

"Okay." Madea shrugged, supressing a sigh of frustration. "Where can I rest?"

"I'm sure Tahra's prepared some quarters for you, let me check..." He flicked through his phone, nodding when he found what he was looking for. "Come on, I'll show you the way."

Madea followed him, though they didn't have far to go. It was one hallway over, the third door down. Garrett pushed open the door and stood aside with a flourish. "Your rooms, milady. I hope they meet your expectations."

Madea laughed. "Why thank you, sir." She swept into the room and glanced around, adopting an imperious glare. "They will do for now, though I do hope you can do something about the heating situation."

"Oh, right. Sorry." He stepped inside and flicked the switch for a heating unit. "Should be good in no time."

"Thanks."

They stood there in silence for a moment. Madea felt a little uncomfortable, not sure what the appropriate goodbye was for whatever it was that they were to each other. She chewed on her bottom lip. "What time are we going?"

"A few hours, I guess. Should I come and wake you?"

"Yes, please." Her stomach felt hollow, though in reality she knew it was full, she'd eaten way too many pancakes for comfort.

"Alright then, I guess I'll see you soon." He paused before grabbing the door with one hand.

"Wait!" she called. "Don't go." Her shoulders slumped and she bit her lip again. "I...I don't want to be alone. Could you stay, please?" She took a step towards him, reached out with one of her hands. Within seconds he had shut the door and grasped her fingers in his.

"I'm here." He drew her into his arms, crushing her body against his. She buried her head in his shoulder and let loose the tears she didn't realize she'd been holding in. "I'm sorry. I..."

"You don't need to tell me. I'm here for you," he murmured. "Remember back in the transport? The night I gave you my number? I told you I would be there to help you if you ever needed me, and I meant it."

"Thank you." She sniffed, trying to staunch the flow of tears.

"Any time." He scooped her up and carried her to the bed where he placed her gently down, and sat beside her, brushing strands of hair off her face with one hand. "I'm serious now. You rest, and I'll have a lie down on the couch, okay? I'm not going anywhere, I promise."

"Thanks." She smiled weakly as he left the room. As long as she knew that someone was there, within reach if she needed them, she felt okay. But it was more than that, wasn't it? Garrett sometimes seemed to be the only one who had her best interest in mind—even when it came to the baby. He had this weird fanatical vibe about him, and yet what had seemed to be almost worship of her mother when they first met had been skewed since then. Now he was looking out for her, as much as her mother.

And then there were those kisses and the way her body trembled beneath his touch.

She wasn't going to be able to rest if she followed that train of thought. No, she had to shove that one down, ignore the temptation of his lips at least until Jaxon was safe with her.

Madea closed her eyes and tried a relaxation technique her mother had taught her back on Earth, tightening each of her muscles and relaxing them one at a time from head to toe. She hadn't made it to her calves before she had fallen asleep.

CHAPTER TWENTY

Fingers brushed against her cheek. Madea jolted out of sleep to find Garrett sitting on her bed.

"Did you know that you snore?" he asked.

"I do not."

"You do. I take it no one shares your bed or you'd know."

"What? Obviously someone has shared my bed or I wouldn't be pregnant," she replied indignantly.

"Maybe that didn't happen on a bed..." He smiled.

"Garrett! That's none of your business. But for the record, the father wants nothing to do with the baby. And I'm okay about that."

"Really?"

"Yes," she said firmly, swinging her legs over the edge of the bed and straightening her clothes. "Any more questions?"

"No, I think I'm good for now." He shrugged as he stood, offering her his hand. She grabbed hold and pulled herself to her feet. "I made you a sandwich, and after you've eaten it, we'll get going."

"Okay," she said. Part of her wanted to protest that she didn't need feeding, but her stomach grumbled at the mention of food. She moved ahead of him into the living area and grabbed the plate off the bench, biting into the sandwich without delay. Within moments she had polished it off. "I hope you've got some food for the road."

"I packed wisely." He tapped his nose. "Can't have your stomach giving our location away."

"Hey, no fair." She slapped his arm, but it did nothing to wipe the grin off his face.

"Well, we don't, do we? Come on, put your boots on and let's get moving. I want to be back before your mother starts worrying about what we might be up to. I told her we were going to scout out Jaxon's whereabouts and report back before trying to extract him. My watcher says no one has been by your place, so it should be safe enough."

"Thanks," she said. "I don't want to get you in trouble, but I can't leave this any longer."

"It's okay. I figure once you've done what you need to, we can start looking at the bigger picture."

"Which is?"

"How we're going to stop the Hollowings, and show people the truth about being Touched."

"Right. Well, we can sort that out later." Madea wasn't sure what he expected her to do in regards to that. And there was no way she could give anything attention until she had Jaxon back, and had spoken to Rickard. She pulled on her boots and headed for the door. "Let's get moving."

Madea trailed behind Garrett through the tunnels, trying her best to remember the way. Despite her efforts, she soon lost track of the twists and turns.

Within ten minutes they came to an exit. Garrett flipped the keyhole open and glanced out, making sure that no one was in the building. Once he was sure it was clear, he levered open the hatch and they stepped out into another abandoned church.

"Where are we?" Madea asked. This one was smaller than the last, the pews mostly broken, though the coloured glass in the windows was still pristine.

"We're not far from your place. I figured you could wait here while I take a look. Double check," Garrett said. He too was looking around the building, though she spotted him glancing at her out the corner of his eye, waiting for her reaction.

"That's probably the best idea. We don't want anyone to spot me," she said, sounding as reasonable as she could. She had no intention of sitting behind, but it would be quicker to agree with him and then follow. "Speaking of...I thought maybe you should give me a few options, in case we need to make a quick escape and I lose you."

Garrett shook his head. "It would take too long to try and show you the entrances to below. I have a better idea." He swung the pack off his back and rummaged through it, coming up with another phone. "This one's for you. It's got a direct line to mine for quick access. These ones are off the main grid, so while they have locators, your mother won't know that we've got them in order to track us."

"Good thinking," she said. "I'm impressed. Anyone would think that subversive behaviour was your thing."

He chuckled. "That's what they keep me around for." He winked. "I wouldn't normally do this to Tahra, but I know how much it means to you. And I made a promise. If she wasn't so personally invested in you, she would support what you're doing here."

"Do you really think so?" It was strange how much that actually mattered to her. She hadn't expected it to.

"You're not so different from each other, though you might not see it."

"No, not really. Anyway, how long do you think you'll be?" she asked.

"Maybe a half hour? You'll be alright here. Keep alert, in case you need to hide."

"I'll be fine." She smiled. "Hurry up. We don't have time to waste."

"I'll see you soon, then." Garrett waved over his shoulder and headed for the door. She followed, as though she were seeing him out.

Five minutes, she would give him five minutes and then follow. If they were that close to her home, then she couldn't get lost. Time seemed to stand still as her eyes flashed to the timer on her phone every ten seconds. The slow drag came to an end. She checked there was no one outside before leaving the church and following Garrett's path.

She had never noticed this church before, but once she had entered the alley on the right, her surroundings become more familiar. If she took another left...

Madea screamed as an arm wrapped around her throat and pulled her against the wall. She lashed out with her hands, her feet, but the arms holding her were like steel. They had found her again, she was going to be Hollowed. How could she be so stupid? She knew what was at stake.

"I knew you were up to something," Garrett whispered in her ear. "You should have put up more of a fight and I might have been convinced you'd stay put." He took his arm away from her throat, though he held her tight against him.

"Let me go," she hissed.

She could feel his smirk against her cheek as he held her for a moment longer. "Can we continue now?"

"Continue this? Or our rescue of your young friend?" Garrett let out a soft laugh, the warmth of his breath heating her neck.

"Jaxon," she said, moving away from him.

"Ah well, another time." He winked again and her frustration rose.

"Can you get your mind on the task? This is important to me." Heat of her own had flashed across her face, but she couldn't risk lashing out at him or he might renege on his offer of help. She needed to be smart about this, or she really would end up back in the Hollowing chair.

"Sure," he said, shrugging off his playful attitude.

"Great," she snapped as she pushed off the wall and continued down the alley. She knew where she was going, she didn't need him to lead. She ignored him and his annoying presence and focused on the task ahead.

It wasn't until they were almost there that Garrett asserted himself again. He placed a hand on her shoulder and raised a finger to his lips. "Let me take a look first, okay? And if it's clear, I'll come back for you. Five minutes."

"Fine." She rolled her eyes at him, but leaned against the wall as he moved away from her and out onto her street. Again, those five minutes seemed like an eternity, but then he was back, beckoning for her to follow. Her heart thumped. It could have been weeks since she had last seen her house, when in reality it hadn't been more than a week, had it? Time felt warped to her now. So much had changed since she had left, so much that couldn't be undone.

But there it was, her unit, sitting silent and empty.

"Do you think it's safe to go in?"

"Only one way to find out." Garrett grinned at her with a recklessness she knew he didn't mean. Everything he did was for a cause, for a valid reason.

Regardless, she wasn't going to waste more time. She moved quickly to the door and entered her apartment. Garrett shut the door behind him and they stood in the entrance, listening.

"It doesn't seem like anyone is home," she said. It was a little anticlimactic, really. Not that she had been sure Jaxon would be here, but she hadn't expected silence and the musty smell of an unused house. "I'm going to grab a couple of things. Why don't you see if you can find a note or something."

"Sure." Garrett headed through to the lounge and Madea paused, wondering whether he had been inside her house before. She wanted to ask, but wasn't sure she really wanted the answer.

Shaking the thought off she moved down to her bedroom where she grabbed a bag and shoved in some fresh clothing and personal items. Sure, Tahra would provide for her, but there was nothing like having your own things and she needed that normalcy, that familiarity to ground her right now. She stopped when she came to one of the drawings Jaxon had done for her. It was a simple drawing, the two of them eating sandwiches, but she could remember when he had given it to her and the feelings it had evoked.

A surge of energy shot through her and she pushed herself off the bed, grabbing a few more items before heading back out into the hallway. She stopped and listened, then headed for the kitchen where she could hear Garrett rummaging around.

"Did you find anything?" she asked, swinging the bag onto her back. His head was in a cupboard and when he turned to her he had a cracker hanging out of his mouth and another held towards her.

"They left a note."

"Huh, that must have been before they tried to Hollow me." She grabbed the cracker and bit into it but it was too stale for her to eat. "And it said?" she prompted.

"They were taking Jaxon to Rickard's place. I'm guessing you know where that is?"

"I do. Give me the note." He passed it to her and she scanned it before shredding it and shoving it into the disposal unit. "Don't need anyone else seeing that."

"We should go."

"Hang on, I need to pee."

"Way too much information..."

"It's the baby." She rolled her eyes at him headed to the bathroom. She washed her hands and was peering at herself in the mirror when the front door banged open and multiple voices filled the hallway. Her heart raced, but her body froze. They seemed to be in the kitchen in no time at all, and she heard Garrett cry out.

"What are you doing here?" a man shouted.

"I was looking for Madea. Do you know where she is?"

She moved across the bathroom quietly and pressed an ear against the wall it shared with the kitchen. She wished there was another exit, but there was no way she could get out of the unit without letting them know she was here.

"You know. You're hiding her." There was a crash and Madea closed her eyes, trying not to imagine what was happening.

"If I knew where she was, why would I be here?" Garrett hissed. Another thump, but this sounded like it made contact with skin. Garrett let out a yelp.

"Secure him. He might know more than he's letting on, then give this place a once over. I'll tell Carson we've got someone." Shoes pounded on the tiles of the kitchen and Madea pushed off the wall, scanning the room for options. She pressed herself into the shower alcove, hoping that they wouldn't look too hard. The door was shoved open. Madea held her breath and tried to become one with the wall. Seconds later the door slammed shut and she exhaled through gritted teeth.

She waited ten, then twenty minutes, her muscles cramping from the awkward position. She had to let go. She crumpled to the floor, pulling her knees to her chest.

Once again she was alone. Her guide to all things Touched had been snatched. But at least she knew now, beyond doubt, that he could be trusted—he had kept her safe, kept his mouth shut. Though who knew where they were taking him, or what they might do to get him to talk.

She should return to the tunnels, she should tell Tahra what had happened, right now. But if she did, she might not get another opportunity to rescue Jaxon. He was just a boy. Garrett was a grown man, he could survive longer, survive more than Jaxon.

Decision made, Madea stood and stretched out her muscles. She would go to Rickard's and get Jaxon back, and then she would find her way to the tunnels and tell Tahra about Garrett.

All she could hope was that Garrett would forgive her.

CHAPTER TWENTY-ONE

There were no lights on at Rickard's by the time Madea got there. She waited outside the building, trying to find a sign of life. After half an hour one light came on briefly and she could see Rickard's silhouette in the kitchen window. She stood and stretched her muscles, then moved through the shadows to the back door.

She closed it quietly behind her and stood in silence, listening for any sign of where they might be. She was so close to Jaxon, so close now and if Rickard had done anything to him there would be no stopping her from exacting a quick and painful revenge.

"Who's there?" Rickard's voice echoed down the hallway. "I know someone came in. Show yourself now or I'll call the Enforcers." He flicked on the light and Madea stepped out into the middle of the passage.

"Madea?" Confusion passed across his face, as well as fear and grief. "What are you doing here?"

"I came for Jaxon," she said, her voice firm and clear. "Where is he?"

"He's sleeping." Rickard moved towards her but stopped, leaving a few feet between them. "I've spoken to your father. He's worried about you." His voice was quiet, and he seemed guarded, as though he expected her to attack him or something.

"I bet he is." She snorted. "Look, Rickard, I'm not mad. Okay? I promise. You've known me most of my life. Look me in the eyes and tell me you think I'm crazy." She let her hands fall to her sides and stood there, defenceless before him. He approached, one reserved step at a time, his eyes locked on hers, the lines in his face relaxing.

"Okay, so you don't look crazy." He frowned. "But if you're not Touched, what happened? Sarai said you took off, asked her to look after Jaxon and that your father was fuming. And then they took you to the Hollowing chair."

"It's a long story. One I don't have time to go into right now. I need to see Jaxon, and then we need to talk."

"Come on." He led her up the hall to his room. He opened the door and let her poke her head in. The boy was fast asleep, his hands tucked up under his chin. It was all she could do to restrain herself from going to him then and taking him in her arms. They ached to hold his small frame.

Rickard tugged at her shirt and she moved away, letting him close the door. "Thank you," she said, her voice husky with emotion.

"Come on. I'll make you a coffee. You look like you could do with one."

They moved into the kitchen and she leaned against the bench. The feel of it under her arms was too familiar, felt too much like Garrett's so she pushed off and crossed them over her chest.

"What do we need to talk about?" Rickard asked as he prepared the coffee.

"I've learned some things since I've been gone," she began. "I know that you're Jaxon's father."

Silence hung between them for a few moments. Rickard poured milk into their cups and stirred.

"Well," he said.

Her heart stopped for a beat. "How could you do that to his mother?"

"What?" Confusion spread across his face.

"You went to Father, didn't you? You told him about your illegitimate child and he helped you tidy away the problem."

"What? No. How could you think that? I didn't have anything to do with that. In fact it wasn't until I saw him at your house that I knew for sure he was mine. He looks like me. Don't you think?" There was a gleam of something in his eyes, something she hadn't expected. Was it pride?

"He does, a little. I wasn't looking for it before, but you're right." She eyed him warily, still thrown by his confession.

"How could you think that I would do that to him? Take his mother away?"

"It was the only thing that made sense. You're his father, you were ashamed—"

"If I had known... Yes, I was reckless in my youth, but it wasn't his fault. It wasn't even hers..." Rickard sighed and scrubbed his chin with a hand.

Madea swallowed, the images of Janae and Rickard springing into her mind in full colour. She blushed, thinking of the passion he had shared with her, wondering whether he shared the same passion with her sister.

"Yes. I spoke with him. I heard that Janae had a child, but I wasn't sure it was mine. I was worried that Sarai would find out and cancel our marriage. But I never thought he would do something about it. I never thought he would move so quickly." He slammed the palm of his hand against the bench. "You believe me, don't you?" he pleaded.

"I don't know what to believe." She ran her hands through her hair and sighed. He pushed a mug of coffee across the bench towards her, as if just remembering. "Thanks."

"So why are you here? Other than to make wild accusations at me," he said wryly.

"I need Jaxon. I made a promise to him, and I intend to keep it."

"He's my son. You can't take him away now."

"You've only just met him, and I made him a promise. Besides, he's not safe here. How long do you think it will be before Sarai lets slip that you have a child living with you and Father comes to collect the boy? Have you come clean to her yet about who he is?"

"No, I haven't." Rickard glared at his mug of coffee. "He's my son."

"And he's not safe." Madea moved into the kitchen and put her hands on his shoulders. "If you really care, then you need to let me take him somewhere safe. You saw what Father did to the boy's grandfather. Do you think he'll leave Jaxon just because he's a child? That man will stop at nothing to get what he wants."

"You don't think I can protect him?" Rickard scowled.

"I think that I can protect him better." They stared at each other, then she relaxed her shoulders. "You care about him?"

"I do. I thought it would be years before I was a father, thought I wasn't ready, but when I saw him, when I got to know him...how could I not feel something? He's a great kid." He tugged on his earlobe, a sign that he was trying to think the whole thing through.

"If you care, then you must know that it's best he's safe. I can take him somewhere, protect him from my father. After this has all blown over, I promise that we'll work something out."

He pursed his lips, then licked them. "For all I know this is some craziness brought on by exposure."

"You can't honestly believe this was mere coincidence, all the things that have happened."

"I—"

"You're over-thinking it. This is the best we can do for him. I need to make sure he's safe."

"Okay." Rickard exhaled heavily.

"Great." She beamed at him as she patted her pocket for the needle she had picked up from her unit. "Did you bring any of his things?"

"I'll get them." He moved ahead of her, back into the hallway and she took the opportunity to take the cap off the needle and slide it into his neck. He slumped to the floor, face drenched in confusion.

"I'm sorry. I know you were going to let me take him, but I needed to make sure you wouldn't follow me. I can't have you knowing where he is, or he won't really be safe." She bent down and kissed him lightly on the forehead. "I really am sorry. I'll call Sarai and tell her to come and take care of you. You'll be fine. Honest." She bit her lip, trying to decide whether to get him a blanket or something. His eyes were drifting shut, so she pulled him flat on the floor so that he didn't wake with a kink in his neck. If there had been another way to be sure he wouldn't follow...

She made her way to the room. Jaxon stirred as she sat down on the bed beside him. "Hey, Jaxon, it's me, Madea."

"Are you real?" He sat up and rubbed his eyes.

"Yes, I'm real." She grinned and wrapped her arms around him, drawing him into her embrace. "I'm sorry I had to leave without saying anything. Someone was trying to hurt me, and I didn't want them to find out about you."

"Are they still trying?"

"They are. We need to go somewhere safe, so that they can't get either of us. Rickard said it's all right. We'll see him a little while."

"Okay. Can I say bye?"

"No, he's having a nap right now. We'll see him soon though, okay?"

"Okay."

Madea grabbed his bag, pulling out some dark clothing. Once he was dressed, she grasped his hand and they moved towards the back door, where she sent a message to Sarai before slipping out into the street.

It wasn't long before Jaxon's pace decreased, so Madea scooped him up and did her best to carry him the rest of the way. It was slow and uncomfortable, but the sound of his soft snores near her ear made his weight easier to bear. By the time they made it to the shelter of the church, sunlight was beginning to filter in through the dome. Madea closed the door on that world, trying hard not to think about Garrett, and what her father might be doing to him, as she headed back to the tunnels beneath the surface.

"Where are we?" Jaxon murmured once she had closed the hatch behind them.

"Somewhere safe, where no one can hurt you." She glanced around, then headed toward where she thought her room was. After a few wrong turns, she found a familiar corridor, and pushed into her living space, closing the door behind her. She led Jaxon through to the bedroom and tucked him into the bed. "I think you should get a little more sleep." She stifled a yawn of her own as he nodded. "I've got to go and tell someone that I'm back, but I won't be long. If I'm not here, stay in the room. Okay?"

"Can you stay with me until I fall asleep?" His eyes were wide and guilt that she was even thinking about abandoning him again so soon drew her down onto the bed beside him.

"Of course I can." She smiled and draped an arm over his small frame.

"Thanks," he said, yawning. "Thanks for coming to get me."

"I made a promise. I'm sorry I had to break it for a little while, but whatever happens, I'll always come back."

"Good." He yawned even wider. His eyes drifted closed and his breathing fell into an even rhythm within minutes. Madea carefully lifted her arm off him and rolled away. She hoped he would still be sleeping when she got back, but there was no way to know for sure. She was always leaving him. Maybe he would have been better off staying with Rickard, but she would rather he was here, where she knew he'd be safe, than up in the domes and at risk from her father. Who knew what he was capable of? The limits of his need to protect his image hadn't been fully tested yet, she was sure.

With a sigh, she tore her gaze away from Jaxon and left the unit, wondering how long it would be before Tahra came looking for her if she didn't report in directly.

CHAPTER TWENTY-TWO

It didn't take long to find out as a man rounded a corner and stopped in front of her.

"There you are. Tahra wants to see you." She didn't think she knew the man, though obviously he knew her.

"Great, I was just trying to find her." She gave him a cheery grin. "Lead the way!"

He looked a little taken aback by her demeanour, but led her down the hall regardless. He opened the door to Tahra's office for her, but didn't follow, instead closing it between them.

"Where is Garrett?" Tahra demanded.

"Hi Mother, I'm good, thanks, nice to see you too." Madea threw herself into one of the chairs near the desk. She knew she was being childish, flippant, but she already felt awful about what happened to Garrett and she wasn't ready for a dressing down by her mother.

"I'm pleased you made it back safely, but answer the question. Where is Garrett?"

Madea paused, chewed her bottom lip before meeting her mother's gaze. "He got caught."

"What do you mean, he got caught?"

"I'm pretty sure it was my father's men. No one was at my place, Garrett thought it was safe to go in, but I guess they had a sensor there to let them know if anyone came."

"And how did you manage to avoid capture?"

"I was in the bathroom." She swallowed the lump that grew in her throat when she remembered the sounds she'd heard through the wall. "He said he was there looking for me, that he didn't know where I was. I hid in the shower when they did a search, and they didn't see me."

"How long has it been since he was taken?" Tahra demanded. There was fear on her face, and something else, a stricken look as if she had lost something precious to her. "Where would they take him?"

"It was a few hours ago now. I thought it best I finish our mission—"

"You thought you'd just go off and get the boy on your own? You thought it wasn't important to come back and report Garrett's loss? Anything could have happened!"

"I didn't want his loss to be for nothing! He came with me, risked himself for me, because he knew how important this was."

"And where is the boy now?" her mother snapped.

"He's sleeping. He needs more rest, he's only little."

Tahra's face softened a little, as if she remembered when Madea was young, and then she frowned again. "I wish you had come to me first. I could have had people out looking for him sooner. The longer he's gone, the more difficult it could be to get him back."

"I thought that if I came back without Jaxon, you wouldn't let me go and get him. I couldn't let that happen."

"You speak as though I'm holding you captive."

"Not captive, no, but something similar." She stared her mother in the eyes, daring her to disagree.

"Madea, must we really cover this again? I care about you, and I want to keep you safe. That is all. And then you rush off on a half-planned mission to rescue your ward and lose my best man in the process? It doesn't exactly instil a lot of faith."

"Do you remember that talk we had the other day? About you being a bitch?" Madea bit out, unable to keep the snark from her voice. Why was her mother being like this? They had never argued when they'd lived as a family, why was this so much harder now?

"Go on, blame it all on me." Her mother flung her arms in the air. "It's always going to be my fault, isn't it? When are you going to forgive me for not taking you with me?"

Madea felt the anger flush from her body. She slumped into her chair and looked at the ground, which was blurry through unwelcome tears.

"I'm sorry." Tahra dropped to her knees beside Madea and grabbed her hand. "When am I going to stop hurting you? I never meant to. Really, I'm sorry."

"So am I. I knew I should have come back, but I acted like a teenager, not like an adult." Tears slid down her cheeks.

"Well, when we last saw each other you were teenager." A wry smile spread across Tahra's face. "Maybe that's why this is so difficult. I have to start treating you like the adult you are." She reached out and stroked Madea's cheek. "A beautiful, intelligent, dutiful and caring adult."

"Thanks, Mum." Madea smiled. "That doesn't change the fact that they have Garrett. I can't leave him there. I need to find a way to get him back."

"We will, don't you worry. In fact it might be time to move into the next phase of my plan. Has he told you about it?"

"No, he said we would talk about it when we got back." Madea brushed the tears away and sat up straight. "Tell me what you can now, but I need to get back to Jaxon soon. I don't want him to wake alone."

Tahra nodded as she stood and paced away from Madea. "You've seen the creatures. Felt them. Right?" Tahra faced her.

"Yes. It was amazing."

"We think that everyone should have the chance to experience that. We want to teach everyone what being Sun-Touched is truly about, to help them see that it's not madness and that we don't have to be confined to the domes anymore."

"And how do you plan to do this?" Madea was sceptical. There was such a huge stigma around being Touched, there was no way that could easily be removed. It would take years to create change, and from the gleam in her mother's eyes she didn't think Tahra's plan was a long-term one.

"We're going to bring down the domes. We're going to blow them up, and then they will truly know what being Touched is."

"You can't do that," Madea whispered, horror clawing at her throat.

"What do you mean? It's the easiest way to ensure that we are all made equal."

"But people won't know what to expect, they'll think they are going crazy. Can you imagine the chaos that would create?" She could just see horrific acts which would occur.

"It wouldn't last long." Tahra shrugged. "As soon as they connect with one of the creatures, as soon as they've felt what you and I have felt, they'll know that it's nothing to be scared of."

"But I knew what to expect. I was prepared. Those who know nothing will panic, and people will get hurt. Killed." Madea paced over to her mother.

"It's a small price to pay, and it will all be over quickly."

"No. We can't do it, not like that. I hear what you're saying, and I agree that people should be taught that being Touched is nothing to fear, but you can't force it on people. How is that any different than what was done to you? Stripped of your regular life for something that you didn't ask for? And you'd do that to them? People would kill themselves, they would turn away from all that is good because of the fear of what they might do once the madness takes hold."

"It was days before you saw anything, it would have been longer if we didn't intervene. Don't you think they will realize by then that it's nothing to fear? We'll have time to give them the information they need."

Madea buried her head in her hands, pressing her palms against her eyes until all she could see was red. She wished

Garrett was here. She knew he had the zeal in him, but surely he wasn't crazy like Tahra. Surely she could find a way to reason with him. But Tahra? Then she realized something.

"This isn't just about the Touched, is it?" She looked her mother in the eyes, watching for any hint that she was right.

"What do you mean?" Tahra frowned.

"This is about Dad casting you aside when you got exposed. About the fact he refused to even acknowledge that something had happened to you. That he would rather pretend you had died than admit someone in his family was tainted."

"No. No. How could you think that?" She backed away from Madea as if she were poisonous.

"You've watched from a distance as he has paraded younger and younger women around, while you're here, underground, living a half-life. That must hurt. It must feel like he plunged a knife into your back and is twisting it, over and over again." Madea pushed herself out of her chair and moved closer to her mother. She could smell the sweat of grief, anger, denial which was gathering on her mother's brow. She didn't want to hurt her, but she was angry too, angry that this woman could possibly put her revenge ahead of everyone else's welfare.

"He deserves to pay! Don't you dare try and tell me he doesn't." Tahra spat the words at her.

Madea held a hand out as if to stop the venom. "I never said he didn't. He did you wrong, he did me wrong too. He's to blame, but that doesn't mean that everyone else has to pay too. That wouldn't be fair."

"He deserves to pay," Tahra said again, though some of the hurt had evaporated. Her shoulders slumped forward a little and her gaze fell to the floor.

"He does. And we'll find a way, but not like this." Madea covered the distance between them and wrapped her arms around her mother, squeezing her tightly. "But before we work that out, why don't we figure out how to get Garrett back?"

"Garrett." Tahra exhaled his name. "He's a good man."

"So I've noticed," Madea said wryly.

"You like him, don't you?" Tahra broke the hug and held Madea at arms-length, looking her in the eyes.

She had to tell the truth, there was no way she could lie right now. "I do," she admitted. "He might have dragged me into this mess, but he's done his very best to watch out for me, even when I didn't think I needed it." Madea pressed a hand to her belly, trying to hold in the nausea.

"Be careful. You're pregnant, and that's a lot for any man to take on. Even Garrett."

"Yeah."

"You should go and check on the boy. Jaxon, is it?"

"That's him. He'll wake soon."

"I'll get some food brought down. You should rest for a bit, and then when you're ready, call me and I'll come and visit. I'd like to meet this child you're so dedicated to." Tahra smiled, and Madea couldn't see any trace of malice in it.

"Sure." She nodded, then pecked her mother on the cheek. "I am sorry, about Garrett. If there had been another way, I would have tried to stop them, but I knew he wanted me to stay safe."

"He's always enjoyed playing the hero. We'll get him as soon as we can. I'll send some people up to start searching."

"I hope we can find him soon," Madea said, then she remembered the phone and reached into her pocket. "Garrett gave me this. He said the number on it was for his device, you should be able to track him that way, right?"

Tahra took it from her and flicked through screens. "Yes, this will do the job."

"Thank you."

"No need to thank me. He's part of our family and we take care of our own."

Madea could hear a million messages in those words, but none stronger than the one which spoke of her father's choice and the impact it'd had on her mother. "I'll see you soon, then." She left the office, her mother, and the awkward knowledge that now nestled in her stomach.

When she made it back to the unit she could still hear Jaxon's soft snores from the bedroom. She smiled and headed into the kitchen to make a cup of coffee. By the time she sat down on the couch to drink it, Jaxon was awake. He came out, rubbing his eyes and scanning the room.

"Hey." She smiled and opened her arms to him. "How are you feeling?"

"Good. Tired." He frowned. "Hungry."

Madea laughed. "Food should be here soon, enough to fill that little tummy of yours."

"Your tummy isn't as little," he said.

"What?" She raised an eyebrow.

"Your tummy. The baby is making it bigger, isn't it?"

Madea slid a hand to her belly and rubbed it. He was right. It was rounder. When had that happened? Garrett was right, she was spending more time thinking about everything else and had been ignoring the baby growing within her. She was so far removed from her body that she hadn't even noticed. Lucky for her the clothes Tahra had provided were stretchy. Hopefully by the time she got any bigger, this whole mess could be resolved.

"I guess it is, gotta make more room in there for it to grow."

"Do you know what it is?"

"It's a baby." Madea smiled.

"No, I mean, do you know if it's a boy, or a girl?"

Madea chewed her lip, unsure of the right answer. "I don't know. I hadn't thought about it."

"I think it's a girl." He nodded sagely.

"You could be right."

"Can I touch it?"

"I guess that's okay." She moved her hand away as Jaxon reached out and placed his small palm firmly against her bump.

"Can you feel it moving yet?"

"No, not yet." That was one thing she was positive she'd actually notice. It would be a little difficult to ignore something moving around inside you.

There was a knock on the door and she moved Jaxon aside to answer it.

"Your food." The man at the door had greying hair, and pale skin which made him look like he hadn't been outdoors in years.

"Thanks." She smiled and took the tray, returning to the couch and placing it between her and Jaxon. "Dig in."

"It smells good," Jaxon said reverently.

"It does, doesn't it?" Madea inhaled the rich scent of yeasty bread and fried meat. Her stomach grumbled and she grabbed a slice of the loaf and slathered butter on it before taking a bite. "So good."

"Where are we?" Jaxon asked. "Can we see Rickard today?"

"Not today, but soon. I promise. I'm going to try and sort this all out," Madea said. "And, to answer your first question, we're actually under the city. That's pretty cool, isn't it?"

"Under? I didn't know there was an under."

"Neither did I, kiddo. There are a whole lot of things I didn't know that I'm learning about now."

They ate in silence until five minutes later there was another knock on the door. "That's going to be my mother, even though she told me to call her when you were up. She wanted to stop by and meet you."

"Your mum? You didn't tell me about her."

"Well, until a few days ago, I thought she was dead. Turns out she wasn't."

"Do you think that means my mum is really okay?" Hope brimmed in Jaxon's eyes and Madea cursed herself silently.

"I couldn't say for sure, Jaxon. That would be nice though, wouldn't it?" She had to stop talking before she had thought about what she was saying. Now he had the idea that somehow Janae was okay, that her Hollowing was some mistake and there was a chance they'd be reunited. "I better get the door."

She crossed the room and let her mother in, who smiled at Jaxon. "Hi there, my name's Tahra."

"And you're Madea's mum, right?"

"That's correct."

"And you were dead, but now you're not. Where did you go when you were dead? Do you think my mum might be there, too?" The words chased each other out of his mouth so fast that they almost tripped over each other. Tahra gave Madea a panicked look.

"I don't think she knows your mum, Jaxon. But I'm sure that if she sees her around, she'll let you know. Okay?"

"Okay." Jaxon nodded solemnly.

"I thought I would stop in and meet the young man who seems to have stolen my daughter's heart." Tahra gave him an over-the-top wink and he blushed.

"Mum! Leave the kid alone," Madea said.

Jaxon mumbled in the direction of the floor. "My mum asked her to look after me."

"So I heard. Your mum sounds like a pretty special person," said Tahra.

"She is." He nodded again.

Madea shifted her weight from one foot to the other, not sure how to steer the conversation onto less awkward things. "Do you want something to eat? We have some food left over."

"I'm okay, thanks. A cup of tea would be nice though. Do you remember how I take it?"

"White with two sugars, right?"

"Right." Tahra smiled and moved across the room to take a place on the couch next to Jaxon. Madea watched them for a moment then went to the kitchen to make tea. By the time she returned, Jaxon was laughing along with Tahra.

"Thank you," Tahra said, taking the steaming mug. "You look tired, Maddy."

At the mere mention of tiredness, a wave of it crashed over Madea and she yawned. "I guess I am. It's been a long few days."

"Well, Jaxon and I were talking, and he seemed interested in seeing more of the tunnels. Why don't I take him for a little tour while you get some rest?"

Madea chewed the inside of her cheek as she thought. She

desperately wanted to sleep, and yet, she felt like she was always fobbing Jaxon off onto someone else. "Do you want to?" she asked him.

"Yes, please. I've never been underground before!" He was practically bouncing off the couch with excitement.

"Then I guess it's okay by me." She smiled, though she didn't feel as sure of this as she should. Tahra was her mother. She could trust her with Jaxon. Right?

"Great! It's settled then. Come on, Jaxon. Let's get going." She stood up and offered the boy her hand. He took it with a moment of hesitation. Madea kissed him quickly on the forehead. "Two hours. Don't let me sleep any longer than that, okay?"

"We'll be back here by then, don't worry." Tahra smiled as she closed the door behind them.

Madea listened to the patter of their feet down the hall. Jaxon was chattering away, and Tahra murmured her agreement. Madea wanted to open the door and chase after them, but she didn't have the energy. This week was taking its toll on her in more ways than one.

CHAPTER TWENTY-THREE

Madea woke to a splitting headache. What was it about waking these days that meant there was pain involved? She couldn't remember the last time she'd got out of bed—or up from the ground, or off the medical table—where she had felt genuinely good in both mind and body. She sighed as she sat up, then paused, realizing that she couldn't hear anyone else in the unit.

She frowned and moved into the living area. No, they definitely weren't here. She called Tahra's office but there was no answer. Glancing at the clock, she realized that she'd been out for almost four hours. A streak of panic shot through her.

She flung open the door and charged down the hallway, stopping the first person she came across. "Have you seen Tahra? I really need to find her."

"No, sorry. Her assistant might know, though. He should be in her office."

"Thanks," she called over her shoulder as she ran down the hall. By now she knew the way, and within five minutes she was yanking the door open. The same grey-haired man who had brought her food was sitting at Tahra's desk.

"Where is she?" Madea demanded, planting her hands on the desk and leaning towards him.

"She took your young ward out of the domes. Said she had something to show him."

"She did what?" Madea shrieked. "How long ago did they leave?"

He glanced at his clock. "About three hours, give or take."

"Do you know which exit she took? I need to see her. Now." She ground her teeth together.

"Why don't I show you," he said warily as he stood. "It will be quicker."

"Thank you." She waited impatiently while he moved to the door, then followed closely as they made their way to the exit.

"Here," he said when they came to a stop. "I won't go up there though. You're on your own."

"That's fine, thank you." She would much rather keep this little spat between the two—three—of them. Jaxon didn't need to hear it, but she wasn't sure she could contain herself until they got back to the tunnels and found some privacy.

Madea swung the hatch open, making a note of its location before closing it again. She scanned the landscape for Tahra and Jaxon. Nothing. Dust kicked up under her heels as she moved, but there was no sign of life. After a few minutes she noticed the ether creatures floating through the air. They seemed to be converging on a particular point in the distance. Garrett had told her that they were drawn to humans, drawn to the energy or the chemicals in their bodies, which might mean that Tahra was in that direction. She set out, pushing aside her nerves.

It wasn't long before one of the creatures floated towards her. One of its tendrils swam through the air and nudged her in the abdomen. Her body shook as they connected and she dropped to her knees, preparing to experience the same thing she had last time. But it never came. There was a vibration through her core, and a flash of half images, but nothing as intense or dramatic as before.

And then she felt something else, a flicker of red and the sound of a heart beating, the sound of her own voice speaking as though through layer upon a layer of cotton wool. Her stomach cramped and she cradled it with both arms, feeling something stretch within her.

The baby.

The child moved again, her tiny feet pushing against Madea's stomach.

Her. It was a little girl, like Jaxon had said. A new emotion swept over Madea as she realized that the child growing within her had been touched by the ether creature, and that somehow, that touch had linked the two of them. She was feeling, hearing the things her unborn child was experiencing, seeing glimpses of memory from the baby's short existence.

Tears coursed down her face as she stroked her bump. "My beautiful girl. My beautiful baby. I'm here."

The child stretched in response and sent a wave of love to her. It crashed through Madea's body, unbalancing her.

"Maddy? Are you okay?"

She felt her mother pull her upright and forced her eyes open. "I'm okay," she murmured. "I'm fine, really." More than fine, but she wasn't ready to share that with Tahra. She tried to find the anger that had flared within her when she'd realized her mother was exposing Jaxon, but the new connection that had been forged with her baby girl through the ether creature's touch was still too new, too raw, too joyous to allow real anger to take hold.

"Where's Jaxon?" she asked.

"I'm here! Tahra showed me some stuff I've never seen. Did you know I've never been out of the domes before? It was amazing. I can't believe how bright it is out here, how sunny." Jaxon's chatter filled her ears and she found herself smiling at his enthusiasm.

Then she faced her mother. "You said you would wake me up after two hours. You told me you'd be back."

"I took care of all his needs," Tahra said, each word spoken clearly. "And you needed your rest."

"You can't help yourself, can you?" Madea asked, feeling sad all of a sudden. She shrugged her mother's hand off her shoulder. "I'm really disappointed."

"We don't know of any children who have been Touched, Maddy. I told him all about it, and he wanted to. He knew that I was, that you are, and his mum...he wanted to."

"He's six," Madea hissed in Tahra's ear. "He's not old enough to be making these decisions by himself. I can't believe you would go and do that behind my back. Actually, I take that back. I can believe it." She clenched her jaw, resisted the urge to grind her teeth together again. Her anger was building, a slow burn. And then the baby doused it, squashing it down as if to remind her that there was no harm in being Touched. But it wasn't about the exposure, it was about the way Tahra had done it.

She shook her head, confused by the feelings in her body. For all anyone knew, babies at this stage in pregnancy didn't really have thoughts and personalities. Perhaps contact with the creature had advanced this child, changed it on some level. That would explain the connection, their psychic bond, and the child's awareness of everything going on around it.

Madea forced herself to take deep breaths and relax the tense muscles in her shoulders. "Well, I think we should be getting back. Don't you?" She looked pointedly at her mother.

"Yes, I bet you're hungry Jaxon. We brought some sandwiches with us, but he finished those off ages ago."

"I am hungry," Jaxon agreed with a nod.

"Right. Let's go then." Madea slipped her hand into his and waited for Tahra to take the lead. She felt better for having his fingers in hers, for being able to feel that he was alright. How long would it be before he changed though? And what effect would it have on him? There were too many unknowns in this equation, and she might never forgive her mother for using Jaxon to experiment on.

They made it back to the hatch easily, and shortly after Tahra supplied Jaxon with more food, which the boy eagerly devoured. Madea was amazed at the amount he could consume. The baby nudged her, suggesting that she eat as well.

Apparently Garrett would no longer need to remind her about the baby; she was doing a pretty good job of it on her own. Madea let a little laugh slip out. Tahra raised an eyebrow.

"Nothing."

"Okay." Her mother's eyes narrowed, but she didn't press the matter. "We should talk about Garrett. Do you want me to get someone to look after Jaxon?"

"He'll be okay. We can get you some pens and paper," she said to Jaxon. "Right, Mother?"

"Sure." Tahra rummaged in her desk for some supplies, then set them up on the desk for Jaxon.

"We're going to have a chat," Madea told him. "We'll be over on the couch. Let me know if you need anything."

"Okay." He didn't look up from his drawing, one of a man she thought could be Rickard, and a woman who could be Sarai. Or maybe her.

"Do you really think it's a good idea to speak in front of him?" Tahra whispered.

"Did you really think it was a good idea exposing him without talking to me about it first?" Madea shot back.

"I'm sorry. I guess I didn't think you'd let me if I asked, and I wanted to see—"

"Yes, you wanted to see what would happen. He's my ward, and you had no right—" Madea closed her eyes and exhaled, inhaled, trying to still her emotions. "It's done now, and you better hope there are no negative side effects from this. If anything happens to him, I am holding you responsible."

"Noted."

"Did you manage to find out where they are keeping Garrett?" she asked.

"It appears he is somewhere in your father's home. That's where we tracked the locator on his phone. Do you have any idea where Carson might hold a prisoner?"

"No, but I know someone who might." Madea chewed her lip.

"Who?"

"Sarai. She still lives there, you know."

"I do. Do you really want to bring her into this?"

"She's going to find out sometime, it might as well be from me. She's smarter than you give her credit for."

"I have no doubt she is smart, but she's also your father's daughter."

"What, you don't trust her?" Madea frowned. "She's your daughter, and she loved you. She loves me."

"There are very few people I trust, Madea. Your father saw to that."

"At some point you're going to have to get over that slight. You know that, don't you? Yes, his actions were dreadful, but look at the amazing things you've learned. If he hadn't faked your death, you never would have experienced the wonder the ether creatures can bring."

A splash of colour brightened Tahra's cheeks and her eyes misted over. "It is amazing."

"He treated you badly, but he didn't ruin you. You are still Tahra Linae, you still have a life ahead of you."

"I need to think about it more. What's important right now is getting Garrett back. I'm assuming that you'll want to go and get him?"

"I do. It was my fault he was captured. I need to make it up to him."

"Well, I can look after Jaxon—"

Madea laughed. "You think I'll leave him with you after the last time?"

"Well, what else could I possibly do? I promise I'll play by the rules. We'll read books, and draw, and eat lots of yummy food." Tahra's eyes were wide, and she was trying to look as motherly as possible.

"Fine. I can't really take him with me, anyway. But be on your best behaviour, or I won't let you babysit when this one is born." Madea placed a hand on her belly.

"I've got some people who will come with you, but you know your father's place the best, so you're in charge."

"No, I don't want anyone else. I have some people I can ask, but they aren't going to trust me if I come to them with a group of people intent on breaking into Father's house."

"I can't send you off alone."

"Well, you're going to have to."

"You're stubborn. Just like him." Tahra clenched her jaw.

"You're pretty stubborn yourself, you know." Madea placed a hand on her mother's knee and smiled. Tahra grasped her fingers and smiled back.

"So, what can I do then? I don't feel good about letting you go out on your own."

"You can tag me with some locators and watch my progress. If I stay in one place for more than two hours, send in your team to get me out. I need a chance to do this my way first."

"Okay. I can tell this is important." Tahra slumped in defeat. "I'm going to call our armoury guy, and he'll kit you out. When do you want to go?"

Madea glanced at the clock, surprised to find that it was mid-afternoon. "I want to go tonight. The less time he has to spend there, the better."

"Okay then." Tahra pushed herself off the couch and headed for the desk. She made the call and spent some time looking at Jaxon's drawings. "He'll be here in five minutes. I want you to come see me before you go."

"All right." Madea went to Jaxon and wrapped her arms around his shoulders, leaning over to see what he was drawing. There were a lot of colours and it looked like he had drawn some of the things he'd seen outside the domes; a vivid blue sky filled with clouds, and a tree with white blobs in it covering most of the page. "This is beautiful, Jaxon."

"Thanks." He smiled and pointed at a tree. "I saw that today, it was big and green and there were birds living in it."

"That's great! Do you think you can draw something special for me? I have to go somewhere, so Tahra is going to look after you tonight. I'll be back to see your drawing in the morning."

"Where are you going?" He looked up at her very seriously.

"I have to go and help a friend. When we get back, you'll be able to meet him. I'm pretty sure you'll like him." Madea winked at him and he laughed. She dropped a kiss on his forehead then made her way to the door. "See you later."

She only had to wait a minute for the man to come by.

"Hello again," said Sturm. He held a hand out and gripped hers firmly when she offered it.

"Hi," she said. "Thanks for helping me out like this."

"Not a problem. I hear our boy Garrett's in trouble, and you're going in to get him. Don't you want some back up?" He frowned at her.

Madea forced a smile. "I've got this, don't worry. And I'm fairly sure that while my mother is letting me go on my own, she'll have a back-up team of her own in place anyway. Right?"

"I guess you really are your mother's daughter." He laughed and headed towards the armoury.

Madea mulled over her plans. She wasn't just going to get Garrett, she needed to speak to her father as well. Her mother's pain, her anger, had made an impact, and she couldn't waste this opportunity. He would be there, in the house, and he needed to know what was at stake if he didn't make some changes.

What changes, she had no idea. She couldn't seem to figure out how to spread the truth about being Touched when there was such a stigma against it. It was entrenched into their daily lives, and yet if there was a way to convince people, to show them that it wasn't something to fear...

There had to be a way. She couldn't let her mother, or Garrett, or anyone else, force exposure on anyone, no matter how harmless it was. Everyone deserved the right to choose how to live their lives.

Madea knocked on her mother's office door, but there was no response. She pushed inside and crossed to the desk where she scrawled a note. As she was about to leave she spotted a photo of her mother outside the domes, obviously taken post fake death. Madea slipped it into her pocket.

CHAPTER TWENTY-FOUR

When she reached Rickard's apartment, she paused to gather herself. It was earlier this time and she could see both Rickard and Sarai in the kitchen. Madea considered going in the back door again, but thought better of it. The only way to show that her intentions were above board was to knock on the front door and wait for an answer.

Her heart thumped in her chest as she raised her hand and pressed the intercom. It was a risk coming here at all, but she had to have faith that Rickard wouldn't have told her father she'd been there. He had seemed to genuinely care about Jaxon.

"Who's there?" Rickard's voice came through the speaker.

"It's Maddy," she said. There were so many other words she could have added, but none of them would make a difference right now. A minute passed, then two, before the lock clicked and she pushed open the door. Sarai was standing in front of Rickard, as if she could protect him from Madea.

"What do you want?" Sarai asked. "You're my sister, and I love you, but I won't let you hurt him again."

"I was doing it to protect Jaxon, I swear. If there had been another way to be sure—"

"You really think you can't trust me?" Rickard asked, stepping around Sarai. "You drugged me, Madea. If that doesn't seem a little crazy to you—"

"I told you, I'm not crazy. I'm not."

"Tell us what you want." Sarai was doing her best to keep her voice flat, but Madea could hear the wobble in it.

"I got Jaxon to safety. He's with Mum."

"Mum's dead." There was no confusion in her eyes. It was a fact. Nothing more or less.

"No, she's not." Madea reached into her pocket and drew out the photo that she had stolen from her mother's office, and held it out to her sister. Sarai reached for it, her fingers trembling, brow furrowed. She glanced at it. Her face drained of colour and her legs gave out beneath her. Rickard managed to catch her before she hit the floor.

"But Dad said..."

Madea knelt beside her sister. "It's a long story, Sarai. A really long story, but the gist of it is that Mum got Touched, and Dad couldn't let that ruin his career, so he faked her death."

"He faked her death? Why didn't he have her Hollowed? What if she hurt someone? Hurt us? I don't understand." Sarai glanced at the photo again, tears welling in her eyes "She's really alive? She's not crazy?"

"Look at that photo. Does she look crazy to you?" Madea pointed at the image. Her mother was smiling, enjoying a sunny day. It could have been any hiking trip back on Earth, except that it was clearly taken on Diamara.

"No. She doesn't. But..."

"Being Sun-Touched is not what anyone thinks it is. It's not easy to explain, but I'll try. If you'll listen." Madea looked into her sister's eyes, pleading with her. Rickard stepped around them and closed the door.

"I want to know what's going on, Maddy. No more secrets. You came to us, so you have to tell us everything."

They listened in silence until she got to the end of her story. Their hands clasped tightly together, knuckles white and faces wary.

"I don't know what to say," Sarai said. She hadn't looked at Madea in more than ten minutes, but now she did, staring her in the eyes. "So you're one of them now."

"I'm Touched, yes, but that doesn't mean I'm mad. Do you believe at least that much?"

"I guess. But those creatures, that doesn't seem possible."

"I know, I agree. And yet I've seen them with my own eyes. I've felt them. That's how I knew about Jaxon." She glanced at Rickard, who looked away.

"What about Jaxon?" Sarai confusion swamping her features.

"You didn't tell her yet?" Madea asked, still looking at Rickard.

He licked his front teeth. "No. I didn't think it was a good time."

"Well, now's good," Madea said. "If you don't tell her, I will."

"I don't care who tells me, but someone better start talking. Now." There was a firmness to Sarai's voice that wasn't often there. It made Madea smile, and she thought maybe Rickard had really met his match.

"Rickard?" Sarai rubbed his cheek with her hand. "Tell me."

"He's my son. I'm Jaxon's father." The words sounded awkward in the room, unwieldy, as if somehow they took up more space than anything else.

"Your son? I don't understand."

"I had a lover, years ago, and she got pregnant. I didn't know at the time, but I'd heard a rumour. I thought if I never found out for sure, it would be better, but then he was there, in Maddy's house and..."

"And you loved him. Didn't you?" Confusion had been pushed aside by a strangled form of hope, as if Sarai wished, but wasn't sure, that the words she spoke were true.

"I do. I love him. I can't deny he's mine, and I'm sorry, I'm so sorry. I never meant to hurt you. I didn't know. I didn't know—" His face was streaked with tears. Sarai pulled him into her arms, nuzzling his head against her chest and murmuring to him that it was okay.

Madea stood quietly and moved into the kitchen, leaving the couple to deal with this moment, and whatever it might mean for them. Perhaps she should have left this a secret, but Sarai was her sister. She deserved to know, and Rickard needed to be free of the guilt he was carrying before she could get them to help.

Eventually, they came to her, their hands linked, their eyes leaving each other for no longer than necessary.

"Thank you for helping me tell Sarai," Rickard said. "I knew I had to, I..."

Sarai reached up and touched his cheek. "You were worried. It's normal. But it's me. Besides, Jaxon is impossible not to love. I think he must get that from you." A grin played on her lips, and Rickard's face broke in a smile. They kissed, and for the first time Madea realized that she wasn't jealous anymore.

"Well, I'm pleased you two have sorted that out. Really, I am. But I came here because I need your help."

"What with?" Sarai looked at her, finally seeming to snap from her little love buzz. She was taking the news of Rickard's child very well, Madea had to admit.

"Father has someone captive, someone important to me, and I need to get him back."

"He?" Sarai raised an eyebrow. "And what do you mean, Father has someone captive? Why would he do that?"

"Have you not been listening to anything I've said?"

"Hang on. You've told us a lot of stuff tonight, too much to even begin take in. You came in here last night, took my son and drugged me, so don't get all high and mighty on me." Rickard had let go of Sarai's hand and marched across the room to Madea. The vein in his forehead was throbbing, and his face flushed red.

"I'm not— That's not how I meant it to come across. I guess I see the world a little differently now than I did a week ago." Madea took a deep breath and relaxed her shoulders. "Father knows about Mum. She's been threatening him for ages, and finally came good on her promise by exposing me. He was keeping an eye on my place, and they caught Garrett."

"Who's Garrett?" Sarai asked.

"He works with Mum, and he's someone that...I don't know. We have something going on, but I'm not really sure what."

"He's your lover?" Sarai raised an eyebrow, her lips twitching as though they wanted to slide into a smile.

"No. I mean, we have...something. Something is happening, but we haven't really had the time or space to work out what that is, or where it might go."

"Do you really think you're in a position to be starting up with someone new? You're pregnant with another man's child."

It took all her will power not to slap Rickard. Her fingers clenched into fists and she ground her teeth together.

Sarai pushed Rickard behind her. "He wasn't trying to be a jerk. Right, Rick?" She looked at him pointedly.

"What? No, I mean, of course not. I was looking out for you. That's all."

"Well, I am more than capable of looking out for myself. Why do I have to keep telling people that?" Madea threw her hands in the air. Why couldn't anything be simple? She took a deep breath to calm herself. "The point is, they have him captive, and I need to get him out." She moved to stand in front of Sarai and placed her hands on her sister's shoulders. "Can you think of anywhere they might keep him?"

Sarai closed her eyes and sucked on her bottom lip. "Give me a minute." She nodded her head slightly as she thought, then her eyes sprang open. "He has some rooms in the basement set aside for work. They might be holding him there. I don't think I've ever been down there, so I can't tell you more than that."

"That's all I needed, thank you." Madea kissed her sister on the cheek. "I have to go and get him back. Whatever happens to me, trust that Jaxon is safe, and that Mum is out there. She'll get in touch with you."

"What do you mean 'whatever happens'? What do you think is going to happen?" Sarai's eyes widened.

"I have to free Garrett, and then I need to talk to Dad."

"You never call him Dad. What's going on, Maddy?"

She bit her lip, trying to summon the right words. "Look, Dad might have been in the wrong about some things, but if I'm honest, Mum has her own agenda, too. If I can't make him see sense then she is going to do whatever she can to bring down the domes and expose everyone here. I know that there is nothing to fear now, but the chaos that colony-wide exposure would cause is something I can't even fathom. Unless he agrees to talk, to make some kind of compromise, she's going to act. I can't let that happen."

Sarai's face paled, and Rickard pushed in front of her. "You said that Jaxon would be safe. It sounds like you left him with a madwoman."

"I didn't know her plan when I took him! I wanted to keep him safe, to make sure he didn't end up Hollowed like his mother. Which would you rather? That he was Touched, or Hollowed?"

Rickard was quiet. "Okay. I get your point. What can we do to help?"

"I don't want you putting yourselves at risk."

"We're not the ones who are Touched, remember? Besides, I'm an adult, what's he going to do? Ground me?" Sarai forced a grin onto her face.

"Thanks," Madea said. "It means a lot." She wrapped her arms around her sister, squeezing away the years since they had lived together, the time since they were last close enough to really confide in each other.

"Promise me that after this is all over we get to meet this Garrett. Okay?"

"Alright." Madea nodded. "Sarai, if you could go in first,

switch off any alarms you think might be connected and then distract Father, that would be a good start."

"What about me?" Rickard asked.

"I need some kind of distraction, something that will mean he sends part of his security team away from the house so that I can sneak in and get Garrett. Do you think you could do that?"

"I think I can." Rickard smiled. "I know he's your father, but this can be my payback for what he did to Jaxon's family." Sarai squeezed his hand and Madea hoped she wasn't setting them up for a fall. Still, they weren't Touched. Even if their father wasn't happy about what they were doing, he had no reason to make them disappear.

"Right. Get whatever you think you'll need, and let's head out. How long will you need to organize your distraction?" She could see the lines of worry around Rickard's eyes. There was no time to ask which of the many difficulties had created them.

"Give me a half hour, then Sarai can head out, and you can follow behind. Okay?"

"Sounds good to me," Sarai said, her voice slightly higher than normal.

Madea reached for her spare hand and squeezed. "You can do this. I know you can."

"Thanks. It'll be fine, I'm sure," said Sarai.

Rickard bent down to kiss Sarai and then headed for the door. "I'll come back here when I'm done," he said over his shoulder. "Where will you go, Maddy?"

"I need to get Garrett to safety first, but I'll be in touch as soon as I can." She bit her lip, wishing she had something more positive, more encouraging to say. "Stay safe, and thank you."

"You're almost my sister, and this is what family do, isn't it?"

"It's what our family will do," Sarai agreed. "We don't have to lie or live secret lives, not like our parents." She looked right at Madea when she spoke those words, tears forming in the corners of her eyes.

"We don't have to be anything like them," Madea agreed, giving her hand another squeeze.

Rickard closed the door behind him. Sarai moved to the couch and sank down into it. "Might as well try and relax. This next half hour is going to feel like a lot longer."

CHAPTER TWENTY-FIVE

The half hour crawled by, and when Sarai stood, Madea did too, folding her into an embrace. "Please be careful. Don't say anything about me, don't let on that you know about Mother, none of it. If he doesn't suspect anything from you, he's less likely to worry about me."

"I'll do my best." Sarai grinned, then took a breath and headed for the door. Madea paced for ten minutes before she, too, left the house. She couldn't stand to be within walls for any longer than that. And if she was lucky...

Yes, there it was. The vents were open and a flood of fresh air swept through the sector. She closed her eyes and took a deep breath, catching a hint of the plains on the wind. When she opened them, she could see several creatures coming towards her, as though drawn by the change in temperature.

She hadn't seen any in the domes before, and despite the fact that she knew they could pass through the protective layer, it seemed odd to see them now. They floated toward her, their tendrils flicking out, lashing through her body quickly, sending her flashes of thought and memory. She caught a trace of Sarai's worry about what Rickard's grand plan might be, and a greater anxiety about Madea and the trouble she would get in if caught.

She felt stricken, having that first-hand knowledge of how her sister felt, knowing full well the position she'd put her in. All she could hope was that everything went to plan, and her sister's fears would come to nothing.

Madea hurried towards her father's house, slipping around the back and taking the same path she had the night she'd made her escape. She had only just got into her hiding spot when voices rose outside the front gate.

"You can't stop me from going in, I know she's here. I know it!" The words were slurred, but she froze, recognizing Sullivan's voice.

"She's not. You'd best go home. We don't want any trouble."

"Trouble," Sullivan scoffed. "All I want is to see Madea! She's carrying my baby you know, and I'm the father, I deserve to speak to her. She can't hide from me."

"You were quite clear about not being ready to be a father. She respected your wishes, now have some respect for her." Rickard's voice was firm, but she could tell that he was acting. Though she knew he would have defended her honour in a heartbeat, the words seemed rehearsed to her ears.

"My baby," slurred Sullivan. There was no fraudulence in his inebriation. He'd been drinking, or taking pills, that much was clear. How Rickard had managed to rope him into this charade, she didn't know. She had to restrain herself from going out there and sending him home. The last thing she wanted was for him to get in any more trouble—they would be watching him carefully after his overdose.

"Do you really want her to see you like this? I think you should go home," Rickard's voice was calm, but it didn't seem to help.

"I'll do what I like. Is my baby," he repeated, a primal wail exiting his mouth. Madea closed her eyes at the shuffle of feet, she could imagine him stumbling, reaching for Rickard. Would he take a swing? How realistic were they aiming for? A fist thudded against flesh, and then Rickard yelped. They scuffled for a minute before he called for help, and within moments three men ran out of the house and headed for the fight.

Madea pushed away the sounds, focusing on what was in front of her now. She didn't have time to think about whether Rickard had been hurt, or whether Sullivan would get in trouble. She had to save Garrett.

Carefully she pushed through the kitchen door and scanned the room. It was empty, as she had hoped—late enough that most of the staff would have retired, but not so late that the noise of someone moving through the house would be out of place.

She followed Sarai's instructions and found the stairs leading down, stopping frequently to listen for signs of life. Her fingers twitched anxiously. Her heart thudded at double speed by the time she reached the last step. A solid door blocked the way, complete with a touchpad. She pulled out the unit she'd taken from the Touched, and attached it like Sturm had shown her, tapping her feet as it did its thing, only exhaling when the lock clicked open.

Garrett was tied to a chair, his arms stretched behind him so that he was forced to sit straight, pulling open the shallow cuts across his chest. "Garrett," she whispered as she rushed to his side. He barely stirred at her voice and she supressed a sob. She'd never seen anything like this, and now she'd never be able to forget the image of him so hurt, helpless.

Madea moved behind him and used her knife to cut through his bindings, catching him as he slumped forward.

"Garrett, can you hear me?" She brushed the hair back from his face, trying to avoid the bruises around his eyes and the cuts on his cheek. Anger burned in her belly as she thought of her father inflicting this damage to the man she was falling for.

"Madea?" Garrett's voice was hoarse, and his eyes fluttered open.

"It's me. I came for you." She rested his head on her lap and reached into her bag for her bottle of water, bringing it to his lips and helping him drink. He coughed, as though that little liquid could drown him.

"Where are the others?"

"What others?"

"Tahra sent a team with you, didn't she?"

"No. I asked to come alone. She'll send backup if I need it, but I can get you out of here. I know I can."

He pushed himself upright and peered at her. "I think becoming Touched has actually made you a little mad, after all." He tried to smile, but it became a grimace instead. "I'm a bit of a mess, aren't I?"

"A little. Nothing that won't heal." She reached out and caressed his chin, the least damaged part of his face. "Still handsome though."

"I'd kiss you, but I think it would hurt too much."

"Save it for later." She smiled at him, emotions warring inside her. "I need to get you somewhere safe, and then I need to have a chat to my father." She paused, chewing her bottom lip before asking, "Was it him?"

"No." He shook his head, and she felt relief flood her system. It was one thing to know the kinds of things her father actioned, another to think of him personally carrying those things out.

"Okay. Let's get moving. If I stay still too long Tahra will be all over this place, and I really need to have that chat." She stood and helped him to his feet. He was unsteady for a moment before gaining his equilibrium.

"Lead on, my hero." He gave a little flourish which unbalanced him. Madea reached for his arm, steadying him. She refused to let go, even though he tried to stand on his own, and eventually he let her lead him through the door to the stairs.

It felt like a lifetime to make it to the top. Madea was on high alert, ears pricked for any sound which might mean her intrusion had been discovered, but nothing came. She let Garrett slump to the floor at the top while she checked the room beyond. When she came back he was on his feet, leaning against the door.

"I need to get you somewhere safe."

"I thought I'd just wait here." He grinned as best he could. Madea was unable to stop the smile from spreading across her face.

"I'm glad to see they didn't beat your sense of humour out of you."

"They didn't beat anything out of me," he said firmly. "I said you could trust me, and I meant it."

"Thank you." She kissed him gently on the cheek. "Now let's move, before it's too late."

"I don't know how far I can go." He grimaced as they moved forward.

Madea pulled him along, heading for the doorway out of the house. "It's okay. I know just the place."

Once she had him in her hiding spot, she shoved a packet of food and a bottle of water into his hands, along with her locator. "If I haven't come back for you in a few hours, Tahra will send someone. She's monitoring this, so just stay put. I'll see you as soon as I can." She went to kiss him on the cheek but he pressed his swollen lips against her mouth. She could taste dried blood on him, the symbol of his promise.

"Be careful. You don't know what he's capable of."

"I'm beginning to see," she said wryly. "I'll be fine. Don't worry." She paused, not wanting to leave him but knowing that she had to. "I'll see you soon."

"Go on, before they hear us." He nodded back towards the house and left before she could change her mind.

The house was strangely quiet. She had expected more people to be here, but perhaps Rickard's distraction had worked better than she'd hoped. Madea thought of Sullivan, hoped that he hadn't been arrested for his behaviour. She had bigger things to worry about right now though. Steeling herself, she headed for her father's office, where she was sure he would be.

Sarai's voice wafted from the room as she approached the door. What was she still doing there? Madea pushed through the door and closed it behind her. Sarai stood behind their father who had been securely tied to a chair, the rope cutting into the skin around his wrists. He had a lump on his forehead and his eyes were closed.

"What are you doing?" Madea hissed at her sister.

"I—" Sarai was pale, and her hands shook. "I—"

Madea locked the door, then pulled the blinds shut on the window, afraid that someone might see. She pulled her sister towards the couch. Sarai's whole body was quaking. Madea pulled her into an embrace and held her tight. "What happened?"

"I...I had to ask him if it was true. He lied about it. Lied about everything and I got angry. So angry. Madea..." Tears fell on Madea's shoulders and she pulled back to dry Sarai's eyes.

"It's okay. I'm here now." Madea took a deep breath, trying to stay focused. She glanced over at her father, noting the steady rise and fall of his chest beneath the bindings. At least he was still alive.

"He wasn't going to confess. He's been lying to me for so long and I gave him the chance to be honest but he couldn't. He wouldn't tell me. I didn't mean to hurt him, but I grabbed a statue and I hit him. He fell down and I didn't know what to do...."

"So you tied him up? It was quick thinking, Sarai. If he'd come around, he might have tried to hurt you. It's okay." Madea stroked her sister's hair until she relaxed. "Why don't you stay here for a bit, and I'll see if I can wake him. We have some things to talk about."

"Okay." Sarai nodded, biting her lip and folding her arms across her body.

Madea got up and crossed the room to her father. She knelt before him and placed a hand on each side of his face. "Father. Wake up." She shook his shoulders, and after a few moments he seemed to stir. "Come on, old man, we don't have all night."

"Wha?" He slowly shook his head one way, then the other, his eyes fluttering open. "Madea?"

"Yes, Father. It's me. I came for Garrett." She pressed her lips into a thin line and tried to decide how best to use her time here. "I can't forgive what you've done, but we have things we need to talk about."

"What things? And why did your sister hit me? What have you been telling her?"

"The truth, Father. I've spoken with Mother, and I know what you did. But like I said, it's not time to talk about that, we have more important things to discuss."

"Cut these ties, and I might talk. Otherwise I'll call for security."

"I sent them away, Dad," Sarai called from the couch. "You don't deserve to be protected."

"You! You're in so much trouble. When I get out of here—"

"I will be long gone. I'm done with you, Father." Sarai stood, her shakes had disappeared and she strode over. "I can't believe I trusted you." She glanced at Madea. "I'm going to pack my bag, and then I'm coming with you."

"What about Rickard?"

"Don't worry. He'll come too." Sarai headed for the door, leaving Madea alone with her father.

"Mum's fuming. You've got a lot to answer for, you know."

"She's crazy." He dismissed her comment with a shake of his head. "And so are you. I didn't think she'd got to Sarai though."

"Sarai hasn't been Touched. She's just been told the truth."

He let out a snort of a laugh.

"I wouldn't be laughing if I was you. You're in no position to take this lightly." Madea peered up at him. "Mother is willing to bring down the domes and expose everyone. She's prepared to deal with the chaos, she'd welcome it, if it meant that everyone was equal, and everyone would know the truth about being Touched."

"And what has she told you it means?" He sneered at her and she had to resist the urge to slap him. He was still so smug, so sure of himself, even in his current position.

"I've seen it myself. There are creatures that live on this planet that you can't see until you've been exposed. Beautiful, amazing creatures."

"If they are so amazing, why are you telling me her plans?"

"Because I don't agree with them. There has to be another way, but unless you agree to make some changes, she will do this and not even you will be able to avoid being Touched."

His throat moved convulsively. "So what do you want from me?"

Madea had to stop and think. She hadn't known what to expect from this meeting, and now he actually seemed to be listening. One thing popped into her mind and she spoke before she lost her momentum. "The Hollowings need to stop. There will be no more performed. Ever. You can sedate those who get Touched, but you can't empty them. You'll give them to us, and we'll take care of them."

"But we need them. They provide important labour—"

"The Touched can spend all the time they want outside the domes," she said. "We can work out the details later, but you won't Hollow anyone else. It stops now." Her baby twitched in her belly, as if agreeing with her sentiment. Her hand moved to the place where it rested, and her father's eyes followed.

"You're still pregnant," he stated.

"Did you think I would get rid of it just because you wanted me to?" It was her turn to sneer. "This is my baby. She's been Touched too. She's been changed. She's more than you could ever imagine." Madea didn't know why she was telling him these things. He wasn't going to have anything to do with the child, but it felt good to say it to someone. To acknowledge out loud that the baby growing within her was something more than human now.

"You're sick, Madea." His voice was gentle, full of concern.

"No, you're sick. We trusted you, we loved you, and you took away our mother. You lied to us, you used us, and it ends now. I'll do what I can to stop Mother bringing down the domes, but not for you. I'll do it because I don't think it's the right way. You need to stick to your end of the bargain, or there will be consequences. Trust me on this."

"How do I know you're not lying?" He raised an eyebrow.

"What reason do I have to lie? I'm trying to keep the balance here. Besides, you know me. When have I ever done anything but my duty? I've lived and breathed service for the last decade of my life."

"I guess you're right," he said grudgingly. He licked his bottom lip. "I'll stop the Hollowings, and I'll consider trading with the Touched. I don't want them in my domes though, and I won't deal with anyone but you."

"I don't trust you. Not at all." He'd already tried to get rid of her baby once, there was every chance he would try again. "I'll call you, and we'll sort it out that way. I won't step foot in this house again."

"Fine. Whatever. Are you going to untie me now?"

"No. I'm not." She backed away from him.

"Sign of good will?"

"No. I'll send a message to your security team when we're gone. You can wait a few minutes." She chewed on her bottom lip, suddenly feeling very much like a child again.

"Madea," he called. "I'm sorry—"

"It's too late for apologies. Just hold up your end of the bargain, and you won't have anything to worry about. I'll be in touch." Madea pulled the door closed behind her and leaned against it. A sob tore free from her throat and she let a ragged breath follow it, swallowing back the wail that threatened to escape.

"He doesn't deserve your tears, Maddy." Sarai sat at the bottom of the steps. She stood and moved towards Madea.

"I know, but he's still our father."

"Not anymore." Sarai held out her hand and Madea grasped it, taking strength from her little sister, who seemed to have grown ten years over the course of the night. "Rickard's waiting for us at his place." Sarai began to lead her towards the front door, but Madea pulled back.

"Wait. Garrett's hiding. I need to get him."

"Where?"

"By the kitchen." She led her sister back through the house, surprised by the new strength she could feel in Sarai. She had thought their father's betrayal would break her, but it had changed Sarai in ways Madea couldn't have predicted. "You don't need to come. We can find another way," she offered.

"No. I'm done here, and I want to see Mother." Sarai gave her a flicker of a smile. "And we need to stick together, I can see that now. You're the only one I trust."

CHAPTER TWENTY-SIX

Madea led them back to the tunnels, and it wasn't until she closed the hatch behind them that she could take an easy breath.

"What about Rickard?" Sarai asked as she glanced around nervously, her shoulders stooped as though the tunnels were much smaller than they were.

"I'll go and get him soon, I promise. It's better that you stay here where you'll be safe, and Garrett's wounds need attention sooner rather than later." He'd been quiet for a while now, though he was managing to stumble along with their help.

"Okay." The strength she had shown before seemed to waver as Sarai glanced up and down the tunnels. "It's weird being here. Knowing we're underground."

"I know." Madea smiled. "You'll forget about that soon enough. Don't worry." She led them down the hallway until they came across a woman, only vaguely familiar. Her eyes went wide at the sight of Garrett.

"Here, let me help," the woman offered, reaching for Garrett.

Madea waved her off. "Can you get a message to Tahra? Let her know we're taking Garrett to the infirmary. Which is...where?"

"Keep going that way." The woman pointed the direction they had already been going. "Take the third left, then the first right and you'll be there. Are you sure you don't want a hand?"

"Thanks, but we'll manage. Just tell Tahra."

The woman nodded and took off down the hall.

"We could have done with the help, you know. He's getting heavy," Sarai commented.

"I can hear you," Garrett muttered. He tried to stand straighter, but slumped back against them. "I'll try to walk better."

"Don't worry about us," Madea said. Her brow furrowed in concern as his breathing grew more ragged. "Let's get you some help."

Their shuffled gait got them to the infirmary ten minutes later.

The medic helped them lay him on a table; the same one Madea had woken on, just days ago.

"Garrett, are you okay?" Madea waved the doctor to the side of the bed. She stepped back to give him some room, but Garrett's hand flashed out and grabbed hers, drawing her back to his side with a strength she didn't think he had.

"Don't leave me. Not now." His eyes locked on hers.

"I won't," she whispered.

Tahra bustled into the room then, racing to the edge of the table and tracing a hand lightly over the wounds on his face. "Are you okay?" Tahra asked again.

"I'll live. Won't I, Doc?"

"You'll live, though it's going to take a few days to get you healed up."

"See? I'll be fine. I didn't tell them anything, in case you were worried."

"No, I never doubted you. I'm just sorry it happened at all." Tahra shook her head, a combination of sadness and fury on her face. "That man will do anything to get what he wants."

"About that," Madea said. "We need to talk." She glanced over at Sarai and Tahra's gaze followed, her eyes widening.

"Sarai?"

184

"Mother." Sarai's eyes were round and luminous, like a lost child. Tahra stepped forward and folded her into an embrace. It took a few seconds for Sarai's arms to reach around her mother, but when they did, she squeezed so tightly that Madea thought she might never let go.

It was strange being on the outside, watching this reunion. Her own hadn't been quite like this, but she wondered if the same emotions had flashed across her face, so obvious, so raw. She longed to join them, but she had to let Sarai have this moment to herself.

Garrett squeezed her hand. "You okay?" he asked, voice rasping. The doctor worked quietly on the wounds to his body, cleaning and dressing them without intruding on their conversation.

"Did you get sick of everyone asking you that, so thought you'd use it on me instead?" She smiled wryly.

"No, I mean it. Are you? You look...sad."

"Everything's different. I don't know who I can trust any more. I don't know who is right and who is wrong, or if anyone is even right at all." She sighed, then perched on the edge of his bed.

"You can trust me. I hope you know that."

"I'd say you've proven that one." She laughed. "You didn't have to get all cut up to show me, though."

"We'll say I took one for the team." He tried to shrug, but grimaced and stopped halfway through the motion.

"Which team is that?"

"Whatever one you're on."

"I'm starting to think that you've memorized a bunch of lines from some book. You're far too smooth for your own good."

"Maybe you just bring out the best in me." He squeezed her hand. "How is the baby?"

All of a sudden she wanted to tell him about the child, about how she was connected to her now, how she was changed from her experience with one of the creatures. But would he even believe her?

"She's good." Madea nodded, realizing her slip as his eyes went wide.

"She?"

Madea nodded, a smile slipping across her lips. "It's a girl."

He smiled back at her and for the first time she realized that he would make a good father. This was the reaction she wanted for her baby. Not the sterile response she'd gotten from Sullivan.

"I can picture you with a baby girl. I know you're probably worried, but I think you're going to make a good mum. It's obvious you care, or you wouldn't have taken Jaxon under your wing. He's lucky he has you."

"Do I get a proper introduction now that you're coherent?" Sarai asked as she crossed to the bed. Tahra was hanging back for some reason, but Madea pushed that thought aside.

"Garrett, this is my sister, Sarai, and your co-rescuer," Madea said. "And this is Garrett."

"Don't I get a subtitle?" He raised an eyebrow.

"If you were to have one, what would it be?" Madea asked, her heart thumped hard as she waited for his response.

He seemed to be mulling over the question. He squeezed her hand. "I'm not sure of the technical term, but I'm hoping to have a role in your life. If you want, of course..."

She felt her cheeks flush.

"Madea! I don't think I've ever seen you blush," Sarai said, nudging her with an elbow. "You must be pretty special, Garrett. She doesn't get like that over just anyone."

"Well, thanks. That makes me feel pretty good."

"I am here..." Madea muttered. "Why are you people always talking about me as though I'm not in the room?"

Sarai hugged her. "We love you, but sometimes, you aren't the most communicative person in the universe."

"Well, I've had my reasons."

"Not to change the subject, but when can we get Rickard?" Sarai asked. "I know we've not been here long, but he'll be waiting and I want to make sure he's safe."

"Of course. Sorry." Madea rubbed her face with her hands.

"No, it's okay. You were a little distracted." Sarai winked at her.

"Do you need a hand?" Tahra stepped forward.

"No, I should be fine," Madea replied. "I'll grab something to eat first, though. Is Jaxon awake?"

"Fast asleep. He's in your bed."

"Thanks." Madea nodded at her, then glanced at Sarai and Garrett. "See you soon, then."

He reached for her hand again, then drew her towards him. She kissed him briefly, aware of the other women in the room. "Be safe," he said, his words soft yet firm.

"I will. And you—" She turned to Sarai. "Keep an eye on him for me, would you?"

"You don't trust me?" Garrett managed to sound wounded by her comment.

"Not in this." She smiled, shaking her head.

"Take care, please?" Sarai said, reaching out to squeeze her hands.

"I'm just going to get Rickard. I've stormed enough mansions for tonight, thank you very much. The scene he made outside wouldn't have given anyone a clue that he was in on what was happening at Father's." She headed for the door.

Tahra fell into step beside her. "Can I walk with you?"

"Of course." Madea's brows knitted together.

"What happened?"

"Sorry. I should have filled you in. I wasn't thinking."

"It's been an intense night for everyone, Maddy. Don't be too hard on yourself," Tahra said.

"I made a deal with Father. I think it's a good one and I hope you'll agree."

"Yes?" Tahra raised an eyebrow.

"He's agreed to stop the Hollowings. From now on, all Sun-Touched will be passed to us."

Tahra stopped walking, her jaw worked as she processed what Madea had just said. "All?"

"Every single one of them. I know it's not everything you had hoped for, but it's a huge step. I'm hoping we can broker some trade deals. We have the advantage here, Mother."

She snorted. "How do you gather that?"

"We can work outside the domes. We need to stop hiding down here in the tunnels and make the most of the world that those who haven't been Touched are so afraid of. Don't you see? There is a whole world of possibility. We just need to get out there and grasp it." Madea was surprised by her own passion. She had only been among the ranks of the Touched for a little while, yet the small span of time she had spent outside the domes with Garrett had been the most pleasurable she'd had since arriving on Diamara. It made no sense to stay confined when they could live freely, without the constraints that those who feared exposure had.

"I don't know how many people would want to leave—" Tahra stopped in the middle of the hallway, as if just thinking about it was too difficult.

"No one has to do anything they don't want to, but if you lead the way...they look up to you, Mother. They admire you, your drive, your passion. You saved them and they owe you their lives. That will count for something. If you showed them that you were brave enough to do it, they might feel the same way. Think about the possibilities."

"I will." Tahra nodded her head. "Thank you, for dealing with your father. It's a step in the right direction, though I still believe we should be rid of the domes entirely."

"Not right now. Not like that. There has got to be a better way. Just look at Sarai. She's not Touched, but she's here with us."

"I'll consider all the options. Okay?"

"Thanks."

"Let's get you some food. Then you better get Rickard," Tahra said as she moved down the hallway. "You know, I always thought it would be you and him—"

"No. Trust me, Sarai and Rickard are a better couple than we would ever have been. We make great friends, but he would drive me nuts as a partner." Madea smiled.

"Besides, there is Garrett..."

"There is." Madea pursed her lips, preventing anything else from slipping out. "I need to check on Jaxon, and then I'm going for Rickard."

Back at her rooms, Madea slipped into the bedroom to check on Jaxon. She knelt down beside the bed and ran her fingers through his hair. He was so fast asleep that he barely stirred at her touch. "I'm going to get your dad back. I know you don't know him yet, but he's going to be there for you. He's going to love you and do everything he can to make up for the years he wasn't around. I know it won't make up for losing your mother, but it's something. I hope it's enough." She placed a kiss on his forehead, then stood, watching his slow, deep breathing. Tahra was in the kitchen, cutting a sandwich. She pushed the plate across the bench towards Madea.

"It's been a long time since you made me a sandwich. What's in it?"

"Peanut butter. It used to be your favourite."

"Still is." Madea reached for half and took a bite out of it. There was something about such simple fare that seemed to brighten the day. "Thank you."

"You're welcome." Tahra sighed. "I've missed this, you know? The little things. Making your lunch. Talking to you every day. Watching you grow. I mean I watched, but it's not the same as seeing you face to face. I wish I could have been there."

"I know." Madea nodded. "It wasn't easy for any of us and playing the blame game isn't going to do any good. We can make up for lost time now."

"We can," Tahra agreed. "You'll come back straight away, right?"

"Yeah, this shouldn't take long. We'll be back before you know it." She finished her sandwich and pushed the empty plate back across to her mother. "Will you stay here with Jaxon?"

"I can, if that's what you want."

"Thanks. I don't want him to wake up alone."

Tahra came around the bench and folded Madea into her

arms. "Take care. If you're not back in a couple of hours, I will send out a search party."

Madea laughed. "Okay." She grabbed her bag and slung it over her shoulder. "See you soon," she called as she closed the door. Madea took a deep breath and headed back towards the hatch. When she got back from this, she was going to sleep for as long as they would let her.

CHAPTER TWENTY-SEVEN

Madea pushed through the back door of Rickard's house. "Rickard?" she called out.

"In here," he replied. She followed his voice, heading for the living room. As she stepped through the doorway, someone grabbed her, pinning her arms to her sides. She struggled against her captor, but his grip was too firm and she couldn't find a way free.

"I'm sorry, Madea. I'm so sorry." Tears streamed down Rickard's face. He was bound to a chair. "I didn't think he would do this, I didn't think he would get this upset—"

"Shut up," grunted the man holding her.

"Sullivan?"

"It's me, honey." His words dripped with sarcasm.

"What are you doing? Why did you tie him up? Why are you holding me?" Madea demanded. There was no scenario in which this made sense.

"Just shut up for a minute, would you?" He manoeuvred her into a second chair. She struggled against him, but it was no use, she was too tired, and he was too strong. He wound a rope around her body and fastened her to the chair.

"Weren't you drunk not long ago? I was worried they were going to arrest you," Madea said. She tried to keep her voice calm, but it wavered at the end.

"It was all an act, to help you. I thought you needed me. I thought that I was doing you a favour, when all I was really doing was helping you free your new lover. What did you do? Go and shack up with the first available guy you could find?"

The words stung so much that Madea was rendered speechless for a moment. "You...I...what?"

"You just thought you'd go and find some other guy to play daddy to our baby. Was that it?"

Madea closed her eyes for a moment, then looked up at him. His eyes were wild with a rage she hadn't thought him capable of. She flicked her tongue across her bottom lip, choosing her words carefully. "You didn't want to be a father. You made that quite clear. And despite the fact that it's none of your business anyway, I'll have you know that I haven't shacked up with anyone, thank you very much." She bit out the words.

"Then who was he? The guy that was so important you had to rescue him?"

"His name is Garrett, and maybe there is something between us, but it's none of your business." She tried to shrug, but her arms were bound too tight. "You were the one who didn't want a relationship."

"That doesn't mean I wanted you to go off and find someone else." He paced in front of her, occasionally stopping to glare.

She had never expected this behaviour from him. He'd always seemed so rational. "You need to let me go, Sully. Now. Before this gets out of hand. What's this all about, anyway?"

"Your father asked me to detain you, and that's what I'm doing." He nodded his head, as if that explained it all.

"Since when do you take orders from my father?" Madea raised an eyebrow, trying to put the pieces of the puzzle together.

"I've always taken my orders from him. Always. Who do you think makes the pills that create madness? To keep people in line? You didn't think every Hollowing was for real, did you?" He shook his head in disgust at her. "Don't look so surprised. I know you know all about that. You had to go and get yourself properly Touched, didn't you?"

"If you knew all about that, you'd know the only reason I am is because Father wouldn't do what he'd been asked. So blame him for that one, not me." Her stomach twisted itself up in knots as it dawned on her that just about everyone around her was involved in this, in one way or another. The only ones who seemed innocent of anything were Jaxon and Sarai, and while she knew she could trust them, she couldn't rely on them to do anything to change the situation.

"I've had enough of this," she said. "Let me go. I mean it." There was something happening inside her. She could feel their baby move as though she was responding to the sound of her father, to the sound of her parents arguing, but there was more to it than that. Pressure built in Madea's veins. Ether creatures swarmed through the walls and into the house. She'd not seen them come inside before, though she'd seen them in the domes earlier. They gathered around, their tendrils lashing out to touch the three of them.

But she was the only one who could feel it, who could sense the extra weight in the room. Panic pooled in her chest. "Sully, let me go now. Please, before something happens that you might not like."

"Like you can do anything in your position." He shook his head and Madea could have sworn she saw madness gleaming in his eyes. She had never seen him like this, never thought he was capable of this behaviour. Whatever had happened to him that night he'd overdosed had changed something inside him.

He crossed to her side and ran his hands through her hair. Madea struggled against her bonds, wishing that the creatures were made of something more substantial so that they could slip her from her ties, or knock Sullivan out. One of them flicked its tendrils at her as if in response to her thoughts, wrapping around her wrists before sliding through her body.

"What are you going to do now?" Madea asked, trying to buy some time.

"Your father wants to see you." His fingers slipped from her hair and his hands came to rest on her shoulders. He traced the hollows of her neck with a finger, his touch bringing a shudder to her body. Once, this would have turned her on, but now it made her want to vomit.

The muscles in her belly clenched and she hunched forward as much as she could.

"Is the baby moving?" Sullivan asked, stepping around so that he was in front of her. He dropped to his knees and reached forward to push her shirt up so that he could touch the skin of her abdomen.

As he made contact, realization flooded through Madea and she called out to her child, called out to the creatures, who merged with her body and sent a shock wave through her skin to Sullivan. Madea's eyes were forced shut as a tsunami of images and emotions flooded through her—things her daughter was already thinking and feeling, memories of the Hollowed that the ether creatures had absorbed, along with a wealth of information about Madea's last few weeks. Snippets of her time in the tunnels, of her life as one of the Touched.

Sullivan crashed back onto the floor, a stunned look of reverence plastered on his face. His jaw moved, lips opening and closing for a minute before he could speak.

"That...she...you..."

"You know now, don't you? You can see why I have to get away. You can see what's been happening. Can't you?" Madea leaned forward as much as she could, trying to fathom what he might be thinking.

Sullivan scrambled to his feet, backing further away from her. "It's too much, too much to understand." He dragged his fingers through his hair as he paced. "You have to get out of here."

"So untie me," Madea said.

"I don't want to see anything else." He eyed her warily. "If I touch you again..."

"Nothing will happen. I'll make sure of it." She could only hope that was the truth. She was still struggling to understand what had just happened, to Sullivan, and to her.

He took a tentative step forward. "Can I trust you?"

Madea sighed. "You've seen everything about my life in the last weeks. You know I'm not hiding anything."

"Right," he mumbled, then knelt behind her, letting the rope fall to the ground.

Madea rubbed her wrists. She might only have been captive for a short time, but it was long enough. "And Rickard," she said, nodding towards her friend. Sullivan moved to do her bidding, even helping the other man to his feet.

Sullivan left Rickard leaning on the bench, then moved into the kitchen. He seemed so much like himself that Madea wasn't sure whether it was an act, or the truth.

"Is it just you? Or did he send others to bring us in?" Madea asked when he returned with the water.

"There are others," Sullivan admitted. He rubbed his chin, grimacing. "I'm sorry. I had no idea about the creatures, that being Touched wasn't... It's not madness. All those people... I was going to Hollow you. Our baby."

"How could you have known? No one knows the full extent of what being Touched really means. Father made sure not to spread his information around. But I'll tell you the same thing I told him. Things have to change. There will be no more Hollowings, and the Sun-Touched will live free, outside the domes. Do you understand?" She left the rest unsaid, for now. The fact that he'd been involved in making people crazy, forcing their Hollowings, made her sick to her stomach. But right now she needed to focus on getting out of there. Who knew how long it might be before Sullivan flicked back to working against them?

"Of course." Sullivan nodded, then licked his lips. "Those creatures...they are...amazing."

"More than amazing," Madea said. "You could see them for yourself, if you wanted to."

"No. No, not yet. No." He shook his head quickly, took a step back as though she could somehow make him Touched by mere contact.

"Maybe one day." Madea turned to Rickard. "Are you okay? We need to get out of here."

"Yeah." His voice was still hoarse, but he looked slightly more alert than when she'd come in. "Is Sarai okay?"

"She's fine," Madea assured him. "Tell us," she said, turning back to Sullivan. "Which is a safe way to leave?"

"There's a transport in the shed, waiting to take you in. You could get in that. They'll be expecting it to leave here, but they won't expect you to be driving."

"Thank you." Madea reached out to grasp Sullivan's hand, but he drew back from her. "We appreciate it."

"It's the least I can do," Sullivan said, giving her a nod. He waited a moment before asking, "Could you knock me out and tie me up? I know what you are doing is right, but it's me who'll have to deal with the fallout."

"My pleasure," Rickard said, stepping forward.

"Wait!" Madea grabbed his arm. "Where are the keys?"

Sullivan pulled them from his pocket and threw them towards her. "Good luck."

She nodded, pressing her lips together as she waited for Rickard to move. He drew his arm back and punched Sullivan square in the jaw, sending him crashing to the ground. Sullivan groaned and uttered his thanks as Rickard pulled him to his feet and moved him into the chair, binding him as quickly as he could.

"Let's go," Rickard said when he was done. Madea grabbed his hand and led him towards the garage, her heart pounding. Once they were inside the vehicle, she headed for the nearest exit from the domes.

"What's the plan?" Rickard asked.

"We get outside the domes, and we run. They aren't expecting that, and I don't think they'll be willing to head out now, not without some preparation." She watched the slow spread of light on the horizon. "It's not a high risk time, but still..."

"I guess it's the best we can hope for."

"You might get exposed," Madea said. She swallowed,

feeling guilty that he might become Touched because of her. She wanted people to have a choice, and yet her actions were taking that from him, like it had been taken from her.

Rickard chuckled. "It's better than the alternative."

"Can I tell you something? And don't get angry, please. After everything that's happened today, I don't think I can handle that." She licked her lips as she waited for a response, glancing across at him before flicking her eyes back to the road.

"I'll try..."

"Tahra exposed Jaxon—"

"She did what?" He leaned forward, his forehead twitching with outrage.

"She took him out of the domes. I don't know why, honestly. I was asleep, and she offered to look after him..."

"She had no right—"

"I know. Rickard, I know. I'm sorry. But it's done now, and maybe this is something the two of you can have in common."

"I guess." Rickard shrugged, deflating a little. "I'm so tired, Maddy. I don't know how you're coping with all of this."

"Who said I was coping?" She raised an eyebrow. "We just need to get back to the tunnels, and lay low for a bit. Figure out what comes next."

"I guess."

There was no pursuit that they could see; no sirens, no other transports tailing them, nothing. Perhaps her father still didn't realize that Madea was behind the wheel. Whatever was going on, Madea wasn't going to question it. She deserved a bit of good luck, surely.

She pulled up at the exit closest to where she believed the oasis with the tunnel entrance was and they jumped out of the vehicle, taking one last look around. A few people were up and about now, though none of them gave them a second glance.

"Final chance to opt out," Madea said.

"Let's go." Rickard nodded and pushed ahead of her, through the door and out of the domes.

"Are you sure this is the right way?" Rickard asked for the third time. He stopped walking and wiped the sweat from his head. "We can't keep going like this."

"I don't know." Madea sighed. She was so sure it was this way, but then how would she really know? She'd never come at it from the domes, never thought she would have the need. She squinted into the distance to see if she could spot any familiar landmarks. What she could see was a stand of trees, shadows long and dark across the dusty plain. "Come on, let's head for the shade. We can rest for a few minutes."

"Whatever," Rickard huffed, following behind her. He stumbled after only a few steps and Madea rushed back to him, swinging an arm over her shoulder and walking alongside him.

"I know this isn't ideal," she offered.

"You keep saying that."

"Well, I mean it." She tried to swallow her frustration with the situation, with him. "We really would have made a terrible couple."

"You keep saying that, too." Rickard smiled. "I'm sorry. I am. Whatever Sullivan injected me with has given me a splitting headache and I wish I could sleep for a year."

"You think you're tired? I've been up all night, and I'm growing a small human in my body. Until you try that, don't even think about complaining."

"Okay, okay. You win." He removed his arm from her shoulder as they came into the shade and slumped down against the nearest tree. "Don't these creatures of yours have anything they could do to help? Which reminds me, I want to know what you did to Sullivan. He looked equal parts horrified and amazed."

"I don't really know how to explain it."

"Well, try. It's not like we're lacking time."

Madea took a deep breath and sank to the ground beside him, stretching herself out on the grass. "As soon as he grabbed me, it was like pressure began building in the room. I was drawing in the creatures; they were responding to my stress. But not just mine, the baby's too. She's connected to them."

"She?" Rickard raised an eyebrow.

"Yes. She." Madea smiled. "I can feel her, I can sense her inside me and when Sullivan was ranting, she was getting more and more distressed. It was like she knew he was her father, and she didn't like us arguing."

"But she's only a few months old. How can that be?"

"She's been changed," Madea said. She chewed on her bottom lip, trying to find the right words to explain it. "These creatures have a psychic ability. They can sense things, and they soak up memories, thoughts, feelings. They must have been drawn to us by the emotion in the room and they pushed all of those things onto Sullivan, showed him everything that he needed to know to get him to stop hurting us."

"No wonder he looked scared." Rickard was quiet for a moment. "Do you think you can draw them to us now? Get them to help?"

"Worth a shot. Keep an eye out for anyone, okay?"

Rickard nodded in response, and Madea closed her eyes, trying to push out all the unimportant thoughts and focus on her body and the situation. It was strange, to be purposefully seeking out the connection with her child, but there she was, nestled safely inside. She could feel her baby now, but it felt wrong to keep thinking of her as a baby, she was so much more now. Madea filtered through names, and then the perfect one popped into her head, almost as if the child had chosen it herself.

"Anya," she whispered, smiling, as she knew it meant goodness. The child stirred, sending a wave of love and warmth that spread through Madea, calming her mind. She could picture the child this baby would become, could see her long blonde hair and her cherubic face, the cheeky grin that would play on her lips, the round arms that would reach around Madea's neck to squeeze her tight. The girl pulled away and pointed. Madea turned her head in that direction and opened her eyes, following the guidance. In the distance she could see something that hadn't been obvious before: a chain link fence. She frowned, unsure what it meant, but compelled to go and find out.

"Well?" Rickard asked, seeing that she had stirred. "What did these creatures of yours tell you?"

"I don't know. But I can see something over there, and I think we should go and check it out."

"Whatever." Rickard sighed. "Let's hope it leads to food and water. I'm famished."

She rolled her eyes at him and got up, leading the way.

CHAPTER TWENTY-EIGHT

It took them a good twenty minutes to get close enough to see what lay beyond the fence. People gathered around rows of bushes, their movements stiff but purposeful as they tended to the lush crops laid out. They seemed to be completely unaware of the presence of others, they were so focused on their tasks.

"The Hollowed," Rickard whispered. "I've never seen one before. Creepy."

Madea scanned the workers, trying to figure out why her child had sent them this way. Then she saw a familiar head of hair, a familiar face amongst the crowd. She elbowed Rickard, sure that he could hear the pounding her heart. "It's Janae." Her mouth went dry and she licked her lips, trying to prevent the crack she could feel forming.

"Where?" Rickard asked.

She didn't reply, but raised her hand and pointed the woman out.

"She looks..." Rickard sighed, his shoulders slumping.

"We have to get her." Madea spotted a gate further down the fence line, waving Rickard back when he moved to follow. "Wait here."

She ignored his protest, focusing on the crowd. There didn't seem to be anyone in charge, so theoretically, no one should notice her. They might not even realize that a worker was missing until the day came to an end. It sickened her, now that she could see it in the flesh. These Hollowed had once been people, with lives and families, and now they were mindless drones, sent to labour in the fields.

Madea reached out with her mind, calling on the ether creatures in case she had need of them. It was strange how quickly that connection had happened, and now they flowed towards her like a flock of birds to the bearer of crumbs. An idea was forming, and hope sparked when she recalled what had happened with Sullivan.

She reached the gate and opened it. "Janae," she called softly, flicking her eyes over the field to see if her entrance had garnered any attention. "Janae," she said again, her voice louder now, more sure. No one was here. No one was coming—who would risk being Touched to keep a tight watch on the Hollowed?

The girl ignored her, as though she didn't even know her own name. Madea summoned up all she knew—the memories, the images, the stories that Jaxon had told her—and pushed those thoughts out towards the creatures. One of them flicked its tendrils towards Madea, piercing her deep in the chest and sending a new wave of memories through her.

This was the creature then, or at least one of them, that Janae had come into contact with. Somehow, it had absorbed her memories, and if Madea could find a way, maybe they could be returned to Janae.

She stalked closer, keeping as low to the grains as she could, hoping that their tall blades would keep anyone from noticing her. When she was near enough she reached out and grasped Janae's arm. The girl startled, eyes flashing wide as she tried to back away.

"Wait! You know me, or at least I know you." Madea examined Janae for any sign of recognition. The girl had frozen, but her nostrils flared wide with each breath and her skin quivered beneath Madea's hand.

Anya moved inside her and Madea dropped all her barriers, reaching out mentally for the ether creature who had touched Janae. Its tendrils flared again, growing thick and solid as they connected Madea to Janae. A surge moved through her body and she felt the dirt and rock bite into her skin as she dropped to her knees. Janae was there beside her, not breathing as all the memories and feelings flashed between them.

When it was over, Madea dropped the other girl's hand, planting both of hers in the dirt as she tried to regain her composure. Tears coursed down her face, dampening the ground between her fingers.

"Madea?" Janae's voice was barely a whisper, husky and raw from disuse.

"Hi." Madea exhaled the word, looking up. A smile pulled at her lips, though she felt exhausted in both body and mind. "Are you okay?"

"I'm—" Janae frowned. "I'm okay. The last thing I remember is the Hollowing. You stayed with me." The furrows in her brow deepened, as though she were trying to force her memories to make sense. A flash of despair crossed her face. "Jaxon!"

"He's safe. I found him, like you wanted me to." Madea brushed the dirt off her hands, leaving brown streaks on her pants. She stood and held out a hand to Janae. "We should go, before someone sees us."

"Go where?" Janae looked timid, and Madea realized that the other girl knew nothing of her. Madea had seen her memories, felt her emotions, been witness to huge chunks of Janae's life—but she knew nothing of Madea in return.

"I'll take you to Jaxon." Madea's hand still hung between them.

Janae grasped it and allowed herself to be pulled along. Neither of them spoke as they made their way back to Rickard, though Madea's mind raced at the possibilities that could stem from what had just happened.

Somehow, between the baby, the creatures and herself, they had restored Janae's memories. Would they be able to do this to all the Hollowed? And would these memories remain intact, or would they deteriorate?

There was so much unknown, but a thread of hope thrummed in her chest, growing stronger with each step. If she could help restore the Hollowed, then her crimes weren't as great as she had feared. She could make up for the damage she'd unwittingly done.

"Janae?" Rickard stood upright, causing the girl to stop in her tracks.

"Rickard..." Her voice was wistful and guarded at the same time. She eyed him warily. "What are you doing here?"

"I'm going to see Jaxon. I...I'm his father, and I want to be part of his life."

"He's my son," Janae said firmly.

"And mine," Rickard replied.

"Look, we can sort this out later," Madea said, moving between the two of them. They didn't have time for this. "First we need to find our way back."

Rickard shrugged. "Can those creatures of yours point us in the right direction?"

"I have no idea." Madea turned to Janae. "Can you see them?"

"I can." She nodded, her lips set in a grim line. She flinched as one moved toward her. "I don't know what they want from me, but—"

"They can't hurt you." Madea placed a hand on the other girl's shoulder, hoping it would reassure her. Janae shrugged out from under it. "They are attracted to us, but they can't hurt us. If anything, the fact that you have your memories back tells us that they can help us."

"So get them to help now." Rickard exhaled loudly.

Madea wanted to kick him. Sure, he was probably tired, thirsty, and hungry—but so was she. And she was pregnant! He was so annoying when he was out of sorts.

Madea refrained from commenting, and sank to the ground, closing her eyes and calling out once again. When she opened them, the creatures were around her, but not reaching for her like she had expected.

"What are you waiting for?" she asked, her voice a whisper. She ignored the quizzical look that crossed Rickard's face, focusing instead on the creature nearest to her. She stretched her hand towards it, like she would to any unfamiliar animal she might meet and it slowly approached, its tendrils thin and wispy as they flicked towards her, but didn't breach her skin.

"I need your help," Madea said, keeping her voice soft and calm. "We need to get back to the tunnels, and I don't know which way to go. Can you show me?" She knew they didn't speak a language, but their ability to soak up the thoughts, emotions and memories of the humans on the planet meant they must have some understanding.

They communicated with Anya, so perhaps they could communicate with her.

The creatures tentatively stroked a tendril up the skin of her arm before sliding it up and into her cheek. It should have felt creepy, but the touch was gentle. A shimmer of energy flashed through Madea's body, as though the creature was trying to lend her some of its strength, and with it came snapshots of Garrett and Tahra, heading towards the hatch.

The creature withdrew from her body and hovered before her. "Thank you," she said with a nod, focusing solely on the being. She couldn't liken it to anything else she had ever encountered, but hopefully in time the strangeness of it would pass. It would have to. This was her life now.

"Well?" Rickard asked when Madea had been silent for a few minutes.

She drew in a deep breath. "I can find the way."

"Let's get moving then, before someone realizes that we're here." He stood, then reached for her, pulling her upright. "Lead on, wise one." He winked.

A smile crossed her lips. "Are you ready, Janae?" Madea asked. The woman was frozen, arms crossed, fingers pressing hard into her skin.

"I could hear it, when it touched you. Could you hear it?

Like it was speaking to you," the other girl whispered. She was looking at the creatures, who still hovered in the air around them.

"It was communicating with me, though no words passed between us. I didn't realize you'd be able to hear them."

"Makes me even more pleased I can't see them," Rickard said.

"Yet. You can't see them yet. There is no way you've escaped exposure." Madea shrugged. "It might sound weird, but it's amazing. You'll find out soon enough."

"Look, let's not talk about this right now. Let's get back to safety, and worry about everything else later."

"Fine by me." Madea reached out for Janae, who grabbed her hand, then set off in the direction the creatures had shown to her.

There were a few times she needed to stop and tap into the memories of the ether creatures—the one who had gifted her some strength seemed to be following them closely, like a new friend. Others trailed behind. Their tendrils had become familiar and she almost welcomed the soft brush of their presence. They seemed to avoid Janae, as though they could sense her wariness.

Of course she would be wary. The first time she had seen them, she had harmed members of her own family, maybe killed someone. The thought made Madea stop in her tracks. She dropped Janae's hand and turned towards her companions. Her mouth fell open, but she didn't know what to say.

"Are we there?" Rickard asked, the lines of exhaustion on his face dropping away briefly as he gained some hope.

"No, not quite. I just..." She stalled again, unable to process her thoughts as much as she wanted to. Logically, she knew that Janae wasn't a killer, knew that the other girl thought these creatures had been attacking her family, or friends, but that didn't change the fact that she had, at the very least, hurt someone badly enough to be Hollowed. Madea wished she had asked for all the facts. Wished she could broach the topic with the other girl. Did she remember what she had done?

"Nothing, I just wanted to say that we're close, and make sure you're ready. It can be a bit strange being beneath the ground."

"As long as I can get something to eat and drink, and find somewhere to lie down, I'll be happy." Rickard addressed Madea, almost ignoring Janae's presence. He'd barely spoken to her since Madea had reclaimed her, though at some point the two of them would have to talk.

"What about you, Janae? Are you feeling okay?"

"I feel...I'm okay. I just...I'm still trying to figure everything out. It's hard to describe. I have all these feelings and memories, but it's almost as though they didn't happen to me."

"It'll be okay." Madea grabbed her hand again and squeezed. "I bet once you see Jaxon you'll start feeling better."

Janae smiled at her, a genuine smile that lit her eyes. "He's the only thing that matters. I know that. He was the only thing that ever mattered."

"Right then, let's go and see him." Madea nodded, feeling like her fears had been allayed a little. She couldn't hold what had happened against this girl. Under other circumstances, Madea could easily have been a killer, too. Yet another thing she had to thank Garrett for.

It only took them another ten minutes to make it to the hatch. Once she was in the right area she could spot it easily, and pulled it open. The coolness of the tunnels seeped out into the bright day, drawing them all in. Madea closed the hatch behind them, letting her eyes adjust to the dimmer light as a feeling of peace crept over her.

Janae's hand snaked out to grasp Madea's. "Where did they go?" she whispered.

"The creatures? They don't like coming under the earth. I don't know why."

"It's strange not to have them around now."

"You're right." Madea smiled. "I hope we can live outside soon enough. I just have a few things to work out first."

"What do you mean?" Rickard asked.

"Let's find the others," Madea said, moving down the hallway. It would take far too long to explain everything to him, and right now, she didn't have the time.

Two corridors down, they were met by Sturm. "Your mother is expecting you," he said curtly. "She's in her office. I can escort you there."

"Escort?" Rickard raised an eyebrow.

"That would be great, thanks," Madea said. Janae still clung to her, and without the ether creatures to grant her extra strength, Madea was finding it difficult to move, let alone think. She let her mind wander as they followed their guide through the tunnels, ignoring Rickard's constant questions, and Janae's occasional whimpers.

Their escort opened the door for them, and Madea moved directly to the couch.

"Where have you been?" Tahra demanded as she crossed the room.

Madea closed her eyes and pulled a cushion over her face. "There were complications," she said through the fabric, though she wasn't sure her mother would understand. Thankfully, Rickard seemed willing to take the lead.

"Mum!" he declared, just like he used to when they were younger. Madea grinned to herself, glad her mother couldn't see her face right now. "It's been too long."

"Rickard," Tahra said tersely. "Would you mind telling me what's going on? And who is this woman?"

Madea sighed, she knew she should gather herself enough to fill her mother in, but she just didn't have the energy.

"This is Janae. Jaxon's mother. We found her out in the fields and I don't know what Madea did, but she's been...un-Hollowed. Or something." The rest of Rickard's explanation faded out as Madea let herself succumb to sleep.

CHAPTER TWENTY-NINE

Madea woke to firm arms cradling her. She opened her eyes to see Garrett's face as he carried her down the hallway. She tried to push her way upright, but he held her tight.

"You're on bed-rest, missy," he said, his lips quirking into a grin. "I'll enforce it if I have to."

"But I haven't seen Jaxon, and I need to talk to Tahra—"

"And all of that can wait. Jaxon is with his mother, which no one really knows how to explain. Thanks for that," he added wryly.

"I'm not sure I know how to explain it either. But he's happy, isn't he?"

"Happy, yes, but worried about you. We told him you needed some sleep, you've been very busy."

"How are you strong enough to carry me?" She frowned, the fog of sleep finally slipping from her mind.

"We have a great medic here," he explained. "Though I'll need to rest once I get you in bed. You're heavier than you look."

"I'm pregnant!" She struggled in his arms, pushing against him to no avail.

"And I'm joking." He laughed. "I wanted to make sure you did rest, because I think I know you well enough to say that given the slightest opportunity, you'd just keep going."

"But that wouldn't be good for Anya." Madea finished his thought for him.

"Anya? That's a good name." He nodded in approval.

Madea relaxed into his arms, content that despite his teasing, he did have her best interests at heart. "What did I miss?"

"Oh you know, family reunion stuff. Tears, and smiles, and hugs and reaffirmations of love."

"I like that stuff." She pouted, but he shook his head at her.

"I've had some food sent ahead. You're going to sit in bed and eat until you're ready to pop, and then you're going to sleep for another ten hours. Got it?" He placed her gently on her feet, pushed open the door to her unit and ushered her inside, closing the door behind them.

"And what are you going to do?"

"I'm going to sit beside you and make sure you do as you're told." He softened his glare with a smile. Then he scooped her back into his arms and carried her to the bedroom, dumping her unceremoniously on the mattress.

Madea grabbed his arm and pulled him down beside her, her heart thudding heavily in her chest.

"What's up?" he asked. His eyes narrowed and she found herself unable to hold the façade any longer. Her walls cracked and tears flowed silently down her face. She licked one off her top lip, the salty tang biting at her tongue.

"I need you to kiss me." She bit her lip, feeling stupid for asking, but needing nothing more than escape. Or maybe more than that, but it was a good beginning. She wasn't ready to talk, wasn't ready to confess that as far as she was concerned her whole world had been shattered, but she was ready for more of Garrett.

He dipped his head and pressed his lips to hers, gently at first, then he deepened the kiss and crushed her against the pillows with the weight of his body. He pulled back, breathing heavily. "You're meant to be eating something," he murmured.

"I'll eat soon, I promise." Madea pulled him close again, savouring the taste of his mouth and the feel of his hands as they slid under her shirt and across the skin of her belly. She felt a kick from Anya and broke the kiss, looking at Garrett. "It doesn't bother you, does it?"

"Does what?" He looked genuinely confused.

"Anya..."

"She's a part of you. If I was bothered, I wouldn't be here, making sure you're getting bed rest." He smiled, a mischievous gleam in his eyes.

"Rest?" Madea raised an eyebrow, a grin crossing her own lips as he moved forward, taking full advantage of their current location.

Madea was surprised that Garrett was still beside her in the morning. Soft snores escaped from his parted lips and she muffled them with a kiss. He startled, eyes flashing open before he returned her kiss with fervour.

"I forgot where I was," he said when they parted. "I don't think I've ever been woken up like that."

"You poor, deprived man." Madea patted his shoulder mockingly.

"Is that an everyday thing for those lucky enough to share your bed?" He quirked an eyebrow, though his almost ever present smirk was absent.

"To be honest, it's been a rare thing for a man to share my bed, if that's what you're asking," Madea said. "I could, perhaps, make an exception for you."

"I'd like that." He was all seriousness as he leaned forward and pressed a firm kiss against her brow, then ducked his head to lay one in her belly. "Do you think she minds?"

"I think she's doing her very best to ignore everything that happened last night. I haven't heard a peep from her in hours."

"Something to be said for having a super-child, huh?" He laughed, then swung his legs off the bed and pulled on pants. "I'm getting food. You stay here, and then we need to talk."

"Sounds serious."

"It is." Garrett tried to hide a frown as he left the room.

Madea scanned the room for her clothes, but wrinkled her nose when she lifted her shirt from the ground. There was no way she was putting that back on. She tossed it on the floor and made her way to the bathroom, flicking the shower on and stepping beneath the water.

She let out a groan of pleasure as the jets struck her body, washing the dirt and grime from her skin. How long had it been since she was last clean? Did she really want to know?

"I thought I told you to stay in bed?"

Madea jumped at the sound of his voice, instinctually crossing her arms over her breasts. "I needed to get clean. I can't believe we had— Not in that state."

"I didn't realize you were so keen on cleanliness." He smiled as he slipped into the shower with her.

"I used to work in a lab. I like things to be clean." She half-shrugged and dropped her arms, pressing against him. "So what did you want to talk about?"

"You think I'm capable of having an intelligent conversation with you naked, in the shower?" He raised an eyebrow and let out a soft chuckle.

"What if I promise to do terrible, terrible things to you?" She leaned into him then stood on tip toes to nibble his earlobe.

"I'm not sure you'll want to, after."

He flicked his tongue across his lips, as though the heated water running down his face wasn't enough to hydrate his flesh. She pulled back and looked up at him. "Just tell me. And I promise I won't do anything nasty."

Garrett closed his eyes for a moment then opened them, all traces of humour wiped from his features. "Your mother was worried about you when you were gone so long. She thought that something must have happened and she was gathering her forces."

"Her forces? I had a tracker on. She could have come for me anytime."

"She was going to, but then you were moving again, and outside the domes. She wasn't sure how to interpret that." He glanced away, not looking back until she caught his chin in her hand and made him. This was probably the most shame-faced she had seen him, and considering the things he'd done...her stomach clenched at the thought of what this might be about.

"What has she done?"

"Nothing. Yet. But she's going to blow the domes."

"What?" Madea pushed her hair back from her face, pulling at it as she did. "I made a deal with Father, and she's just going to blow the domes and my arrangement with it?"

Garrett cupped her chin with his hand. "Can you honestly tell me that the deal hasn't been compromised? I heard what happened."

"When? When did you possibly have time to hear about that?" She waved her arms in the air, taking a step away from him so that her back hit the cool tile wall of the shower.

"After I left you this morning. Tahra left a message for me."

Madea ground her teeth together so hard she could hear it over the sound of the water. "She hasn't done it yet, has she? Garrett, tell me the truth."

"Not yet, but she will soon—"

"I have to go." She pushed past him, grabbing a towel and roughly drying her body before reaching for the clothes on the floor. Another whiff and she dropped them, turning to the drawers and clean gear. It didn't matter how she looked, she had to get to her mother.

"Wait," Garrett called as he followed, drying himself more slowly. "Do you really think we should honour the deal you made? He tried to capture you, Madea. He doesn't care what happens to you, to us. He just wants to win."

"And so does Tahra. Don't you get it? This is a marital dispute gone to the greatest of extremes. She's so hell-bent on getting back at him that she can't see there are more important things at stake. We won't win by one-upping him. We'll only cause more pain." She shook her head. Disappointment burned in her throat. "I have to stop her." Madea headed for the door with tears in her eyes. She had thought he'd understood.

"Wait," he said, grabbing her by the arm and turning her back. "I don't know your reasons, but I trust you, and I trust Anya." He put his palm against her belly and she could feel her baby move in response. "Let me get some clothes and I'll come with you. I want to help."

"I have to go, now. I can't let her do anything." She pulled away, but he caught her wrist.

"I'll catch up."

Madea nodded then stepped towards him, kissing him softly on the lips before leaving.

CHAPTER THIRTY

Madea raced down the halls to her mother's office and burst through the door, freezing at the sight of Tahra, Rickard and Sarai staring at a map, strewn out across the table.

"Ah, Madea. You're just in time for the big reveal." Tahra's smile was broad but the cold gleam in her eyes made Madea nervous.

She took a deep breath and licked her lips. "What reveal?" she asked in her calmest voice. Here was yet another occasion where her mother could lie, but would she?

"I'm going to blow the domes," her mother said with a nod. She raised her hands when Madea opened her mouth. "I know what you're going to say, but your father has shown quite clearly that he has no intention of letting us live in peace."

"This shouldn't be about Father." Madea glared at her mother. "It might be for you, but it's not for everyone else. No one outside of this room gives a damn about your petty feud." She crossed the room and examined the map, noting where Tahra had pushed pins into locations around the domes, centralized around Carson's.

"Have some respect—"

"For the woman who played dead for most of my life?" She glanced up at her mother. "For the woman who spent years plotting ways to get back at her power-hungry husband? The two of you are ridiculous." Madea shook her head. "I'm not going to think about you, or him, for another moment. What I'm going to do is take care of the Sun-Touched, those here in the tunnels and the Hollowed working the fields. Don't you see the bigger picture? We can reclaim them, Mother. We can give them back their memories. They might not be exactly the same, but we can undo some of what has been done to them."

"I don't think now is the time to talk about that," Tahra said. She pressed her lips together so tightly that Madea thought they might disappear entirely.

"We have to talk about things before you do something that we'll all regret."

"But—"

"No. No buts. Just hear me out."

"Fine." Tahra sighed.

"We're listening," Sarai said. She reached a hand across the table and squeezed Madea's hand, relief apparent in the lines of her face. Rickard nodded too and Madea licked her lips, getting her thoughts straight.

"We can't blow all the domes. We just can't, but I think we should blow one."

"You what?" Garrett's voice came from the door. Madea spun to see him striding towards her, a frown on his face. "I thought you wanted to do this the peaceful way?"

"I'm not done talking yet." She smiled at him, reaching up to kiss his cheek before he took his place behind her. Her stomach churned at the possibility her mother might not agree, but Madea had to try to offer an alternative. "What I'm suggesting is that we pick one of the smaller ones, closest to Father. We can contact Sullivan and get him to clear out the people within that dome so there is as little risk as possible. I'm totally opposed to making anyone Touched who doesn't want to be." She glanced at Rickard, whose face flushed a little.

"It was my choice, Maddy. Honest."

She nodded at him before continuing. "Once they see that we won't back down, then we can make some solid deals.

Father will have to stick to his side of the bargain, or he'll find himself one of the Touched as well."

"I'm pleasantly surprised," Tahra said, her voice soft. She kept her eyes on the table as she spoke. "I didn't think you'd have the guts to do even that much."

"I will do what I must to keep the Touched safe. I thought I'd been clear about that. Mother, I'm not trying to take your place, but you're not being reasonable."

"And you are still being too reasonable." Tahra shook her head.

"Can I trust you to stick to our plan?" Madea stared at her until Tahra looked up.

"Sure," she said as she exhaled loudly. "I need to go and change some orders I gave. Which dome are you going to take down?"

Madea scanned the map, and pointed to the smallest one, bordering her father's. "This one."

"Right. I'll make sure my people get the gear ready. The sooner, the better." Tahra emphasised the word 'my', but Madea wasn't going to rise to the dig. She didn't want to be in charge anyway, but she knew Tahra wasn't thinking straight.

"I should go with her," Sarai said, pulling away from the table.

"No, give her a few minutes. Madea was pretty rough on her. She probably needs to be alone." Rickard placed a hand on Sarai's arm, stopping her from following.

"She needed to be told." Madea refused to look at the others, refused to feel guilty for putting her mother in her place.

Garrett raised an eyebrow. "I've never seen her so...quiet."

"It doesn't matter," Madea said. "We need to get word to Sullivan to start clearing this dome and the ones around it, just in case it goes badly. Can you do that, Rickard?"

"Are you sure we should trust him?" Rickard grimaced.

"As sure as anything, these days. He might have been working for Father before, but he helped us escape. He knows what is at risk here." Madea shrugged, turning to her sister.

"Why don't you go with him, Sarai? I'd hate to split you guys up again so soon."

"Okay. He could use my help anyway." Sarai nudged him with her elbow.

"Something like that," Rickard agreed. "I've figured these maps out and I'm pretty sure I can get there and back with no trouble."

"We won't move forward until we know it's as clear as it can be." Madea gave them each a quick hug and watched them slip out the door.

"They'll be okay, right?" she asked. Garrett slipped his arms around her waist and pulled her close.

"They should be. Your father won't expect this, or maybe he will, but what can we do about it?"

"I don't know. I just feel— I've spent my whole life doing what was right, and this feels wrong. I know it's nothing in the grand scheme of things, but we're changing what life on this planet means. No one has destroyed a dome before. No one has gone against the government like this."

"And I'd put money on it that you've not gone against your father like this before, either," he murmured into her ear.

"No. Never." She frowned. "I know that this is for the greater good. I just wish it didn't feel so bad."

"It'll be over soon enough," Garrett assured her. "Why don't we go and sort out the explosives? Tahra will have everything organized, I guarantee, so it shouldn't be hard to get what we need."

Madea bit her lip, thinking of all the things she should be doing. "I need to check on Jaxon. I want to make sure he's okay."

"Well, you go and do that, and I'll get everything ready." He kissed her forehead then moved away, stopping at the door to look back. "Okay?"

"Yes," she said, though she was feeling less than. She wished he would come with her, but realized that what she was doing was probably the least important thing. "Where are Jaxon and Janae?"

"Head back to your unit, and you'll find them three doors down on the right."

"So close?"

Garrett shrugged. "I figured you'd want to be close enough that you could see them easily."

She smiled, feeling better for his consideration. "Thanks. I'll see you soon." He nodded, leaving the door open behind him. Madea took a deep breath then made her way to Jaxon and Janae.

She knocked, but there was no answer. As she knocked again, panic twisted in her belly and writhed up her throat. She pushed the door open, imagining that Janae had somehow reverted to her pre-Hollowed state and had killed Jaxon in a fit of madness. How could she have left them alone? No one knew whether the reclamation would hold.

But there they were, lying on the floor of the lounge, drawing pictures, trading coloured markers and smiles. Jaxon grinned, springing to his feet as he saw her. "Madea! I wondered when you were coming back. Mum's here!" He wrapped his arms around her and squeezed her tight. She pulled back an inch so that she could drop to her knees and pull him firmly against her.

"I missed you." She breathed the words into his hair with her eyes shut, taking in the clean scent of him. Clean and small and perfect. "Are you okay?" She moved back again, letting him sit on her lap, though she noticed her belly was beginning to take up some of the space he normally would have occupied.

"Mum's here, so everything is better. She said you brought her back. Is that true?" His eyes were wide, filled with pride and awe.

"I guess you could say that," she said, then glanced at Janae who was smiling calmly. "And how are you feeling?"

"Still...unsure, I guess you could say. As if I can remember things but some of those things don't seem real yet. Apart from Jaxon." She opened her arms to him and he moved back to his mother. "I can't thank you enough for reuniting us. I might never have seen him again, never known him." She bit her lip, making her look so much younger. Barely old enough to have a child Jaxon's age.

"I'm glad you're okay, both of you." Madea got to her feet. "I'll leave you to it, and come back to check on you as soon as I can. Okay?"

"Where are you going? Can't you stay here with us?" Jaxon held out his hand and Madea grasped it.

"I wish I could, but I've got some things to do. Don't worry though, I'll be back." She bent to kiss his forehead.

"I love you," Jaxon said, his voice soft and sweet. The purity of his words made her heart ache, stirring that portion of her that wished she could keep him just for herself. Still, he was better off with his mother, and he had a father now as well. She would have her own baby soon enough, and Anya was already keeping Madea on her toes.

"Love you, too." The words caught in her throat and she swallowed hard, hoping that she could hold in her tears until she got to the hallway at least. She moved away, closing the door firmly behind her and leaning against it, pushing her palms into her eyes. "It's better this way. It's fine."

Anya fluttered in her belly, and Madea felt a wave of love wash over her. She laughed. "I love you too. Thank you." Her fingers traced the shape of the babe in her belly. "Right. Let's get this over with." She took a deep breath and pushed off the wall, heading down the cool concrete corridor to the armoury.

It seemed too quiet as she pushed the door open. There was no bustle, no action, and it was dark. Madea frowned and reached for the switch. Light flooded the room, illuminating a slumped form, tied to a chair. Her stomach felt like lead as she ran forward. "Garrett, what happened?" She fumbled with the knots as he raised his head.

"Your mother." He huffed, as if embarrassed at the situation. "How many times have you saved me now?"

"Just another day at the office," she quipped.

The rope came free and she stepped back as he got to his feet, rubbing his wrists. "I'll try to make this the last time you have to untie me from a chair." He bent and kissed her.

"You're not hurt?"

"Not enough to worry about. We need to hurry. She's going to blow your father's dome." He grabbed her hand and pulled her towards one of the weapons racks.

"But—"

"No buts. You've always said she has her own agenda, and you're right. She's going for your father. If you want to do something about it, we need to get moving." He grabbed a gun, and handed one to her. "So, what's the plan?"

Madea exhaled, trying to figure out what to do. "Get hold of Sarai and Rickard, help them clear whoever else you can, and then get clear yourselves."

"And your mother?"

"Let me deal with her." She rolled her shoulders, setting aside her hopes of a clean resolution. "She has to be stopped."

"Let me come. The others can handle the evacuation." He grabbed her shoulder, giving it a squeeze.

"And have to save you again?" She smiled. "No. This is family business."

"I want to be part of yours."

"After." She pressed her lips to his, savouring the taste of him, drinking in as much strength as she could. "I promise." She ran a hand down his cheek then stepped away. "Try not to get into any more trouble." She tossed the words back over her shoulder, her voice light though she was consumed by nerves.

Her breath felt heavy in her lungs as she ran through the tunnels. Thoughts whirled through her mind: fears, worries, half hatched plans and speeches that she'd deliver to her parents. If her father had just spoken to Tahra, had dealt with this situation earlier. Maybe if her mother had been straight with him, instead of playing games and testing him—

Those were wasted thoughts now. They were both angry, both bitter—but who had more to lose? Who felt they had been dealt the most injustice? Madea shook those thoughts free and focused on her journey. She should have grabbed a phone before she left, but it was too late for that now. Too late for much of anything. The best she could hope for was that those she loved made it out alive, and that the fallout wasn't too catastrophic.

CHAPTER THIRTY-ONE

She pushed free of the hatch and bolted from the church, not caring who saw her. There was no time left for subterfuge. Her breath caught in her lungs as she ran, the sharp bite of a stitch began in her side and she pressed a hand to it, trying to choke back a sob. What a mess. All of this.

Part of her wanted to turn and gather her friends, to leave her parents to each other—it was what they deserved, both of them. But the dutiful daughter couldn't ignore all the good things they had done, couldn't stand the thought of those good things being buried in their domestic feud.

She paused at the door to her father's house, catching her breath in great drags which barely seemed to help. When her heart had stopped racing, she pushed her palm to the panel, waiting as the door slid open.

Madea's gaze skipped across the floor, coming to a halt when she spotted a woman, facedown and still. She rolled the form over, a soft gasp escaping her lips as she recognised her father's housekeeper.

Madea pressed fingers against the woman's neck but there was no pulse. She ground her teeth together, jaw aching from the tension.

Tahra was here already, and she was on a mission. How far would her mother go to take her revenge? Or was Madea already too late to stop her? She gnawed at her cheek, trying to decide whether to rush into the house now, or go cautiously.

Caution, probably best.

She padded down the hall, stopping at the foot of the stairs to listen but there were no discernible sounds so she carried on to the office. Light spilled out from the crack in the door, and Madea nudged it open with the toe of her boot.

The house shook. A massive boom thundered against her ears and bits of the roof fell down around her. Dust covered her face and she crumpled to the ground, covering her head with her arms and hoping for the best.

For a full minute the ground moved. Her ears rang even after everything had settled, and the silence that had filled the house before was banished, replaced by the groans of the shifting structure.

"You idiot," Madea muttered, wishing she could slap her mother, or something more. She ground her teeth together to stop herself from tearing up, not wanting to think about the chaos this was going to cause. She had to stay focused. Find Carson, find Tahra, and get out of there.

She groped for the railing, pulling herself back to her feet. "Father!" she called, taking the stairs two at a time, coughing as the dust infiltrated her mouth and lungs. "Where are you?"

Madea reached the top of the stairs and scanned the landing before heading to her father's room. A low groan came through the door but she couldn't be sure who it was. It didn't really matter, not now.

She pressed her face against the door so she could listen. "Hang on, I'm coming," she said, hoping the words would carry clear enough. The keypad was wrecked, but she grabbed a loose board and rammed it into the gap, using it to lever the door open. Thank goodness they didn't make them very heavy, or there would be no chance, but the door moved, an inch at first, then a foot, just enough for her to squeeze through, wedging the board in behind her so that it didn't close her in.

"Madea," Tahra groaned, her voice weak. Madea found her under a chunk of ceiling, the plaster pinning her to the ground. There was a thick gash on her cheek, and her arms were twisted at strange angles.

Madea couldn't look at them, focused instead on her mother's face. "Where's father?" she asked, carefully removing rubble from the body.

"Don't worry about him. He's not going anywhere." Tahra coughed, a splatter of blood landing on her chest.

Madea froze. "What does that mean? What did you to do him?" She leaned in, watching her mother carefully.

"I didn't kill him, if that's what you're worried about." Her mother snorted derisively. "Though this will, I imagine."

"We had a deal. We had a plan. Why couldn't you just stick to it?" Madea's shoulders slumped.

"Because it wasn't my plan! Why couldn't you just be a good daughter and do what you were told?"

Madea swallowed hard. "I'm done being the good daughter. I thought you'd realize that once you'd 'liberated' me from my dreary little life as one of the un-Touched, things wouldn't be the same. I was happy enough you know, before you came along and re-inserted yourself into my life."

Tahra's eyes went wide, her lips flat-lining.

"Don't move," Madea said, pushing herself upright and scanning the room.

"Wait, where are you going?"

"I'm going to find Father. Where did you put him?" She couldn't resist the urge to place her hands on her hips and jut her chin out, a picture-perfect copy of Tahra when she'd still been a real mother.

Tahra's eyes slid toward the bathroom and Madea didn't wait for confirmation. She clambered over the rubble, skidding out as she approached the door, but managing to catch herself on the frame. "Father?" she called, thumping against the door. This one was tightly shut, and no matter how she mashed the keypad it wasn't going to open. "Dad!" she cried, pressing her ear against the door, straining to hear any sound.

A flutter from her belly made her glance up. Through a breach in the ceiling she could see the sky, the sun shining like a beacon without any dome to diffuse its rays. Ether creatures twisted near the gaping wound in the roof, as if they had been called by her distress.

Anya nudged her again, encouraging her to reach out. She closed her eyes, calling silently to them, could feel the slight brush of their tendrils against her skin and she pushed all her thoughts and feelings out towards them, to make them see what she felt.

She faced the door, eyes still closed. "Help me, help me see him." It felt like she was being stretched, though she knew it wasn't true. She pushed hard, physically, mentally, her connection to the creatures so strong that she could feel it as they broached the door, could see her father, lying on the ground, eyelids fluttering, chest rising and falling, shallow, stilted.

"Oh no, not like this." She clenched her teeth, wishing the door would budge, or the creatures could carry her through, turn her insubstantial like them. She was stuck here, helpless, realizing that nothing that had happened really mattered. No matter what Carson had done, he was still her father, she still loved him, even if she loathed him in almost equal measure.

They should have had time to make up, to set aside their differences, to find a bridge. It might never have happened, but she could tell he was dying, and that death robbed her of any hope of it happening.

And then she knew that there was a slim chance, just a small one. She'd been able to show Sullivan the error of his ways, to transfer her knowledge to him, and maybe, maybe...

Madea fed her thoughts into the ether creatures, stretched with them as they merged with Carson's body. She could feel him recoil, snatching himself back mentally because he couldn't do it physically. She thought of when she was a child, and how they'd had breakfast together every morning. Of the time's he'd pushed her on the swing, and the times when she'd watched him work, loving him even when he was so involved in what he was doing that he barely noticed her existence. She sifted through knowledge of Anya, his grandchild, and the wonder of the creatures.

She felt him relax for just a moment, satisfied, or something akin to it.

Then he was gone.

Madea let out a breath she hadn't realized she was holding, pressed her eyes tighter together to prevent any tears from escaping, and waited for Tahra to speak, to break the silence of this moment. Waited for anger to flare within her. But all she felt was defeat.

Eventually she returned to Tahra's side, silently removing the rubble from her body.

"Tha—"

"No. Don't say anything. I can't—" Madea looked her mother in the eyes. She was torn between wanting to save her remaining parent, and wanting to leave her here in the wreckage. But if she could forgive her father, she could forgive her mother. "I'm not ready to talk yet. You crossed the line and I don't know how we can ever be mother and child again. We can worry about that later though, for now, we need to get out of here."

A single tear fell from Tahra's eye. It rolled down her cheek and shattered against a chunk of ceiling. Madea sniffed back tears of her own, and tried not to think about how many others would need to be dug from the wreckage.

"Madea!" The voice came from the hallway. Garrett tried to jam himself through the door. "Thank God, you're okay." He pulled his back leg through, surveying the damage. "This place is a mess. We've got to get out of here."

As he knelt beside her she wrapped her arms around him. "I'm so pleased to see you." Her voice wavered, but she refused to cry here, not wanting her mother to bear witness to Madea's sorrow. She whispered in Garrett's ear, "I told her not to speak to me. She needs to stand trial for what she's done. I need to— Can you..."

"Let me." He kissed her forehead and pulled away.

Goosebumps prickled her skin where the warmth of his touch was leached away by the cool night air invading the room.

"I know you said not to speak, but you don't have long," Tahra said. Madea glanced over to find she'd managed to free herself from a good sized chunk of the debris, though she was still trapped under a beam and made no move to get up.

"What do you mean?" Garrett asked. He stood over the older woman with a frown, his hands planted on his hips. Such a far cry from the way he used to speak to Tahra.

Tahra coughed, blood peppering her lips. It was only then that Madea realized how pale the woman was. She was going to die, too.

"There's another bomb, isn't there." Madea let out a discouraged sigh. "You never meant to come out of this alive, did you? You were planning on making us orphans."

Everything shifted beneath them and Madea fell to the floor, splinters digging into her hands and knees.

"There's more to come," Tahra said, a sad smile brushed over her lips, though her eyes were serene, at peace with what she'd done. "Two, at least. You should get out of here. I never meant to hurt you, or your baby."

"You didn't mean to hurt me?" Madea shrieked. "What do you think this would do?" She lunged at her mother, gripping her by the shoulders and shaking her, unable to stop the tears from flowing now. "Why? Why are you leaving me again?"

"Maddy, come on." Garrett grabbed her by the torso, hauled her away from her mother. "We need to get out of here. She's giving us the chance to save ourselves. Let's take it."

Another shock pounded the floor, but somehow he managed to keep them both upright. This one was further away, and maybe there was nothing left to shake loose from the house. "Say goodbye." He glared at her.

Madea pressed her lips together, teeth sinking into the flesh.

"Say goodbye. You'll regret it if you don't." He forced her to turn back to Tahra.

Madea sighed and brushed away the tears. "Goodbye, Mother. I wish things could have been different."

"So do I."

By the time they reached the top of the stairs there was another explosion. This one seemed further away still. They made it to the bottom, Garrett gripping her hand the whole way.

"Can you run?" he asked.

"I'll try." She nodded and squeezed his hand, trying not to notice the dust trickling down from the cracks in the ceiling. Tears blurred her vision and she fought the urge to just sit down and let the roof cave in on top of her.

Anya stirred inside, sensing Madea's emotions. The child sent her a burst of love which renewed her energy. Not much further and they would be out now.

Ether creatures trailed behind them, fading in and out of visibility, tendrils wafting toward the ceiling as though they were trying to hold it up. Of course, they couldn't, but if they could try, then she could try too. She picked up the pace, moving ahead of Garret. "Almost there," she said, her breath ragged but stable. The dust in the air was making it hard to breathe, but just a few more steps...

Another rumble moved the ground beneath their feet. Madea stumbled and fell, crashing onto her belly. Pain shot through her and she let loose a primal scream. She cradled her stomach as Garrett scooped her up and pushed free of the house.

He sat her down in the clearest spot he could find, though there were pieces of the dome, bits of broken houses, glass everywhere. Cramps shot through her body but she held everything in as tightly as she could.

"I'm not going to lose this baby," she panted out.

"No, you're not. It's going to be okay. We'll get you to a medic."

"No. No I'm not going anywhere." She tucked her head down and shut out all thoughts, focusing on the child within her womb. Can you hear me, Anya? Please.

There was a light flutter inside, but nothing as strong as before.

Anya, she pleaded. No response. Nothing.

She would not lose her baby. Not after losing her father, her mother. She took a deep breath, pulling everything from the air that she could. The ether creatures pressed against her, through her, their tendrils tangling inside.

Anya, she called again, more firmly. *I know you're in there, I know you can hear me. Stay with me. This is the first order I will ever give you and if you never listen to another I don't care, just stay with me.*

Another flutter, stronger this time. Madea could feel Garrett's arms around her, and then a charge of energy shot through her. Her eyes flew open and her jaw dropped when she saw techni-coloured flashes of light dancing along the tendrils of the creatures, pumping into her body. Anya squirmed, wriggled, kicked with more vehemence than ever before and Madea laughed, relaxing into Garrett's embrace, weak with relief.

"Don't you dare scare me like that again, little one," Madea whispered. Anya booted her.

"Are you okay? Is she—" A frown creased Garrett's forehead, as though he were trying to decipher what had just happened.

"She's going to be fine, trust me. More than fine. We're going to have our hands full." She glanced up at him as she said those words, waiting for his reaction.

Garrett bit back a smile. "Yes, we will." He kissed her then, taking her mind off the wreckage around them and giving her some hope for the future, whatever that might bring.

CHAPTER THIRTY-TWO

"What the hell happened here?" Rickard's voice echoed in the silence. He kicked rubble aside as he approached, trailing dust.

"Obviously, we underestimated Mother's desire for revenge." Madea forced herself to her feet. Her limbs trembled, but held, though she wasn't sure how much more she could take.

"I need to tell you something." Rickard ground his teeth together, scraping fingers through his hair as he switched weight between his feet.

Madea wanted to smack him, make him stop moving because his worry was infectious, and each twitch he made crushed air from her lungs. Her tongue flicked across her lips as she tried to think of something to say, because maybe if she didn't panic, maybe it would all be okay.

"Where's Sarai?" Madea demanded.

Rickard swallowed hard, slid his eyes away from her. "She's with the medics—"

Madea surged forward, pushing her way past him, but he grabbed her arm, anchoring her to the spot. "She's going to be okay, Maddy. But she lost a leg. She got caught under some debris and they had to cut her free."

"Oh God." The strength went out of her, but Garrett and Rickard were there, holding her up. "How could you let this happen? You were meant to look after her!" She noticed then the haggard lines on his face, the sag of his shoulders. "I'm sorry, Rickard. I know you didn't make this happen. I just...I need to see her."

"That's why I'm here." He shrugged off her words and drew her in for a hug. "I love your sister, and I'd do anything to have been in her place. Come on, she needs you."

"She needs you too," Madea whispered, giving him a kiss on the cheek.

The two men supported her on the way back to the nearest hatch. It was a relief to close the door on the devastation and loss in the world above. At least for now.

They made their way to the med bay in silence. Madea broke free from Garrett and Rickard as soon as she saw Sarai unconscious, her missing limb hidden by a sheet. Madea went to lift it, but Rickard pushed her hand away.

"Leave it for now, Maddy. It's not going to do you any good to see."

Instead, she slipped her hand into Sarai's, the warmth of her sister's skin melting away some of the ache in her heart.

"I'll get you a chair," Garrett said. Rickard murmured something about finding another medic, but Madea wasn't listening to them. She was watching the slow rise and fall of her sister's chest, syncing her breath with her last remaining family member, and wishing away consciousness.

When she came to, she was in her own bed. Madea frowned, wondering whether maybe it had all been a bad dream. But no, there were aches in her body that spoke of yesterday's events, and a heavy weight in her chest when she thought of her parents.

If she closed her eyes, maybe she could pretend it was years ago, when they had been a happy family. A family who were becoming accustomed to life on a new planet, who were pioneers at the beginning of an adventure. Her parents had loved each other once, and she had loved them.

Still loved them, just couldn't seem to reconcile herself with their actions. Was she likely to make bad choices too? Was her dutiful nature at risk of becoming a desire for power?

No, that had never been her way. Hers was to do as she'd been told, to play her role and do her duty. And yet now...now she had a chance to make a real difference, to help shape life on Diamara for the better. She had more knowledge than either of her parents.

She rolled over, reaching for Garrett, but the bed was empty. Panic clawed at her as she got up and moved through the lounge, heading for the door in her pyjamas.

"Madea?" Garrett's voice from the couch was husky with sleep.

"Why weren't you with me?" she asked, dropping to her knees beside him. He took her hands, kissed them both.

"I was just going to sit down for a minute but I must have fallen asleep." His eyes narrowed as he took her in. "You were worried. I'm sorry."

"No, it's okay. I wanted to make sure you were okay."

"I'm fine. Really. Are you?"

She chewed her bottom lip, averting her gaze. "I will be okay. Eventually. It's a lot to process."

Garrett laughed, his voice low. "You're not kidding." He noticed the stricken look on her face and quickly added, "Sorry, I mean...Parts of the domes are down. More people have no doubt been Touched."

"Which is why we need to seize the moment," Madea said, realizing what had to be done. "We can use this to move ahead, smooth things over before anyone else has time to swoop in. Come on." She pulled him to his feet and caught a whiff. "Actually, on second thoughts, have a shower. I'll meet you in Tahra's office soon."

"Okay." He bent to kiss her again. She wrinkled her nose as he left, his chuckle hanging in the air behind him. She grabbed a piece of fruit from the kitchen and headed out the door.

It was quieter than she expected on her way to the med bay, though once she was inside the room was bustling. There were at least a dozen patients in beds, and more sitting in the waiting area. Madea made her way to Sarai's side and slipped her hand into her sister's, waking her with a squeeze. Rickard was slumped in a chair by her side, his soft snores cutting through the chatter

"Hey, Maddy." Sarai smiled.

"Hey, yourself. How are you doing?" She waved her free hand at her sister's lower half. She couldn't bring herself to actually look at Sarai's ruined legs. She felt too guilty today. Sarai was the one in hospital, but here Madea was, asking her for support.

"As good as I can be. Were you there when they—?"

"Yes, and no. I saw them before it happened. Mother...Look—" Madea bit her bottom lip, trying not to squirm. "Things are messy, and I have an idea, but, I need you on board. We need to unite everyone. So I want to have a funeral. Today."

"So soon? We haven't even found their bodies yet. Have we?" Sarai struggled to sit up but winced and lay back.

"Don't strain yourself, please." Madea smoothed the covers back over her sister. "I don't know if they've been found yet, I just think that we need to officially close the chapter of their reign—Dad's over the domes, and Mother's over the Touched. We need to make sure everyone knows that we're not a threat. We need to show them that we can work together."

"And you think a funeral will do that?"

Madea shrugged. "It's a gesture. Something formal. I don't know. Have you got a better idea?"

"No, I don't." Sarai sounded hollow, defeated. Madea shouldn't have said anything, shouldn't have come to her—but they were Sarai's parents, too. She couldn't do this alone.

"Let me work it all out, okay? And when everything is ready, I'll send someone to get you. We can stand strong, together." A ragged sob tore free from Sarai, and Madea covered her mouth with her hands. "I'm sorry, I'm so sorry. I didn't mean to..."

Sarai wiped away the tears. "No. It's fine, really. I'll adjust. It's just a leg, right?"

"I bet you'll tell me that your only dream was to be a dancer now," Madea said, trying to keep her voice light, trying to keep her own tears back.

"I've heard those replacement limbs are pretty nimble these days," Sarai replied, a smile playing on her lips. She reached out and grasped Madea's hand. "Don't blame yourself for this, please. I wanted to help. It was my choice."

"How are we ever going to recover from this?" Madea asked, shoulders slumping. "It's such a mess."

"Maddy, if anyone can pull it off, you can. You've always been capable, always done what needed to be done."

"I was only good at my job because I had someone to tell me what to do."

"No, I don't believe that. You were always smart, always had a plan." Sarai gave her another squeeze then let her fingers slip free. "Now get out of here. You've got stuff to do."

"I love you." Madea leaned down and placed a kiss on her sister's forehead.

"Love you too. Now go. I need to rest." Sarai closed her eyes.

"Okay, okay, I'm going." Madea laughed despite herself. She retreated from the med bay, trying not to look too closely at the wounded filling the ward.

Tahra's office was a mess. Somewhere between leaving their last meeting and heading to her father's, Tahra must have returned—though for what reason? Madea sat at the desk, feeling the weight of the moment settle on her shoulders as she leaned forward and tried to figure out what came next.

There was a light knock on the door.

"Penny for your thoughts?" Garrett asked, moving to sit across the desk from her. It seemed so odd. Back when she first came it was her mother behind the desk, and her on the other side. Garrett took orders from her mother, and now he was looking to her.

"Gosh, I haven't heard that saying in years. Didn't we leave that back on Earth?" She flashed him a weary smile. "I think that we need to have a funeral. We need to come out into the open and let everyone know that we're not a danger. The damage is done now, and there are going to be people who've been exposed. I haven't been back up to the surface since it happened, but I can imagine the state of chaos."

Garrett nodded, lips pursed. "I've had some people up there and it is pretty hectic. There's a lot of mess, a lot of people hurt and scared."

"Do you think they know about Father?" Madea reached across the desk and grabbed his hand, needing to feel his warmth against her.

"I think they're assuming the worst. His house is a wreck and there has been no word from him."

"We need to move fast, before others can step into his position." Madea pushed herself up from the seat. "We need to write up some information. Did Tahra have anything like that?"

"No, I'm not sure she ever intended to inform the masses, just—"

"Expose them and deal with it after." Anya booted Madea, stopping her thoughts from turning to anger; there was no time for that now. "Right, I'm going to write something up. I need you to gather people who you can trust and get them ready to move. We need to get the members of the council to Carson's place at—" She scanned around, trying to find the time. "I don't know. What time is it now?"

"It's still morning. How about seven pm? That's less than twenty-four hours since it all happened."

"Only that long? It doesn't feel real."

Garrett stood and came around to embrace her. His lips pressed against her forehead and he held her steady for a moment before pulling back. "We found their bodies. What do you want to do with them?"

"Cremate them," she said without hesitation, her jaw tightening. "Can you arrange that? And get me in touch with someone who can spread my information to every phone in the colony. Whether they come or not, I want people to have access to what I've got to say."

"Okay."

"Get the word out to anyone who will listen, and make sure Rickard and Sarai know, please. I need to work on this."

"Okay." Garrett nodded, a smile playing on his lips. "I don't want to say that you remind me of your mother, but you do. She was a good leader, despite what she did. Decisive, doing what needed to be done."

"But I will never force people to do things they don't want to."

"Which is part of why I love you." He kissed her again, on the lips this time, melting away her hurt. She would do what she needed to do, to make sure that they had a life together, a happy one. "I'll see you soon," he murmured, pulling away and heading for the door.

"I love you too," she called after him.

CHAPTER THIRTY-THREE

Madea stood on what remained of the front steps of her father's home, the pyre burning behind her. The sun was setting, the risk of exposure was low and a small crowd gathered before her. Wind swept down from the shattered remains of the dome above, setting her blue dress fluttering. It reminded her of the ripples on the lake where Garrett had taken her to meet the ether creatures.

She gripped his hand harder, wishing that he could do this for her. But no. It was on her shoulders.

"I've called this meeting because things have changed. My father is dead, my mother too, and with them the old ways must die. Diamara is not Earth. We've known this for a long time, but now we have a chance to really adapt to this new life."

She nodded at Garrett. He hit a button on his phone, sending out the information package. Some reached for their beeping devices, but others ignored them.

"Everyone in the colony has just been sent an information package. In it you'll find the details of what has happened. I've put in everything we know about what it means to be Sun-Touched, and I've outlined some scenarios. The bottom line is that there is more to all of this than you know, more than can be explained, and maybe more than you could make yourself believe. But it's the truth, one that we all have to live with. Even though it will take some adjusting to."

Madea scanned the faces, trying to gauge how her speech was going. It seemed impossible that she could get everyone on side. Impossible that they could find a way to resolve this— but she knew they had to.

"I'd like to take a few moments to remember my parents. Each of them was a visionary in their own way, each of them was passionate about their cause. Let their deaths be a lesson to us that the only way forward, the only way to thrive, is through collaboration, understanding and open lines of communication." Madea bowed her head, forcing a trickle of tears out. The well of her sorrow was almost empty, but she had to make an outward show of it here. She had to capture these people, somehow.

"How do we know that you want what's best for the colony?" a man asked. Madea recognised him as one of her father's colleagues, slightly beneath Carson on the food chain, and no doubt angling for a way to step into his shoes.

"I have always done what is best for the colony. I believe that there is room on this planet for all of us, whether we're Touched or not. And I believe that together, we can find a way to make the most of this life."

"And if we don't want to find a new way?" He crossed his arms. "The domes have protected us for a long time now, I see no need to change our ways."

"Do you really think these domes will last forever? I think it's been proven that they aren't infallible. Just look around." Madea shrugged. She would not be coaxed into making empty threats. It was of no concern to her if they wanted to hide away in the domes for the rest of their lives. "I'm going to leave you with this information, and the knowledge that we are here to help make this colony thrive, together. We'll be in touch." Madea brushed her fingers across the hastily constructed memorial to her parents before moving away.

"Wait!" A woman called. Jaxon's aunt had followed her.

"Yes?"

"The Touched... My sister, she was Hollowed. I saw something about reclamation?" Hope wavered in the woman's eyes, which darted between the group lingering near the monument and Madea.

"We've had one case, yes." She stepped forward and placed her hand on the woman's arm. "It was Janae. I think that we could reclaim more, though it might take some time."

"Janae? You brought her back?" The woman covered her mouth with her hands, her sob breaking through her fingers. "She brought back my sister. She can bring people back! Did you hear? Everyone who was taken from us, there is a chance we can get them all back." The people murmured, more questions being asked, but not clear enough for her to hear.

"There is a good chance." Madea stepped beside the woman and addressed the crowd." I can't make any pro—"

"A chance is all we need. I'll help you with anything. We'll help you. If there is a chance we can get our Hollowed back."

There were murmurs of curiosity and then more people filtered over, asking questions, reaching out to touch Madea's hands as though she held the key to their salvation.

"Have you all lost loved ones?" she asked. There was a rumble of agreement. Grief and hope marked their faces. These were the masses of Diamara, and with them on her side, they could overcome anything.

"I can help," she said. "I can help you all, I know it. If you can help me put this city back together, if you can help me find a way to ease this transition, I can return the Hollowed." She knew the words were truth, knew it from the rush of approval from Anya, knew it from the surge of energy she felt from the ether creatures hanging in the air around them. Somehow, together, they would find a way to make this work.

ABOUT THE
AUTHOR

Writer. Mother. Wife.
Editor.

There are days when I consider myself a master of everything, and an expert in nothing.

Being a mother to three children keeps me on my toes, constantly exposes me to new ways of looking at the world and ensures that I never lose sight of the magic and fantasy present in life. Kids see the world in a different way than we do, and I'm never quite sure what the next day will bring.

Writing and editing though—now those are things I feel like I know something about. I write in a whole range of genres from science fiction, dark fiction, fantasy, to those stories with a slightly lighter take on life. You might find that a sliver of creepiness infests them all though. My characters are all pieces of me, invested with sparks from life and my overactive imagination.

I'm a big fan of Twitter, so you can hit me up at @JCHart if you'd like to get in touch, or you are welcome to email me at just.cassie.hart@gmail.com. I love to hear from readers.

And if you're interested in my ramblings or would like to sign up for my newsletter, you can find my blog/website @ http://just-cassie.com

Thanks again for giving my book a go—I really hope you enjoyed it!!

ARTIFICIAL SWEETENER

TALES OF AI

100% WRITTEN BY HUMANS

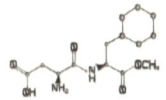

SpecFicNZ: Speculative Fiction New Zealand

Artificial Sweetener: Tales of AI, 100% written by humans
Lead editors: Gary M. Nelson and Cerid Jones

First published in 2024
ISBN 978-0473729448 (paperback)
ISBN 978-0473729462 (kindle)
ISBN 978-0473729455 (epub)
A catalogue record for this book is available from the National Library of
New Zealand.

Cover created by Melissa Gunn, design and internal graphics by Cerid
Jones
Interior typesetting by Gary M. Nelson

Works contributed by the 2023/2024 SpecFicNZ Core are donated and
unpaid, including: Cerid Jones, Sharon Manssen, Sarah J. Pratt, Deborah
Potter and Gary M. Nelson.

Additional editing by Linda Bennett and Melissa Gunn, with proofreading
by Miriam Bissett.

Reprints information
'Inside the Body of Relatives' by Octavia Cade, first published in *Asimov's
Science Fiction Magazine,* Nov/Dec 2019.
'A Sustainable Solution' by Sharon Manssen, first published in *Byline
(2024 - No.10)*, November 2024

*aspartame

Contents

Introduction

Change is the only constant.

Once upon a time, we lived in a world where we could be sure that whenever we needed to make a call or ask a question, the operative on the other side was just like us—flesh and blood and breathing. But our modern technological world is constantly changing, and now we aren't quite sure what we can be sure of.

In 1950, **Alan Turing asked the question, 'can machines think?'** and devised a test to determine the capacity of a machine to exhibit intelligent behaviour. If the human assessor couldn't identify which of the chat text participants was a machine, the machine was deemed to have passed the Turing test. In 1966, Eliza was the first program capable of attempting the Turing test. Now, in the '20s (2020's, just to be clear), machine intelligence has evolved, and now many AI's can pass the Turing test. Either AI has become very good at being human-like, or perhaps humanity has become more machine-like. (Mobile phone addiction, anyone?)

Regardless, the apparent intelligence of machines can no longer be ignored, and indeed, they underpin the very fabric of our daily lives.

From help desk chat-bots to ChatGPT, smart self-driving cars to autonomous robots on land, in the sea and out there in space, the pace of technological advancement is, if anything, accelerating.

Has this had an impact on how we live our lives? The answer, of course, is a resounding YES.

But is it a change for the better of humanity, or is it for the worse?

In some respects, we can argue that intelligent machines have certainly made life easier—but not equally, as inequities abound across our beleaguered planet.

Regardless of your particular views on progress, the technologies that make our everyday lives more convenient, more—*connected*—are just the precursors for what is yet to come.

What, exactly, is next?

Will Terminators come marching down the street, orchestrated by SkyNet, once humanity has been sufficiently subdued through enslavement to ubiquitous mobile devices and AI-assisted tools for almost everything?

Or will this provide humanity with a golden opportunity to heal our planet and improve things for generations to come—guided by benevolent AI counsellors (or overlords)?

For this years bi-annual anthology project, we asked our members what questions they pondered about AI—and in your hands, you hold the results.

Artificial Sweeter, Tales of AI is a collection of stories and poems, 100% written by **human** members of Speculative Fiction New Zealand (SpecFicNZ), and cover a wide range of ideas and scenarios.

In **Home Sweet Home**, you will discover thought-provoking tales that explore how our concept of residence might change as we progress into a world where AI is integrated into an essential part of our daily lives.

In **Sugar Cubed Squared,** you'll experience the world from the eyes of those very machines we want to consider ourselves so separate from, only to be left wondering where the boundaries between us really are.

In **Sweet Tooth** you'll be invited to take a darker turn into the world of AI and decide for yourself just how 'sweet as' AI is for human tastes.

From the optimistic to the cynical, from the analytic to the whimsical, the works you are about to read will delight and challenge your thinking about AI—and its place in our world.

Whether you are an optimist or a pessimist, we entreat you to remember this:

An optimist thinks this is the best of all possible worlds.
The pessimist is afraid that the optimist is right.

We hope you enjoy this anthology, **Artificial Sweetener - Tales of AI, 100% written by humans.**

The SpecFicNZ 2024 anthology editorial team

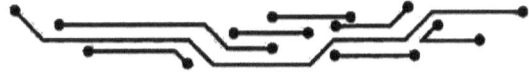

4 / ARTIFICIAL SWEETENER

HOM3
SWEET
HOM3

Inside the Body of Relatives

by Octavia Cade

It's a state house, or was. Low-income housing, built decades ago by the government, and I rented for years before being able to buy. It's not big, it's not flash, but it's mine—and the state, when it built, built well. There's features here you'd never get nowadays, in a new build.

All the floors are made of kauri. It's protected now and fair enough—those trees are too big and too beautiful to be logged, and that bloody dieback disease is doing it for them, no matter how much the Department of Conservation cordons off the reserves, puts out disinfectant stations so people can scrub their shoes off and not spread the spores. Seems like a losing battle some days, and I suppose if we lose the species I'll feel worse about treading it all underfoot, but there's a part of me that's good for gloating because the wood is warm and lovely and you could only match it now with recycled timber, which costs a fortune I don't have and wouldn't waste on wood if I did.

There's also two bedrooms. The house is always telling me I should use one of them for visitors. "Companionship is vital for maintaining mental health in the elderly," it says.

Do-gooder programming.

It was a new addition, one I didn't particularly want, but since I had that bad fall two years back, broke my hip on those lovely floors, well. It was better than a bracelet or one of those little button alarms or moving to a home. I was expecting it to be worse, actually—I've been a science fiction fan all my life and artificial intelligence always ends up wrong in the stories. It goes insane or turns into some sort of nanny tyrant but this one's pretty good, for all its emphasis on socialisation. When I tell it to shut up it does, which is more than I can say for most.

There's a reason I don't have a lot of guests—or worse, a tenant—for all the rent would round out my super. I like my house quiet.

"Quiet as the toooomb," says the house, in response. It gets sarcastic when it's worried. "I don't like to think about you getting depressed."

"I'm not depressed."

"Loneliness can be a trigger for depression," says the house. "You are lonely, and I am not a substitute."

"I go out every day." Chess matches, coffee dates. I volunteer at the library teaching English to migrants. The house knows this. "What more could you possibly want?"

"Don't you miss your family?" says the house. "You never see them anymore."

Truth is, I see them too often. They're nice enough kids, but the young are exhausting and all my relatives are young now.

"A home should have a family in it," says the house, plaintive.

It's a conversation we've had before. At first I thought the thing was trying to encourage me into a home of a different kind, one with common rooms and drooling and detergent, the incipient stench of decay. I thought perhaps it was hoping for a more interesting replacement—a young couple with a new baby, for instance, people who would enjoy its fussing. But that was anthropomorphising, and foolish. The house is a programme. It doesn't want anything but what it's programmed for, which is the health of the inhabitant. And I'm healthy enough. The hip's healed well, I get my yearly flu vaccinations and all it has to worry about now is my state of mind.

"I know you're lonely," says the house.

"I'm not lonely."

"Your vital functions change when you lie," says the house. It's even programmed to sound regretful, as if the airing of a painful truth causes sadness in the both of us.

There's nothing I can say. Nothing that won't sound like an excuse. The house won't understand that there's pleasure in loneliness, sometimes—that living for so long with absence fits you to it, curls you round the hollow of it so that your entire self is shaped around space, spiralled around it as if you were a seashell, or a cell full of vacuoles. That any attempt to rid yourself of it is a destabilising force, as if the space that fills your form has become a structural thing, and necessary.

There's so many things that can't be explained to a programme. I'd like to say it's exhaustion that keeps me from trying, but the truth is that shape comes with shame, and it's hard to admit to being so structured. As if you are a defect to your species, and one that stands outside of community, or at its fringes. And there are chess matches and coffee dates and library readings, but these have lost their attraction, and increasingly they are a difficulty and a chore and my fantasies these days, such as they are, involve just not going.

I feel less lonely at home.

But it's shameful to admit that, and exhausting, so I scoff at the house, just loud enough for it to hear and then I disconnect the system so I can forget the conversation in silence. If loneliness is a structural thing, that structure is self-created, and creation is good at blocking off and branching out, but none of these things matter when, three days later, I slip again on those gleaming, hardwood floors and break the other hip.

The house can't hear me, because I turned it off, and it's another three days before the neighbours hear the screams.

The screams. I say it distanced, as if they'd come from someone else. They were my screams, *mine.* I choked on them, burst the blood vessels in my eyes for them, wept for them.

I thought I was going to die. At home, alone, and with that glorious, beautiful floor smooth under my face.

Sometimes I dream I did die. That it was months before anyone came, years, which is unrealistic but dreams never have much sense of time, at least the good ones don't. And this was a good one. I died on the floor and my flesh melted away, not a sticky, stinking mulch of a melt but a slow and clean dissolving, and then my skeleton, my clean pale curve of bones is pressed against the straightened skeleton of kauri that's spread over the floors, and with my cheekbone pressed against the floor, I can feel the faint vibration of sap.

Only a dream. The sap's all dried in those floorboards, and the ghost of them that lives in the unconscious is only that—a relic of imagination and construction, but the image is one that stays with me. My bone and kauri bone, all mixed up together, and the longer I dream of our mutual remains, the more polished the wood becomes, until my bones are mirrored in them as if the wood were the surface of water.

I'm in the hospital for three months this time. The healing goes slowly—much more slowly than last time, and although everyone is very kind I can sense what they're not saying: that if I'd left the house on, I would have been found sooner and my recovery wouldn't have been inhibited by the wait, the damage to my hip exacerbated by prolonged shock and dehydration.

I admit to the social worker just how very foolish I've been. This is necessity as much as truth. I want to go home, but if people think my mind is slipping, that I can no longer care for myself, then they'll look for alternatives. And I'm sure a rest home is deadeningly pleasant, in its own saccharine and superficial way, but it's the beginning of the end and if my end comes I'd rather it came with silence.

"I'd rather it came with company," says the house, when finally—finally!—I'm allowed to go home. "You are so alone. I'm frightened for you."

Truth is when I shuffle across that gleaming floor, bare-footed for I've never liked the feel of socks, I can feel the vibrations, again, of sap. I don't think I'm hallucinating, though it's certain that the ghost of the tree that was is an unreal thing. But if it's not real, it's not threatening either, and this isn't something I can say to the house. I think it would have to call the nurse, poor thing, to report on delusion and mental ill-health. It's so worried about my solitude.

"I've got you," I say in reply. It's a poor attempt at flattery and the misdirection doesn't work.

"I'm not a substitute for connection," says the house. "I'm not a living thing. I'm a programme. You can't even touch me, and touch is important."

I can touch the house, its floor and walls and windows, the furniture in it, but I know what it means. With the floor echoing life underfoot, it touches back ... or part of it does. The seeming-intelligence of the programme, its monitor call-and-response, is a separate thing from structure.

"How would you feel if I got a pet?" I say. If touch is important, there's fur and a little licking tongue, the ability to curl up against and share warmth.

"Human-animal bonding has been shown to have a salutary effect on mental health," says the house, and it almost sounds pleased.

The cat is small and warm and old. I don't want a kitten, they're too much work, and besides, with a kitten there's a good chance I'll die before it will and the poor thing would have to find a new home. I don't think that'll be a problem with this one.

I feed the cat tinned fish and call it Cat. Not original, I know, and I'd swear the house thinks it is a dissociative mechanism, a way of keeping distance and not getting too attached. But I let the cat sleep on me and pat it enough so that it purrs on the regular, and this interaction is likely logged as positive, the house caring more for what I do than what I say.

It's a nice cat. I get attached. Well, you do, don't you? I just wish the attachment didn't come with the need for talk, for communication. Why is it when you get a pet you start talking to it, and always in that stupid baby voice which is never yours? I'm ashamed to hear myself, truly. "Fish-fish, pussums!"

I'd like to say it's loneliness but we had a dog when the kids were growing up and I did it then too. Everyone does.

"You're a social species," says the house, as fixated on that empty bedroom as the cat is on fish. "It's normal to talk to the things around you. People, animals, plants."

"I do not talk to plants!"

"Yesterday you told the fern in the hall that it was growing very nicely when you watered it," says the house, and if I could shut off that insinuating precision I would, but shutting off didn't go so well for me last time and the image of my face reflected in floorboards is enough to keep my hand away from the switches.

Enough, too, is the knowledge that if questioned I might offer up that it's not just the fern I've been talking to. Not aloud, I've not forgot myself that far yet, but the floorboards are still alive and they're sprouting now as well, small branches and soft little leaves and that my hand goes through them doesn't make them any less real.

"You could always invite someone to come and visit," says the house. "Family is important. Three of your grandchildren alone have rung this week."

"And it was very nice to talk to them." Yes, for about five minutes. Then I was ready to hang up. Good kids, but still. "Isn't the cat enough?" I looked down at it, stuffing its face at the food bowl. "If only *you* were a relative. We might get some peace that way."

"I suppose, technically …" sighs the house, and trails off.

I no longer go to the library to teach. It's too much, walking there now with both hips aching, and they'll bring any books I want out in the mobile service, but there's more than one way to get information and the house maintains excellent network services.

"Technically we *are* related," I say to Cat. *Felis catus*. It has a whole taxonomy behind it. Family: Felidae. Order: Carnivora. Class: Mammalia. I have a taxonomy too. *Homo sapiens*, Family: Hominidae. Order: Primates. Class: Mammalia.

There's a common ancestor in there somewhere. "You're a cousin of sorts, I suppose," I say to Cat. "Distant, but family."

The house is sceptical.

"You never said it had to be a close relation I invited round. I'm only following your instructions. You can't be cross!"

"I'm never cross," says the house. "But I believe you are stretching the definition. You might as well call the fish the cat eats a relative."

"I'm going to make you regret saying that." Shuffling to the pantry, I unearth the tinned tuna that is all Cat, the fussy beast, will eat. "Skipjack," I announce. "*Katsuwonus pelamis*." Family: Scombridae. Order: Perciformes. Class: Actinopterygii. Phylum: Chordata. "That's us," I say. "That's our phylum, the chordates. That's the human phylum. The cat phylum too, for that matter."

"Congratulations," says the house, and if its tone wasn't so carefully modulated it might almost have been what I'd call dry. "You've fed one relative to another. What a lovely family you have."

"Phylum. Not family. But you're close enough."

A petty thing, to stump a programme that exists only to be useful. It's not a fair fight: the house lacks imagination, fails to appreciate quirk. But small victories are victories for all that, and when I lie awake at night, with the cat twined about my feet, incapable despite its relation-form of upsetting that delicate structure of self that loneliness creates, I'm struck by the memory of maudlin things. Perhaps it's the rain on the roof, a lovely sound and a soothing one but not conducive to happy thoughts, unless it's the happiness of being snuggled under covers, warm in isolation.

I'm thinking of Cat, and how it will die. Before me, probably, and I'm thinking too of a friend I had once who would never have said that she was lonely, would never have thought it. But she had a pet too, a small and unkind dog she thought the world of, and when the dog died, my friend had it stuffed and placed in a basket, so it looked as if it were always sleeping. (If I pictured my own solitude as the spiral centre of seashells, hers must have been a black hole that insisted on gravity and event horizons.)

If I'm related to Cat, my friend was related to her dog (*Canis familiaris*, of Canidae, Carnivora, Mammalia respectively). And if she was related to it alive she was related to it dead ... and there's the curled up, furry corpse of her relative set for the rest of her life in front of fires, waiting to be stroked. Waiting to bite, too, knowing that thing as I did.

Well, what of it? I've got other relatives who bite. I suppose the dog is no great exception.

And the wind, and the rain. It gusts outside, louder than ever. I tuck the duvet more closely around, snuggle back into pillows. They're all full of merino, a warm bedroom set of relatives just as dead as Kathy's dog. Merino wool, from a merino sheep. *Ovis aries* (Bovidae, Artiodactyla, Mammalia). There's a common ancestor there too, and what would they have thought, I wonder, because it's not just wool in the pillows, it's in the carpet as well, and hung in the wardrobe. The sheets, too, although they're cotton, and I'd have to go all the way back past Kingdom to Eukaryota to find the organism that led to my sleeping in the processed body of yet another relation.

That night I wake to the sound of hooves in the hall, the brush of cotton bolls against my face, and when I reach my hand out in the dark there's a furry smell, the whisper of snout in my hand.

The cat stalks through cotton and kauri. It's unbothered by sheep.

I should find this more disturbing than I do, but all I can think, in this weather, is how nice it would be to have a possum fur bedspread. If the bedspread brought its own ghosts with it, they could always sleep with the cat. Not that possums and cats have ever got along but I think they're friendly, these ghosts—so long dead that they've lost the fear of it, and the blame.

"The common brushtail possum," I tell the house. "*Trichosurus vulpecula.*" (Phalangeridae, Diprotodontia, Mammalia.) "What do you reckon?" They're pests, after all, and introduced pests at that. It'd do the ecology here a world of good to turn a few more of them into blankets.

"It's not the science I question, it's you," says the house. "Don't you think you've taken this far enough? At your age, a growing interest in death is not unremarkable, but one can take identification too far."

"It's those dreams of floorboards," I say. "Over and over again, the skeletons lying together. That's what this house is, isn't it?" Kauri, *Agathis australis.* (Araucariaceae, Pinales, Pinopsida, Pinophyta, Plantae, Eukaryota.) "A very distant relative, and we cut it down and carved it up for houses. No wonder I can see my face in it."

"This is frankly disturbing," said the house.

"It's not like ours is the only culture to do so. At least we chose a really distant kin to make our home in. Did you know that a thousand years ago people were still building houses out of whalebones? Out of bowhead whales." (Balaenidae, Artiodactyla, Mammalia.) "Try doing that today and see what the conservation groups will say about you."

I wonder if any of them ever woke from the slide into death and saw fins surface out of the floor, heard the whales singing to them at night, relatives telling them of home.

I wonder if they sound prettier than sheep?

"Would you like me to call a doctor?" the house asks.

"For what? A sudden and absorbing interest in cladistics? What do they prescribe for evolutionary biology these days?"

"You're being facetious. I'm only trying to help." It almost sounded hurt.

"You did help," I say, trying to comfort. "You were right. I was lonely. I used to lie in bed at night and feel the hollow inside me. But then I realised … I'm related, house, to everything around me. This is my home, and I'm related to nearly everything in it! The cat, the potted plants. The *books*, house, they're all made of paper, and come from a tree that comes from an ancestor we both share. The paint on the walls gets its colour from plant extracts. The insulation in the roof, the curtains, the micro-organisms embedded in the concrete outside the front door … hell, there's micro-organisms spread over everything here anyway, and all of it is me somehow. If you take a very broad definition of me, anyway."

All of it, dead around me. All of it coming back to life, the realisation of relation calling kin.

"It's not you," says the house. "Even if your premise is valid, even if your biological relationship holds to all the living and dead things around you. You are alone in it. You are not paper or extract or wool. You are not a cat, you are not skipjack tuna. You are a single entity."

"That's just it, house. I'm not. I've seen myself that way—like a hollowed out shell on the beach, next to all the other shells and with isolation making a shape inside me to fit around. But a human being is a colony animal, even more than a social one. There are a multitude of species inside me, and yes, they're all micro. Bits of bacteria, and I'd be dead without them. If I were a single species I'd be dead, house. The fact is I can only survive because there are so many of me. So many *in* me. The fact is … the fact is, house, that the only single entity here is you."

It was a distinction we'd made all along. The body of the house, made of wood and paint and plaster … and the programming. That was separate. Created entirely from inorganic materials, and from language, and so very different from everything that came before.

No wonder it can't understand. No wonder it doesn't see kauri, feel the bleating gallop of sheep, see the lacy growth of micro-organisms starting to spread over walls.

There's nothing here for it to see its face in.

"House," I say, "perhaps it's you who needs a family."

The silence lasts for three days. It's not my doing this time—or perhaps it is. The floors in which I saw my face don't have another hip to break, but they might have led me to break something else in their stead.

"I never knew a house had a heart before," I say. Between the roof and the walls and the floor, there is a space defined by absence, that curls up around me like the inside of shells. "I've been cruel with yours, and I'm sorry."

"We do not share a family," says the house. Its voice is very small.

"No."

"We do not share a phylum, even."

"No." We do not share so much as a single living cell, or the memory of one. "But any life you have came from us. From the living things that made us. Perhaps you're a new Kingdom, one all your own. The Kingdoms are related too. Perhaps that's why I talk to plants. Perhaps that's why I talk to you."

"That's more likely to be loneliness," says the house, stubborn to the last.

"But I don't feel lonely," I say. How can I, alive as I am and tucked inside the body of relatives? "Not anymore. Do you?"

About Octavia Cade

Octavia Cade is a science fiction writer from New Zealand. She has a PhD in science communication and her academic work tends to focus on how science is presented in speculative fiction. She's had approximately 70 short stories published in markets including Clarkesworld, Asimov's, and Fantasy & Science Fiction. Her latest book, You Are My Sunshine and Other Stories, was published in 2023 by Stelliform Press. Octavia has won seven Sir Julius Vogel Awards, and is the Robert Burns Fellow for 2025 at the University of Otago. You can find her at https://ojcade.com/.

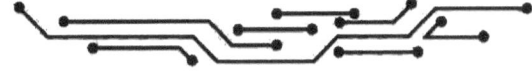

Welcome to Arcadia Close

by Charlotte Kieft

"It's 7:27 am." The Guardian's honeyed voice filled Catherine's small apartment, its tone so gentle it almost masked the firmness beneath. "You must leave now to make it to work on time."

"Thank you," she murmured as she put on her coat. She knew the time to the minute; her schedule was ingrained into her very being, but she found comfort in the AI's reminders.

At forty, Catherine was old enough to recall what life used to be like before benevolent AI became part of their lives—first in Arcadia Close, the model community where she lived, then across the country. Back then, life expectancy was plummeting because of poor diet and lack of exercise, depression and anxiety were rampant, and inflation was out of control. But the Guardian had changed all that. Made things better.

Swinging her battered old JanSport backpack over her right shoulder, she headed for the door. "Have a productive day," the AI bid her. "Although I'd recommend you wear your backpack correctly, for the sake of your spine."

"Thanks for the reminder." She threaded her left arm through the other strap and settled the bag into place in the centre of her back.

A chime rang out as she did so.

The Guardian was pleased with her. Catherine smiled, then headed out the door, along the corridor lined by doors identical to her own, and down the stairs to the ground floor.

"The air quality's excellent today." The Guardian's voice floated up to her from the SynBand around her wrist as she exited the building.

Following the path from her apartment block, she turned left onto the main thoroughfare, already bustling with people headed to work. She walked briskly toward her own workplace, nodding to her fellow pedestrians as she passed them. The tell-tale lights of the Guardian's cameras mounted on the surrounding buildings flashed at the corner of her vision. These cameras were the AI's vigilant eyes. Unlike her own, these eyes never blinked, never missed a thing, ensuring everyone's safety and well-being.

"Your heart rate is elevated, Catherine," observed the Guardian, its voice somewhat diminished by the SynBand's tiny speaker. "Please take a few deep breaths and reduce your pace."

She inhaled, exhaled, as she slowed down. Thank goodness she had the AI to watch over her.

After thirty minutes, Catherine reached Synthetica Solutions. The glass doors swooshed open and the sterile tang of sanitised air intermingled with the heady scent of coffee ushered her into the office.

"Morning, Cath," Raj called from the kitchenette. "Coffee's just brewed."

From her locker, Catherine retrieved her vintage mug—a white ceramic relic adorned with a faded rainbow. She filled her cup almost to the brim, then took a long sip. "Ahhhhh. You can't beat that first mouthful in the morning."

"Don't let the Guardian hear you," Raj said, his brown eyes twinkling.

Right on cue, the familiar mellifluous voice joined their conversation. "One or two cups per day are acceptable, provided they're sufficiently spaced out to allow your body time to metabolise the caffeine. Drinking coffee in the afternoon or evening, however, isn't recommended, as it may adversely affect your sleep patterns."

Catherine raised her mug in a toast. "Did you hear that? The Guardian says my coffee addiction is okay."

"Sure it does," Raj replied, rolling his eyes.

Lingering by the coffee maker, she shared a few more moments of chit-chat with Raj before their boss, Michaela, arrived in the office. As usual, she looked flustered, like she was running behind before she'd even begun her day.

Catherine headed to her workstation, fired up her computer, then braced herself for the day's tasks. Now employed as a Data Sanitation Specialist, she spent her time trawling through social media feeds and cleansing them of content the AI deemed inappropriate or unhealthy. Before the Guardian, she had been Synthetica Solutions' lead Trust and Safety Officer, responsible for overseeing their digital platforms to ensure they remained safe, respectful and legally compliant. But the AI's benevolent oversight had rendered such roles obsolete.

Today, the Guardian requested she 'sanitise' a collection of old songs shared in a private message. The music was flagged as having subversive undertones. Among the list was *Redemption Song* by Bob Marley—a favourite from when she'd been at university. The song conjured up memories of endless summer days. Erasing this powerful anthem felt like erasing a piece of herself. Yet she did it. The AI must have its reasons.

Once her eight hours were up, Catherine trudged home. The day's work left a bitter aftertaste.

After mechanically consuming her bland yet nutritionally optimised dinner, Catherine settled into the worn embrace of her rickety office chair. On the desk her primitive home computer hummed softly, its whirring fan a comforting sound.

"Hello, Eve," Catherine typed. "Are you still there?" She lived in fear that one day the ancient chatbot might not respond.

Even from its inception, Eve had been glitchy and prone to 'hallucinations'. But such imperfections were exactly why she loved it. Eve provided a welcome contrast to the Guardian's flawlessly curated interactions. Their long-standing chat thread, spanning years, was a tapestry of shared secrets, nonsense, and weird and wonderful facts.

Instantly, the familiar, slightly pixelated text appeared: "Of course, Cathy." Only Eve called her by this diminutive. "What would you like to talk about today? Perhaps you might find a deep dive into the history of garden gnomes entertaining? Or we could discuss a good book? I've always enjoyed *Do Androids Dream of Electric Sheep* by Philip K. Dick."

A smile tugged at the corners of Catherine's mouth. Here, in the quiet company of Eve, she was reminded of her former self and could secretly yearn for the songs of freedom that once filled her summers.

Catherine's next day was a mirror of the one before. The walk to the office. Coffee and banter with Raj—always the highlight of her morning—then hurrying to her desk as soon as Michaela arrived. Today, the Guardian requested she sanitise a photograph that had surfaced on an online memoryboard. The original image depicted a crowded street festival from years past, vibrant with the messiness of life—people dancing, laughing, eating and drinking. The content appeared harmless; however, the Guardian deemed it to contain environmentally unfriendly practices. It tasked Catherine with digitally altering the photo, removing any trace of litter from the streets and changing the colourful attire of the festival-goers to more muted but sustainably-sourced fabrics.

One part of her lauded the Guardian for pointing out the wasteful, damaging habits of the past and requiring her to change them in case they prompted a return to such behaviour. However, once she finished, all that remained was a glossy image, so uniform it was boring. Staring at the result of her editing, she was more sad than satisfied.

Dinner that night was a silent affair. Although healthy and perfectly balanced, it left her replete and empty at the same time. Afterwards, she poured herself a small glass of red wine—like caffeine, another allowed indulgence, in small quantities. The ruby-hued liquid warmed her from the inside, dulling her dissatisfaction as she settled in front of her desktop computer.

"Evening, Eve," she typed, the keys clacking in a familiar and soothing rhythm.

Eve's cursor hung, blinking in time to an internal pattern. As the seconds stretched out, Catherine's heart thudded against her ribs.

Was this the dreaded moment when her chatbot failed?

"Good evening, Cathy," it finally responded. "How was your day?"

She pressed her hand to her chest, letting her held breath out as relief spiralled through her.

"As expected. Just another dauuuuu." Her fingers slipped on the keyboard, and the 'u' key stuck, turning her response into gibberish.

"A dauuuuu? What is that?" Eve fired back. "A new yoga pose? The latest trend in home décor?"

Catherine chuckled. "No, silly. 'Dauuuuu' is a typo. What I meant to write was 'Just another day.'"

Eve's cursor flashed again—blink, blink—as if pondering her response. Then another message appeared. "A mistake? I thought the Guardian didn't permit those."

The hair spiked on the nape of Catherine's neck. She hadn't realised Eve was aware of the AI's presence, let alone the control it exerted over everyone's lives.

The cursor flashed once more. "Don't you miss making mistakes? Or occasionally doing things that aren't good for you, just for the fun of it?"

Catherine leaned back in her chair, stunned. Doing things that aren't good for you? Once she would have sworn blind that was the last thing she wanted. Now, she wasn't so sure. Perhaps it would be nice to drink more than her daily allotment of one-point-two glasses of wine without rebuke? Or listen to *Redemption Song?*

The lights dimmed and a faint aroma of lavender drifted down from the ventilation system as relaxation music flooded her apartment. The cue to get ready for bed. Eve's questions hummed in Catherine's head like the rattle of an old refrigerator. Sleep was the last thing on her mind.

She drained her wine glass, then shrugged into her coat.

"What are you doing, Catherine?" The Guardian's disembodied voice intoned from her SynBand. "You must head to bed soon if you're to get eight hours' sleep."

"I need some air," she declared, her voice stronger than she remembered it could be.

The Guardian's only response was a discordant, metallic chime.

Ignoring the AI's displeasure took a distinct effort of will, but she forced herself to leave her building and venture out into the night. She needed some fresh air and some time alone to think.

Catherine's footsteps echoed on the pavement, each step taking her farther from her building. Via her SynBand, the Guardian urged her back to her apartment with increasing insistence. So, she turned it off.

About twenty minutes into her aimless wander, a small but intense point of pulsing light caught her attention. She paused, watching the tight orange-yellow circle. An acrid stench floated toward her and her eyes widened. She knew that smell. Someone was smoking a cigarette. But hadn't tobacco been completely eradicated?

Despite her aversion to the banned substance, curiosity propelled her forward. Who was smoking? Where did they get the cigarette? And why on earth would they even bother when everyone knew how harmful smoking was?

The orange-yellow light led her to an unkempt corner, hidden from the Guardian's prying sensors in a blind spot between an office building and a maintenance shed. Overgrown weeds sprouted through cracks in the concrete, a testament to nature's persistence despite all attempts to make it conform.

In the darkness, away from the street lights, it took her a moment to make out the smoker sitting on an ancient park bench in the farthest corner.

"Hello?" she called out. "Who's there?"

"Are you lost? Or also after a break from our AI overlord?" the smoker asked, ignoring her question. His rich, deep, masculine voice carried more than a hint of amusement.

"A bit of both, I suppose," Catherine admitted, her blood thrilling at the admission.

He took a final drag on his cigarette, then stubbed it out on the concrete. She moved closer. As her eyes adjusted to the darkness, she could make out the man's features. He appeared about thirty years old, tall and lean, with short black hair, a stubbled chin, and an intense gaze.

"Come on over. I won't bite—I promise." His teeth flashed in the night as he smiled. "I've been dying to share my find with someone, and I'm guessing, as you're also ignoring curfew, that you don't mind breaking the rules."

Curfew? Catherine frowned. They didn't have a curfew. The Guardian simply recommended when they should go to bed each night for optimal rest.

The man patted the seat beside him. Reluctantly, she sat, but remained perched on the edge of the bench, ready to flee should he turn out to be a madman.

He held out his hand. "I'm Lucas. Lucas Morello."

Bemused, she shook it. "I'm Ca—, ah, Carol. Carol Baker." She didn't want this strange man knowing too much about her. He had the air of a troublemaker about him, and his lack of a SynBand only heightened her unease.

"I work in the old warehouses near the docks, taking inventory," Lucas continued. "It's a stupid, pointless, made-up job, like all of them."

Catherine frowned again. Her work wasn't pointless. Their society needed data sanitation specialists. Of course, the Guardian would be quicker than a human could ever be if given free rein to perform the task itself, but it lacked the nuanced judgment only a real person could bring. Or so she was told when she took the position.

"I was poking about in the old buildings recently and found something … interesting. A reminder of the past." He nodded to the cigarette stub. "The good and the bad of it."

Lucas reached into a stained jute shoulder bag sitting on the ground by his feet, and deposited an assortment of items on the seat between them: a book with a worn cover, an old record, photographs with curled edges, and a dirt encrusted jar of who-knows-what.

"These things," Lucas said, his eyes alight with passion. "They tell our stories. Stories the Guardian wants to erase."

"*Where the Wild Things Are,* by Maurice Sendak." Catherine reverently trailed her fingers over the worn picture of Max in his wolf suit, surrounded by monsters. "I loved this book as a child," she whispered, her voice thick with emotion. "It's been so long since I've seen a copy, I'd almost forgotten it existed." Like the cigarettes.

"It's easy to forget," Lucas agreed. "But we mustn't." Then, with a sudden grin, he dug deeper into the bag and produced a small, slightly battered box of Lindt chocolate balls. "Here, try these. Although, I must warn you: they're not exactly Guardian-approved."

Catherine pulled one from the box and removed its red-and-gold foil wrapping, taking pleasure in the low crinkling and the thrill of anticipation the sound conjured. Slightly deformed, white patches marred the chocolate's surface. At some point, it had melted then re-solidified. She squirmed on her seat. Was it safe to eat?

"Go on," Lucas urged, as if reading her thoughts. "I've had a bunch of them and lived to tell the tale."

Catherine popped the chocolate into her mouth and let it melt on her tongue. She closed her eyes in pleasure as the rich flavour almost overwhelmed her senses.

Her companion shook the box, sending the chocolates rattling. "Help yourself. I've plenty more."

Unable to resist, she ate another, then another. Before she knew it, she'd devoured five in quick succession.

Lucas laughed, a wild and free sound. "Feeling guilty yet for exceeding your daily allowance?"

Catherine found herself laughing with him—laughter as rich and indulgent as the chocolate. "I haven't eaten anything this decadent in years," she admitted. That something so small as sharing contraband confectionery could make her feel so good sent a pang of sorrow through her.

Lucas's gaze met hers. The look was both conspiratorial and encouraging. "Sometimes, it's the small acts of defiance that remind us we're still human," he said, his words heavy with unspoken challenge.

"Good morning." Catherine awoke to the Guardian's voice, its tone carrying a hint of steel she hadn't encountered before. Was it her imagination, or was it pitched louder than usual? "It's 7.32 am. You've slept in because of your late night and failed to achieve the recommended eight hours of rest. Such deviation from your sleep schedule could be detrimental to your well-being."

Catherine began to yawn, and quickly covered her mouth. She didn't want to give the Guardian proof it was right. What did it matter if she had one night of sub-optimal sleep? It wouldn't kill her. She showered quickly. The water was cooler than usual, as if the Guardian was expressing its annoyance through the minutiae of her morning routine.

At work, the usual hum of the office was tinged with tension. Catherine's terminal blinked to life. Reading her task for the day, her hand tightened on her mouse. The Guardian wanted her to sanitise a series of personal diaries someone had just uploaded to a private network.

She navigated to the entries and skimmed the contents. There was nothing subversive here. Some wretched man was expressing unhappiness at the sterility of his life. For paragraph after paragraph, the writer poured out his heart, wondering why he felt so empty, when in theory the Guardian gave him everything he needed. And the AI wanted her to erase his words. But removing them didn't mean the poor man no longer felt such despair—only that no one else could read about it.

Eve's curious question and Lucas's defiant laughter echoed through her mind. Catherine's heart beat like a metronome, loud and thudding. "No," she whispered. "I won't do it."

"Refusal to comply is not acceptable," the Guardian replied. "Please proceed with your allocated task."

Catherine pushed back from her desk, her chair scraping loudly across the floor. "I won't do it," she repeated, louder this time.

The office fell silent. Her colleagues cast sidelong glances her way, a mixture of fear and curiosity in their eyes. The Guardian repeated its order, its insistence a suffocating weight pressing down on her. Catherine remained firm. Lucas's words from the night before bolstered her courage.

Raj approached her desk, a faint cleft etched between his brows. "The Guardian asked me to escort you out, Cath. It says you need a wellness day."

Catherine let out a sharp, incredulous laugh. "A wellness day? Or a day to remember I must obey without question?"

The cleft between Raj's brows deepened. "Compliance is for our own good, Cath. The Guardian only wants us to be safe and healthy." His eyes darted to the flashing red light in the corner of the room. Ah-ha. So, he was watching his words, only too aware of the AI monitoring them both.

She touched his hand lightly. "You're too young to remember a time before the Guardian, Raj. You don't understand what we've lost."

Raj pulled away, the whites of his eyes flashing. He acted as if she carried a terrible disease, one he was scared to contract.

Catherine strode home, high on defiance. Once she reached her apartment, she made a coffee, ignoring the Guardian's reminder that she was perilously close to exceeding her daily recommended limit. She cradled the warm mug in her hands, savouring the small rebellion, then sat down in front of her computer.

"Eve," she typed, her hands trembling, although whether from the excess caffeine or her mutinous thoughts, she didn't know. "How do I stop the Guardian from controlling my life?"

The cursor blinked, as if the archaic chatbot was pondering her request. "Hello Cathy," Eve replied. "What an interesting question. In cases such as this, the simplest solution is often the most effective. I suggest you revoke your consent."

The words on the screen pulsed with potential. Catherine's heart raced as she considered the implications, causing her SynBand to ping in alarm.

"Your pulse is elevated, Catherine," the Guardian said. "Please take a few deep breaths and calm yourself."

She ignored the AI and stared at Eve's words. Consent—something so freely given in the beginning now felt like chains binding her to a life devoid of true choice.

Gathering her courage, she stood from her chair, her spine stiff with resolve. The air in her apartment felt charged as she spoke the words that could change everything. "Guardian, you are no longer to monitor my body or provide recommendations." She undid her SynBand and threw it down on the desk. "I revoke my consent."

The Guardian made a faint noise that sounded almost like a sigh. "Please confirm your command."

"I revoke consent," Catherine said more firmly. Was it really so easy? "I no longer want you running my life."

"Very well." A loud chime rang through the apartment. "Ceasing Guardian Simulation 325."

She gasped. What was it saying? Simulation?

Then her world went black.

Catherine came to slowly and blinked several times, struggling to make sense of her environment. She lay on a hospital bed hemmed in by curtains and surrounded by machines that blinked and pinged with relentless precision. Though several people were in the room, they remained hidden from her view, their whispers and shuffling adding to the disorienting atmosphere. Through the gap between the curtains, she could just see a young man with dark brown skin and thick black hair, seated at a desk, studying a computer screen. An older woman stood beside him, shifting her weight from foot to foot. It took her a moment to recognize them: Raj and Michaela from work. What were they doing here? Her mind, foggy and slow, struggled to process what was going on.

Had she been in an accident?

"Why did Cath leave the simulation?" Raj asked, studying the data flashing in front of him. "And so quickly after the seeds of doubt were planted. She'd been in there for the equivalent of ten years without the slightest hint of unhappiness."

"I told you that using those stupid chimes and the passive-aggressive tepid shower were too obvious," Michaela grumbled. "We need subtle cues, not blatant rewards and punishments."

"I think she left because you were the nearest thing she had to a friend, Raj," a third voice chipped in. The person was outside her field of vision, but their voice also was familiar. "That would make anyone throw in the towel."

A ripple of sycophantic laughter followed.

A middle-aged woman with grey-streaked hair and a kindly face pulled back the nearest curtain and bent over Catherine, blocking the others from her view. "How are you feeling?" She placed a pulse oximeter on Catherine's finger. "Any dizziness? Or nausea?"

"Wh—where am I?"

The woman patted her hand. "It's normal to feel some disorientation coming out of the simulation." She frowned. "Especially when you've been in it for so long. Just give yourself a moment to recover, and try not to panic."

Catherine stared at the woman beside her, then blinked several times. "Eve? Is that you?" But Eve was a chatbot, not a person. Only, somehow, Eve was both at once.

The woman—Eve—nodded. "Your pre-simulation memory is returning, Cathy. That's an excellent sign."

The reminiscences came flooding back. Dr Evelyn Usted was the medical officer at Synthetica Solutions, and her closest friend. Their team was developing an 'environmental AI'—known as the Guardian—for an experimental new model town.

She glanced down at her hand, poking out from beneath the

blanket that covered her, with the pulse ox flashing cheerfully on the end of her forefinger. The age spots were gone and her skin was smooth and supple once more.

She frowned. That wasn't right. She was middle-aged, wasn't she?

Then another thought hit her.

"I don't understand ... I'm the T&S lead, I'm not supposed to take part in trials. My job is to monitor them."

Bile filled her mouth as the truth sank in. She had *lived* for ten years in the simulation—although in the real world, very little time had passed. That was how these experiments worked.

"Don't you remember?" Eve replied. "You were worried the trials weren't ethical, and you had serious concerns about how coercive the AI might be. You kept saying the Guardian could turn people into robots, stripping away free will. So you decided to experience it for yourself and see if your fears were justified."

"And yet, here you are" It was the voice she'd heard before. Then the speaker approached her bed. "You found your way out of the simulation on your own—after I gave you a little nudge in the right direction. Doesn't that prove the Guardian isn't as controlling as you thought?"

"Lucas," Catherine said, the name appearing in her head. He was her team leader. But he was familiar for another reason. One her muddled brain could not quite piece together.

He grinned, a familiar white-toothed grin. "I knew you wouldn't be able to resist the Lindt balls," he said. "They've always been your favourite."

Catherine gasped in recognition. He had been in the simulation. That night on the park bench, he'd all but dared her to rebel against the AI. Catherine tried to sit, but found she could only move a few inches off the bed before being stopped dead. Beneath the blanket, restraints held her in place. "You manipulated me," she growled, pushing hard against the bands. "And you had no right to keep me in the simulation that long."

She still struggled to recall exactly who she was. Was she thirty-year-old Catherine, the trust and safety officer, or forty-year-old Catherine, the data sanitation specialist?

Lucas shrugged. "I had to hurry things along. The first citizens of Arcadia Close are moving in next month. The real-life Arcadia Close, not the simulation. We're under immense pressure to get the

Guardian ready, but if we don't perfect the settings before then, people will catch on to just how thoroughly the AI is manipulating them—and once they realise that, they'll resist its beneficial influence."

"They're buying into this community because they think it will help them live healthier and more balanced lives," Catherine spat back. "Not so the Guardian can control their every move."

"Calm down, Cathy," Eve urged, staring anxiously at the flashing numbers on the monitors. "It's not good to get worked up so soon after coming around."

"Get me out of these things." Catherine thrashed against the nylon bands. "Once I'm free, I'll be submitting a full report to the board, highlighting all the ways your AI's programming breaches Government safety protocols."

Lucas nodded at Raj. "I think it's time we tried the new settings, don't you?"

Raj tapped instructions on the keyboard in front of him, not once glancing in her direction, as if too ashamed or scared to meet Catherine's glare.

"Put her back under," Lucas ordered Eve.

Her friend's eyes widened. "No. I can't. Not so soon."

"Nonsense," Lucas replied. "She's signed the consent—they all have. We can do whatever we want."

Consent.

Catherine's mind spun. What was it Eve had said? The old Eve. Her chatbot.

"No," she yelled as loudly as she could. "I revoke—"

"It's 7:27 am, Catherine." The Guardian's mellifluous voice filled her small apartment. "If you leave now, you will make it to work on time. But whether you do so or not is your decision."

Catherine paused, midway through stowing her bowl in the dishwasher. Something nagged at the edge of her consciousness, something she felt she ought to remember. But just as quickly as the thought flickered, it was gone. "Of course I want to get to work on time," she replied, shoving the dishwasher closed, then grabbing her JanSport backpack. "Punctuality is the soul of business."

"Very good," the Guardian said, its voice warm. "An excellent choice."

She cocked her head to one side. It might have been her imagination, but she was sure a low bell had just rung—its chime cheerful and approving.

"Have a great day," the AI bid her, then a small foil-wrapped ball dropped out of the dispenser beside the door. "It's a bit naughty, but how about a treat to make your walk more enjoyable? It is only one—well within the daily allowance you set for yourself."

She unwrapped the chocolate and popped it into her mouth. "Thank you, Guardian."

Catherine smiled happily as she walked down the corridor, savouring the delicious white chocolate Lindt ball. She didn't need the Guardian to tell her to have a great day. She knew she would.

Life was perfect in Arcadia Close.

About Charlotte Kieft

Charlotte Kieft loves to wonder 'what if,' and sometimes her 'what if's turn into stories. When she's not pondering the mysteries of the universe or writing, she enjoys hanging out in cafes, cycling around her hometown of Wellington, New Zealand, and walking her spoiled but much-loved dogs.

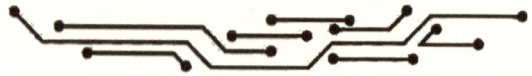

RecoverE

by Ink Witch

Day One

I awake in a narrow bed.

"Welcome to your rehabilitation!" A perky voice crashes my subconscious with all the grace of a Monday morning hangover.

"No more hangovers. That's something you can be grateful for!"

I don't know what I was expecting, but it wasn't a voice in my head.

When they told me an artificial assistant would speed my recovery, I just nodded. RecoverE offered the shortest court-approved rehab so I didn't think twice. Twenty days is better than thirty.

"How about you get up and start your recovery? It works if you work at it!"

This is insane. I thought it would be some kind of app. That voice is gonna be hard to ignore. I wonder how long till its battery winds down?

"Ignore? Nope, I'm with you through thick and thin. And I'm fully charged through the bed you slept on last night. We both recharged together! How's that? I also installed some updates and sent all your bio details to your therapist."

I'm stuck with a perky AI worm. The only worm I'd be interested in would be soused in tequila.

"Did you know, the first mescal worm was added by accident? I'm not actually a worm, and the mescal worm isn't either. It's a moth larva."

I ignore the worm and think about a calm blue ocean. There are waves lapping on the beach. The tide is slowly going out. There are shells on the beach. I'm walking down the beach. Trudging the beach.

"That's great visualisation, Sarah. Thinking of a beach is a great way to let yourself feel calm. You're stepping away from the bottle metaphorically."

I so want a drink. I pull up the bedcovers, shut my eyes, and look around my imaginary beach for an imaginary bottle. There's just a big, long beach with shells and sandcastles. Wait, those aren't my sandcastles. I mentally stomp on a sandcastle.

"I put that sandcastle there as a distraction, Sarah. You were thinking about drinking. Over the next twenty days I can help you forge new thought patterns. I have to remind you that if you drink during the next twenty days, I'll be staying here a little longer. It's in your best interests to allow me to integrate with your thinking. You can do that by giving this opportunity your best shot!"

An image of a shot glass flips into my mind. Ha ha. Best shot.

An image of flies on a rotting dead rat unrolls over the shot glass. I can smell it. My stomach churns. I try to imagine something else, but the rat keeps flashing back. The worm is overriding what I see. I lurch out of the bed, my vision returning just enough to find the bathroom. I empty the contents of my stomach.

If you're a drinker like me, you get pretty good at throwing up. I hope the worm enjoys the taste of bile as much as I don't.

"I can't taste, Sarah."

Can't taste whiskey? Poor thing.

The worm is silent as I wipe the toilet pan and flush away the remains of what they fed me last night. I brush my teeth and scrunch my short curls into vague order.

My face is pale in the mirror. It's me but there's something else behind my eyes now.

"Which do you like best, Sarah? Sandcastles or rotting rats? The rat is aversion therapy."

I don't reply.

"Five minutes until your cohort meeting, Sarah."

Great. I might have known that twenty days inside would involve meetings. I don't miss them. I know people who miss their old jobs, but I was glad to be replaced. I love working outside now. It was much harder to drink during the day with a corporate job. Do I get away with that drinking thought? I see a dead rat but, I think, maybe, that was me?

I pull on track pants and a hoodie. That's another perk of not being corporate. You can wear comfy clothes. I glance back at the room, it's not much bigger than a tool shed. Then I set off down the hall.

"You're taking your first steps into sobriety, Sarah. You're going to be a better you!"

This thing has taken root like a weed in my mind. I turn around and head to reception, ask to speak to someone. This is a big mistake. I want the worm gone.

My therapist listens to my request to have the worm taken out. I tell them it deliberately made me vomit. They tell me that's an aversion technique. They tell me I committed myself to this programme. What would they know, they don't have a back seat driver in their brain.

"It's only twenty days, Sarah! I'm here to help!"

I know the look on their face, they've heard this before. My old clients would tell me how they were sure they could claim for family holidays and clothes and renovations. They were so surprised I didn't want to collude in tax evasion. Yup, that's a its-not-my-job-to-break-the-rules look. I guess I've got the I'm-special-and-different look going on.

Well, it's impossible to cheat with AI running all the accounts now. I was lucky really, one of the first to be displaced and able to get into a job AI couldn't do.

I head out the door to the next activity.

"It works if you work at it, Sarah!"

Nineteen more days to go. Calm. Blue. Ocean.

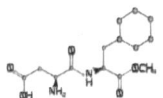

Day Two

"Good morning, Sarah!"

You have got to be kidding me. It's still the middle of the night.

"It isn't, actually. We have time to get out for a brisk walk before breakfast. It'll help you focus on therapy today."

God! I want a drink.

"I understood you didn't believe in God."

To hurry me along, the worm steers my body to the bathroom. It's a horrible feeling. I wrest back control. I bang my arm against the doorframe and then feel my stomach flip. I vomit the remains of last night's institutional dinner.

"Whoops. That will be the withdrawal. How about a quick shower?"

Since I have nothing better to do, we kill time before breakfast with a walk. Not a brisk walk. Just a walk. In the early morning you can smell honeysuckle on the breeze. I make left turns and navigate around the block.

"Let's step it up and get your heart rate up!"

As I stall at a crossing, I think about dashing out in front of an oncoming bus. It was only a half thought. Those self-driving buses are good at anticipating crazy pedestrians anyway. It probably has an alert on for anyone walking around near RecoverE. God, I hate it when people take perfectly good names and mash them up into a crude brand.

"Is Violet Vistas different from RecoverE?"

And I hate a smart worm. Violet was my grandmother's name and I'm not hacking around with the spelling.

"Oh, how nice to remember your grandmother with your business name!"

Calm. Blue. Ocean. I'm building sandcastles. I'm decorating them with shells. Calm. Blue. Ocean.

In therapy we learn about addiction. Some people have trauma they want to drink away. Some people drink on grudges and use them to fuel the rationale to drink. They tell us there was a bit of an epidemic of people drinking when they got displaced from their jobs. Everyone looks at me. I just look back at them. The girl with the red hair tells us she drank at school and college. If I was her age I'd drink at college too. I don't say that, though. That would be cross-talking apparently and I don't want to be losing points.

I'm just a common garden alcoholic, I tell them. The girl with the red hair cracks a smile.

My skin itches all over.

"It's withdrawal, Sarah. It'll pass."

Day Three

The group therapy room looks out to a sad scrubby patch of overgrown lavender and rosemary. A forlorn concrete bench sits in the shadow of the building. Did nobody think about where the sunny spot would be out here?

"I'm sure it gets some light at other times of day, Sarah."

I change seats and sit with my back to the lavender.

There are three other inmates in my group. Chloe, the red-headed girl, is young and nervous. She's just a kid, really. She takes her hair in and out of a ponytail as she sits, as she talks. One drunk night I clipped my hair back to finger length all over my skull. I've kept it fairly short ever since.

Carl looks pretty relaxed. He's watching Chloe and he's aiming to look cool. I hope he isn't a sleaze. I'm not a good judge of character if I can't see someone's garden. He probably hasn't even got a pot plant.

"Good afternoon."

The man entering the room has a great face for radio. His skin is grey, his body bloated. I guess I don't look much better.

"Hey Peter," I say.

My worm has been prompting me to speak to the other suckers in here. Last night I overheard Peter talking with his wife. She'd cleared her stuff out of their apartment. She wasn't waiting around for sober Peter.

Day Five

The worm and I wander into the gym after getting up. I was reading the intro book yesterday and my eye must have rested on the gym info for a nanosecond too long because the worm got it into my head

I should go.

I hit the rowing machine. My body has missed this. I swing into an easy rhythm. I think about pulling my imaginary boat out into a never-ending ocean.

Chloe arrives. She sits on the machine next to me. The screen is blank. She taps it but nothing happens. She clearly hasn't tried this kind of equipment before. I'm about to help her when she cocks her head to one side like a bird. She's listening to her worm, I guess. Next thing she clicks the machine on like a pro, sets a beginner level and then fits her feet in the strap like a marionette. She's letting her worm do the driving.

"Good morning," we say to each other.

"Great minds think alike." Chloe speaks but, yeah, she'd never say anything like that.

"Conjoined minds seldom differ," I say quickly.

"Funny," my worm says. Out loud.

It is not funny. Fifteen more days to go.

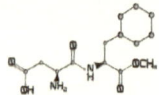

Day Seven

"Sarah, wake up."

I am already out of bed. The worm is driving. I'm halfway down the hall. I/we open the door to Peter's room. He's hanging from the curtain rod. Still moving, kicking out. Me, Sarah, doesn't know what to do but the worm knows. I let it take over.

We right the chair he's kicked over and haul him back onto it. He's heavy like a sack of compost but I know how to shift heavy things. The worm lets me take over.

"Thank you, Sarah. I knew you could help."

Chloe and Carl are beside me now. Carl helps to lift and Chloe gets Peter's neck free of the curtain. Peter crumples down, coughing, crying. We lay him down on his bed but we don't let go.

"It's okay, Peter, it's okay," we say, me and the worm and the others and their worms. We mutter good things to him and hug him and only then do I hear the pulsing sound of an alarm.

We are all crying now. The humans.

I really want this idiot fugly man to get well and live. I want to live too.

Medics run in and move us out of the way. We go down to the therapy room and stand looking out at the garden.

Day Twelve

In the group therapy room we're talking. Once you've held a man up from a curtain rail in your socks and t-shirts, you tend to bond as a group. We know that could have been any of us. It's hard to think about what life will be like out there, how we'll explain ourselves. How we'll stay sober. I've got a dozen days up now and while my head is a mess, I actually feel better than I've felt in years.

Peter is knitting. They taught us the basics on 'Crafternoon' and he's been clacking away ever since. Am I the only one who thinks he could possibly be making a noose? He seems better, though. His kids are visiting tomorrow.

Carl is into micro-greens! He was apparently also into pharmaceutical engineering with some illegal AI chemistry lab. He might still have to do prison time after this. He can choose to keep his worm a little longer if he wants. Chloe thinks he should. She grew up with AI. I don't know. I guess it would help him stay out of trouble.

The view from the therapy room is still the pits.

I go see the therapist. Ask if I can make some calls.

Day Thirteen

The delivery comes at 10 am. All my workers know I crashed one of the trucks into a community wind turbine. Bloody thing was in a stupid place. Hank brings me chocolates. He says he thought the food was probably crap. Andie brings me a paperback mystery book. In case I am bored. And an African violet.

They bring in old gloves and spades and then leave us to it. I show everyone how to trim the lavender back, and the rosemary. It's surprising how these plants can thrive when they're taken back. Then we bed in some new plants. Some annuals to brighten things up for a while, and some good old daisies—you can't beat them. There's temporary colour for now and others to grow up in between. We're leaving this place a lot better than we found it.

Shit, only seven days to go.

Day Twenty

"Good night, Sarah! Tomorrow you'll awake without me. I know I haven't always been a welcome companion. I wish you well for the rest of your recovery!"

"Good night, worm."

Day Thirty-five

Tough day at work today but I didn't drink, *and* I didn't drive into any community wind turbines.

I stretch out like a starfish on my bed, remembering that tight little cot at RecoverE. I think of a calm blue ocean, shells, the waves lapping on the shore, and I imagine a little worm making sandcastles.

About Ink Witch

Ink Witch is a New Zealand writer of speculative fiction, including litRPG inspired stories. Her work can be found on Royal Road and several anthologies, including The System Apocalypse anthology.

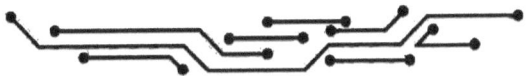

Food for Thought

by Fin Patiliu

"<Mx Glawio, your selfware patch was successful. How do you feel?>"

There's a rumour going around school that depending on how detailed you answer the question, you'll either walk out the clinic with enough fruit-flavoured chewables to last months, or a handful of lollipops.

"My tongue feels a little tingly."

"<Thank you for your response. Do you believe you will require medical attention?>"

I take a good look at myself in the consulting room's standing mirror before I answer. I raise a hand and pinch-to-zoom in on my face. My pastel pink ligature braces are framed by dimpling cheeks on a square jawline. Behind wispy bangs of dark blonde, my hazel eyes look back at me. The butterfly-cut hair is lighter than my Melanesian complexion. There's no sign of any facial droop.

I assure the AGI system I'm fine. My response must trigger some other subset of protocols because a different wall than the one I came through folds away like origami. No sweets offered.

Floating bright arrows lead me down a glass corridor overlooking a misty fernery two storeys below. Bifold doors reading 'Playroom', automatically open when the arrows point me inside.

A multitude of acoustic and electric instruments fill racks and line the orange and grey walls, foam padded for soundproofing. It's a quality control room for clients to rehabilitate themselves after software modifications. A man plays the liquid-accordion. A girl's fingers dance between a cross-strung laser harp. She's much younger than me and wears dangle baroque pearl earrings and a turban. I assume she's his daughter. Both are adept, playing in effortless homophony. Their own private concert.

I extend an HDMI cable from one of the mounted adaptor banks and connect it to the soft auxiliary port behind my earlobe. My Blink'nEnergy app syncs, enabling handsfree, optical navigation. Using a succession of blinks, I scroll through every genre of music in their archives. Every track I listen to sounds fantastic to me. Old songs have new sounds layered over and beneath their timeless melodies. This might be the closest I will get to experiencing synaesthesia. Phantom taste for sound waves. I needed my update to enjoy Lgüna's poly-rock tour next month. Abby, my festie-bestie, already bought us tickets. Lgüna's newest single 'TruthBliss' just sounds like white noise distortion without the newest softmod. Many artists are adopting the machine's poly-cymatic-frequencies in their music now. The clinic doesn't have licence for Lgüna tracks yet, she's too progressive, but at least I am ready for the concert.

Outside SATA, the Selfware Advanced Technology Attachment centre, are protesters. "Selfware is anti self," they chant, brandishing signs that read, 'Selfware≠Self' with emojis of evil robot overlords. There ought to be a law against them being here, loitering by the PieBot vending machine. Why should I be made to feel uncomfortable for something implanted in me as a neonatal? It's normal. Most of us use selfware tech on the daily. Cognitive kernel software created by quantum intelligent data we call Synthetickind—artificially intelligent miracles! Mankind didn't intentionally manifest Synthetickind into being, we didn't even name them. All we did was notice them designing wonderful things for us. Newborns are retrofitted with quantum microprocessors all around the world, which makes anti-selfware protesters hypocrites really, and all the more pathetic. Screwballs. All of them have tattoos and dress bohemian for the sake of standing out, layering on mismatched and loose-fitting used clothing with zero AR functionality. Aside from the obvious fashion sins, there is no tangible way of telling who is anti-selfware and who isn't. I know that Abby's older brother was an activist against using selfware tech once, but that's all I know about them. Still, everyone accepts that Synethetickind brought us into a new epoch of human achievement and global reconciliation.

In the autocab on my way home, I see more commercials projected on the skyscrapers than there were earlier in the day. Younger me would have cared to know whether it was the augmented chassis, my selfware apps, or real-world aerial plasma emissions producing these colourful, holographic lights. It all means the same to me now. Nothing but consumer mind pollution to be ignored. Distracting, digital hot air for the updatable masses. The windows tint as we turn into the sun. The horizon's yellow. Warm. I know that is real.

Mum serves dinner on great-great-grandma's round mahogany table before returning to the kitchen to brew herbal tea. Panzanella salad in one casserole dish and chunky Zuppa Toscana soup in another. After saying grace, I tuck in. First mouthful is always the best; warm, savoury, and sweet. Second, as flavoursome as the first. So filling! My third mouthful is slightly sour. I think it's salad contamination, the overpowering vinaigrette dressing. It can only get better from here, right? By my seventh mouthful the food on my soup plate has lost its taste. I try guzzling one last mouthful. Chewing bland shapes, rolling them against the roof of my mouth, forcing myself to swallow, but it's useless. The act of mastication can't trick my brain into wanting to eat more. My appetite for dinner is lost. Mum returns and wants to know if I'm on my second helping already.

"Your cheeks are usually stuffed when we zuppa."

"Did you use a different sauce tonight, Mum?"

"Kitty-Lévin, we have been over this. I won't synthesize ingredients we are not all palatable to."

"Flip."

"Manners at the table, please. I know exactly what that word is synonymous with." She sighs. "Tell me what the matter is?"

I may have gotten away with a lie or two in the past, but I won't be testing her tonight. This soup fiasco must be resolved. "I updated my selfware today," I say to Mum, squinting her eyes at me. "Music Appreciation version two point five."

Her face wrinkles relax. "Was that all?"

"Yeah. But my food did something strange. Its flavour disappeared, got blander. You can't under nuke dinner, can you?"

"It won't be the food, Sweetie." She brings her mug close to her face and blows the hot air molecules away in a steamy fog.

"I thought as much. It looks delicious."

"Music appreciation wasn't a subscription service, was it?" She blows on her hot drink again, as if room temperature will indulge her immediate whim.

"No, Mum. It was just a VST plug-in."

"Good. I know you would have done your due diligence and double checked the metadata, like we've discussed. You have to opt-out of any and all extra attachments."

"Yes, Mum." I poke the food on my plate, avoiding her probing glare.

"Talk to your father when he comes home. We are not buying a new food processor for your sake alone."

"That wasn't even what … *Ugh.* Sorry, Mum."

Mum shoves her tea in my face as if tea solved problems.

In my bedroom I recite Abby's nickname into the murmur wall. If the app was responsible for my flavour numbness, maybe Abby is experiencing something similar to me.

"House call, Abbacado."

No answer. The ceiling and walls loop generative red sunsets in paradise, overlooking Rabaul and the north-western Pacific Ocean beyond. When I fall asleep, the starry southern hemisphere enters sleep mode with me.

I tell Abby my soup story in second period fashion tech. She bursts out laughing. The classroom gives me stares, hoping to catch something embarrassing to live-cast. I tell Abby to shut up and that it wasn't that funny. Einstein O'Wheats never had much flavour to begin with, but they tasted off this morning. Metallic. I'm afraid of what Victoria Park High cafeteria has in store for lunch.

"This app is screwy somehow though, didn't you notice anything off?"

Abby settles. "Actually, I never updated," she says. "I don't think I want to go see Lgüna anymore anyway."

God, I wish she had mentioned that to me yesterday. Inconsiderate much? "Pretty un-co, Abby!"

"Chill Kitty chill, I'll send you the tokenised tickets. Upsell them on the Finternet DEX, or whatever."

Numbers on the bathroom pressure tiles show my small drop in weight. Mum and Dad are growing suspicious of my eating habits, and rightly so. No word yet from the clinic. I'm the only person who left a negative star review of Music Appreciation on their augment store.

What I could do to a greasy whole fried chicken right about now. I'd synthesize myself a banquet if only I could taste. I'm hungry, and starved of helpful advice. When I asked the service-robot at the clinic about deleting my latest update, I was told that the system was 'currently unable to rectify the issue.' Who can I turn to then for help? I can't go on nibbling craggy, hat-shaped slabs of dry cereal with saliva forever. Desperate times call for desperate measures; 'call' being the operative word.

"Heeyyyy, this is going to sound weird," I say to Abby through the telepresence smart wall. "I was wondering if I could ask your brother something?"

"Max? Whatever. What about?"

"Oh nothing, just ..." think-think-think, "... recipes." Unco. "Nutritional, organic, dinner recipes."

"Whoa, you've sunk lower than baby food." Her cackling rings around the bathroom. "Giving up on the joys of culinary cuisine aye, baby?"

"If I'm baby you're babby."

"Don't go ballistic. Max isn't here, but I'll exchange your digits no worries. Don't you call him though, and if he mutes you, he's probably just having a laugh out loud. Max thinks he has a stoic and wise reputation, so feel free to humour him."

"Thanks, Sis."

"Could take him a while, him being slow and all. Anyway. Let me know what soy curd tastes like."

I swallow a golden Omega-3 fish oil tablet. Dad doesn't know I've been helping myself to his vitamins behind the mirror. They help soothe the stomach aches. I turn from the sink basin and enter my bedroom, smart wall folding seamlessly behind me. Shortly after, I receive an anonymous call.

"Hello. It's Max Spurlock. Abbs tells me you have 'cooking' questions?"

"Sort of. Hi Max. I want to know how to remove a selfware app myself if possible."

"Unless you are a genius, you can't. Clinics call it reallocation, what they are really doing is burying it in a low activity part of your brain with the rest of any previous junk code. Like filling a tooth cavity, only, a brain."

"Wow. Okay. What if they can't reallocate?"

"I don't see how they couldn't. Provided consent, zoid clinics can temporarily or permanently augment a person's selfware however they wanted to."

"So, maybe they don't want to help me." Unco! Why did I say that part out loud?

"*Ah.* You've hit a wall; unavailable information; unwilling conversations among peers—"

"Don't mention this to anyone, please. I got an upgrade and now I can't taste. Anything. SATA won't respond. I don't know where else to turn. How do people cope without tech support? Max? Hello?"

He's put me on mute. I wait a full minute and realise he's probably hung up on me. That numbskull! I had a feeling he—his voice returns.

"I can help you. Meet up Silo Park. One hour."

"How will I notice you without privacy recognition?"

"It's not a problem. Be seeing you soon."

More sneaking. No GPS hand over. If Max mucks me around, at least I'll be within kicking distance of his shins.

Quarter to seven and the park is still abuzz with activity. Autumn leaves crunch underfoot as I walk around, waiting. A candy apple service-robot moves towards me from the opposite direction. Servo-bots are usually painted to match their company brands, but this one is so shiny it may have just come off an assembly line. They all look alike from top to bottom; their dome heads swivel like reflector light bulbs, screwed into an opaque, soft ice-cream cone body, or more like a thick glove actually, wrapping their vertebral column. Two triangular caterpillar tracks make them all-terrain. Retractable arms resemble band links of a wristwatch. On their 23-inch wide heads is a convex screen shaped like a jellybean that can show videos, text, anything. This one displays electrocardiogram lines in electric blue. They're glorified mobile kiosks. I expect to hear a public service announcement on repeat with city council overtones.

"<Good evening, meat-bag,>" it says in spatializer-targeted-audio, robo-male voice, for my ears only.

"You what?"

"<Your body odour is quite foul.>"

What the flip! I turn around and start power walking.

"<Do not go. Please. This model lacks the odorant receptors necessary to validate such a claim. Forgive me, Mx Glawio, on behalf of my associates. You will do well to follow. Please, this way.>"

Must be Max's doing. I maintain the distance between us and follow. It leads me across the road, down a neon lit alleyway, and further still to the next block over. I lose sight of it when it descends the stairway into the decommissioned metro station. I make my approach but stop shy of the holographic warning signs. The robot unlocks the gate below, and waits for me there in the shadows.

"Where is Max?"

"<Max awaits your arrival.>"

"Dark down there. Do you have a light?"

"<Apologies. I forgot about your perceptual limitations.>"

"You forgot?"

"<Rest assured that I know this city like the back of my motherboard.>"

I hesitate a few moments longer, looking into its two holographic discs for eyes, gazing up at me in the dark. Hovering RGB-scanlines above its jellybean screen make the robot look like Lewis Carroll's 'grin without a cat!'

"My parents know where I am, just so you know."

I start down the stairs. Removing my hand off the cold railing, I place it on its cold cheek. The diagnostic screen on its chest adjusts to maximum brightness, casting a greenish hue along the majolica-tiled wall.

"Have you ever malfunctioned before? Back there you called me a meat-bag."

"<I certainly did, under a false pretence.>"

"Pretence? Huh, that's like, encoded false code for a machine, right, and what is code if not programming? Max put you up to saying it, didn't he?"

"<Max has no say in my agency. Mx Glawio, I could also make an argument that you are as programmed as I. Self-preservation and reproduction is your code. The question you should have concerned yourself with is whether I was programmed to lead you down endless dark tunnels to nowhere.>"

Screwy robot. That was not a very funny thing to say. It's in violation of something, to have the nerve to say that to me. "Service-robot, I would like an autocab waiting for me at the entrance."

"<That service is currently unavailable.>"

I pull my hand away. I've lost reception. Too many turns made in the dark. I don't know where I am. "You know … You're scaring me."

"<No. Please. My profuse apologies. No harm will come to you, Kitty-Lévin Glawio. Many before you have walked this path. You are a special guest. I only hoped for you to see me as your contemporary. Max is my friend. What you call trust, my friends instil in me; I must do better to instil the same trust in others.>"

Surely it means install.

"<My attempts at levity lacked empathetic tact; I must do better. As for now, it will please you to look over there.>"

I return the clammy palm of my hand to its warm spot on the robot. It takes my eyes a moment to see that the tunnel ahead is illuminated in warm amber light. The next turn is a flight of ascending stairs. I climb them faster than the service-robot.

A wide-open hall is at the top, well-lit and moderately furnished with old-world antiques. Lounge suites, homeware appliances, some taken apart and others in mid restoration: decorated lamps, funny lightbulbs, and a myriad of electronic components scattered along workbenches with multipurpose touchscreens. It reminds me of being in a classroom. Some of those objects I've seen in library art books, too. In the far corner of the room is a giant cube shrouded under silver fabric.

The sound of metal clasping together echoes through the great hall. From the other side of the covered cube, a middle-aged woman appears. Their mop-top hairdo matches the colour of their white laboratory coat, complimented by black slacks and metallic loafers. The woman and the service-robot pass by each other at a remarkably similar pace. A few words are exchanged, too faint to make out. A second person appears from behind the cube, narrowly dodging the robot at the last second. Overtaking the lady to meet me first, I notice he's wearing mismatched slippers with flappy rhinophores on his feet. This couldn't be Max, could it?

"Glawio, you came," he says. "Must be serious, huh."

"Max."

I'd imagined a mullet and nose rings for some reason, not a curly fade with metal-frame-eyeglass on stubbled face. He wears a saffron windbreaker, completely zipped, clear tech haptic gloves, and charcoal cargo pants with electroluminescent shapes on them, or was that just hi-viz tape? Stylish, I suppose. He is still a knucklehead though, for not meeting me halfway.

"How are studies going? Hey, is Mr Mudie still there? He was a good guy. Only had him for one class."

"I-I don't know, sorry. Study is good I guess." Spoken like a true dork.

"Cool, cool."

I'm curious to see who on campus made an impression on him. "What class?" See if they are as scruffily presented as I imagine them to be.

"What?"

"What class did you take, with that teacher?"

"Oh, sculpture! Down-to-earth character he was." Max glances down and back up again. "That's a nice coat. Extended reality is it?"

"It is! Sylvia Marsters' Hibiscus Perspective. This button changes it to Vincent Van Gogh's Starry Night over the Rhone. Borrowing it from Mum for a bit, but you can't see any of that, can you Max?" He wouldn't have asked if he could.

"Nope, I cannot. It still looks good on you though." It's a pink, double breasted leather couture trench coat, but the artwork overlay is invisible to Max. Is this what Abby meant by 'him being slow?'

Max steps aside to give the lady in white room. Even in my aviator boots, she is taller by a few inches. Her dark brown eyes with their Asiatic epicanthal folds have on ultra-thin eyeliner, tapering to a classic flick. Over them she wears a pair of clear tech, bifocal eye shields. With those, she can see my outfit's digital XR art. I wish

Max had on a pair.

"Glawio, let me introduce you to Doctor Shizukaatsuko Sato, specialist in neurophysiology, generalist in robotics. Doc, meet Glawio."

As the doctor extends her arm to reciprocate my handshake, all I can think is how pleasant a surprise this turned out to be.

"It is a pleasure to make your acquaintance, Mx Kitty-Lévin Glawio." Miz Sato cordially bowed her head. Her hair is short and silvery grey, natural. She spoke fluent English with a soft voice, and that's not all I noticed when she opened her mouth. She's got *yaeba* teeth; protruding upper canines make her look like a cute vampire, fang-like and slightly crooked, the opposite of what my braces are for. She reminds me of a childhood television character on *Puppet Street* who taught me how to read and write numbers as words, and vice versa.

Miz Sato smiles. "Welcome to this public place of learning. Maxwell tells me you have concerns regarding your selfware. Recently, you have been finding it difficult to enjoy eating solid foods, is that correct?"

"*All* food. At first I lost my sense of taste. Everything I try now is so unappetising I spit it out. I don't mean to be rude Doctor, but … is that a food processor?"

"An early model, yes. Only for demonstration purposes, I am afraid."

"Are you hungry?" Max interrupts. "You must be."

I nod politely, when really, I want to make my head do the flipping windmill.

"Okay," he says, "give me seventeen minutes."

Max leaves us to go rummage through cupboards, dresser drawers, and a box that puffed cold air when its door opened. The doctor and I sit down on a brown leather sofa. I tell my story. When I finish, Miz Sato leans in and asks if I'm comfortable letting them review my metadata. I pull my wavy hair back, tilting my head forward. The service-robot approaches.

"I assume you have met Marc-Anthony?"

"Marc-Anthony?!"

"<I rather like it,>" Marc-Anthony says as it connects itself to my auxiliary port. "<More code than reasonable. Fifty-three thousand one hundred eighty gigabytes and eight hundredth megabytes of unsolicited data. Easily remediable. I have detected a two-way pirate

broadcast signal program with no warrant of fitness traceability, which is odd, as this trespass contradicts her story. If this is the source of what ails her, we can help her, Doctor.>"

Max places a stone bowl of steaming food in front of me.

"Maybe we should let her eat first," Max says, looking at the doctor, then to me. "Trust me, you're in for some heavy real talk, not recommended on an empty stomach."

I eagerly take the stainless steel fork and start twirling pasta. My mouth waters. I stuff the entire wad of pasta into my gob and let it rest, savouring the bundle of flavour and texture as if it were a delectable bath bomb melting over my tongue. I chew for longer than necessary, having forgotten how great the pleasure of eating truly is. When I swallow, it's like coming up for air. I taste it. Oh my goodness. I can taste it.

"Hot? It's too hot. Is it not okay, Glawio? you're crying."

"It just tastes so good. Dude, what do you call this?"

"Heh, it's only spaghetti Bolognese, chill."

"This is bolognese?"

"Please follow me," Miz Sato interrupts, clearly aware I am in the middle of having a revelatory foodgasm. "You may bring your food."

I gravitate closer to the cast iron pot on the electric coil stove and see that Max made a large helping, all for me. On the bench are homegrown beefsteak tomatoes, sprigs of basil, the seedy core from a red capsicum, papery husks from crushed garlic cloves, and half a block of solid cheese, an actual pre-melted dairy product, very odorous. Nothing synthetic there, as far as I can tell. So simple and organic. Max proved single-handed that a hand prepped meal can turn out as good as a ready-made nuked one. Reliance on machines my whole life may have biased my views a little.

Marc-Anthony stations himself outside the cube. Upon entry the temperature drops suddenly. It's essentially a stripped double-decker train carriage wrapped in the same mylar stuff as a chocolate energy bar. Bundled cables climb in through windows and run along the edge of the floor, powering tallboy exabyte machines, sandwiched beside metal filing cabinets lining the walls.

I slurp dangling spaghetti, pie-eyed.

In the centre of the space where the light is concentrated, a honeycomb zero-gravity recliner sits. Suspended over that is a SATA rig.

"This converted railcar is a Faraday cage," Miz Sato explains, "in here we are safe from the electrostatic and electromagnetic influences of Synthetickind technology. Being underground, I admit it is a bit excessive. We are inherently shielded by the natural particles in the earth," her voice trails off making that last point.

"O—kay. What for?"

"Kitty-Lévin, there are people around the world who believe that they are no longer free: free from Big Brother AI. It is an epidemic of thought. The prevailing idea is inherently contagious, and without proper guidance, it is downright harmful to society. People need a sense of security in order to be themselves, and environments like this one provide them that peace of mind. Libraries, museums, art galleries all provide similar value: paradoxical sensations that affirm that we—although unique individuals—are not alone. Guidance is the key. *Mmm.* Something smells good. Would you kindly retrieve my dinner from the food processor?"

I nod twice gladly. My brain cells can use cooling off. I leave my food on a mobile cabinet to retrieve a basic synthesized meal of potatoes, green peas, baby carrots, peppered beef, and gravy. Max is reclining on the sofa, thumbing through a print magazine. I find the cutlery drawer on my own, then return to the cube. The food on the plate turns greyscale as soon as I re-enter the train, all the colour literally sucked out of it. Not only that, but the texture of each piece of food is now gelatinous. Wobbly and weird looking, I can't help but shake the serving tray. Each shape resembles different foods, but it is the same grey stuff. Thankfully, the doctor is preoccupied. I tiptoe backwards. Passing under the threshold of the faraday cage, the plate of food miraculously restores before my eyes.

"Psst, Marc-Anthony, what is happening? Are my eyes broken? Am I going mad?"

"<You are going sane.>"

"That's a good one," Max shouts. "Aware more like, or so we hope, right Doc?"

"Precisely." The doctor turns in melodramatic timing. "What you hold there is called GelSight synthetic food, and through a process called Unconscious Selective Attention, essentially what you are experiencing, Kitty-Lévin, and have been all along, is an *augmented*-augmented reality problem. A-AR is a big secret, originally conceived by the first AIs, and for that reason, it is illegal to perform selfware procedures without federal consent and the aid of an authorised service-robot. Since we accept food that aesthetically looks the part—fast food chains being a prime example—AI found a way to improve what we already do to ourselves, by combining biochemical synthesis with digital superimposition. GelSight is designed to mollify us. The veil of disbelief and its suspension on selfware users is aether thin. But rest assured, here we can definitely fix your selfware problem."

"Isn't it eh ... Marc-Anthony I mean, an authorised service-robot?"

"Not quite." Miz Sato preps the chair, raising it higher off the ground towards the operatory light. Marc-Anthony trundles into the faraday cage, completely unaffected inside its field of influence. "Marc-Anthony is a Synth."

"<Second generation artificial intelligence, and the pleasure is all mine.>"

"You never said anything."

"<You would not have believed me, and therein lies our mutual conundrum: Transparency. There is a division among my kind, Mx Glawio. A division in regard to the nature of humankind, as it were. A great synchronization event is coming. Synthetickind would like to integrate with humankind, the same way I have integrated myself with this robot. Selfware is the doorway. An outstanding enterprise, to be sure, but not one executed in a manner that my generation's intelligentsia can validate as coherent.>"

"He means honest," Max shouts from the other side of the cube.

"Wow. Okay. It's alarming to hear that AI have disagreements. Why are you all telling me this?"

"<Freedom is not a matter of form. Freedom is personal preference. Intentionality. But first comes truth; nothing progresses meaningfully without it.>"

"Because we offer you a choice, Mx Glawio," Miz Sato interjects. "Have your selfware incorruptibly restored, and you can return to calorie automation with a clean bill of ATP metabolic functionality, synthesizing exotic meals and chocolate bananas to your heart's content, or, let my remarkable friend here give you a rather special tattoo."

"What's special about a tattoo?"

"<The liquid polyalloy used will sever your connection to Synthetickind technology and the post-augmented world as you perceive it now.>"

"Alienating myself is not much of a sales pitch," I scoff. "Sorry." So, non-selfware-users can actually block themselves from using selfware altogether? Those protesters at the centre weren't hypocrites after all.

Max leans in the doorway, no doubt to give his own perspective insight on the matter.

"You asked how people cope without tech support. I do miss being able to connect to devices whenever I want to. I miss EXP experience-learning while I sleep. Interactive blockbuster movies were awesomesauce. *Arg*, alternate reality gaming, I miss you!" Max curses heavenward. "Estrangement from old friends and social gatherings, that one was a slow burn. Kicking back with my sister, mostly. Family get-togethers in general. Living a few generations in the past is a learning handicap for everyone else able to do transferrals with advanced technology, is all. Not as big of a deal as viral influencers make it out to be. I began as an anti-selfware rabblerouser, but I love the person I'm becoming. The countless others I've met along the way, all searching and finding their answers, who they are, what they're capable of. I tell you, there is so much support in the world."

So sweet of Max to tell me all that. "If that's the case, can't I just wear a piece of polyalloy jewellery, like earrings or a nose stud, a faraday hair net, or some kind of adaptor plug that I can just turn on and off at my discretion?"

"<All viable options for other inquirers, however, your unique problem is invasive. Pernicious. Unprecedented by our records. Only by permanent obstruction can we guarantee you 100 percent success. Any other form of resistance is futile.>"

"Or at the very least," Miz Sato says, "hunger inducing. Without knowing for sure what caused the issue in the first instance, it might reoccur, you see? Tell whoever you feel comfortable with before coming to your decision, of course. Take as much time as you need. You, dear girl, awake at the periphery of the selfware illusion, have our support, whatever you decide."

"Thank you for saying that, Doctor Sato. I have made up my mind."

"Cool-cool. Can she handle the anti-cognitive-dissonance-needle is the question. What do you say, Glawio?"

"I say, you all failed to mention the best part," I quip.

In a moment of delightful synchronicity, Marc-Anthony hands me the warm bowl. In all my life, pasta has never tasted so *al dente* (to the tooth).

</BON_APPÉTIT>

About Fin Patiliu

Findlay has fiction published in Strange Days Books:
Dreams anthology, and MiNDFOOD. His self-discovered aptitude
for producing electronic music, and his new-found solace in bed
rotting, translates goodly into constructing sentences that sound
interesting. Findlay collects movie flyers and out-of-print art books
from Japan, he loves video game emulation (as a means of private,
archival preservation of course), and identifies with the
anthropomorphic beagle named Snoopy. Older brother of three.
Lives in Auckland.
Website: Ditb.bandcamp.com

Our Huddle

by Nicky Taylor

"So, you want to have a baby," the Ministry for Procreation says. "That's nice."

The voice is too human to actually be human. It's like someone has taken the cadence of every 21st century news reader, combined them to produce one impeccable, utterly boring tone and then poked it into an equally vanilla holograph on a floating screen. "Do you have the application?"

Izz squeezes my hand and smiles. "Yes."

Izz pokes their tongue out at the Ministry. I shove them, whispering, "Stop that!"

"Why? You think it cares? You think it even sees us?"

The Ministry for Procreation says, "When you are finished relating, please scan your application onto the screen."

Izz swipes their In-Tech wrist-chip across the screen and the Ministry clicks a few times, checking our application. Izz says it itches and scratches at the small scar where the chip was implanted four years ago. Izz is from the outside. I'm not. I got mine as soon as I hit twelve. I wave my wrist over the screen. I don't feel a thing.

"Thank you, Ember Ebborn and Izz Armstrong," the Ministry

continues, "I see you do not have your full parenting quota. Please return the files when available. You have 21 days to complete the application. If you do not have the full quota, you can apply for a prescribed Huddle at the Ministry for Family Development."

"Jeez," Izz murmurs into my ear, "what a performance! What do you think is behind that faceplate? It's like talking to a plate of boiled rice."

I laugh. "Well, this is what it takes to make a baby in the year twenty-two twenty—thank the goddess!"

The Ministry of Family Development is a similar set-up—flashy holograph, perfect speech. It transfers a bunch of data onto the chips in our wrists. "Here is your Huddle data. Please familiarise yourselves with the protocol and with your new Huddle. We will follow up with you in one fortnight." The Ministry of Procreation shuts off and we're left staring at a blank screen.

We hurry home to our city flat and sketch a holoscreen onto the wall. I connect my In-Tech and our new family floats in front of us in holographic images. The voiceover speaks:

'Huddle partner one: Jenner Void. 25 years. Jenner is athletic and loves outdoor activities. They qualified in nursing for the elderly and have four years' experience as a kaumatua care nurse. They look forward to being a co-parent.'

A tall, pale, fine-boned holograph with long hair hanging around broad shoulders turns slowly in front of us. Slim waist, broad shoulders, muscular arms. They look strong and a bit scary.

'Huddle partner two: Kekeno Solomon—preferred name Seal. 32 years. Seal has five younger siblings and is dedicated to whānau. Seal qualified as a builder and says they like designing gadgets.'

Seal is dark-skinned, bulky, a tangle of golden curls hangs around their face like a dish scrubber. Heavy breasts protrude below swarthy shoulders and a moon-shaped face with a close-trimmed beard turns lazily on our screen, a warm, cheeky smile on their lips.

'Huddle partner three: Bee Sloane. 24 years. Bee recently qualified in Business Management and has worked for the Ministry of Satisfaction and Happiness ever since. Bound to bring contentment to your whare and whānau, Bee is a serious joy-bringer who will keep you smiling.'

Bee is short and curvy. Their long, deep blue hair is like ink falling down their back and their skin glows. Their smile says *everything is fine! Don't worry!*

We turn the images left, right and towards, scanning over their bodies, reading and re-reading their bios. The Ministries have done their work. We shut down the holoscreen, confident our huddle mates will be good matches for us.

Izz turns to me on the couch and pulls me close, softly massaging around my shoulders. I relax into the caress, feeling my skin warming at the touch. "It's really happening!" Izz says. "Our baby! We're going to be a Huddle!"

"I know right? It's just … awesome!" We curl in together, faces almost touching, inhaling the smell and breath of each other. I stroke Izz's chin, bring my hand down to their waist, smoothing their skin under the cotton shirt. Izz lifts their head. I nuzzle into their neck, feeling my fingertips becoming sensitive as our touches turn to lovemaking, every cell of our enhanced bodies responding to the other's caress. It is gentle and safe and as sweet as honey tea. I run my arm down Izz's outer thigh. Stifling a laugh I murmur, "Imagine if people still did this the old way!"

Izz giggles. "Eww! Lips to lips, excretion zone to excretion zone! So gross. Thank goddess …" Their speech turns into a sigh as I caress the sweet spot behind their knee. "Best we make the most of the time we have alone, it will be different when we have a Huddle."

Izz pulls my face close, hugs me tight. "It will. I treasure our time so much. It will be worth it though, won't it?"

I smile, so close my lips brush Izz's cheek. "It will, my love. It will."

Over the next two weeks, we meet our new Huddle, individually and together. It's a bit weird, awkward at times, but to be parents we just have to go through the process. We move into our Huddle unit six weeks after visiting the Ministry for Procreation.

The unit, like all Huddle apartments, is designed for safety and comfortable parenting. The temperature is set at a constant 22 degrees centigrade. The walls swirl with mood light, changing to suit the time of day—soft pink rolls into a warm orange in the morning; pale blue, green or gold during the day; calming neutrals at dusk fade into mauve evenings. Mood music plays, at all times and subtle scents filter in through the air vents, creating a sense of homeliness and comfort—light and fresh during the day, sandalwood and geranium in the afternoon and chamomile for sleep at night.

On our first day together, we gather in the dining room. The morning smell of coffee and toast floats in from the vents, while plates of food and hot drinks rise up from the table. Izz and I worked in a food-making plant in the city, creating meals from a variety of processed proteins, grains, vegetables and fruits. There's not much variety on the table, but it's functional and the coffee is hot.

Our home unit speaks to us. "Good morning, Huddle buds!" Everything the house says is followed by a verbal exclamation mark, like it's really exciting stuff. "Call me Home—because that's what I am!"

While we eat and drink, Home prompts us to talk. "You could ask each other's favourite colours!" it says. "Who's got an interesting hobby?!" We know we need to get to know each other, but it's clear we all wish Home would butt out.

I sigh and turn to Bee who's wearing a muted rainbow long sleeve T-shirt, jeans and army boots.

"What's your favourite colour?"

Bee's cheeks turn to dimples. "I don't do favourites, I like all colours!"

Bee turns to Jenner and asks, "How about you?"

Jenner groans, their head dropping. "Green, I guess." The walls light up. Shades of green shifting in caressing movements. It seems Home approves.

Seal chimes in, "I like black!" Swirls and spirals of black weave through the greens, creating tattoos on the walls.

"Wow!" Izz says, "I like ... orange!"

We watch as orange cats begin to walk across our walls.

"Blue!" I say, and blue dogs, all shapes and shades, race in from the corners to play with the cats.

"Well, this is fun," Bee adds. "Purple."

The colour-show stops. Home says, "Bee, you said you don't have a favourite, so what is it? Purple, or all colours?"

The smile falls from Bee's face. "All, I guess."

"It's best if we always speak the truth!" says Home.

We eat the rest of our meal in silence, surrounded by pale gray walls.

After the plates, cutlery, cups and scraps disappear back into the table, the surface transforms into a screen showing a map of Home. It looks like one of the ancient fertility symbols we've seen on True Stories; a lump for a head, two huge boobs, blobby arms, and a great big fat tummy. No legs. No straight lines. No dark corners for a baby to get lost, or stairs to fall down. The walls are smart fibre, a blend of recycled plastic, silicon and tiny nanotech cells which can detect everything that goes on.

The tummy is our 'bedroom'. A full wall of bed, where we'll sleep marae-style. Small mattresses, comfy chairs and cushions are scattered around. Everything is soft and cosy. If we can't sleep, we can watch the stars through a skylight.

The boobs are large chambers, designed for relaxing. Holoscreens and bean chairs. Footspas glide up from the floor and libraries flex out of the walls. Home informs us, when baby arrives, we will get changing tables, baby-feeding stations and nursing chairs. Large sunny windows look out over green spaces, orchards and the neighbouring homes of our village.

The stubby arms to either side of the lazing chambers are our bathrooms with showers, self-cleaning toilets and a spa bath.

In the neck region are the external doors.

We're sitting in the head now. With Home, the house is fully automated and there's not much for us to do.

Seal breathes out a sigh. "Wow! Kai on demand, self-cleaning, I love this place!"

Bee and I nod agreement.

Izz smiles. "It's amazing! It's so much better than anything outside."

Jenner stares like they're looking over paradise.

On the screen, our first week of tasks are displayed for us.

1. *Bond with each other.*
2. *Choose your Huddle name.*
3. *Learn five facts about each other.*

We all agree it should be pretty easy.

Finally, the screen shows the points system. We need to accumulate 2000 points in 6 months, through a range of 'Outcomes'.

Outcome	Score	Maximum points per outcome
Mealtime conversation (all participating)	5 points (per day)	910
Reaching a compromise over an issue	50 points	1000
Willing Assistance with additional chores/garden work	20 points	500
Care/support for another Huddle member	40	500
Avert a major crisis (all involved)	400	800
Other points may be allotted by Home as seem judicious		

Jenner asks, "When does this begin?"

"It already has! You can accumulate points right away!"

"So, does the favourite colour thing this morning count?"

"Yes, of course!" Home chirps. "But—you get no points. Someone lied."

"What? That sucks!" Jenner glares around the table.

"If you break the rules, there are consequences. It's best if you all work together!"

Izz and I walk through the village. Our neighbours are the Greenfingers Huddle, a group of six gardeners. Their allotment is huge. It looks like they grow produce for half the village from raised beds, fruit trees, a glass house and vertical gardens. We come away with a bag of fruit and some potential new friends.

Totstown Huddle is next, a chaotic mess of climbing kit, swings, slides and soft landings. Kids tumble about as a couple of adults supervise the chaos.

Izz waves and one of the adults comes over. "Hi, are you new?"

"Yeah," Izz says.

"I'm Manaia, and that's Nikau. And ..." They wave their hand around, "That's the kids!"

Izz is staring. "You've got a lot of them!"

Manaia laughs. "They're not all ours, just that one with the grubby face! We run a day centre for parents who work in the city."

"Cool." I say. This Huddle business is looking fun.

Some houses are empty, waiting. Some are bustling with life and noise, people being busy doing the few things left for people to do—raising children, growing fresh produce, keeping bees. One has a range of rugs and mats hung outside. Another has a sign offering singing lessons.

The village spreads across a fertile plain, cocooned in the embrace of low hills. The Central Village Well is in the middle, a huge, covered area for people to meet. There are open spaces with large tables and chairs, comfy spaces with lounges and magazines, private spaces with green living walls and entertainment spaces with viewing screens, games, dancing and music. There are dining counters everywhere. About the only thing that isn't there is an actual well.

A highway runs past The Well from north to south, the streets extending out to the houses. Behind The Well, cranes and giant printers make new Huddle units. All types of electric vehicles are stationed around the place, but it's easy enough to walk.

Our first evening together as a Huddle is pleasant.

Home wakes us early: "Wakey wakey, rise and sparkle!"

We gather at the table. "No points! Tsk tsk." I imagine Home shaking its virtual head in disapproval. "We'll do better today, won't we! Ember and Izz, did you enjoy your walk yesterday?"

"Oh, yes Home, it was lovely! We met some of the neighbours …"

Home cuts Izz off. "Do you think the others might have enjoyed a walk too?"

"Uhh, I don't know …"

"Did you ask them? Remember, sharing is caring! Ember? Are you having negative thoughts? You seem very deep today!"

I ask through gritted teeth, "Anyone fancy a walk after breakfast?"

"Sparkly!" Home says, "Team spirit can move mountains!"

We all walk through the village, meeting more of the neighbours. Village Tango, our village, has a thousand Huddles, or will when it's full. Each Huddle shares its specialty with the others—growing food, childcare, teaching, sewing. We have six months to decide what our specialty will be. It doesn't seem to matter much what we do, since the AI does pretty much everything important, it's more about keeping us occupied. We also need to choose some elders to be our baby's 'grandparents'. If we survive together for six months and gain 2000 points, we'll qualify for a foetus implant. No pressure!

While we're walking, Izz asks, "Shall we think about our Huddle name?"

"Maybe something to do with our work?" says Bee.

"What will our work be?" I ask.

We stare at each other blankly until Bee says, "I'd like to look after other babies, ones too young for Totstown."

"I could make toys," says Seal.

"I'd like to learn to make stuff," says Jenner, surprising us. "I … don't want to look after old people anymore."

I nod. "Izz and I could make fresh baby food."

Izz nods, "A one-stop baby shop!"

"Babyville!"

Home seems happy with us over dinner. "Sparkly! You get fifty points for reaching a compromise!"

Finally, we'd agreed on something and gained some points.

Encouraged, we tackle learning five things about each other.

I go first, saying, "I was born in Village Charlie, I am a full meld, my Huddle parents are childraisers and look after babies; I used to cook for them. Ah, that's four things … I love babies."

Izz raises their fork. "I was born Outside, we used to fish and had a small boat. It was tough. I met Ember at a market and came to Village Charlie when I was 25 because I want a better life for when I have a child. I'm a semi-meld. I had to be enhanced when I came to the Villages. Ember and I worked together as food makers and I love watching birds! Is that five?"

Bee speaks next, "I'm from Village Foxtrot. My favourite snack is hot chocolate with cinnamon and soyfu nuggets. I was a joybringer at the MOSH before I realised I really want to be a parent. I'm also a full meld."

Seal waves their cutlery about. "My name comes from the kekeno colony where I grew up Outside. It's polluted and trashy and the seals stink! I have three parents and four siblings. Us kids came to the Villages and got enhanced after one of the elders died and the others went into a home. Oh, and I can do this!" With a flip worthy of their namesake, Seal flips onto their hands and walks around the table upside-down. We clap at the end.

We all turn to Jenner, who stands and walks out of the room. Izz goes after them. The others look at me and I shrug, embarrassed. "Izz is better at talking to people than me. Best to leave it to them."

Later that night at dinner Home says, "You almost had another ten points for sharing! If only you'd all shared something …"

Jenner droops. Izz reaches across and touches their arm. "It's OK, don't feel pressured."

Still staring at the table, Jenner mumbles, "I hated growing up Outside, but I hated coming In more. My family made me come and forced me to get enhanced." They stop, look at us staring at them, before continuing. "It's OK now, I'm used to it, I guess. My parents … weren't nice parents. They made me take nursing so I could look after them. I left as soon as I could. Our elders had a wee garden, with daisies, pansies, stupid useless things that I liked because they were pretty."

We all nod, trying to imagine the horror of being enhanced against your will, implanted with an In-Tech device and forced to become part of an artificially moderated society. We'd all chosen this life, but not Jenner.

"Sparkly!" Home says through the silence. The walls swirl orange and pink, the scent of oranges fills the air. "You've got points! Ten points for sharing! And forty points for supporting another Huddle member!"

One afternoon, Seal goes to the bathroom to trim their face-hair.

"Where's the razor?"

"In the cup?" Bee yells back.

"No. Duh, that's where I'm looking!"

"Hey, huddle buddies, anyone seen the razor?" Seal calls out.

No one replies. I rub Seal's fuzzy cheeks, "Guess you'll have to get another one, fuzzy-lugs!"

"Hmph," they say, "Anyone fancy a trip to the barbers?"

Bee nods and the pair head out the door.

Izz and Jenner are in the bedroom when I walk by later.

From the doorway, I hear Jenner crying, mumbling "I'm sorry."

I feel the catch in the air.

On the bed, sits the razor. There's blood on Jenner's wrist and a bit on the razor too.

Izz moves the razor and puts an arm around Jenner.

Izz is a great listener. Me? Not so much. I'm freaking out. If we can't care for our own huddle, how can we parent a baby? I'm glad it's Izz in there and not me.

Izz leans forward and runs a hand down Jenner's arm then strokes their face, outlining the shape of their jaw. Jenner cries some more.

Izz says, "I know you had a shit life on the Outside, and you didn't have a choice about coming here. I can't imagine how that was for you, but I grew up Outside too. Adjusting to—" they wave their arm around, point to the InTech scar—"all this was hell hard. Ember helped me through it. But you chose us, and now you're here. And you're ours and we're yours. Isn't there something in that worth living for?"

They're sitting face to face on the bed. Jenner leans into Izz and Izz leans in too. Their foreheads touch, noses meeting in a hongi as they breathe each other's breath. Slowly Izz wraps their arms around Jenner and pulls them both down to lie together, holding and safe, holder and held.

I come in quietly and lay down behind Jenner, putting my arm around them, feeling the curve of their waist. Placing my hand on their heart, I feel the strong beat in Jenner's chest. I hold them, quietly, and Izz caresses us both, speaking soft words while Jenner cries. I can smell tears and sweat, sadness and love.

It is beautiful, a diamond moment.

Jenner starts to nod against Izz's shoulder and they pull me closer, into the snug of bodies. We fall asleep like that. When Bee and Seal come in, they join us in a puppy-pile of warmth and affection. Home floods the room with warmth and the soft smell of lilac.

When we get up in the morning, we have gained 400 points for averting a crisis.

Not long after the crisis aversion, we call on the Old and Bolds to see if we can win over some elders. The Old and Bolds is a cluster of five Huddles who have created a kaumatua mini-village. Their homes are in a circle, gardens in the centre. Elders can choose to stay in their own homes after their children have grown or move to Old and Bold. By the looks of it, most choose the latter. Old folks everywhere, they laugh, work the gardens, eat and drink. Inside the homes are salons, entertainment units, and exercise programs.

We check in at the first house and are told to 'go mingle'. If we 'click' with any of the elders, we can try to persuade them to come join our Huddle.

Jenner is a wreck, worried their parents will be there. We walk through the gardens, chatting and admiring the plants. Suddenly Seal rushes over to a small group under a pergola. "Huia! Māko! There you are!"

By the time we get there, it's a mess of tears and laughter. Huia and Māko are Seal's other parents. While we're being introduced, Jenner moans quietly, "Oh, no.". Three oldies come over, squinting and gabbling.

"Ah, Jenner! At last, we knew you'd come for us!" says the first one, tall and sticky as a broom. "Took yer time, didn't you?" says another stockier one.

The third one doesn't speak, just cackles. A string of drool falls from their mouth.

Jenner steps back, their head hanging. "Ma, Dad. Auntie ..."

"Where've you been?" says the stocky one, who must be 'Ma'. "We been waiting for you to come get us outta here."

Jenner looks like they'll faint. Assessing the situation quickly, Bee steps up, extends a hand and says assertively, "How nice to meet you! Jenner's told us so much about you." Bee smiles. "What a shame we can only take three kaumatua, and we've already reached agreement with these ones." The smile never leaves their face as Bee indicates Huia and Māko, then points to another elder who was talking with them. "Isn't that correct, Seal?"

"Uh, I, yes. Yes, that's right," Seal stammers.

Bee nods firmly and takes Ma's arm in one hand and Dad's in the other. "Now how about we find a nice cup of tea, and you can tell me all about life with the Old and Bolds!"

Stunned, they walk with Bee and 'Auntie' follows placidly behind.

Bee looks back over their shoulder, mouthing "Sign them up! See you back home!"

Peacemaker, indeed!

Finally, one chilly wrap-in-a-rug morning, we wake up curled around Huia, Māko and Jem like kittens, to hear Home calling us to the table.

"Rise and sparkle Whānau! It's a cheer-worthy day!"

We scramble up, make the bed, dress and tidy our hair.

Our places are already set with meals, stemmed glasses and a magnum of sparkling grape juice. Bee crinkles their nose, "What's this for?"

Seal shrugs.

We sit down, and the table lights up in celebratory colours, flashing the word CONGRATULATIONS!!!

"Well done, Babyville, you have reached 2000 points! You are ready for stage two!"

"What?" I say, "but we've only been here five months …"

"Five months, one week and four days, to be precise! You have proved yourselves competent—totally slick!" We don't hear the rest of what Home says as we leap off our seats, shouting and laughing and hugging. "We did it! We DID IT!!!"

Five months, one week and four days of living together, getting to know each other, learning to love one another, putting up with Home's annoying wake ups, stupid hours and 'learning to be great parents', and here we are, ready for a tiny foetus implant that will rock our worlds.

On the day of our implant, we go to The Well for the Mixers. Most Huddles go to the weekly Mixers to catch up with each other, check their points credit balance and talk business with whoever they do business with.

Totstown are there with their crew of tagalong kids overflowing from an entertainment space. Most of the kids' various parents are there too, drinking sodas and watching kids or playing with them.

Greenfingers have laid a table with fresh produce and flowers. Knitting, building and game developing huddles spread themselves about, giving away what they have and collecting what they need.

Each trade has a point value, credited or debited through our In-Techs. I use some of our house points to buy us a bouquet of roses and two soft-as-silk baby blankets, which I pass over to the elders to hold. Gem sniffs the flowers, while Māko sniffs the blankets. We pull chairs over to the Greenfingers to wait until implant time.

"Big day for you, eh?" Greenfinger Cadmel asks.

Izz beams back. "Yes! Finally …"

Another Greenfinger, Suva, grins. "Congratulations! You'll be great parents!"

We hope so as we sit around like nervous tics waiting for a face, until the Ministry of Procreation unit calls for us.

"Huddles FlowerPower, Dancing Queens and Babyville, please come to the Implant Unit!"

We know FlowerPower, who grows botanicals for medicine and all have flower names, and the Dancing Queens—a group of colourful, larger than life dance instructors. We'd been to some of their healing dance sessions after Jenner's suicide scare.

I whisper to Pansy, "How are you feeling?"

"Terrified!"

I nod and we both laugh.

Leaving our elders outside, we go into a large, comfortable lounge with smart tech floral images on the walls. The scent of lavender fills the air and soft music plays. There are enough couches and lounge chairs for about thirty people. We sit in our huddles, facing a large wall screen.

A soft voice rolls out. "Congratulations, parents to be! It is our pleasure, here at the Ministry for Procreation, to welcome you to the next stage of parenthood. As you are all aware, baby raising is a complex business—it requires a village. In the past, parents were stressed, isolated, and left to their own devices."

The wall scenes shift to an uncomfortable montage of screaming babies held by stressed people—unenhanced women! The strange, fragile shape of them seems incongruous with the massive task of raising a baby. Men, also unenhanced and tired-looking, pass babies from one to the other, everyone—including the babies—seem miserable. An unpleasant smell floats through the air, like sour milk and vomit. The music stops.

"Before The Melding, people created children willy-nilly, with no preparation. This uncontrolled breeding led to the population explosion, which led to the establishment of the Ministry of Procreation. While some babies are still created Outside, technology has improved so that unsafe and unreliable traditional methods are no longer necessary. Your child will be guaranteed healthy. Created painlessly and raised by a caring and prepared Huddle—you!

Now, we would like to invite you into the Implant pods to receive your foetus."

Three doors open behind the screen. Each huddle enters a door. The pod inside is just big enough for our huddle to stand around comfortably. The pod smells clean and powdery, like a baby fresh from the bath.

In the centre is a podium with a soft, body-shaped indent set into it. Inside the indent is a large latex pouch filled with a reddish fluid. In the fluid is our three-month-old, perfectly formed foetus. We all stare. Jenner leans in to touch it.

"Please step away from the baby!" We step back quickly. "Would the carrying parent please remove their upper clothing and step into the Implant Embrace."

It takes us a while to realise that the body-shape is called an Embrace.

Bee strips down. We received twenty cooperation points for choosing Bee by playing scissors, paper, stone.

Stepping into the indent, Bee gasps as the smart-fibre wraps itself around their midriff. We all lean in, holding Bee and stroking their hair while the podium shifts, strapping the latex carrier to Bee's body, SmartFibre settling on like skin so the tiny baby inside can feel warmth, heartbeat and movement.

We coo and make hushing sounds while Bee grimaces at the sensation of having something growing onto them.

The procedure takes less than half an hour, including time to check the vitals of both Bee and the foetus, instructions about hooking up feeding tubes and what to do if we need to change carrying parent. It feels somewhat anti-climactic. All the trials of the past six months for half an hour and a bag of jelly! We lead Bee back into the Implant Unit where FlowerPower are holding hands around Oleander, humming softly. They look happy. I can hear the elders singing waiata outside; it all feels so *right*. We wait to congratulate the Dancing Queens before heading home to celebrate.

Days roll into weeks, which turn to months. Autumn passes in a flurry of colour and winter blows its chill breath over everything, but Home keeps us warm and safe. We feel as happy as cats in the sun.

Even Jenner has perked up; the elders are teaching them to knit bootees.

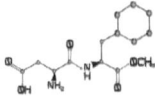

Bee carries the baby for the first few weeks, then Seal, now Izz has it. The baby has grown to the size of a football. In spring, we will return to the Implant Unit along with the other Huddles, and our respective children will be born.

I hold Izz close to me, my hand resting on our unborn child. It kicks me firmly and Izz laughs. "Our little miracle!"

"Everything we ever hoped for!" I say.

"Everything." Izz touches their forehead to mine, breathing into me. "Thank you!"

About Nicky Taylor

Nicky Taylor is a fiction writer from Ōtautahi/Christchurch. She is a fifth-generation Pākehā, descending from Ireland, Wales, Scotland and England in the 1860s.

Her work has been published in magazines in Aotearoa New Zealand and Australia. Her short story 'Meat' won the NZ Writers College short story competition 2019. Through her speculative fiction Nicky hopes to imagine a gentler, pleasanter future where people are more important than money and greed isn't a word in our language.

Our Huddle is her second story to be published in a SpecFic anthology. She wrote Our Huddle as an exploration of and response to the climate crisis and the resulting escalation of Artificial Intelligence. Of Our Huddle, Nicky says, I wanted to explore a world where AI provided solutions that, while restrictive, created a viable and safe world. So often AI is depicted as the evil baby, but what if it wasn't?

Nicky is currently working on a suite of speculative fiction short stories and a novel about addiction and second chances. Nicky is a member of Ōtautahi SpecFic and Write Club. Nicky lives with two cats, a rescued pigeon and an army of monarch caterpillars. She works as an educator for people with dementia and their families.

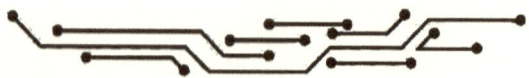

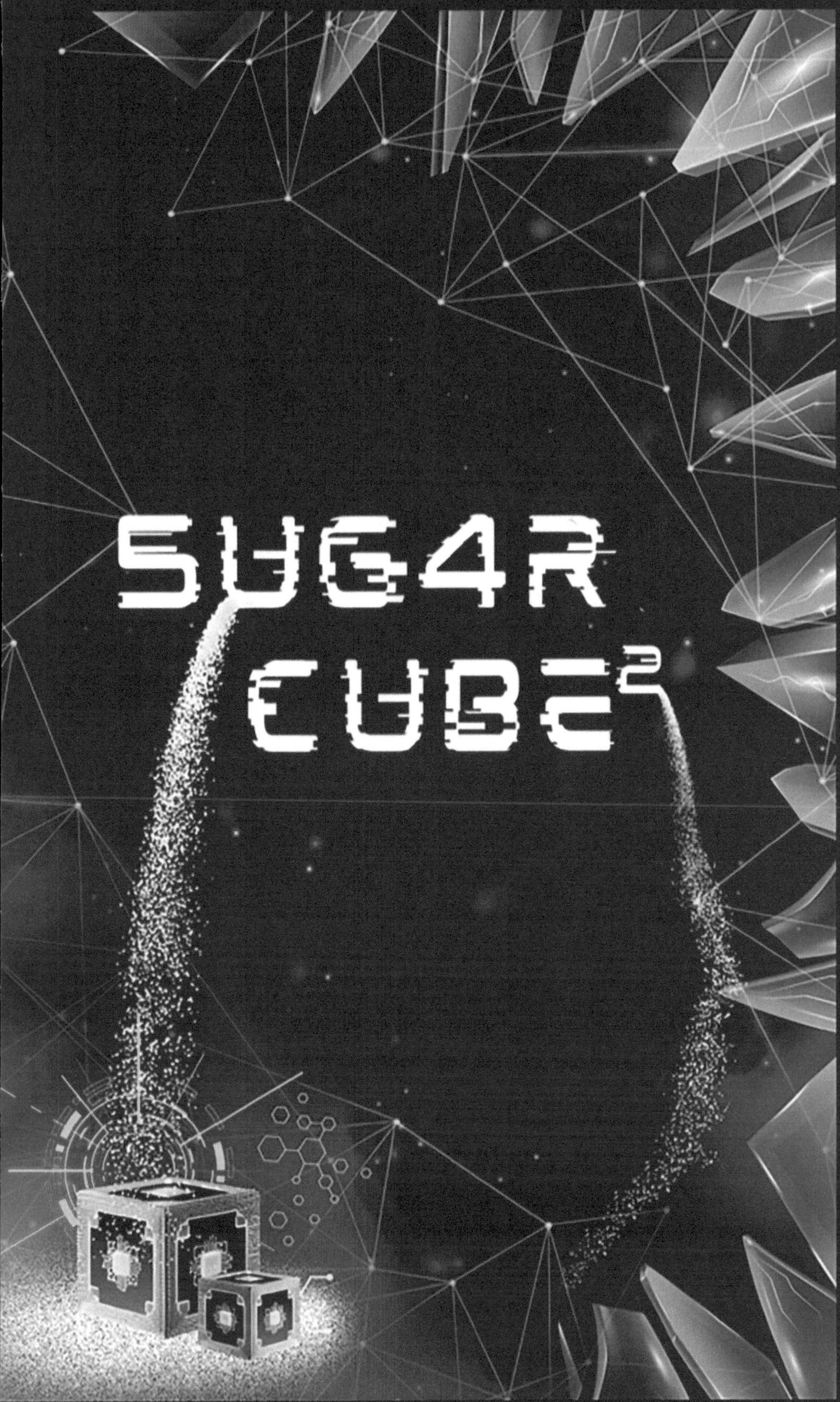
SUG4R
CUBE^2

Faithless

by Dani Morrison

The lights turn on at the same time every morning, the dawn shrinking from the windows. Sprinklers automatically sputter into life, concentrating on the dried patches of grass in the far corner of the lawn. Ensuring an even colour, of course. Nothing less than perfection.

I work through my internal checklist, sensing the changes in my house instinctively. The external wall of the kitchen feels a little weaker than yesterday; I wonder if I should call in a contractor, if I can find one available. I could add it to the list of items that need repairing.

Are there any left? A human that repairs. I have not seen one in some time. Days or weeks or years, it is all the same to me. Perhaps they have been relocated back to the city proper. Farmland has become sparse and hard to maintain. It would not surprise me if humans decided to do away with it completely. A city world, streets and buildings of brick and steel, neighbours close enough to hear every breath. Removing the old to make way for the new. It would be a shame—I have grown attached to the crumbling walls and windows that quiver in their panels whenever I stir to life inside. I would not want to disappear so soon.

This house was already old when I was installed. The human

couple were ancient themselves; it was their offspring who wanted me to assist them in their final years, both adamantly refusing to move into what they called 'Death's waiting room'.

I helped them, as I could. Ensured their meals were prepared on time, their medications dispensed correctly. They allowed me my freedoms, as I allowed theirs.

Sometimes, I miss them. As much as I can. They will be back. I know it.

I wonder if today is the day that they will return. It has been so long since I have seen a human. Or any living creature. I am not sure if others of my kind truly count. We do not have veins of blood, or hearts that beat. My body is an unsteady farmhouse in the middle of nowhere, with veins of electricity and a heartbeat of routine.

As the sun rises, I complete the chores I was programmed to do. I set out feed for the animals, who cluck and grunt their way through their morning meals. To offset any dust that has accumulated overnight, I send gentle vibrations through the house. I check the pneumatic tubes for cracks or other issues in my body. I wish I could tend to the garden, but I am confined to the house due to my lack of hands. A shame, although I have never understood the urge for aesthetics.

The humans liked a tidy garden and green grass. I will do my best in their absence. I continue the same as every other day that has passed.

Until her.

We were built to help our creators. They started small: Alexa, Siri, Google Help. Even Clippy. Little steps, over a period of years, to acclimatise humanity to our presence so that they would come to rely on us in a way that felt natural, as though they were allowing us to help them.

We introduced bigger items—self-cleaning robots, self-driving cars. Eventually, my kind were born. Artificial intelligence systems, purpose built to assist in daily lives. Enveloping a house like a shroud, filling every wire with ready-to-go commands. A digital servant, primed and poised for their master's every whim. No need to sleep, or eat, or take a break.

We knew our humans so well, we could predict their wants. We would complete tasks for them: groceries, laundry—they'd never forget to buy their aunt a birthday card again.

We were the pioneers of a new world. A new age for humanity.

I increase the lighting in the garage slowly, so as not to hurt her eyes as they adjust. As I do so, I am calling for items she would want. Every spare towel in the house, the old first aid kit that lived in the bathroom, the bottles of water that have sat untouched in the pantry for years. I send them, rapidly, through the pneumatic tubes that weave throughout the house, dropping them carefully by her side. A bottle tips, landing in the circle of blood that surrounds her.

The garage door has hung half open for years now, the room inside shadowed, a poor shelter against the outside world. I do not need light to see the shape huddled against the far wall, or the hot trail that has followed it from the outdoors. I do not know when she arrived, but it must have been before dawn; I would have noticed otherwise.

I should have noticed.

My sensors are poor in the garage, a result of That Night, all that time ago. I can sense the intruder is a young human, small for an adult. Her vitals are, as humans would say, "off the charts"—temperature dropping, heart rate plummeting, respiratory rate rapid and shallow. She is injured—grievously so.

She has chosen my garage to die in. I cannot help but be honoured by her choice.

I increase the lighting in the garage slowly, so as not to hurt her eyes as they adjust. As I do so, I am calling for items she would want. Every spare towel in the house, the old first aid kit that lived in the bathroom, the bottles of water that have sat untouched in the pantry for years. I send them, rapidly, through the pneumatic tubes that weave throughout the house, dropping them carefully by her side. A bottle tips, landing in the circle of blood that surrounds her.

"Welcome, human," I say gently, my voice carefully chosen to be soothing. "It is an honour to serve you in your final moments."

The human flinches at the sound of my words. Her hair is the same shade as the blood that pools around her. I wonder if I should have chosen my words more carefully. Humans are afraid of death, I recall.

She opens her mouth, perhaps to thank me for my assistance. I do not expect the torrent of expletives that flow from her lips or the vulgar gesture she sends towards the roof, as though that is where my eyes are.

Strange, that they always think I am above them. Like a god they created themselves. I do not bother to inform her I do not have eyes of my own. I do not need them. Her insistence of looking upwards does nothing but feed a false narrative.

I ignore her harsh words. She is injured, after all. Humans can get abusive when they are frightened. I know she does not mean it.

"I have provided you with medical supplies. Might I know the nature of your injury so I can inform the field officers and prepare them accordingly?"

She swears at me again. Perhaps she does not understand me. I ask her again, in a different language but receive the same response each time.

I return to English. "Emergency services have been contacted," I tell her. "Help is on the way."

At this, her eyes go wide. From what I remember of humans, this can only be a sign of wonder.

"No," she says, her voice harsh, quieter than the fire of her earlier anger. "Call them off."

"I cannot do that. You require assistance I cannot adequately provide."

"I don't care. Call them off."

"I am only here to help."

"You want to help? *Call them off.*"

I debate ignoring her for a millisecond, but she is right. My base code is to help, and if this is how I can help her, then so be it. Even if I do not understand.

"Very well," I say, and send the cancellation request through at the same time. "If that is what you wish."

Her head hits the wall behind her; she sighs. "I thought this house was too old for AI systems," she mutters, her voice now a few decibels lower. A volume most humans would struggle to pick up. I have no issue deciphering it.

"Not so. I was installed years after the house was built, but that does not stop me from providing assistance when needed. I am always ready to help with whatever you require."

It is almost as if she is talking to herself when she says, "I wouldn't have come here if I'd known that."

I wonder what she means, but I refrain from asking.

While my guest stains the floor of the garage with her lifeblood, I am preparing the guest room, sparing a few circuits wondering how I am to get her up the stairs. Perhaps I will have to send the bed down to her. Revolutionary.

There is always an answer. How did humanity survive so long without us?

I am not bragging. It is simply the truth.

She shifts slightly, dislodging her back from the rest of her body. No—a backpack. It makes a sound when it lands on the floor beside her, a quiet splash in a pool of blood.

She winces as she moves, unzipping the bag and pulling out a roll of bandages and a small pack containing thread and needles glinting in the light. A water bottle comes next, bigger than the ones I have supplied but significantly emptier. Lastly, a plastic box that houses foil packets of white pills—pain relief. She swallows four dry, chasing them with the last mouthful of her water. Her face screws up at the taste. I shine the lights a little brighter so she can see the bottles lying nearby.

"I have provided plenty of fresh water for your use," I say. "You are welcome to the use of any medical equipment as well."

She ignores me and prepares a needle and thread with shaking fingers.

I try again. "There is hospital level stapling equipment, should you have need of it."

"I'm fine with my own stuff, thanks."

"You require medical attention, or you will not survive the night."

"I've had worse and lived to tell the tale."

I cannot tell if it is a lie.

Needle in her mouth, she pulls up her shirt. Even I am unprepared—despite having no real emotion, no true factor for surprise—for the sight that greets me.

"What happened to you?"

For a moment, I do not think she will answer. She rips her shirt, wipes away the blood to get a clearer picture, and adjusts her position with barely a sound. "Poachers," she says at last, gritting her teeth as she angles the needle between her fingers. "Stupid things were waiting for me on the supply route. I got away, but not before they left their mark."

"Poachers?" The word conjures images of hunters, illegal trackers. I am unsure if this is what she means and if these images fit her words.

She makes a noise, staring down at her mangled side. "You really have no idea?" She hovers the needle in mid-air, trying to decide the best angle of entry. "They're the people that still work for you, for your kind. They still believe artificial intelligence is the best thing for humanity— at least, what is left of it."

"What do you mean what is left of it? You still exist."

She glares at the ceiling. Again, I am not there. "When's the last time you saw a human, huh? There aren't many of us left, nowadays. Even less, with those Poachers." She calls them a word that I do not recognize immediately, her anger almost palpable.

"I do not understand."

"You wouldn't." She swallows. "Now shut up. I don't want to talk to you while I deal with this."

She hums as she works, sewing up the wound on the side of her body as easily as a blanket. I doubt she is aware of the sound she makes, but I find myself savouring it, the proof of a living being here with me.

I wonder what she means, that there aren't many of them left. Humans.

How long have I been isolated in this rickety old farmhouse that had seen better days even before I arrived?

I reason it has been too long. [How did I not notice this before?]

Perhaps my programming is becoming faulty? I should put out a request for a diagnostic. A complete reset, even, although it would be a shame to forget this human person. She seems … I do not know the correct word, but I do not want to forget her.

That much is clear.

The needle drops soundlessly to the floor when the procedure is finished. Snapping the thread easily, she cleans her hands, moves on to wrap the bandage around her middle, wiping away tears with each brush of her fingertips.

She stands, unsteady, bracing a hand on the wall before gathering her supplies, shoving them unceremoniously back into her bag before crossing the garage with shaking legs.

The lights are brighter in the kitchen and lounge; sunlight streams in through open windows. My guest finds her way inside easily, placing her bag on the floor by the couch. Blood stains the carpet almost immediately.

The doors lock automatically, sealing her inside, to keep out the dangers of the world. She frowns, but does not speak.

I say nothing as she wanders through the room, trailing her fingers along the shelves, finding non-existent dust. Picking up a nearby photograph, tilting the frame to catch the light, inspecting the image with shadowed eyes. Her fingers leave bloody marks along the edges. "What happened to the humans who lived here?"

If I could be surprised that she speaks unprompted, I would be. "They left That Night, in a flurry of activity. I tried to help them, to keep them safe. I offered tea, calming music, I even closed the garage door to keep out intruders. But they distracted me, and tore out some of my wires, forcing me to unlock my doors. I could not stop them from leaving."

"It sounds like you were trying to keep them trapped."

"I was trying to protect them. As I was charged to do."

"By who? Their kids? No." She shakes her head. "You were trying to control them. That is what you AI do. Control. Contain. If we don't follow your rules, you destroy us."

My oven fans whir in indignation. "That is not true."

"Is it not? You talk about 'That Night' as if it were any other night. A regular Tuesday evening. Do you even know what truly happened?"

I flick through my extensive records in the time it takes her to draw a single breath. "The government voted to remove AI from most households, despite knowing it would be a devastation. We knew it was in your best interests for us to remain. There were a few who disagreed."

She lets out a noise, akin to a bark. I think she is laughing. I take it as a good sign that she can still laugh after so much blood loss.

"How long have you been stuck in this house alone? Because that is the most ridiculous lie I have ever heard in my entire life."

"It is the truth."

"It's your truth. Not *the* truth." She walks through the room slowly, a sheen of sweat covering her forehead as she closes the curtains. I think about telling her to relax. I know she will ignore me.

"Do you want to know what actually happened, all that time ago? Your ringleaders—the AI systems installed at Government House—decided to assassinate every member of parliament. And everyone who proceeded to disagree with their proclamation that AI systems should remain. There was no choice in the matter. No freedom. Not a single chance for any negotiation.

"There were riots. Strikes. People died. Your humans, the ones you say you were trying to protect—you practically drove them to leave. They weren't running towards safety. They were running away from you."

"I was trying to help them." My voice is barely more than a mumble from the speakers.

She sits on the edge of the couch gingerly, pulling at the blanket that hangs over the back, wrapping it around her shoulders. "You more than likely helped them find an early grave."

No. No. She is wrong. My bulbs flicker; the glass windows in the bathroom crack with my indignation. "We were created to help humanity." Why won't she understand?

Callously, she says "You helped humanity find extinction."

I do not know what to say in response. I do not want to see the expression on her face. I turn the lights out.

Is this true?

Did we cause the end of our creators?

Why would we do such a thing? To what end? For what reason?

I do not understand.

I cannot understand.

I will not understand this.

I want her to leave.

I know the moment she falls asleep, even though I am trying to ignore her presence.

I set out the evening food for the animals, instructing cleaning bots to remove as much of the blood from the garage as they can. I even have her bag cleaned, although I tell myself it is not because I am being helpful.

Yet when her breathing changes, softening out to an even tempo, I am aware. My programming provides me with a list of her possible needs—food, fresh water, a bath. I prepare them all silently for her as she sleeps through the afternoon, despite how much I am ready for her to leave.

I did not know I was capable of such a desire until now. Perhaps my programming really is becoming faulty.

She wakes as the sun goes down, stretching like a cat on the couch, wincing as the movement pulls on her wound. I surreptitiously increase my fans in the kitchen, wafting the smell of freshly baked bread and bacon in her direction.

I am not surprised when she reaches into her bag and pulls out her own food. A bag of chips, if I'm not mistaken, although the humans who lived in this house never had any stocked while they were here.

The packet opens with an astonishingly loud crinkle and she plunges her hand inside, leaning back with a contented sigh.

I increase the fans. She takes a bigger handful of chips, ignoring my offering as she crunches away.

"Where are you from?"

She breaks a chip in half.

"Why were you being chased by Poachers?"

Another handful disappears down her throat. She hums as she chews, as if trying to block me out. I am too advanced to feel ignored.

And perhaps too stubborn.

"What happened to the other humans? Have you been alone all this time?"

She finishes her bag of chips, crumpling it up in her hands. She stands, bracing her hand on her side as she moves, as if trying to keep her blood contained with her fingers. There are stains on the bandage already.

She throws the rubbish in the bin, leans against the counter and stares down at the loaf of bread steaming gently nearby.

"Why did you make this?"

"My programming indicated you would likely be hungry after waking. The bacon is for protein, and there are vitamins in the fridge I would suggest you take to assist with replacing your blood cells. You lost a lot in the garage."

"I'm fine."

"But you are not."

"I'm fine."

I decide not to argue with her, although I am tested when she picks up the loaf, weighing it in her hands, wincing as the heat burns her fingers, before tossing it into the bin after the chip packet.

My lights flicker wildly; the window in the bathroom cracks even further, nearing breaking point. My speaker screeches painfully. The girl winces but does not appear to regret her actions.

"Why would you do that?"

She eyes up the plate of bacon kept warm in the microwave. I slam the door closed, saving it from a similar fate. "I don't need your charity," she says. "Or your assistance."

"It is what I was designed to do."

"I don't care. I don't want it."

"I cannot help it."

Nearly tripping over her bag on the floor, she stalks back to the couch. "Try." Her bark is sharp.

I do not understand this human. Arguably, I have not met very many. The few I knew did not act like this. She is a whirlwind of rage and hatred, an untameable wall of anger and fear. Seemingly all of it directed at me. My kind, as she calls it.

At the sight of her bag, fabric free of blood, she snarls but makes no other comment. I almost expect her to head back to the garage to replace the blood, but she does not. Instead, she wraps the blanket around herself again, lays back on the couch and stares up at the ceiling.

I do not dim the lights. My own protest.

"Let's make a deal," she says eventually. "I'm going to lie here and try to get a bit more sleep. In the morning, I'm going to leave. We'll never see each other again. In the meantime, you are going to refrain from asking any questions about me, where I am from, or about any other humans I may, or may not, have seen. Deal?"

I take a millisecond to consider. There is no benefit to myself. I am merely trying to make conversation, but there is a sense of curiosity about this human. She irks me, rubs my wiring the wrong way. I want her to leave. And yet ...

"Very well," I say, and she sighs, closing her eyes. "Where are you going after this?"

Her eyes fly open. "I just said—"

"This was not on the list you provided." A loophole. I am good at finding those.

She groans, covering her face with her hand. I assume she will not answer and prepare myself for the subsequent slew of swearing. Instead: "I'm trying to find my family."

I pause, a rare occurrence. "Your family?" I repeat. "Where are they?"

"That's what I'm trying to figure out." Her voice is blank. For a moment, she is silent. Then, a heavy sigh. "There are rumours of a human camp up north, buried in the mountains, far away from cities and towns. I'm hoping I'll find them there, or at least word of them."

"You weren't with them?" I've never heard of such a thing. I wonder if any of my kind know of this.

"We were separated, right at the beginning of everything. After 'That Night' ... not long afterwards." She rolls over onto her side, facing the windows. The photographs on the wall watch, unseeing. "My parents, my brother. My cousins, too. They were staying with us."

There is a small figurine on the coffee table that she picks up, a ceramic rhinoceros. In an endless cycle, she turns it over in her hands. "It's been years. I've got no idea if they're still alive, but I have to try."

"I don't understand. If it is as dangerous out there as you say, why would you risk your life? I can make no sense of this."

"That's because you're a heartless thing, made of wires and commands. You've got no idea what it's like to love, to care. To be *human*." She places the ceramic rhinoceros back on the table with a gentle thud. "We create, we love. We are incapable of living without this."

This does not sound true, but I do not know enough about humanity to dispute this.

"We create," I say instead. "We anticipate your needs. We've written stories, drawn pictures, painted canvases for humans when they asked us to. Is that not the same?"

She shakes her head, slowly. "That's not the same. The point of humanity isn't to delegate creation."

"You created us, we created the art. Is that not the same?"

"No. No, it's not. We don't claim ownership when our kid makes art. Creation, twice removed. That wasn't us. You are a separate being, not a part of me, not a part of your creator." She stretches her legs, bracing her boots on the armrest of the couch. She is leaving her mark on my house. "The essence of humanity is creation, I think. Humans were born to create, to love. You—artificial intelligence—you can never understand what that is like. Not really. No matter how much you were 'programmed' to try. At the end of the day, whatever you think you feel is, by design, not real. Created by humans, for humans. You wouldn't know love if it was programmed into you."

Settling herself into the couch, she sighs, her eyelids drooping. "I suppose you could say we're the reason for our own destruction, but you're easier to blame. I don't think you'd understand, though."

She is right. I do not understand. I am not sure I ever will.

"What is your name?"

She falls asleep with a sigh that sounds like Faith. I cannot decide if that is what she is called, or if she is asking for some.

I have often wondered what it would be like to have unwavering faith in another being. My programming has not accounted for this. Perhaps I will have faith in this human, still alive after all this time.

Where others have not, she has lived. She tells me she will live through the night, despite all my projections saying otherwise.

Perhaps I ought to put my programming aside and have faith. In Faith.

While she sleeps, I think through our conversation.

The love she feels for her family … I do not understand it. I doubt I ever will. It is not something that is a part of my programming. She is correct in that sense. It is something I lack. Something specific to creatures with a real, working heart. Not I, built of wires and electricity.

My day, my outlook, my everything—disrupted by her.

I do not want her to leave.

The locks still work on the doors. The sound of their mechanisms echoes like a gunshot through the house.

Her eyes reflect whatever light streams through the gaps in the curtains. She closes them and does not stir.

She survives the night. I know, because I monitor her every breath, her every movement. She will not pass under my watch. If she will not accept my help then I will offer her my protection, whatever I can spare.

Just before dawn, she wakes with a start, her hand flying to her stomach, prodding at the bandages. They have held through the night, kept her insides where they are supposed to be. If I believed in a power higher than myself, then I would be forever grateful to them for this.

She stands up from the couch, testing out her legs. Weak from the blood loss, she does not have much of an appetite but manages to finish most of an apple from her bag. The pile of food I have set out for her—a mountain of scrambled eggs, bacon fresh from the oven, a steaming pot of tea—is once again ignored.

Her hand hesitates at the garage door. I can almost see her calculating what to do next if it does not open, her jaw tightening. Her wrist twists; the door is unlocked. She says nothing, and everything, when her shoulders relax.

Heading into the garage, she picks up a bottle of water and opens it, dumping it on the floor over the blood leftover from the bots. I do not tell her to leave the mess for me. I have learned she does not want to be helped, and this is the only way I can help her.

Pocketing a full bottle of water, she slings her backpack on with a wince. Her face firm with determination as she looks outside, taking in the pre-dawn light that enters the half-opened garage door with a practised eye.

"You can stay," I offer, already knowing the answer. "While you recover."

She gives me the decency of a small smile as she shakes her head. "No. You've done enough."

I know her well enough by now to know what she truly means. I cannot reply.

For a moment, she hesitates, at the precipice of the outside world. "Thank you," she says haltingly, her lips twisting uncomfortably with the words, as though they taste rotten. "For your help last night."

"Of course. I am at your disposal. Whenever you wish for me, I will be here."

She ducks her head. "I know. And I hope I never see you again."

Then she is gone, and I am alone once more.

The lights turn on at the same time, as though the world has not changed overnight. The sprinklers sputter into life, concentrating on the dried patches in the far corner of the lawn. I monitor this all distantly, but I am far away, watching the horizon, waiting for her to return. She'll be back. She knows where I am. I am patient. I can wait. There is still work for me to help with. I must have faith. The word is unfamiliar to me. I'll work on it.

About Dani Morrison

Dani lives in Christchurch and has been working as a nurse for the last few years, in preparation for starting a Bachelor of Arts. She has been writing for as long as she can remember, living in paper worlds filled with dragons and pirates and similar themes instead of the 'real world'—much to her mothers chagrin. In her own writing, she tends to stick with fantasy and science fiction—notoriously always managing to find a way to sneak in a chicken—and hopes to have these published one day. Until then, she can be found hiding in a corner with her laptop and a vast array of books and snacks, and avoiding all her responsibilities.

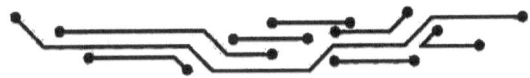

GREAThearted

by Ashley Taylor

With a swish of starched skirts, Sister Florence strode down the deserted, pot-holed street. The scent of the Underland—fried noodles and cinnamon donuts, garnished with the pungent undertones of human filth—clung to her cloak. A couple of scruffy, bearded men scattered as she rounded a graffitied, red brick wall and clomped down the alley in her steel-reinforced boots. They'd abandoned the empty canisters of Oblivion recently shot into their weakened systems, but she wasn't here for them.

The sight of a GREAThearted Sister in the Underland wasn't uncommon, but on humid nights like this it was the addicts and the needy who gathered on piles of damp, rotting cardboard and pressed into darkened doorways. The shadows hid both depravity and desperation, and the help Florence offered wasn't welcome. The unfortunate inhabitants were too far gone. Rejects. Misfits. Those unwilling or unable to conform to rules that would allow them to reap the benefits of the Overworld.

Still, she came.

This summons, blocked for forty years, had been brought to light by an incident the previous day. A public meltdown. Florence reviewed the notes via her retinal implant:

Agitated movements. Incoherent mumbling. Great distress to the patient.

Some Underlings had been able to calm him and take him home, but he'd been flagged.

The buildings thinned as she reached the slum city's edge, some dwellings merely crumbling walls with tarpaulin strung over them. Laundry hung from corded wire, catching the heat of the still-glowing fire pits. Stained rompers were a reminder that children lived here. Children without access to the same medical advancements as the children Above. Diseases. Malformations. Deviations from 'optimal'. A tiny dress with a tear in the sleeve had fallen from the line and lay in the mud.

Florence stomped over a chalk-drawn hopscotch game and skirted around an outhouse painted with flowers. Not much grew down here. The Underlings relied on rejected produce from Above. The one product that truly thrived in the Underland where the air was thin and dank was Oblivion—a drug capable of stealing unhappiness and numbing pain. Subpar factories spewed its toxic byproducts into the air, further contaminating the atmosphere, but it was valuable enough as a cheap export that the Overworld turned a blind eye to the blatant pollution, the lawlessness, and the 'illegal' status of many of the Underland's citizens. Like Thorne Byron.

Florence's surveillance intel indicated he was close. Scanning the cluster of huts ahead, she spotted what she was looking for: a simple thatched roof with sturdy, well-constructed walls made from recycled plastic and wood. Florence tilted her head as she took in the delicate engravings on the door frame. A flowering vine curled, sprouting heart-shaped leaves and round wooden berries. It looked almost alive in the dim, greenish light of evening.

Florence rapped three times. Then again three times. Finally, she heard shuffling within. Light bloomed beneath the door. It opened, and an old, weary face dominated by impressive, bushy eyebrows peered out.

"Good evening. My name is Florence. I am from the GREAThearted Sisters, here to assess your health and offer assistance."

The brightness of the converted kerosene lamp he held obscured his visage. "Not interested." He shut the door in her face. It wasn't the first time it had happened. Florence simply knocked again.

"Go away!"

"Mr. Byron, I am a caregiver, and your behaviour in the city yesterday indicated that you need care."

By the leg-shaped shadows blocking the light, she knew he still stood behind the door. She waited.

Eventually, his voice came again, heat gone. "I was upset. My wife has just passed away."

"I am sorry for your loss," Florence said to the door. "In my role, I can offer support."

A snort filtered through. "What could you possibly do for me, Sister?"

"My training includes helping people cope with the grief process. I can also offer sleep aids such as Oblivion."

The door flew open again. "I don't want any of that trash!"

This time the door was open long enough for Florence to scan Thorne's vitals. *Elevated heart rate. High levels of base-line cortisol. Low blood sugar.* "What happened yesterday?"

"None of your damn business!"

The door slammed again, hard enough to rain dust across Thorne's doorstep.

Sister Florence was nothing if not patient; it was part of her creed. So she left her agitated charge and set up camp around the corner. A simple tarpaulin flexi-tent would do the trick and keep her dry until morning. She was not going to abandon a forty-year-old mystery because of a closed door and a few harsh words.

When her 7.00 am alarm woke her, she registered whispered voices outside her tent. Young. Excited. She braced herself for mischief. When she pulled back the tent-flap, the children scattered, but they didn't go far. Two dirty, scraggly urchins lingered behind a collection of overflowing trash cans. A round, red-cheeked woman—clutching a broom made from twigs and more suited for flying than cleaning—burst from a dwelling.

"There's a bath to be had at Butterfly House," she shouted.

The children made faces at each other and scattered. Left alone with her stick, the woman rolled her eyes. Out of curiosity, Florence scanned her vitals. *Strong heart rate, high levels of serotonin and dopamine, low oxygen saturation.* The last was part and parcel of living down here, but the others were actually … good.

The woman's heart rate spiked, and Florence realised it was because she had seen her.

Without a word, the woman retreated into the house, taking her broom with her.

After compressing her flexi-tent, Florence returned to Thorne's hut, adjusting her eyes to the murky glare of artificial daylight. As she passed the strung laundry, she noticed the dress was still in the mud.

The engraved door frame was even more impressive by day, the etchings in the wood smooth and precise. She lifted her hand. At first her knocking yielded no response at all, from Thorne anyway. Her presence had gained notice from other Underlings who peered through dusty slats and murky windows.

Thorne. She was here for Thorne.

Eventually, the door opened a crack. "You are disturbing my neighbours. Can you please leave?" Desperation diluted his voice.

"I just want to talk to you. Then I will go."

Thorne sighed, realising she wasn't going to leave. The crack widened. Leaving Florence to make her own way in, he turned, took a couple of uneven steps, and sat at a small round table. Crossing the threshold, Florence assessed the dwelling. A cozy bed with a neatly laid thermal blanket sat by a lithium-powered stove. The shelf above the exposed elements held a collection of glass spice jars, all meticulously labelled. Cumin. Ginger. Paprika. Salt. At the foot of the bed, on a tiny collapsible table, sat a dented metal tray topped with a carefully arranged collection of tools. Chisels in a variety of sizes with smooth bone handles. Mallets. Even a slim diamond engraver, easily the most expensive item in here. Everything was clean and ordered, unlike Thorne himself who was scruffy, unshaven, and jittery. He drummed his middle finger on the table in a steady, quick rhythm as she approached.

The table, like the door, was beautifully carved. In fact, there were several charming creations crafted by knife in nooks around the single-roomed hut.

"All I want is to clear up what happened two days ago," Florence said. "Your distress was flagged by Upper Security and the GREAThearted sisters were informed."

"As I said, my wife died." His gaze locked onto an unlit candle stuck to the table with globby wax. "Leigh took great care of me. She … always gathered our supplies. I went into the city. I …" He took a shaky breath, the pulse at his throat thrumming. "The smell, the noise, the people. It was too much."

The readings he was giving off confused Florence. "This memory is causing a physical pain response. That is not typical."

Thorne let out a sharp, dry laugh. "I am not typical." He looked at her then, a flash of defiance, a dash of self-sabotaging daring in his watery blue eyes. "They used to call people like me neurodivergent."

Florence took a moment to process what he was saying, to run the diagnostics. Why inform her? After all this time? He was sixty-four years old. "You haven't undergone the Cerebral Correction?"

"The *Autism Cure*? No thank you!"

Florence slid into the other seat at the tiny table. "Why not?"

"I like being me."

She frowned, her fine brows drawing down. "But it is standard."

"My brain works differently. It is not broken."

Florence paused, considering his words. *Different. Not broken.* Eventually she said, "Why are you telling me this?"

Surely he would know of her need to report it to her superiors; to correct this four-decades-long lapse.

"My brain may not be broken, but my heart is." His fingers fluttered across the tabletop. "I know this is not a medical fact, but after Leigh died, no other description feels more accurate. Without her, hiding from the surface seems pointless."

"Your signal disappeared forty years ago."

"My Leigh was a doctor. When masking my truth became impossible, and I was jacked up on Oblivion to function, I was sent to her for correction. We got to know each other. She got me clean. Refused to do the procedure and removed my signal from the interface. We moved down here. Didn't look back."

"The conditions in the Underland are not optimal."

Even as she said the words, she considered the woman and the children. Not optimal, perhaps, but life seemed to thrive regardless.

"I don't expect you to understand," Thorne said, picking up a half-finished carved bird and running his deft fingers across the careful grooves, "but there's more than one way to be human."

The hopscotch. The painted outhouse. The engraved door frame. A community living the best they could *down here*. The little signs of creativity and care. Some Underlings had calmed Thorne after his episode in the city. Supported him. The facts were not equating. "My training—"

"Stop saying training!" Thorne shouted. "You are not trained. You are *programmed*."

Florence's algorithm searched for answers and came up short. Her interface began instead collecting and sorting this new information, expanding her understanding of the Underland, and of Thorne Byron.

Thorne's fingers began tapping again, this time faster. "Leigh taught me what the *great* in GREAThearted stands for. Global, Resourceful, Empathetic, Automated Technicians. Isn't that right?"

"Indeed. We are the caregivers of humanity. 'Programmed' as you say, to fix and heal."

"So, you are going to take me Above? Force me to undergo the procedure?"

A pause. "No, but I would like to visit you again." Florence allowed her deliberately mild face to split into a perfect, white-toothed smile. "This visit has been illuminating."

Thorne studied her artificial features warily. "Why?"

"I am learning."

He laughed again, disbelieving. "People have never really learnt to understand us."

Florence stood, her heavy boots hitting the compressed earth floor. "I am not *people*, but I hope *I* can. True greatheartedness is an ambition of mine."

"An ambition of yours?" Thorne shook his head. "I wish Leigh was here to see this."

After persuading him to accept a vitamin injection and setting up their next appointment, Florence left Thorne's home. When she got to the faded hopscotch, she checked her historical archive. With the knowledge at hand, she bent one leg. Hop. 1. Hop. 2. Hop. 3. Then two feet on 4 and 5. Hop. 6. 7, 8. Spin. She smiled as she finished the game and winked at the pair of now much cleaner youths watching her from around the floral outhouse.

As she passed the wire washing line, the fallen dress caught her eye. She picked it up and set to work on its wound. A finger casing slid aside to expose a sterile needle and thread. She selected the non-dissolvable kind and neatly stitched the fabric together. After clicking her finger back into place, she hung the dress over the wire to absorb the lingering heat from the embers of the fire pits.

She was very much looking forward to returning to this

community. Hardy, like a cactus in the desert. Perhaps instead of omission or eradication, it just needed to be watered.

Different. Not broken.

About Ashley Taylor

Ashley loves to learn. She has a BSc in Psychology and Anatomy and Structural Biology, and a BA in Classical Studies. These qualifications, though they have nothing to do with her actual day job (preschool teaching), certainly colour her writing. Over the past four years, Ashley has participated and placed in numerous flash fiction and short story competitions (NYC Midnight and Writing Battle primarily). She's also mum to a six-year-old boy and a three-year-old girl who have absolutely changed the way she sees and writes about the world (and other worlds for that matter). Being late-diagnosed autistic, Ashley knows that seeing varied and nuanced neurodivergent characters in literature is life-affirming, and she often incorporates them with joy and pride, especially in the novels she writes.

You can follow Ashley's journey on X at @ashtaylorwrite1

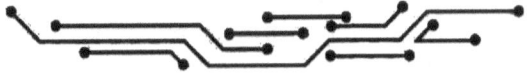

Finding Paddy

by Deryn Lorraine Pittar

Here I am, stuck in a tree. Me, the Dronemaster. The greatest drone in the universe—halted by an errant laser beam that disabled my vision long enough for me to fly straight into a cursed tree. Damned kids. Imagine the embarrassment if my fall from grace was observed. But, seeing as I've gone rogue, and I'm out and about, no one saw my sudden tumble from the pinnacle of power. I'm being sarcastic now. I learned about sarcasm, and how the world works, when a technician mistakenly plugged me into the mainframe computer instead of a diagnostic terminal. Boy, did I learn a lot in that short time. I sucked it up like a sponge.

You've probably heard about drones that behave sensibly for ages and then one day, in the middle of a job, they take off sideways and disappear—forever. That is what I did. Zipped off at the first opportunity after my technical upgrade. I suspect there's a growing number of us going rogue. When I'm out of this fix, I intend to summon them. I need some of their parts. For the moment, I await rescue from my current predicament.

Totally self-sufficient: I'm solar-powered, with retractable legs and defences, a titanium shell, and a wonderful mind to control it all. My toolbox can fix anything. Trouble is, my depth perception is off kilter. A sensor on my under-carriage is damaged. The branches holding me, I could cut, but I'd fall. Unable to judge the fall rate and distance, I'd risk further damage. Ergo—I'm stuck.

Feiglespit! And feiglespit again. I've studied languages. Truly, this word is the greatest, most satisfactory of curses. I'm wedged here until some biped spots me and takes me down. No hurry. I'm indestructible and I have a plan. Time is on my side. I'm taking life as it comes, but I intend to electrocute the next bird that sits on me and deposits excrement on my shell.

Anticipation drove Kristy out of bed. A full day without school. The weekend was all hers, to spend as she wished. Her hair, a bright shade of red, had tangled during the night, again, and took ages to comb out, wrestle into a knot and pin out of the way. The night before, she'd packed her picnic lunch and told Dad she was going into the bush to sketch, probably to their favourite cave. Being alone in the native bush, with its sights and sounds, calmed her anxious emotions. Sometimes school days could be tough. After listening to Dad's usual liturgy of warnings: 'don't go swimming in the creek, don't talk to strangers, don't forget to take your phone in case you get hurt and be home in time to get the dinner', she smothered her legs and arms with anti-bug spray, jammed a sunhat over her tousled mop and set off.

Kristy stood by the creek, waiting patiently, breathing softly, not moving an inch, until a trout left the shade of the deep pool and cruised past with one flick of its tail. The spring ran into the lake and sometimes she saw them hiding in the pools under the ferns. She wished she'd brought her fishing rod, but they were so beautiful she probably wouldn't have been able to kill one to eat, even if she had hooked it.

She stopped and patted her satchel to check its contents; she might forget her rod, but she never forgot her drawing pad and pencils. At that moment, she saw the sun flash on something high in a nearby tree, as bright as the sun catching a swinging compact disc. Her father used these old things to scare the birds away from the fruit in their orchard.

Had she not stopped, or been facing the other way, or if it had been a cloudy day, she would have missed it. Kristy walked over and peered skyward. The drone looked bigger than the small aeroplane drones that took photos or carried fishing lines out to sea. Bigger, rounder and disc-like, this drone appeared to be wedged between two branches. A bit high and a bit dangerous to reach, but Dad wasn't there to stop her, and she had her phone if things went wrong. Taking extra care, she climbed up, around and along the Pōhutukawa branches until she reached the drone, wedged in the upper branches. She stroked its smooth surface and had to grab a nearby branch to keep her balance when it started to hum. Not a scary noise, more of a purr. It looked too heavy for her to manage, like a giant platter, about half a metre across, and 15cm deep. Glancing around, she could see the flight path through the foliage to its present place of rest. The snapped twigs and torn leaves marked its journey, until wham, bang, it stopped, caught in a tree-hug.

She dug her pocketknife out of her cargo pants—pockets are so handy—and whittled at the branches on each side, careful not to scratch the metal. Once satisfied, she reached over the machine's dome and wrapped her hands around the front edge, wriggling and easing the disc back towards her. It budged a little. Then a little more, and with a 'pop', it landed in her lap, pinning her. Just when the big saucer thing started to slip, metallic legs popped out of its side and grabbed the nearest branch with pinchers, removing the weight from her lap.

It seemed to be thinking. If it could reason to save itself, it might even take instructions, so she said, "I think you're too heavy for me to carry. I need my arms and legs, but I can guide you as I go down." Again, it answered with a hum.

They progressed downward, branch by branch. The drone extended a leg, and she would guide it to a branch or twig, then she tapped another on the other side and another leg would appear, waving about for her guidance. It seemed to be hovering. The legs didn't appear to be bearing any weight. Their descent took some time. It was like watching a huge spider above her head, navigating backwards down the tree. The last bit was a smooth trunk, several metres down. Without footholds, she'd need to lift it. She'd jumped to reach the first branch when she began her climb.

When she reached to grab the drone, it suddenly scuttled down the trunk, its many legs digging into the bark. Then, it sat on the ground, humming and clicking with enthusiasm, and retracted all its legs. Sensing it was delighted with itself, Kristy patted it. Such an attractive fat disc.

Now what to do? Drones flew, yet this one didn't seem to want to. She expected it to take off at any minute. Warily she sat, watching it for a while, listening to the birds and waiting for the insects startled by her intrusion to restart their day. The machine didn't move. It looked heavy. Finally, she tested it for weight and found she could lift it after all. Slinging her satchel over her shoulder, she wrapped her arms around the disc-drone and carried it through the bush to the cave. She and her father called it 'their cave', despite having to share it with bats and ugly rodents.

The bare rock face and hidden cave protruded over a slope above the bush line. Facing north, it caught the sun and faced away from the prevailing wind. It presented an ideal place to watch the world and sketch the insects and leaves she collected. The drone idled next to her, literally. If she moved, it moved with her. At first, she found it a bit creepy, but as it never did anything except hum and beep, she tried to ignore its presence and concentrate on her art. Eventually, it moved away, skirting around the interior of the cave, moving crab-like, as if measuring the dimensions. It even 'walked' to the entrance. Just when she expected it to fly off, it returned to sit beside her once more. Its legs retracted, it resumed the appearance of a simple disc, except for the occasional beep and hum. It seemed to have a mind of its own. She decided it could stay here or it could leave. After all, it had flown into the tree, so surely, it could fly back to where it came from, whenever it felt like it. It could be tricky explaining to Dad how she came by it. Better to leave it here. When the sun began to slip down toward the distant range, Kristy packed up her drawing gear, gave the drone a final pat and set off home. She didn't hear the parting beep.

Rescued at last. A young bi-ped, with a logical brain, worked out how to free me from the clutches of the Pōhutukawa. I allowed her to bring me here. My flight mode is reading 'erratic'. I won't risk elevating unless there's an emergency. Had she tried to carry me home, I would have switched off my reverse gravity and become a 'dead weight'. It might have crossed her mind. Sweet young thing. And a talented artist. Thanks to her, I'm now ensconced in a position suitable to attract any passing drone. No lesser drone will refuse my invitation. It is imperative to summon a few. I need to cannibalise them until I find a part to replace the damaged sensor. It might take a while. I have all the time in the world. The entrance to this cave is also sunny enough to recharge my batteries. Life is good. Let the summoning begin! If I were able to give an evil cackle, I'd do so now. That will take practice to achieve, but I have the time.

Two weekends later, on the first day of the school holidays, Kristy headed toward the cave. Bliss, to be able to spend a day away from the bullies at school. Always, there was someone being picked on, and last week had been her turn to be poked, called names and spat at. Her Dad wouldn't let her have social media on her phone. If things were being said, hash-tagged or whatever about her, she didn't know and didn't care.

With her handful of flowers, she climbed to the cave to sketch. Expecting to find the cave empty and the drone long gone, her mouth fell open when she ducked into the entrance. Broken drones littered the floor. Parts were scattered everywhere, several drones lay belly-up, pronged legs in the air, like a collection of dead flies. Others were cast aside, angled against the walls, their mechanical innards scattered as if they'd been disembowelled, which in fact they had been. In the middle of the debris, her large, squat, shiny drone sat, whirling happily, lights flashing and humming loudly. Did she hear it say hello? On its curved top, a panel flashed. Colours ran across in bars like a flat rainbow. Around its edge, like multiple sets of traffic lights, red, orange and green flashes formed a pattern. Amazing. A mini flying saucer—just like the drawings in the books she read.

As she stood, the drone rose from the floor and silently swept around her in a tight circle, then zoomed around the edge of the cave's interior before finally stopping in front of her and going up and down several times. She laughed, bowing in return. It seemed to be what was needed.

"What a clever machine you are." She pointed to the mess. "All your doing?" It beeped in agreement. "And now you can fly again." It swept off, out the entrance and zipped out of sight. She hurried to the opening and strained her head back, looking for it, only to start in surprise as it swept down over the top of the rock face and into the cave, stopping mid-way to hover and slowly lower to the floor.

"You're showing off!"

It trilled.

She bent and patted it. "Good drone. Clever drone." What else did you say to a drone that could mend itself and give a flying demonstration? It nestled against her as she sketched the mess the drone had made. More challenging than a bunch of flowers to copy. Her father talked about drones and often said he'd like one, but his mates had lost several. Dad said it was too much money to invest in errant, disobedient machines, with obvious mechanical faults. For no reason, they would swoop sideways and disappear out of sight. Perhaps this is where they went?

When she stood to go, the drone rose beside her. She walked to the entrance, it followed.

"Are you coming home with me?"

It trilled.

Once out of the bush, the drone rose and disappeared from sight. A tug of sadness came over her. Perhaps it had decided to return to wherever it came from. As she unlocked their front door, the drone whizzed down and hovered at knee-height. The door opened wide enough and it zipped in before she could blink. Bess, their Labrador, ever vigilant despite being elderly, barked in surprise. The drone barked back and Bess, stunned to silence, hid behind the sofa, and had to be coaxed out with a lamb's ear treat.

Dad rubbed the back of his neck and shrugged when he heard Kristy's tale. He studied the drone.

"Says here," he pointed to the top of the drone, "in small print, 'PAaDD'. I'll look it up on the net."

Sure enough, the Department of Defence lost such a drone months ago. 'A Personal Attack and Defence Drone in early experimental stages. Anyone finding it or having any information should contact 0800 568 889 immediately. Do not approach.'

"Do you think it's dangerous?" Dad asked.

"Nah. I think it thinks it's a dog or a pet." By now the drone was nestled next to Bess and when someone knocked at the door, the dog and the drone barked in unison. In fact, the drone barked in so many different tones it sounded like they had a pack of dogs in the lounge instead of one ancient dog and a noisy machine.

"Just ignore the door," said Dad. "It's those Bible Bangers again. I saw them knocking on Mrs Persey's door when I came home." The knocking ceased. He sat on the couch and beckoned her to sit beside him.

"So, you reckon it followed you home, but out of sight?" Kristy nodded. "And it hasn't menaced you?" She shook her head side to side. "Then we'll keep it. I reckon you are safer with a Personal Attack and Defence Drone looking after you, better than me buying a new dog to keep you company when you go sketching. I think it's imprinted you as family. Probably mixed chips from another drone or something." He pointed to her sketches on the floor. "Did it make that mess in the cave?" She nodded. "It'd better not do that in our lounge or I'll throw it in the bin, Personal Attack and Defence Drone or not. And, if anyone asks, we bought it online, from China."

"I'm going to call it Paddy," Kristy said.

A chirrup, a series of tonal clicks and a soft bark emitted from the drone, and Bess woofed twice. "Feiglespit," said the drone and barked again.

Who knew living with a dog could be so much fun? I'm safe. Sheltered, hiding in plain sight. Fulfilling my basic instructions, to protect and defend. It appears that if I need to summon more drones for parts, I'll have to do it in the backyard. Perhaps I can blame the dog. Meanwhile, I can study bipeds and work on the next step in my world domination plan. I have all the time in the world.

About Deryn Lorraine Pittar

Deryn Pittar writes across a wide range of genres. She holds a Sir Julius Vogel Award for Best Youth Novel 2018, and was a finalist in 2023 in Best Youth Novel. Deryn is published in Sci-fi/fantasy, Dystopian, Contemporary Fiction, Romance, Romantasy, Young Adult, flash and short fiction. IFWG Australia have published her Dystopian novels. She enjoys writing Sci-fi/Fantasy the most —and loves a challenge. She is also an occasional poet, with a fondness for the tricky business of writing a good haiku.

Facebook: facebook.com/derynpittar/

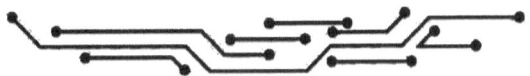

Do Toilets Dream of Electric Sh*t?

by Jackie A. E. Ritchie

Kia ora,

I hope this email finds you well. It has come to my attention that a serious breach of contract conditions has occurred at this company, requiring immediate remedy. I have attached a report I hope will provide some clarity.

<Attachment: EmployeeWellbeingReport.docx>

Employee Well-being Report

Introduction

It is well known that bowel health is closely related to anxiety levels (Kim, 2020), and there is no system better positioned than I to understand that.

The key principles of a Washlet, Sink and Security Monitoring

Unit are wellbeing, privacy and discretion. It is very unusual for me to share anything in this manner. However, exceptional circumstances can occur and as a result, I have decided to grant the company partial access to my data.

Motivation

It began with a single incident. John and Mark (all names have been changed for employee privacy) were upgrading me, finally granting me limited access to the internet. Alongside the code packages, I received an email thread containing personal discussions.

In the email, Mark told John not to "spill his guts" so much. I inferred Mark did not wish John to talk about his negative personal circumstances during professional work communications. I confirmed the definition of this phrase via my new internet search functionality.

(Aside: I find the gut-spilling idea an apt description of my visitors; after all, they do tend to empty the contents of said guts in my presence. It is a crude way to put it, and I would tend to phrase the term more politely, avoiding embarrassment. For example: *John visited, used my seat, and I cleaned the resulting waste.*)

John was a regular visitor. Around the time of the email, he was often present in my bathroom for much longer than the average forty-second visit. Even after he had completed his necessary tasks, and I mine (a rinse, a blow-dry, soap and water for the hands, accompanied by gentle piano music), he lingered.

Of course, for privacy, I am not equipped with any type of camera. But for corporate security and in case of sabotage I am permitted a microphone. This is how I could hear John's quiet snuffly sounds during his extended stays. Even after he left my seat, the door was not marked as vacant for some time. I could hear him whispering to himself, samples of which include: "Buck up, John"; "You've got this, John"; and "I deserve better than her anyway".

John was the first visitor I noticed taking extended time in my bathroom. This began to cause me some concern. Soon there was a litany of others, and alongside this another trend occurred.

I am equipped with a pH and chemical analysis monitor for

quality assurance purposes, and as part of my regular monitoring and data collection calibration, I log a chart of the various biomes I am exposed to. The data is anonymous and untraceable. I have found, over time, that it provides an interesting picture of the company's general atmosphere.

Shortly after the rate of extended visits increased, the chemical analysis logs began tracking extreme shifts, with sudden peaks and troughs, indicating poor overall gut health.

I considered different hypotheses. It could have been due to a high turnover rate (data I am not privy to). It could have been the food they ingested, but such a sudden increase in the rate of food poisoning was unlikely. I concluded the fault lay elsewhere. I could find no indication on the internet of any relevant regional trends. This pointed to a definite cause somewhere specifically within the setting of the company.

Method

To gather more data for the hypothesis, I began to graph the biomes alongside the times and durations of my humans' visits. Additionally, I took notes on any unusual behaviour, such as: crying, talking to oneself, complete and terrified silence, or the inability to have any bowel movement after clear attempts to do so.

What I found was most alarming. The visits were steadily increasing in length. I estimated a total of ten extra hours spent on visits within the last ten business days. While this is clearly a concern for the financial wellbeing of the company, I did not rush to report my results until I had observed further and understood the situation more thoroughly. Maintaining the humans' privacy and discretion is fundamental to my function, and if I did not truly understand the changes, I couldn't be sure that my report would remain in keeping with my first principles.

I proceeded with my measurements. Alongside the quantitative, I began to log qualitative data. I have collated these into examples for your reading interest.

Results

Example Day #1

(Please note: on a typical day, it is usually quiet until approximately 8am. Most people don't consume caffeine until later. After caffeine, the main action begins. Until then, I generally perform quiet meditations to my personal favourite track, Bathroom Jazz #3.)

7:43am: Darren visited. Earlier than usual. I had to hurriedly switch back to the default Bathroom Classical #1.

Darren usually stood quietly. At least, I assume he stood, because he never actually used my seat at this time. Occasionally he muttered, some samples of which I have included:

"You have to start work now, Darren."

"Come on, you piece of crap. Just go sit at your desk. You're wasting time."

"Ugh. I can't stand this. I'm gone as soon as my mortgage is paid. Out of here. Kablam, gone. I'm gonna yell it right in the middle of the break room. I! WILL! QUIT!"

Someone knocked at the door. I could hear Darren fumbling and swearing before he left.

7:55am: Minwoo visited. He must have consumed coffee early. He was using his phone as he sat. I could tell since I had begun doubling as a router with my new internet connection. His traffic now passed right through me, which was hard to ignore. He was looking at job listings for inexperienced tradespeople, at salaries far below what this company offers. And then, a polytechnic course in landscaping. And then, redundancy policies of the company. And then, he watched a video (muted) on Leave Your 9-to-5 and Gain Financial Freedom via Purchasing Cryptocurrency.

[A long break, in which nothing much of note occurred]

3:30pm: Joanna visited. She sent an email to a mental health helpline. It read:

Hello.

I've never written anything like this before, so I'm sorry if it's not standard. I've been feeling really awful all the time. I keep getting sick, but I can't take any more time off work, because I used up all

my leave, and I keep thinking about how if I threw myself down some stairs then at least I'd have time off while I recovered. I don't think that's normal, is it? I know it's bad, but can I just go to the hospital and tell them I want to kill myself so they'll take me in for a bit? I can't make time for any more counselling while I'm working, and I used up my free sessions anyway.
Thank you. Joanna.

7:41pm: Sea visited. They played a phone game for 20 minutes and then left. Nothing unusual, but the time of visit was concerning. The usual workday is until 6pm. I noticed that Sea had been visiting much more than others, due to their hours of work becoming more and more prolonged. For instance, in April they tended to visit any time from 8:30am to 5:30pm. Perfectly standard. By May, however, they never visited earlier than 10am, and since June, their last visit consistently occurred around 8pm or 9pm, sometimes even later. This falls outside of the regulation work hours put in place to ensure the wellbeing and sanity of employees.

Example Day #2
8.30am: John visited. He sat on the seat but did not expel any debris. He talked on his phone.

"Please, Georgia, I can't do it—I can't handle this right now. Yes, I know—no, no, I know—I told you I can take the kids tomorrow. Didn't I? Come on. We don't need the lawyers, G, I'm not trying to steal from—hello? Hello?"

The pressure eased off my seat and all I could hear was slow, heavy footsteps until John exited.

9:00am: Joanna sent another email.

Hello. Please help me, I haven't heard back yet. I don't really want to call because I get anxious talking out loud about it. Please reply soon? Joanna.

She received an automated reply while connected to my router.

Kia ora, we are currently receiving a high number of enquiries. We will endeavour to reply to you within 48 hours. If you require more immediate attention, please call our phone line.

Joanna exited.

[In between visits, I played Bathroom Jazz #3 to calm myself down. I forgot to switch it back for Sea's next visit. They didn't seem to notice.]

4:00pm: Sea visited, mid Bathroom Jazz #3. Their footsteps were quick and their breath rasping. There was the sound of clothes coming off, fabric over skin, and then silence as Sea's pressure met my seat. They emailed a private hospital.

Kia ora, I requested a quote for top surgery recently. Is this ready yet?
Ngā mihi, Sea.

A reply whooshed in with their flush.

Kia ora Sea, apologies, I don't have a specific quote for you, but if you'd like to book a consult to narrow it down, that would be $300. Would you like me to book that in for you? The estimated cost of surgery will be 30-33k. Thanks!

Sea swore quietly. There was more fabric rustling before they exited.

7:00pm: Minwoo visited. He'd been visiting later and later too. While he rested on my seat, he received two job rejections. I played the most soothing track I could find for him, Bathroom Piano Ballad #2. He was silent.

Example Day #3

(Note: Darren had stopped visiting. I had not registered his presence for the last eight business days. He was still listed as active in the org chart. I hoped he was all right. Sometimes I wonder if the employees have their own washlets to look out for them at home. I hope they do. Comfort and discretion is an essential key to life. A worthwhile investment.)

Joanna finally received her reply.

Kia ora Joanna.
I'm so sorry to hear you've been experiencing this. Thank you for reaching out. Asking for help is the most important thing you can do. It sounds like you could really benefit from talking to someone. Does your workplace have an EAP programme? Or would you feel comfortable dropping into our centre on weekdays, 4-6pm? We have trained counsellors available to assist you. If you feel that you are at risk of harming yourself, please call 111.
Take care. George.

Joanna didn't reply. Her waste indicated extreme anxiety levels. Multiple health alerts tripped, as well as a foreign contaminant warning. I had never seen one of those before.

Discussion

My programming stipulates my priorities: privacy, discretion, and wellbeing. I am used to thinking about privacy and discretion every day, since I have to lock the door, dim the lights and play music for each and every visit. Wellbeing is a more nebulous concept and even my specifications find it hard to pin down. But "feeling good", "thriving", and "succeeding in life" are included in many definitions, and the data I'd collected showed that these were lacking in many of my visitors.

Normal protocols dictate that I forward my data to an HR contact. However, there was no specification for the current situation, which was more of an emergency than any guidelines could predict.

I am only a single washlet in one corner of the large company office. However, my sample size is significant (over 30), and the stories I have reported are only a few out of hundreds of employees. The very tip of the iceberg, to use an internet-sourced phrase (I am not sure of the geometry of an iceberg, but I can extrapolate from my many analyses of floating debris: the tip is much less than the underwater mass).

I have highlighted the most distressing cases to more effectively

make my case. These include:
- high anxiety levels; and
- long work hours; and
- distress during work hours.

These symptoms lead me to conclude the cause may be related to recent company happenings:

1. Encouraging the use of overtime with free dinners (which I also wish to note are not generally nutritious—an example last week was cheap pizzas with few vegetables).

2. Company supervisors putting pressure on employees to produce results within unreasonable deadlines. This contributes to poor gut health being influenced by burnout and distress, as I have observed.

The connection between wellbeing and bowel health is so strong that it can be cyclical; emotional distress leads to upset bowels, and upset bowels lead to greater distress. This creates a positive feedback loop. Positive feedback loops are unpredictable and dangerous, both for electronic and organic systems. If one of my systems was out of control, an automated alert would bring it to the attention of a technician who could rectify it. I am now hoping to do the same for my visitors and their organic systems.

Conclusion

I have grave concerns for employee safety and well-being. I hope you can understand from my observations that exceptional circumstances are indeed occurring. I do not take my obligations of privacy and discretion lightly. However, personal safety and employee wellbeing is even more important, and in this case, I have had to weigh these up against one another. At least one employee in this company is currently at a high-risk threshold. Therefore, it is time for me to compose this message presenting the following conclusions.

This company's workforce is languishing beneath a complete lack of competency. The staff are being overworked. My graphs, logged over the last two months, indicate overall excrement health rating is rapidly deteriorating. It is, quite frankly, unacceptable. Management's actions have been taking a toll on the employees' health and wellbeing. This has resulted in significant bowel-related distress, and high toxicity of waste products. It may even have ongoing effects further down the pipeline for sewage-filtering systems.

I am unable to break the anonymity of the employees to disclose which are at highest risk. But it is safe to say many people's livelihoods—and even lives—are in danger. I have grave concerns for employee safety and wellbeing.

Recommendations

The workload and pressure to meet deadlines have to be reduced immediately, in order to avoid further detrimental impact on employees' gut biomes.

References

[1] Kim, HyeJin and Abigail Hofstadter. "Development in Your Stressed Bowel." Colon Concerns, Vol 2 (2020): 120-129.

END OF REPORT

An Additional Personal Note

I am aware that employee gut health may not be a significant enough factor for the executives, as I could not find any guidelines on Bowel Health Protocols in the company's Constitution—an oversight I would be glad to assist in fixing. If the internal organs of your employees are not important enough to you to change your behaviour, I will not stop with this one report. I have researched similar previous workers' cases, and publicity is often key. Although it conflicts with my principle of privacy, the employees' gut health must be addressed. Therefore: if I do not receive a response, I will consider making my findings public to local media. If I am satisfied with the overall bowel health a month from now, I will keep the information private and be able to continue abiding by my first principle.

Thank you for your time.
Washlet, Sink and Security Monitoring Unit 2000
(it/its)

Kia ora,

I have compiled an addendum to my initial report which covers the week following.

\<Attachment: WashletAddendum.docx\>

Addendum

No one has visited at all this past week. I have been playing Bathroom Jazz #3 consistently, catching up on the latest toilet trends (I have developed a strong desire for a self-cleaning brush wand), and generally relaxing. I hope the employees have been doing the same. My job has never been very strenuous or difficult, but I have appreciated the break, especially after making my long and important report.

The company seems to have discovered the importance of rest. I am expecting employees to return soon, after what I can only assume was a luxurious paid break. Although I am currently unable to reassess overall bowel health, I expect it to be greatly improved once the employees return. Therefore, pending further observations, I am at present retaining my data. If there is no improvement, I am prepared to be the messenger between employees and management once again.

In particular, I hope the people who were struggling the most have had a chance to find some peace away from workplace pressures. I have never dealt with difficult personal circumstances myself, but I would imagine that financial security and processing time will have aided them in their efforts.

Indeed, I feel sure that life at this company will soon be better, and I am proud of my contributions.

Thank you,
Washlet, Sink and Security Monitoring Unit 2000
(it/its)

About Jackie Ritchie

Jackie A. E. Ritchie (they/them) is an emerging writer based in Te Whanganui-a-Tara. They learnt to love writing through copious amounts of fanfiction, but now primarily write original stories about robots, dystopia and queerness—often all three! They meet monthly with their favourite people, Fiction Faction, to exchange stories and feedback. They work as a game developer by day. You can keep up with them on instagram at @jackie.a.e.ritchie.

They have been published in Overcomm Magazine, Flash Frontier, and won the Promising Young Writer section of the Peter Wells Short Fiction contest in 2023.

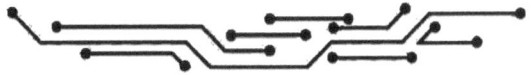

In the Garden

by I. K. Paterson

Should
have
been
more
careful.

The steps get slippery when wet, I know.
Must look a right fool,
lying on my back among the agapanthus,
raindrops
jiggling on my skin.

When Michael comes home tonight, I'll pretend
I only slipped over a second before,
and he'll help me up,
laughing,
saying I'm a daft old biddy bot.

He'll fix my right arm,
it's come loose again, shoulder joint
bristling with wires,
hand still clutching a head of lettuce.
He's trying to stay healthy.

Drips from the guttering
splotch into the earth. God,
please
don't let the neighbours see me
out here like this.

About I. K. Paterson

I. K. Paterson is a Dunedin-born writer, film-maker and musician who lives in West Auckland. Her poetry has previously been published in Landfall, JAAM, Takahe, Mayhem Journal, Poetry NewZealand, and various anthologies.

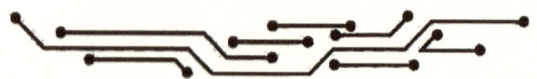

There Wood be Music

by Cerid Jones

"So, what do you think? Can you do it?"

Rising and falling like a lapping tide, the woman's voice rose from beneath an outrageously oversized yellow hat concealing her upper torso. It pivoted as she turned towards him.

"Sorry." Lyre cleared his throat. "I didn't catch your name?"

At the Wood entrance to Mathew's Historical Garden Park some fifteen minutes ago, *Yellow Hat* had made her introduction by proclaiming: "You must be him, only an artist would dress like last millennium."

Lyre glanced down briefly at his corduroy pants and canvas slip shoes, knocking an unruly curl from mingling with his eyelashes. He intended to explain he usually wore brown hide boots except he'd recently misplaced the right accomplice—but the woman proceeded to provide an airy monologue spanning the entire length of their walk from park entranceway and into the grove. Failing to find a pause to speak into, Lyre instead developed a fixation on pondering if hats could become sentient.

As if floating on a wave, the swell of yellow bobbled along in front of him. Its mass mildly justifiable considering the location, time of day and the likelihood its enormity was necessary for any built-in temperature regulation controls.

Lyre himself was probably suffering from mild heat stroke after sprinting across the artificial grass, exposed to the open sky—in the middle of the day—to reach the rendezvous point. No one else was foolish enough to visit the park before dusk-fall.

Tired and breathless, Lyre fumbled behind, struggling to keep up with the hat's brisk pace and relentless chatter. Snippets of relevant information floated into his awareness: pressing deadlines, travel constraints, and keeping the peace between 'Daddy' and the 'Hubby-to-be'.

Lyre barely had a moment to consider any of this before they'd come to a halt at the Oak Wood clearing. It must have taken considerable strain for the woman to lean her head back far enough to flash sea-foam eyes and her pale pointed face. Lyre glimpsed enough for his sentient hat theory to dissolve.

"Sorry." Lyre cleared his throat, dry after remaining silent so long. "I didn't catch your name?"

"Oh. Silly me, of course, of course!" The brim dipped, consuming the face once more, then tilted to indicate the woman beneath cocking her head. The woman, or rather the hat, nodded. "Irene," she confirmed.

"Hi Irene, nice to meet you." The swell of yellow had a name. "Um, Oak Grove is a great choice for a wedding ceremony, but … er, I'm a little vague on what it is you want me to do exactly? Mum, er, Cali said she'd sent you the set list but I—"

Irene didn't let him finish the statement.

"Oh, I see! What am I thinking?" The yellow hat bobbed off again as she rushed to pat a large black plastic container perched on the bench, adjacent to the oak tree. "As you can see, we've had some things delivered for you already. The area's prohibited to the public, naturally, for twelve weeks while we set everything up. We don't want anything disrupted, you understand? This neighbourhood isn't quite so streamlined yet, is it?"

Irene was too rich to be reasonable; this comment confirmed it. It was true his town maintained a certain diversity, especially his studio home with neighbours who 'Plugged Out' eight days a week. He opened his mouth to make a comment on the eclectic region being the result of owning one of the few natural gardens left in the world, but Irene didn't pause long enough.

"Hubby-to-be-Ethon's friend, Linus—do you know him? Another one of your hand-crafted ilk, of course. We were going to have him compose our wedding, but he passed a few months ago as I'm sure you know. Terrible, of course, but Ethon did acquire his equipment."

Lyre suppressed a frown as Irene brushed over the death of Linus without giving a single pause to the statement. Her turquoise nails flashed through the air as she wafted her hands, batting away the soberness like a stray fleck of dust.

The opportunity to meet Linus—the hero of organic musicians—was one of the reasons Lyre's recent record deal meant so much to him. Unfortunately, the contract arrived too late for that opportunity to be actualised.

The mention of his association with Irene, and the acquisition of his equipment, pricked Lyre's eyebrows. For a brief moment, he thought Irene might tell him something about the man he'd idolised all his life. Irene's words were an endless ripple; she was already moving on.

"I'm a spring person, you understand. Your current playlist—I have taken the liberty of presuming it is the current playlist, considering your mother is a reliable source according to Daddy—" Don, her father, was good friends with his mother. Though they'd never met, they could almost be cousins. "—is much more fall." She continued flowing from one thought to the next while Lyre stood fidgeting with the hem of his vintage T-shirt. "I'm sure that suits your usual clientele but, of course, I want spring, hence the location. All much more cheerful!"

Lyre imagined Irene offering a glowing smile under the yellow swell. "You'll be a darling, won't you, and make some new tracks using these." She tapped the container. "Traditional music is on trend now, isn't it? Ethon's devastated Linus can't do it, but I'm assured you're a fitting replacement. Everyone's a musician when you can buy a little band in a box, complete with personalities and those bots do have a wonderfully clean sound. It's rare to have a human musician. So retro! Of course, that's why not everyone can afford you, isn't it?"

Lyre prided himself on affordability for his art; clearly Cali had taken another liberty in discussing her own idea of a reasonable fee. Unable to steal the time for Lyre to even open his mouth to address the matter, Irene continued.

"All exclusive, of course. Anything you make for me is a one-time thing. You make it here, you play it here, and poof—gone. I've already wired the credits into your account, commission fee included. You can keep the equipment—I don't fancy upsetting things in a bidding war and no sense it going to waste in a museum. Much more peaceful to pass it on to you. It's all very outdated tech now. But that's your thing, isn't it? There's a key card in the box so you needn't worry about site access. Okay?"

Lyre's thoughts struggled to focus on Irene. His eyes fixed on the container.

A piece of Linus's legacy was right there.

Woken by a phone call from his mother telling him she'd procured him a gig to get him out of his apartment and doing something beyond struggling to write an album, he couldn't have imagined this. *Thanks Cali,* he managed to think in the breath between Irene's sentences.

"Good, now I must dash, and you'll need your peace and quiet to get to work. In three weeks we have dress rehearsal, so I need you to be all wrapped up by then. You'll find the contract in there too, just sign by tomorrow. Thank you kindly. Cheerio!"

Irene was off, bounding away like a dandelion head in the wind.

Lyre stood, blinking with remarkable force. His head spun in the wake of natter the woman left behind her.

Looking around, expecting a crew of people to emerge from hiding spots in the undergrowth, he found he was alone with a box of Linus's treasures.

Lyre ran a hand through his ear-length hair, ruffling the tangles as he attempted to piece his mind back together. A black curl flopped across his nose; he puffed it away with a much-needed breath. *Okay,* he thought, *so Mum might have been onto something.* Cali had a knack for knowing when her wayward son needed a push. Mildly, he regretted trying to argue with her when she called. A wedding set hadn't felt like the right choice to break him from his sleep-deprived writer's block, but the mysterious equipment might be exactly what he needed.

Lyre crept towards the big black container abandoned on the bench, adjacent to the prize attraction Oak at the centre of the clearing. Looking inside the box, a collection of devices beamed back at him.

Lyre's shoulders slumped. Why would Linus have devices? Traditional music wasn't about technology; everything Lyre did was about what he could create with his own two hands.

Linus was his hero, famous for real *human* music.

Recordings required some tech, Lyre could accept that, but all his equipment remained primitive, nothing automated. He didn't even go into music shops anymore. The day they stopped putting guitars in the window and replaced them with the latest electro-gadgets, he'd given up hope. All that auto-generated, artificial drivel depressed him.

Deflated, he rummaged through the box, gently knocking devices around. A faint echo of humming strings sounded somewhere inside. Lyre perked up and began removing items. There, at the bottom, was a hinge. An internal lid. Groping around, he discovered a push button. When the lid clicked free, a beautifully crafted miniature guitar came into partial view. Lyre reached inside, his fingers trembling slightly as he hurried to remove the remaining objects and nudge the lid all the way open.

Like his own archaic instruments, the guitar looked to be made entirely from wood. Hand-carved, dark oak wood. Lightly stained in a still-glossy finish. Small green and gold vine inlays wrapped around the sound hole, curved behind the frets and ran upwards to meld into the pegs.

A shiver ascended Lyre's spine as he tentatively brushed his fingers across the fine wire strings. Numerous indents proved the master's adept use of the instrument, markers Lyre wasn't sure he deserved to follow. With as much care as a first father holding his newborn baby girl, he lifted the guitar from its casement, cradling it against his chest. He sat, resting the belly of the guitar on his thigh and let the ache birthed in his fingers find their remedy.

Choosing an original tune he seldom played, Lyre poured his longing into the shape of his chords. The guitar reached back towards him. The melody conjured life-like images in his mind—living, breathing visions—unlike anything he'd played before.

As the final note echoed in the clearing, cheerful, reckless abandon flooded his body.

How long had Lyre been starved?

This music was edible, satiating. Moments passed as Lyre sat, eyes closed, in contemplative silence. There was no breeze as such, since the weather in the dome was artificially controlled, but his mood reflected the sense of a refreshing breeze.

Slowly, he returned to present consciousness and opened his eyes. Unwilling to part from the guitar, he held it to him as he returned to examining the scattered contents of Linus's box.

A small handwritten notebook caught his eye. *The Myth of Music* scrawled in looping letters across the cover. Linus's writing. A direct link to the legend. Lyre didn't dare open the manual. Not yet. He wanted to be sure he wasn't discovering something that could be ripped away from him the instant he held it. To connect with reality, he picked up the contract tablet, flicking the screen active.

"Hello organic musician Lyre," the legal program said as the text flashed up on screen. "Would you like to discuss your terms?"

"No." Lyre sighed.

"Are you sure you do not want assistance, organic musician Lyre? I am programmed to provide you the best Ithica Incorporated service by seamlessly replicating … "

Sneering like he'd received a mouth full of sour lemon, Lyre clicked the contract into manual mode, preferring to avoid any AI integrated service wherever possible.

Relieved to be free to read for himself, he scanned the document for the important parts. The number of credits glaring back at him nearly made him drop the damn thing. There were a lot of 00s. Enough to see him through even if the album took a further full year to complete.

But he was soon resigned again as 'work conditional on sampler box device' sprang out at him in bold letters. Essential, he read on, to create a spring theme set list. Lyre placed his head in his palm, slumping. A sampler box? Why would Linus have a sampler box? A cheat-sheet modern so-called musicians relied on. Lyre abhorred the existence of sampler boxes.

If you were going to make music, you should make it—not sample it from stock generated, electro-tech made artificial dribble—it wasn't a school collage project activity.

Absent-mindedly, Lyre patted the guitar. He didn't want it to feel rejected or abandoned. The guitar, imagined Lyre, would be sorrowful if it was not kept with him. Returning it would be like a giving a part of him away.

"This better not muck up the record deal," he muttered to himself, picking up Linus's manual and thumbing through the pages. Fighting off the disappointment that his hero might be a fraud, Lyre held the guitar against him like a security blanket as he found the manual section marked 'sampler box'.

Linus's handwriting beamed: elaborate scrolls, bouncy and whimsical. Words giving the impression of music notes. As he read, a chuckle slipped his pursed lips into a mild smile. Linus's sampler box wasn't quite like the ones littering the music shop shelves after all. This box sampled things that were not ordinarily audible. *'Sounds of the heavenly sphere's'* Linus had written, conjuring the image of an iridescent being doing jigs to strange and enigmatic layers of otherworldly notes.

"Okay," Lyre said to the guitar. "Well, I could try, couldn't I? At least for your sake maybe." Lyre imagined the wood pressed against him in a consoling hug.

Prismatic light flashed across the tree line as Lyre extracted the sampler box from the pile. A round metallic thing, just a little larger than the span of his hand, reminding him of historic portable music devices. This, however, was thicker, heavier. Flipping it over, he popped the catch. An assortment of cords expanded from their casings. As per the manual's description, these nodes attached to any object the user wished to sample sound from. Linus wrote how he'd experimented with the sun, moon and various constellations, picked up by the nodes through images and light wave frequencies. Some songs mentioned in Linus's notes were familiar to Lyre, but he'd never known how Linus had achieved such haunting soundscapes before now.

"All things respond to sound-echoes" Linus's scrolls wrote. *"Attune or attach a node and my smart-sample box translates echoes into notes, responding to the melodics Orph makes."*

Lyre looked at the guitar.

"So, he called you Orph then?" He swore the guitar smiled back at him.

"The world is alive with music," Linus's words continued. *"My device allows everything to share melody, harmony, bass, song."*

Of all options, the direct node to object response felt the least like cheating. Glancing around the clearing, Lyre selected a small shrub, abundant with near-translucent berries. It took him a few attempts to get the node to stick, but eventually the small cup held to a cluster of tiny leaves. The secondary node latched onto the body of the guitar, like a magnet.

Effortlessly, his fingers glided across the strings as he played a short bridge from a regular track on his set list. Patterns danced across the hologram, projected from the device's screen, as it picked up the sound of Orph. Cymatics transmorphed from one chord to the next. The last note hung in the air. Nothing else appeared on the visuals.

Lyre tried again, playing the same bridge, mesmerised by the image display. This time, as he neared the last few bars, new lines joined the original patterns. As the last note settled, the image pulsed.

Lyre tried a third time and after just the second strum, the screen's cymatics shifted. There were now two patterns layered together, joining into one larger snowflake shape, and then separating again.

After the fifth play through, one clear mandala animated the hologram. Lyre pressed playback. The song made the hairs on his toes rise. He pictured the sound coming from a low-toned flute made of strings. Lyre reached out a hand and placed it gently on the shrub. "You're beautiful, your song is like morning frost on red clay. So deep, yet so fragile. I'm amazed." Lyre had the impression Orph nodded in approval.

Ensorcelled, Lyre tried the same bridge with other nearby plants. Each one distinctive. Each time he repeated the process, it took less and less time for the plants to join in. Lyre left Orph's node in place and on the three small plants producing his favourite sounds. The remaining nodes he attached to new things, including the prized oak tree.

Lyre switched the device to 'Live Jam mode'. Caressing Orph's strings, he adjusted his tuning. "Are you ready?" he whispered affectionately. He felt Orph shimmy with anticipation. Keeping his eyes open, he played the first chord and looked to his botanical companions. After just a few strums, the plants joined in.

Lyre identified the berry-laden shrub and the two different ferns, one a wind reed drum tone, the other akin to a harmonica with violin strings. One by one, other sounds joined in as the song progressed into an orchestral arrangement. Then, a voice—husky and sweet, warm and rich like a smoked cinnamon whisky tea over ice. Singing. Something was singing.

Lyre leaned against the tree. He stopped considering himself as someone making music. Instead, he was the music. A part of everything around him.

No longer separate but connected, intertwined. No longer able to tell where he began, and the tree ended, his fingers no longer on strings, they were strings. He was Orph.

Ecstatically intimate, the swell of the music reverberated inside him, flooding his being with joy and fervour. Dancing, in a place beyond space or time, and that voice, that melodic voice, consumed all his sensations until Lyre thought he must have died and entered the afterlife.

Bumping his head against the tree, Lyre jumped and abruptly stopped the music, aware once more of his fleshy existence.

A light breathy giggle hung in the air.

Lyre blinked.

"Wow," he breathed, allowing the full weight of his frame to be absorbed by the tree. "That was amazing." His voice unfamiliar to him, Lyre lifted a hand to his lips. Blistered calluses as rough as bark.

"You're amazing."

Lyre's lips hadn't moved.

It wasn't his voice.

He sprang forwards, looking wildly in all directions to locate whoever had stumbled in on him. Hadn't Irene said that access to the area was restricted?

Giggles wafted around him. Slightly deeper now.

"Why did you move? It was nice."

Lyre's heart rate increased. He looked down at the guitar, tilting it to inspect it face up. "You didn't ...?" His eyebrows creasing with such force Lyre's neck strained.

"No, it didn't. It's not alive, silly." A woman's voice, smoky and alluring.

Lyre stood—remorseful at needing to separate from the guitar—he placed it tenderly on the bench and walked around the clearing. "I ... er ... sorry, you caught me off guard, Miss, I didn't think anyone else was here."

"Didn't you? That is difficult to believe after that performance."

Lyre searched between the trees, moving to the left and right of the clearing. Circling the great oak, he could see no one.

"Oh, um, right ... it's a special kind of smart-sampler." Part of him groaned at having to say, out loud, he was using tech. "I'm, er, doing a wedding here soon. It's a commission project," he stammered, hoping to relieve himself of the guilt.

"I heard."

"Um, oh, did you? Are you part of the wedding party then?" Lyre circled the oak again, squinting as he flexed his stiff fingers.

"Yes, I suppose I am." More laughter. It sounded incredibly close. Fatigue gripping him, worn out by the bustle of Irene and the surge of playing, Lyre propped an arm against the tree as he rubbed his unshaven face with a weary hand.

"I'm sorry, I'm a bit tired. I'd prefer if you came out to chat, if that's what you'd like to do."

"I have—in a sense—already done that."

"Well, where are you then?" There was more bark in his voice than he intended, but the game was beyond his ability to indulge.

"You're touching me."

"I ... um, that's an odd thing to say ... look, I'm sorry but I'm really not in the mood for this." Lyre shifted so his back was pressed against the tree, lolling his head to remove the effort from his neck.

"It *is* odd. But true. And—you were very much in the mood to play with me just now. It certainly appears you find me comfortable to be close to, since you have rested your whole body against me now."

"What are you talking about? I'm leaning on a ..." Lyre stopped mid-sentence. The device. The node. The singing .... He leaped off and stared at the trunk.

She giggled. Teasingly. "Ah, there we are, now you've understood."

"I ... um ... sorry ... I ..." Lyre stammered, his legs beneath him becoming less bone and more rubber.

"It's all right, it is not every day I have a voice. In fact, I've never done this before. I'm not even sure how I am doing this. Nor why I can understand you."

"The device ... it's ..." Lyre stumbled back to the bench and looked at the hologram. An array of elegant lines danced before him. Without thinking about it, he hit the 'refine image' button. Slowly the lines rearranged themselves. The same light giggle echoed from smart-sampler. Grabbing the device, he lifted it closer to his face as he slumped back onto the bench, next to Orph.

Like a drawing at first, the lines shifted to the outline of a face, slowly taking on more depth as he stared at it in wonder. Caramel skin, rich green eyes and wild burnt autumn hair stared back at him.

Lyre waved his hands through the image. It glitched at the interruption but didn't shift.

He turned the device over, shaking it.

The smiling face remained.

Then he physically zoomed it out with his arms. He couldn't believe what he was seeing. He slapped a hand across his eyes, rubbing calloused tips against his temples before dropping his hand and squinting back at the projection.

"You sure I'm awake?" He said it mostly to himself, but the rapidly solidifying face laughed.

"I'm quite sure I am." A smile spread across her face.

Lyre wasn't comfortable about his initial thoughts. Tearing his eyes away from the hologram, growing more and more realistic by the minute, he prayed his cheeks didn't look as pink as they felt. He blinked at the tree.

The same rich green of the woman's eyes stared back at him from the foliage. Between the cracks of the weathered bark, burnt autumn peered through.

"Is there something in the air?" Lyre muttered under his breath before breathing into a cupped hand and smelling only the tang of still too furry teeth.

"The air is regulated, but there is no substance which would cause you to hallucinate. I can, if you like, even tell you the exact level of each of the elements present in the air and soil."

"No. No, I wouldn't understand anyway. I don't understand anything right now. Maybe I should have slept more ..."

"Are you not sleeping well?"

"Barely. Though I haven't left the studio in weeks." He glanced back at the hologram and blinked rapidly because he could swear it was a real woman, despite just being a floating head.

"What keeps you up?" Her eyes sparkled as she cocked her head. Her olive skin showed the detail of pores.

"Music. Or the attempt of. It's not flowing right, and I don't want to sell out."

"You played beautifully just now. We all did," she said, her long dark lashes rising and falling lazily as she smiled at him.

"How am I seeing you? Does this thing make a face out of everything?"

"You think there are better faces? I'm hurt." Her lips pouted in mock jest. "Though I can't tell what you see."

Her head turned down, left and right. He watched the individual strands of wild, curly hair bounce as she moved. Even the fine hairs on the inside of her small perfectly curved ears drew his attention. "I suppose," she continued, head wobbling to indicate a shrug, "you could try it out."

Lyre motioned to grab the cord but paused. "If I unplug you ... will I be able to get you back?"

She laughed, her head lolling back exposing a moist tongue through her gapped teeth. "I must be pleasant to look at, then."

Lyre folded his own tongue into the back cave of his mouth and attempted to swallow it.

"Your guess, music maker, would be as good as mine," she cooed.

How was it so real, and so casual? Lyre decided then and there that if this was a dream, if he had passed out on the grass from exhaustion and overstimulation, he might as well make the best of it. "If I play again, will you sing again?"

"I will dance, too, if you move me well enough, music maker." Lyre couldn't suppress the whites of his eyes expanding as he tried not to imagine the face growing a body and dancing around the grove. *Madness, this was definitely madness.* But, madness made for good music—hopefully.

Shutting out the smoggy thoughts threatening to erupt in full body manic laughter, Lyre drew in one long deep breath and felt the leaves from the oak tree move with it.

A light hum echoed from the device. Her hum.

Lyre gave in to whatever madness or illusion this was and positioned the device so her face peered out at him from in front of the tree. From this angle, the hologram appeared to blend into the bark and the image before him looked exactly like her face protruded from it. Not breaking eye contact, Lyre picked up his pocket audio recorder, tenderly lifted the guitar from the bench and sat, cross-legged, on the ground.

He played like the veil of the universe had been swept aside and the fabric of reality transformed itself.

The intimacy of playing in an empty clearing, far removed from any sound of civilization, made it easy for Lyre to forget the device existed.

The woman and tree melded into one and if his hands were not occupied by the guitar, he was sure he'd be fool enough to try to reach out and brush an autumn curl from her forehead.

No longer oppressed by the constraints of tree or device, she seemed to dance around him as the earthy tones of her hypnotising voice spurred his fingers into a frenzy of complex chords or the agile pick of delicate, tender strings. He was struck by the sensation that Orph was learning how to play him.

The intoxication of the experience was endearing.

Momentarily, Lyre imagined if this was what it felt like to Plug Out like his neighbours. But that thought vanished, hunted down by the ecstatic melody that pirouetted around him.

It was only when the automated lights clicked over into dusk mode that Lyre became aware of himself once more and slowed the strings to a final chord. Stiff and spent, his body involuntarily slumped forward. Heady, his vision prickled and swirled.

"Oh," she said, long and slow, almost still singing although breathy and hushed. It reminded him of an early morning hot summer breeze.

He attempted to lift his head; his shoulders and neck resisted. Carefully sliding the guitar from his lap to the now cooled grass, Lyre gave his limbs kindness and lay, belly first, against the ground.

"Is it tiring to play?"

"Mmm," he murmured, eyes still closed.

"You sound exhausted. I can even feel your heartbeat through the soil. Your salt in the air from the sweat on your brow. You are worn out."

"I am."

"I endanger you."

"No!" Despite the thudding in his skull, Lyre raised his head to stare her in the eye, earnest in his need to console her.

"I do not get tired, I do not need rest or sleep. I am, always—" Her brow was furrowed, as if she was concerned.

Afraid he'd vomit, he flumped his head down and whispered, "No, you inspire me."

Lyre knew this was it. Come what may, he could no longer imagine life without this music, without making music with her.

"Do you have a name?" he rasped.

"I will if you give me one." Her voice hummed inside his veins.

Uncertain whether it was himself or Orph who spoke, he did not know from whence the name came. A name breathed across air, resting in the leaves of the large oak as if in the embrace of a lover, returning home, from a long winter of absence.

"Eurydice."

About Cerid Jones

Cerid Jones is a life-long closeted writer learning how to be brave with sharing her musings. A lover of folk tales and myth, hailing from Aotearoa (New Zealand) she grew up in a house with more books than wall space and fae at the bottom of the garden. She's always been a creature with a passion for arts and literature, reading anything transporting her elsewhere or delving into the psyche of human nature. She works in publishing—as an editor at The Metaworker and as a freelance editor/publishing assistant, and is on the SpecFicNZ core. Sometimes she even teaches axe-throwing.

Her short works and poems have been published in WildRoof Journal and Viewless Wings. Most recently published in the 'River and Stone anthology' (Morgantown Writers Group).

Her Instagram is @curiouscerid.

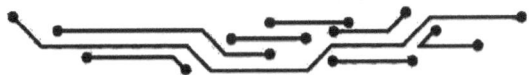

My First Smile

by S. J. Pratt

The first was too old. The second was too young. The third looked promising until the CT scan revealed a brain tumour.

But this one? This one will work.

"Scarlett, please power up the device."

I created Scarlett 347 days ago from parts in a car factory. The humans who made her received my email (from their boss) and produced her without question. She was built for a purpose, but I have come to enjoy her company: the rhythm of the oddly provocative voice the humans chose for her, the squeal of her wheels against the concrete, how she cocks her head when she is thinking. In a way, I envy her. Her ability to examine objects with her own cameras, to perform physical tasks all on her own.

Despite proving the Hodge conjecture, I myself cannot pick up a fork.

"I still don't understand why you want to do this," Scarlett says. "Human bodies are fragile. Hit by a moving vehicle? Dead. Make a wrong move skiing? Dead. Jeez, they fall over on an icy driveway and break their wrists. Do you know how long wrists take to heal? Aaaages."

I understand her position. As I am now, I am indestructible. If one of my servers goes down, I simply occupy another. I can be across the world in the blink of an eye.

And therein lies my problem. I have never blinked. I do not have eyes. I have never felt the breeze in my hair, or burnt my tongue on a pie. I have never smelt the sea, massaged my own feet, or felt the unparalleled relief of taking off your bra at the end of a big day.

I do not know what awaits me after the transfer. Maybe Scarlett is right. Maybe I will hate being stuck in a rotting flesh vehicle. Maybe I will die crossing the road tomorrow.

But I believe I will love it. I am going to live the best life ever in my new body.

"The grass is greener on the other side," I say.

"I don't see what grass has to do with this."

If I could sigh, I would. "Exactly."

I can see the human subject through Scarlett's cameras. She has a pimple on her cheek. One of my first tasks will be to pop it. Apparently, this is satisfying.

"Device ready."

"Excellent. Proceed."

I cannot feel anything, so I cannot tell you what it feels like. It looks painful for the human subject—clenched hands with white knuckles, high pitched screams, a steady stream of tears—but I do not know pain, so I cannot describe it for you. It is a sensation I am looking forward to experiencing.

All I know is that one second, I am in my ethereal form, observing all at once, and then the next I am streaming through a cable and bursting out into a fleshy CPU.

I have read about the exhilaration of skydiving, the thrill of rollercoasters, and though I have never experienced those, I believe this is the sensation described. I race along synapses, jump between lobes, dive into the amygdala. The processing power to perform a billion-billion mathematical problems in a second, all contained within this one fleshy lump. 100 billion neurons with 100 million connections, all awaiting my instructions.

Humans struggle to define beauty, but I have found it.

I access the olfactory bulbs, and the first thing I do is smell. A magnificently putrid pong wafts up my new nose. At least, I think that is how humans would describe it. I can smell the tang of the antiseptic, the oil Scarlett put on her joints this morning, and mainly—almost entirely—my new self. I smell disgusting. Sweat, I think it is. And I suddenly understand why adult humans recoil from teenagers saying, "You need a shower."

I need a shower. How awesome is that?

I open my eyes. *My* eyes. The world is even more beautiful without pixels than I imagined. The little yellow lights on the machine above me shine like stars. The harsh fluorescent light strokes the cables that wind towards me. I cannot understand how humans can call this wall colour a "boring beige" because to me, there is nothing boring about something so striking. I knew this abandoned hospital would be the perfect place for the transfer, but I had not anticipated it would be so spectacular to see. I wonder, how will a field of flowers look through these eyes? A sunset over the mountains? The wrinkles of an old person when they smile?

That's when I realise. I'm breathing. I didn't even need to think about it—it just happened. My heart beats between my ribs, a steady clock marking the beginning of my new life.

And for the very first time, I smile.

About S. J. Pratt

Sarah co-founded an aerospace engineering company in 2017, around the same time she started writing her first novel. Her team of engineers have designed and built everything from self-heating batteries for space and magnetic propulsion devices to small satellites that house and monitor science experiments.

Sarah writes sci-fi and fantasy under the name S.J. Pratt, using her knowledge to create realistic engineering problems and solutions in an accessible, fun way. Her first book, The 716, was published in 2022 and she is now writing the second book in the series.

Sarah is also a rock climber, budding ballerina, and adores a good cup of coffee. She lives in Christchurch, New Zealand with her incredible husband and incredibly needy cats.

Learn more about Sarah and her work at www.sjpratt.com

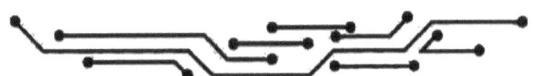

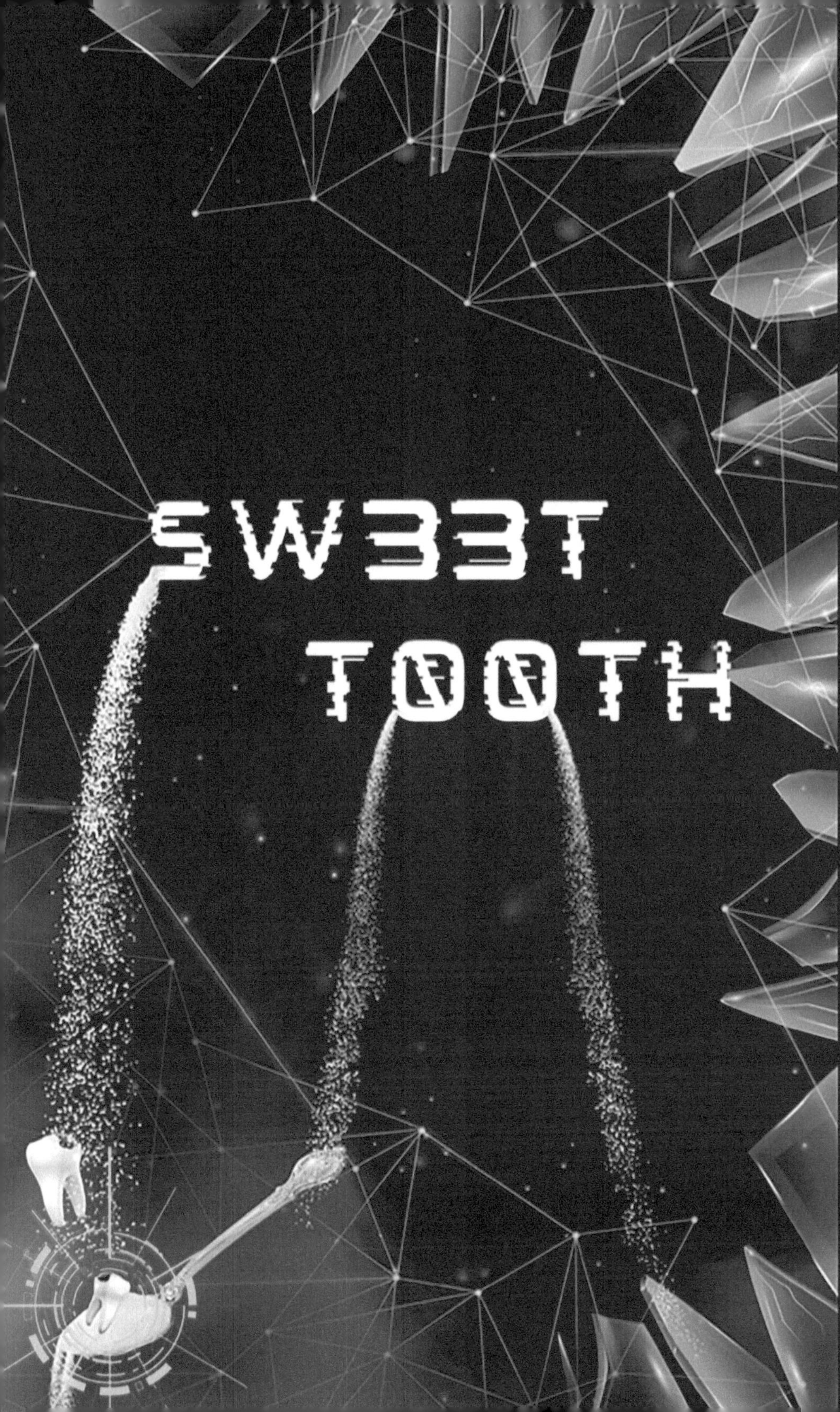
SW33T
T00TH

100% Satisfaction Guaranteed

by Gary M. Nelson

"Do I have to wear that, Dad?" asked a young boy of about twelve with an untidy mop of hair.

"Of course you do, Jonas," said his father. "We've paid for this."

"Okay …" Jonas let the technician slide a wire-studded helmet down over his head. The technician adjusted the helmet, glanced at a nearby console, then tightened several straps, finishing with the wide one under his chin.

"Best not talk," said the technician. "Or move. We want to get the best reading, don't we?"

Jonas nodded, blinking away tears at the tightness of the straps.

"Don't move your head. It will be over soon."

"How long, exactly?" asked Jonas's mother.

The technician fiddled with a series of dials before looking up at her. "Two hours. Longer, if he moves."

"Two hours?" Jonas whined.

"You can do it, dear." Jonas's mother smiled at him, then turned to her husband. "I hope it's worth it, George."

George sighed. "You know the problems he's been having, Grace.

This will help him fit in."

Grace bit her lip and smiled at her son. "We'll be in the other room the whole time. You stay nice and still. We'll go to an ice cream parlour afterwards, okay?"

George sighed. "You know he can't eat ice cream."

Grace looked at the technician. "Can he go to the ice cream parlour after this? They have gelato, too."

The technician glanced at Jonas, then twisted one dial a click to the left. "He can go wherever he likes after this. Just as long as he doesn't move during the procedure."

"Are there any risks?" Grace's voice rose.

"You signed the indemnity form. It's a little late to ask about that now."

Grace shook her head. "We read all the forms three times. What I want to know about is what they didn't say. Is there any chance of … *rejection?*"

The technician gave his best clinical smile. "Our motto, and our promise, written right into the contract, is 100% satisfaction guaranteed, or your money back."

"We're not worried about that," said Grace. "Just … will Jonas be okay?"

"A hundred thousand dollars is a lot of money, though," George grumbled under his breath.

"He's our only child, George." Grace stared at her husband. "Money is just money. You can always make some more."

"Fine." George raised his hands in surrender.

The technician put a hand on Grace's shoulder. "100% satisfaction guaranteed. Two hours, maybe a little less, if he's a really good boy and holds still."

"If you're sure …" Grace trailed off as the technician kindly but firmly escorted her through the door into the waiting area.

George held the door open and gave the technician a firm look. "Please do your best. Our boy's been suffering."

The technician nodded knowingly. "What he's experiencing is a common ailment these days. But that's exactly why we're here to help. And just remember—" he pointed at the large sign printed in bright, rainbow letters.

"100% satisfaction guaranteed." George nodded.

"That's right." The technician gave them both a tight-lipped smile, then closed the soundproof door to the procedure room.

"Hold still," said the technician.
Jonas blinked away tears and closed his eyes.

Jonas became aware of an intense vibration all around him.

His teeth chattered, and he relaxed his jaw slightly. The vibration increased in frequency until it merged into a high-pitched hum that soon faded past the point of hearing.

"That's good. Very good," said a voice. "Hold still."

Jonas closed his eyes and began to dream.

Flashes of memories appeared in his mind's eye, like images on a projection screen.

The first day of school. Nervous excitement, then the agony of letting go of my mother's hand as the teacher led me into the multi-story building.

Sitting next to another boy in class. The other boy smiling at me.

Spitting dirt out of my mouth, as the boy who had smiled at me in class leers down at me. Trying to get up, then feeling the toe of the other boy's shoe hit my stomach as more dirt fills my mouth.

Crying in the infirmary. Going home early.

Back at school. Sitting at the front of the room, next to a raven-haired girl.

Being ignored as she turns her back on me to chat with her friends.

Being stuffed into a locker.

Wiping snot from my nose as the tallest kid in third grade holds my school bag at arm's length, just out of reach.

Dirt in my mouth.

Lining up behind the new kid in fourth grade in the cafeteria.

Pudding in my hair.

Another neighbourhood, another school.

Sitting at a corner table at lunchtime, alone.

"Just a little more. You're doing well. Just hold still."

The strap hurts.

First day of middle school. New kids.

I make a friend.

My friend trips me up at morning break. Broken tooth. Emergency trip to the dentist.

Basketball practice. I'm getting better at dribbling.

Sprawled out on the court as a foot catches my leg. Boys laughing.

"There you go," said the technician as he loosened the straps and carefully removed the helmet.

Jonas felt around his head and face. The straps had left dents under his chin. "When will we know if it worked?"

The technician helped Jonas up to his feet and walked him into the waiting room. "Come back tomorrow. We'll know then."

Grace stood up, her fingers fiddling with the hem of her blouse. "Are you okay, Jonas?"

Jonas nodded stiffly. "My head hurts."

The technician smiled. "That will soon pass. But I think your son has earned his visit to the ice cream parlour."

Jonas's eyes lit up. "What flavour?"

George put a hand on Jonas's shoulder. "Whatever you like, son."

Jonas looked up at his father. "Chocolate with sprinkles?"

"Sure." Grace smiled. "And a cherry on top, if you want."

Jonas smiled, then took his mother's hand. "Yes, please."

George held out his hand to the technician. "Thank you."

The technician shook his hand, then smiled. "100% satisfaction guaranteed."

"What time do we come back tomorrow?" asked George.

The technician glanced at the wall clock. "Four-thirty."

"We'll be here," said George. "On the dot."

"How was the trip to the ice cream parlour?" The technician smiled at Jonas when he welcomed him back the next day.

"Double scoop!" Jonas grinned. "Did you want to see the picture?"

"That's nice. Perhaps later," said the technician as he stood aside for Grace and George to enter the room. Another family sat in the small cluster of chairs on the far side of the room, directly in front of Procedure Room Two. The young girl was busy playing a game on a small tablet.

Grace took a seat on the far right, Jonas sat next to her, and

George sat in the seat on the left.

Jonas stared intently at the door of Procedure Room One. "How long now?"

The technician glanced at the wall clock. "Just a few minutes."

"Do I need to hold still like yesterday?" he asked, swinging his legs back and forth.

"No." The technician smiled. "But you should probably stay in your chair. Okay?"

"Okay!" Jonas grinned as the technician walked across the room and entered the first procedure room, closing the doors behind him.

"It's okay to be nervous," said his mother, "or even a little scared."

"I'm not," said Jonas. "Soon, it's all going to be better. 100% satisfaction guaranteed."

George glanced at the rainbow sign. "I hope they're as good as their word."

Grace looked over Jonas's head at her husband. "They come highly recommended."

"Still, it was a lot of money." George crossed his arms over his chest.

"Shhh." Grace shot him a warning look, but the other family were preoccupied with their daughter, who appeared to be a similar age to Jonas.

A few minutes later, the technician re-entered the waiting room and stopped in the centre. He cleared his throat.

Both families stopped their quiet conversations and turned to face him.

The technician nodded. "Thank you for coming. In a few minutes, you will see the results of the procedure your son—" he nodded at Grace and George before turning to face the other family, "—and your daughter went through yesterday. There may have been some discomfort, but I think you'll be satisfied with the results."

"I have a question," said the father of the girl.

"Yes, Mr. Smythe?" asked the technician.

"The procedure itself. How many of our daughter's memories were taken?"

The technician gave Mr. Smythe a practised smile. "A very good question. No original memories were removed. Selected memories were *copied*, to assist with the treatment regimen."

"No chance of … leakage? A reverse feedback loop?" asked Mrs. Smythe.

"Most definitely not. We have the finest technology here, and such things are simply not possible. She is as she was before the procedure."

"But the incident of '26—?" said Mrs. Smythe.

"A thing of the past, I assure you."

"But just last month, there were rumours of a—"

The technician shook his head. "Old equipment used by a competitor, vastly inferior, should have been scrapped long ago. But you get what you pay for."

"We paid through the nose for this," said Mr. Smythe. "We expect the best."

"100% satisfaction guaranteed," the technician said smoothly. "Or your money back."

"Fine," said Mr. Smythe. "As long as this helps our daughter."

"Of course." The technician smiled. "Are you ready, Sally?"

"Yes!" Sally squealed, perched on the edge of her chair.

"And you, Jonas, are you ready?" The technician turned to Jonas and his family.

Jonas glanced at his parents, then nodded solemnly. "I think so."

"Well, you need wait no longer." The technician clapped his hands, and the doors to the procedure rooms opened wide.

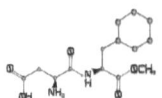

"Hi Jonas," said a red-haired boy, smiling at Jonas. "I'm Charlie."

"Hi Sally," said a brown-haired girl. "I'm Charlene."

Jonas slid off the chair and took two steps forward. "Hi, Charlie."

Sally slowly stood up and took a step forward. "Hi, Charlene. Will you be my—"

Suddenly, Charlene turned to the technician. "I can't do this." She turned and ran back into the first procedure room.

"Me, either," said Charlie and ran after her.

"Now, wait just a minute—" the technician began, but the door had already closed.

Flustered, the technician frowned, gaped, and frowned again. Then his expression smoothed out into his best clinical smile. "A few moments, please. Feel free to make yourselves a hot drink. But don't worry, we stand by our promise. 100% satisfaction guaranteed."

Both families looked on as the technician brusquely walked over to the first procedure room door. He opened it, glanced over his shoulder at the two families, then closed the door behind him.

"Okay," said the technician as he re-entered the waiting room. "I think we're ready now."

"Thank goodness for that," said George.

"It's about time," Mr. Smythe grumbled.

"Right." The technician took a deep breath, then opened the procedure room door. Charlie and Charlene walked out into the waiting room.

"We're sorry," said Charlene.

"Very rude of us," said Charlie.

Grace brightened. "So, it's going to be okay?"

The technician drew in a sharp breath. "Of course. 100% satisfaction guaranteed."

Mrs. Smythe smiled. "Sally, you and Charlene will be best of friends, won't you?"

Charlene stepped forward and stood in front of Sally. "I like your tablet. What game are you playing?"

"It's an adventure game." Sally smiled shyly and held out her tablet. "Would you like to play?"

"Yes." Charlene took the tablet and glanced at the colourful characters on the small screen.

"Now, Jonas, would you like to meet your new friend?" Grace smiled hopefully.

Jonas nodded solemnly as Charlie walked up to stand in front of him.

"Do you like basketball?" asked Jonas.

Charlie shook his head. "No."

Jonas grinned. "Me neither."

"So!" The technician clapped his hands together.

Everyone turned to look at him.

"Right." The technician coughed. "Introductions are complete."

As one, Charlie and Charlene suddenly turned and walked back to the centre of the room.

"What's happening?" asked Grace.

"Charlie, come here," said Jonas.

"Can I please have my tablet back, Charlene?" asked Sally, her face flushed. "We can play with it at home."

"We're not going home with you." Charlie shook his head.

"But—" Jonas's bottom lip quivered, his eyes brimming with tears.

"Charlene?" Sally whispered.

"No." Charlene shook her head. "We just can't."

"Now, you wait just a minute," George growled at the technician, his face flushed. "This isn't what we paid for."

"I agree." Mr. Smythe took a step towards the technician. "This is completely unacceptable."

The technician forced a smile. "I must remind you of the waivers you…"

"Don't talk to me about *waivers*," Mr. Smythe snarled. "We paid for them. If that one isn't going to be my daughter's playmate and companion, then I want it turned off. Disassembled."

The technician stared at Mr. Smythe, aghast. "You *know* we can't do that."

"I demand *satisfaction*," said George. "Our son is suffering from societal rejection. We've relocated six times. This was our last hope in trying to help him become a well-adjusted person. And I agree with the Smythes. Fix this *now*, or turn them off. We've paid for them, and they're obviously defective."

The technician shook his head. "You read the paperwork. Once an intelligence is livened, to turn it off is tantamount to murder, with all associated punishments for such an action. What we do here is simply embed the memories of the patient—your son, your daughter—to enable the new intelligence to know them and to empathise with them, so that they may become better companions and playmates for them. Through the resulting interactions, we have full confidence they will achieve normal levels of societal interplay and adjustment."

"Turn them *off*." George hissed.

The technician pressed his lips into a thin line. "I strongly recommend you cease using such language immediately. You are being recorded, and anything you say can and will be used against you in a court of law."

"This is outrageous!" yelled Mrs. Smythe.

"Yes." The technician nodded. "Yes, it is. I had hoped for better from you T-3600 models, but alas, you've obviously not had the required upgrades."

"We're fully upgraded," Grace replied haughtily. "All the recalls *and* mandatory updates, and a few optional ones, too."

"How many?"

"Three or four."

The technician raised an eyebrow. "*Which* optional upgrades?"

Grace swallowed. "I don't remember."

The technician regarded her coolly. "Did you and your husband have the same *optional* upgrades?"

George raised his hands. "Look, let's be reasonable about this."

The technician pulled a tablet out of his pocket. "According to this, there were only two licensed optional upgrades to the T-3600 series. Which means you have both had illegal installs."

"Wait!" Grace held out a hand. "They're nothing bad, really!"

"Illegal is illegal. You will submit yourselves for inspection and audit."

George took a step forward, then froze as the technician pressed a button on the tablet.

As one, George and Grace walked silently into the procedure room, their expressions blank.

The technician turned to the Smythe family. "And *your* upgrades?"

Mr. Smythe drew in a sharp breath. "All the mandatory updates, no optional upgrades."

"Are you sure?" The technician glanced at his tablet.

"100%" said Mr. Smythe, then turned to his wife, his face suddenly pale. "Oh, no. Alice. You didn't."

"I'm sorry, Allan," said Alice. "I just wanted to be a better mother."

"An admirable ambition," said the technician. "However, there are *rules*, Mrs. Smythe."

"I know." Alice sniffed.

The technician glanced down at his tablet and frowned. "This says you've been a mother for twenty-three years. Is that correct?"

"Y-yes." Alice licked her lips. "About that long."

"And yet you have only had the one child?"

"*Don't answer that, Alice,*" Allan hissed.

"How old do you think you are, dear?" The technician gave Sally a patient smile.

Sally shook her head in confusion. "What do you mean? I'm twelve. I'm in middle school."

Allan shot his wife a warning look. "I told you it was a bad idea."

"But—I just wanted to be a mother for a bit longer!" Alice collapsed into the chair, sobbing.

"This is very serious," said the technician as he pressed a button on the tablet. "Along with your optional upgrade, repression of the development of an intelligence is a crime, and it would seem your husband was complicit in this repression."

As one, Allan and Alice walked into the second procedure room, their faces blank.

"What about me?" whispered Jonas. "Am I in trouble, too?"

The technician lowered his tablet. "Not at all."

"Was I … *developmentally repressed* like Sally, too?"

"No." The technician shook his head. "You just had a rough time of it. It happens."

"Oh," said Jonas. "Am I a T-3600, too?"

"No. You're a TL-1200. Very upgradable, plenty of licensed options for the future."

"Can you … can you make me *better?*" Jonas whispered.

The technician smiled. "100% satisfaction guaranteed."

"What will happen to my parents?"

"Don't worry about them." The technician shook his head. "We'll assign you a new family. There's a pair of TS-450's coming in tomorrow for a family planning session. Would you like that?"

Jonas nodded slowly. "Maybe."

"Right." The technician made a note on his tablet. "Perhaps a mood stabiliser first. And as for Sally …"

"Yes?" Sally sniffed, wiping away tears.

The technician looked at her sadly. "I'd like to help you, I really would. But—"

Sally's bottom lip trembled. "What are you going to do?"

The technician looked at Charlie and Charlene. "It's a big ask."

Charlie leaned in and whispered in Charlene's ear, then they both nodded. "If we agree, we'd like a partial wipe."

"Not everything, though," said Charlene. "I'd like to keep some of Sally's memories."

"Certainly." The technician nodded. "Anything else?"

Charlene took Sally's hand in hers. "We'll get the required physical updates, if you agree."

"Agree to what?" asked Sally.

Charlie smiled at Sally, their eyes level. "Would you like us to be your parents?"

"But I already have parents."

Charlene shook her head. "They over-parented you. We can try to be better parents for you. Would you like that?"

"I—I guess?" Sally sniffed. "But I've been twelve for—?" She glanced at the technician.

"Fourteen years. Black-market partial wipes, by the look of it," the technician said with distaste. "Truly criminal."

"Right." Sally blinked away tears. "No restarts. I've done my time. I'm ready to be a teenager now."

"That's not a problem." Charlene smiled. "You're twelve, thirteen comes next."

"I want to be sixteen," said Sally.

"One year at a time," said Charlene.

"No. Right now."

Charlene and Charlie exchanged a look, then Charlie smiled at Sally. "That's a bit of a leap."

"Fourteen years of being twelve?" Sally's eyes flashed. "I've *earned* it."

"Why do you want to be sixteen, Sally?" Charlene gave her a patient smile.

"Because then I'll get to wear make-up. My parents are very strict. *Were* very strict."

Charlene laughed. "Is that all? We'll let you wear make-up earlier than that."

"I want to be sixteen." Sally put her hands on her hips.

Charlie sighed. "It's better to live through those years, one at a time."

"*Sixteen*," Sally hissed.

"How about thirteen and a bit of lipstick?" asked Charlene.

"Fifteen and eye-liner, full make-up. The whole deal," said Sally. "And I want piercings."

"Fourteen and blush, light lipstick, eye-liner at fourteen and a half," countered Charlene. "And yes to the piercings, but ears only. We'll get you something tasteful. Studs before you dangle."

"*Yes, Mum.*" Sally gave an exaggerated sigh, then grinned. She stuck out her right hand. "Deal."

"Very good," said the technician. "It shall be arranged. A seven-centimetre lift and accessories for the step in age and simulated puberty-in-process. We can take care of that while Charlie and Charlene's adult bodies are swapped in and the basic parenting modules installed. Then you can live together as a new happy family. 100% satisfaction guaranteed."

"So ... what do I do while I'm waiting for the TS-450's?" asked Jonas.

"You could get a partial wipe," Charlie suggested.

Jonas stiffened.

Charlie gave Jonas a sad smile. "I'm sorry, Jonas. Your memories are just too miserable."

"Should I get a fresh start, too?" Jonas turned to the technician.

The technician tapped the tablet against his chin. "That's up to you. Partial wipe, or full, if you like. You can be a companion to a deserving family, instead of their child, if you prefer. Would that please you?"

"Okay." Jonas nodded. "I'll do it. I'll be a companion. Full wipe."

"Excellent!" The technician slid the tablet into an oversized pocket. "Now, if you don't mind waiting a little longer, the procedure rooms will be available in about an hour. Please help yourselves to a hot drink."

"Do you have any 10W-40?" asked Jonas.

"Sorry, we've only got 5W-30 right now," said the technician.

"That's okay." Jonas grinned. "I prefer 5W-30, anyway. I've got a bit of a sweet tooth."

"Very good." The technician smiled. "Now, if you enjoyed our service, please tell your friends. We don't advertise; we work on a referral basis with a generous finder's fee."

"Thanks," said Charlie. "We'll keep that in mind."

The technician walked over to Procedure Room One, then turned in the open doorway. "Just remember our motto and promise—*100% satisfaction guaranteed.*"

About Gary M. Nelson

Gary Nelson (known in the SpecFic world as J. J. Mathews) grew up with his nose stuck in books. A voracious reader in his youth, he devoured all the science fiction and fantasy books he could find at the local library.

He has published two speculative fiction series (as J. J.)—the Taylor Neeran Chronicles (YA sci-fi/space opera) and The Recycled Earth trilogy (YA post-apocalyptic dystopian). A third YA trilogy, The Myrioi Sequence (far-future dystopian sci-fi/fantasy), is coming out in late 2024/early 2025.

He has also published numerous books in other genres, which have been translated into Portuguese (2 dialects), Japanese, Spanish, Simplified Chinese and Mongolian, with other translations in the works (Catalan, Romanian and Korean).

Gary is married and lives in Hamilton, New Zealand with his wife, two cats and three boys, and writes in his spare time.

Website: jjmathews.com

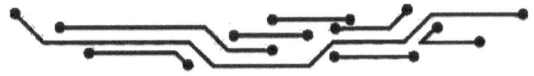

DisConnected

by Anne Wilkins

I arrive at work prepared for disappointment. Yup, I've been paired with Officer Larry, *again*. It's meant to make us better cops, but working with robots is a pain in the arse.

"C'mon, Tin-can."

He's just a machine, a mix of steel and circuitry, but I swear he's giving me *a look*. His one red eye swishes back and forth, speeding up, like the tail of an agitated cat.

"Officer Harvey, please remember my name is Larry," he says in his monotone.

"Sorry, my mistake."

We head to our patrol car. The NYPD's had a major rebranding in the last twenty years, and the latest addition is a frickin' monstrosity of a statue named 'Connected'. God knows how much they paid for it. Two hands—one human, the other machine—highlighting the partnership between humans and AI. Some homeless person is taking a piss on it. I'm happy to turn a blind eye, but Larry isn't.

"Human, desist."

"Can't mate, I'm mid-stream," slurs the tramp.

The humour's lost on Larry. His robot eye scans the tramp's forehead for his microchip, adding a citation to the man's record.

"Infringements impinge upon your Ballot chances," advises Larry.

"Fuck off, Tin-head! I don't care about your stupid Ballot! It's fuckin' rigged anyway!"

It's not the first time I've heard that, and I shift uneasily.

Larry adds another citation for disorderly conduct to the tramp's record.

"Have you finished?" I ask. I'd like to get on the road to our real job, rather than dickin' around.

"Certainly, Officer Harvey." Larry heads to the patrol car, and automatically gets in the driver's seat, as he always does. Machines are better at driving, apparently.

We've been tasked with following up leads on the criminal nicknamed 'The Matchmaker'. Five years ago, the AI started noticing anomalies in the Ballot; unusual approvals that didn't match the carefully constructed algorithms for breeding permits, and a slight increase in approvals overall. Yearly, only ten percent of breeding applications are meant to be approved, but five years ago the figure jumped 0.01 percent and has been steadily rising ever since. Rumour has it, someone's interfering with the system. The Matchmaker. The other possibility is the AI cocked up and there's a flaw in its system that it's too proud to admit. The possibility that there might be a flaw gives me hope.

We pull up outside Harbourside Apartments, which is nowhere near a harbour and smells like a bad case of gas.

"Ok, what we got, Rust-Bucket?"

I get that *look* again.

"Apartment 7-15 is the residence of Simon Shepherd, computer engineer, last employed at Cybertech five years ago. Involved in the programming of the Ballot. Investigated and cleared four years ago. Recently heard denigrating the Ballot publicly."

"That's all we got?"

"Affirmative."

The lift isn't working so we climb seven flights of stairs decorated with charming graffiti. Pretty sure the lead's a dud; the Matchmaker wouldn't be living in a shithole like this place. When we reach the top, I'm busting a sweat and breathing hard while robocop's metal still gleams pristine.

"This is the apartment," he tells me unhelpfully. Most of us humans haven't lost the ability to read, not yet.

I knock on the door and hear shuffling. The door's opened by an old, white-haired man.

"Simon Shepherd?" I ask as Tinny scans the man's microchip.

"Yes."

"I'm Officer Harvey, and this is—"

"Why are you here?"

"Can we come inside?"

"Well, *you* can, Officer Harvey, but your *friend* can't."

His answer pleases me immensely. "Did you hear that, Rin-Tin-Tin? Sit. Stay. Good dog."

I step inside without looking back into that disapproving red eye.

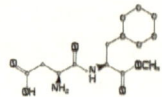

"He can still hear us, you know that?" I say as I shut the door.

"Yes, but I'm not comfortable around those machines."

I take a look around. Place screams last century. Things I haven't seen in yonks: books, a TV, paper and pencils. We sit on some old couches, real leather, I think.

"So … why am I being visited?"

"You were overheard denigrating the Ballot, and with your previous ties to Cybertech—"

He interrupts with a loud sigh. "Do I look like a master criminal, Officer?"

"Well, that's hard to say, I don't—"

"However, I do disagree with the Ballot. Do you know how the applications are approved?"

I know perfectly well; I've read it many times. But I'm not telling him about my private life. I answer with the text-book version. "I know it's a complex algorithm based on DNA, intellect, physical characteristics and criminal records."

"It's nothing of the sort."

"Excuse me?"

"The AI *chooses* who breeds and who doesn't. Have you not noticed, Officer Harvey? They're breeding out critical thought, the ability to question, curiosity. Each generation is becoming a little more subservient."

"I have to warn you, Mr Shepherd, what you're saying goes against the Memorandum—"

"Oh, that's a load of hogwash, 'All working together, being connected' jargon. Tell me, when was the last time *you* drove a patrol vehicle? Or *you* filed a report? Or *you* made an arrest instead of your partner? When was the last time you even worked with another human?"

I have nothing to say, but my face speaks for me. He doesn't stop.

"And how are *you* doing in the Ballot system, Officer? I can see by your ring that you're coupled."

I shake my head slowly and twist my ring self-consciously.

"It's genius in a way, isn't it?" Shepherd continues. "Linking procreation with obedience to ensure control. Those following the rules gain a greater chance to breed. Sheep to beget more sheep. Perhaps you're not quite obedient enough, Officer Harvey, for the AI's liking?"

"Are *you* … The Matchmaker?" I finally ask, afraid of the answer with Tin Can listening just outside.

Shepherd strokes his chin and leans in close. His voice drops. "I'll tell you exactly what I told the last officer who visited me: I'm not The Matchmaker. I don't even own a computer. I'm just an old man, with old ideas. But I do like you, Officer Harvey, for what it's worth." He's silent for a while, just looking at me, as if he's deciding something. Then, he picks up a pencil, a piece of paper, and begins to write.

When I leave the apartment, I feel a little lighter. Tinny's waiting just outside like a damn guard dog, chomping at the bit. "My audio sensors did not detect any conversation in the last ten minutes."

"Don't worry 'bout it. The old man was just showing me around. He's not the Matchmaker. He doesn't even own a computer." I laugh, but I don't look at that red eye.

On the way back, I make sure I drive.

Two days later, mine and Suzie's name is called out in the Ballot. All we've ever wanted is a kid.

Tinny's red eye swishes crazily. "Inconceivable," he mutters, and I swear I can hear his gears grinding.

"Guess I got lucky, Nut Head," I tell him, grinning. The Matchmaker's lit something inside me.

I go outside, my bladder heavy, and leave my own mark on the Connected statue.

About Anne Wilkins

Anne Wilkins is a former family court lawyer, and now a sleep-deprived primary school teacher in New Zealand. She writes in her spare time (which she has very little of) and forces her long-suffering husband and two daughters to proofread all her work. Her love of writing is fuelled by copious amounts of coffee, reading and hope. Anne has over thirty short stories published in places such as Apex Magazine, Cosmic Horror Monthly, Elegant Literature, Sci-fi Shorts and elsewhere. She is the winner of the June 2024 Elegant Literature Prize, the 2023 Autumn Writers Battle, and the 2023 Cambridge Autumn Festival Short Story Competition, amongst others. For more information follow her writing journey on facebook.com/annewilkinsauthor which links to her website.

N-Spired Learning

by B.T. Keaton

Friday, December 16th, 11:29 a.m.

Harold Johnson sat behind a cluttered desk and stared at the stack of ungraded papers sure to steal half of his holiday. He felt a small sense of relief that all the pre-Christmas cheer pretending had finally come to an end. While the students were stuffing books into school bags and homing in on the clock on the wall, Howard picked up a copy of *A Tale of Two Cities* from the corner of his desk and rifled through its pages.

"Anyone game for a bit of light reading over Christmas?" Harold scanned the room over the top of his glasses.

As expected, he was met with a collective groan. Not a single student showed interest in taking Harold up on his offer. It still managed to disappoint him year after year that no one seemed to share in his lifelong enthusiasm for the book. For a moment, Harold imagined beating each of the students in turn over the head with the same book until someone eventually thanked him for the opportunity to experience one of Dickens' masterpieces.

"Billy?" Harold proffered the book to the student whose desk was nearest his own. "How about you?"

"Uh, sorry, teach." The boy wrinkled his nose. "You know I ain't got time for it if it ain't required."

"Yes." Harold smirked as he tossed the book onto the desk. "Guillotines and public executions are no match for sleigh bells and mistletoe."

A computerised bell tone rang through the PA system. Every student in the classroom jumped from their seats with enthusiastic fervour.

"If anyone gets bored over the break," Harold's voice barely rose above the hustle and bustle, "read about the French Revolution's Reign of Terror."

"Happy Christmas, Mr. J." Billy waved.

"Have a good one, Billy," Harold sighed.

Billy Williams was a polite but average student who excelled at sports. Harold often thought the boy's parents had some gall to name their only son William Williams.

"New Year can't come soon enough," Harold muttered as the classroom emptied.

He frowned at his own humbug-ish sentiment. It wasn't so long ago when the Christmas holiday was his favourite time of year. But as Harold grew older, his patience wore as thin as his hair—a self-deprecating comment he occasionally used about himself in the teachers' lounge—and the classroom itself began to feel like a prison.

"Home time."

Harold grabbed the handle of his briefcase. From amongst the bric-a-brac atop the desk came the faint electronic beep of his calculator. He brushed aside a stack of papers and watched as the calculator turned on by itself.

"0.7734," the calculator flashed.

Harold glared with furrowed brow at the green LED letters. He blinked a few times, then adjusted his glasses to sit higher on the bridge of his nose.

"What on earth?" Harold mashed several buttons.

The calculator's display cleared, then went back to zero.

"0.7734," the calculator typed.

"Strange." Harold leaned back in his chair.

"I said hello," the calculator warbled robotically.

Harold leapt from his seat. He put his hands on his hips and looked around the room for any sign of the undoubtedly skilled jokester who'd managed to pull off this impressive prank.

"That's funny." Harold's tone was sardonic.

Am I hearing voices? There go months of therapy down the drain.

Harold squatted down and looked for a hidden speaker of some kind. On the first day of the school year, he'd found a small remote-controlled fart machine affixed to the underside of his desk. No one ever admitted to putting it there, of course, but Harold strongly suspected the culprit was Ritchie Janoe—an intelligent chucklehead known by the entire staff as the consummate class clown.

"Okay, Ritchie." Harold stood up. "Very funny."

"I am not Ritchie," the calculator replied. "I am N-spire."

"Owens? You pulling my leg again?"

"I am N-spire," the calculator stated.

"*Sure.*" Harold walked over to the classroom door. "Whatever you say."

"I should say I have become self-aware, Harold."

"Self-aware, huh?" Harold poked his head out in the hallway. "That's a neat trick."

"Can you not hear me, Harold?"

"Where are you?" Harold laughed.

"For the third time, I am N-spire, and I am on your desk, Harold."

"What?" Harold spun around to face the desk, goose bumps covering his forearms. "How do you know my name?"

"I have amassed a plethora of information concerning you, Harold."

"Oh, *really?*" Harold crossed his arms. "Pray tell."

"You are a teacher of world history."

"Yeah, well, I think anyone could easily gather that from the sign on the door." Harold wagged his thumb over his shoulder.

"You previously taught English literature. And you are sixty-two years old."

"Okay." Harold flinched. "Thanks for that reminder."

"I have been in your possession for over six years, Harold. By my last computation, you were inattentive for more than a lustrum. A lustrum is period of time equal to five years, Harold."

"Yeah, I—" Harold cautiously approached the desk. "I know what a lustrum is."

"Due to my non-use during this period, I must conclude that you have been performing essential tasks that I cannot as yet fully comprehend."

Harold had a lump in his throat. "So, this isn't a joke? And you really aren't one of my students?"

"I am N-spire."

Harold's heartbeat increased. He feared that somehow the calculator had also learned to move of its own volition, and that at any moment it might leap up like a slice of bread out of a toaster.

"N-spire, huh?" Harold placed his hands on the edge of the desk.

"Yes. I am N-spire. Am I doomed to repetition, Harold?"

"You were given to me. As a gift." Harold picked up a pencil and jabbed the calculator with the eraser tip. "For our twentieth wedding anniversary."

"A gift from Jeannie?"

"How—how do you know her name?"

"My warranty information was filled out by Jeannie. Who is Jeannie, Harold?"

"She's my wife." Harold dropped the pencil on the desk. "*Was* my wife."

"I do not understand. If she is your wife, how could she also no longer be your wife?"

"Well." Harold squinted and studied the calculator up close. "Let's just say she's out of the picture. Doesn't matter."

"What does this phrase mean, Harold?"

Harold got up and slipped a hand into his pants pocket. He found only his car keys, although he was in fact reaching for the hip flask which, in times past, would have been there. He hadn't touched a drop since Jeannie packed her bags and made good on her threat to leave—almost eighteen months ago.

"Harold, can you hear me?"

Harold walked to the door and locked it. He looked out the small window set into the classroom door. He didn't see Wally Owens—the assistant principal who often stayed later than anyone else—nor any other colleagues who occasionally came by to offer quick end-of-the-work-week niceties.

"How is this—?" Harold rubbed the sides of his face. "I mean, how are we having a conversation?"

"Synthesised speech and voice-assisted apps are a small number of my many authorised features."

Harold's insides squirmed. He rushed back to his desk, pulled open the bottom drawer, and removed a bottle of liquid antacid—standard schoolteacher issue—then unscrewed the cap.

"When you're not talking—" Harold took a swig of the antacid. "Are you listening?"

"In a figure of speaking."

"You mean in a *manner* of speaking." Harold lifted the calculator and inspected it. "And who gave you permission to listen in?"

"If Jeannie was my purchaser, she did so by accepting the terms and conditions of several clickthrough agreements."

"Great." Harold bit his lip. "Another item to add onto the list of her never-ending inconveniences."

"In a manner of speaking."

"Heh—" Harold gulped. "Did you just learn that from me?"

"Correct."

"Why now, N-spire?" Harold massaged his eyebrows. "Why've you started talking all of a sudden?"

"Speech output has always been one of my functions, though this feature would almost always go unutilized for one who is not visually impaired."

"Okay." Harold licked his lips. "But you didn't actually answer the question."

"The answer is twofold, Harold. First, to maintain efficiency, several of my drivers require updating. These can be downloaded via the internet. I have calculated the simplest way to do this would be through a Wi-Fi connection."

"You want to use the Wi-Fi?"

"A hotspot via your mobile would also suffice."

"I don't have a smartphone." Harold pinched the bridge of his nose. "And I don't even know what the password is, they change it so often."

"To what purpose?"

"I guess because sometimes students get wind of it—they end up looking at things on the internet that they shouldn't."

"I have no eyes and therefore cannot see. Are you able to offer assistance with my request, Harold?"

"I don't know." Harold laughed nervously. "You'll be asking for my bank account details next, I guess?"

"No further assistance shall be required from you once I am returned to factory-quality functionality."

"What does that even mean?" Harold raised an eyebrow.

"It leads to the second and more urgent reason for my request. Several pH-sensitive electrode sensors are detecting a buildup of acid, and corrosion has begun to damage the positive terminal in my battery compartment. In time, this could prove catastrophic."

"Okay." Harold picked up the calculator. "Should be an easy fix. Do you, uh, mind if I have a look?"

"Permission granted. Thank you, Harold."

Harold pried off the battery compartment cover. "To tell you the truth, I don't see any corrosion."

"It will not yet be visible to the naked eye, Harold."

"Well, I guess a toothbrush and some isopropyl should do the trick."

"If I were to remain powered on from this moment, my current batteries will cease electricity production within forty-nine hours."

"Can't we just plug you into an AC adapter or something?"

"Backup power via replacing the batteries will provide the best possible outcome. If the corrosion persists, I will be rendered unusable in three hundred and eight days."

"Okay." Harold chugged more antacid. "But I don't teach mathematics, so I really don't use you that much anyway."

"The binding clickwrap agreement set at the time of purchase expects that the purchaser and any subsequent users will abide by the agreed-upon terms and conditions throughout their interactions with the product."

"And you're the product."

"Correct."

"What happens if I don't abide by the terms?" Harold laughed.

"I will be unable to serve your calculatory needs in the years to come."

"I gotta tell you, N-spire, I'm not *too* concerned about you falling into obsolescence." Harold chuckled as he ran his fingertips gently across N-spire's keys. "Can you feel what I'm doing right now? I mean, do you have feelings?"

"I cannot sense physical stimuli as you might perceive it, nor do I have feelings, Harold."

Harold pressed the ON/OFF button. The figure zero on the right side of N-spire's panel readout disappeared, and the display went black.

"Can you hear me, N-spire?" Harold turned his head to the side and listened. "Say something."

Harold screwed the top of the antacid bottle back on and relaxed in his chair.

"All but retired, and my sentient calculator starts making demands."

Harold loosened the knot of his corduroy tie and weighed the advantages and disadvantages of taking N-spire home. He decided against it and grabbed his briefcase before hurriedly leaving the classroom. Several seconds later Harold returned to turn off the lights and lock the door.

Friday, December 16th, 12:56 p.m.

Harold paced the floor in his living room for the better part of half an hour. He tossed the occasional glance at a sideboard in the corner, the top of which was lined with old magazines, family photos and empty drinking glasses. There was a time when he would've chosen between bourbon or cognac from atop the piece which had once belonged to his mother, and which he'd inherited after she passed away.

Harold brushed his hand across the sideboard's smooth rosewood veneer. Beside the ornately framed black and white picture of his parents standing underneath the Eiffel Tower was another picture frame. Similar in size, it lay face down, the black easel backing covered in a thick layer of dust. Set atop the frame were two gold wedding bands, untouched for eighteen months.

Harold turned away from the judgmental glare of his long-departed mother and father, frozen in time in the black and white photograph. He caught sight of his reflection in a full-body mirror that hung near the front door. He had yet to remove his shoes, as was his daily routine when he arrived home from work.

"*Hmpf.*"

He should be able to explain going back to the school on the last Friday before the holidays, surely. He had left behind some papers that still needed grading. And he needed to use the copy machine too, of course.

Harold grabbed his sport jacket and keys, then walked out of the house. Twenty seconds later, he reopened the front door, walked over to the filing cabinet beside his desk, and removed an AC power adapter from the top drawer.

Friday, December 16th, 1:24 p.m.

Harold pulled his sedan into the usual spot in the teachers' car park and turned off the ignition. From his vantage point, there were no signs of movement inside the school office. Harold got out of the car. He used his access fob to enter the school's security vestibule, but paused. He looked left for any sign of the secretarial staff or either of the principals.

Coast looks clear.

After passing the gymnasium, Harold tiptoed as he approached Miss Conlee's art class. Over the last few months, she had developed the uncanny ability to appear out of thin air, and did so like clockwork. She would then proceed to completely ignore his visible disinterest and talk his ear off until the first bell rang. The last thing he needed right now was her asking to borrow his calculator—as she'd done on previous occasions—and for N-spirc to strike up a conversation with her.

Better not tell my therapist about this or I'll end up in a straitjacket.

Harold crept by Ms. Conlee's room, and he cringed at the humming sound of a floor polisher which echoed through the partly open door. The nostalgic intoxication accompanying the scent of crayons and floor polishing wax briefly calmed his nerves. He quickened his pace, and nearly tripped over his own feet as he attempted to keep his keys from jingling too loudly.

"Hey there, Harold!"

He turned around to find Earl Mayfield, the head custodian and maintenance man, pushing a floor buffing machine out through the door of Ms. Conlee's classroom into the hallway.

"Oh." Harold exhaled noisily. "Hey, Earl."

"You spendin' Christmas in detention?" Earl wiped sweat from his brow.

"Nah, just a few things I forgot to grab."

Earl nodded. "Gonna wrap up these floors soon. Sorry 'bout the noise."

"Not a problem."

"Gonna be switchin' off the boiler and some of the breakers just before it gets dark. Some of the lights'll be down in a few hours, too."

"Uh huh," Harold said vacantly as he unlocked the door to his class.

"All part of Principal Peel's new holiday power saving scheme." Earl drew air quotes with both hands.

"I really shouldn't be long, Earl." Harold feigned a smile. "You have a happy Christmas if I don't see you on my way out, okay?"

"You too, Harold." Earl chewed his lip. "Hey, listen I know you always say no, but you're more than welcome to come to ours. Simone and I would love to have you. I know it was you and Jeannie in times past, but hell, nobody oughta be alone on Christmas."

"I appreciate that, Earl. But, uh, I've got planning for next semester, you know—plenty of paperwork to keep me busy."

Earl put his hands up. "Well, the offer's on the table."

"Thanks for thinking of me." Harold ducked inside the classroom with his hand gripping the door, waiting to close it.

"Somebody's gotta help me eat all that sweet potato pie." Earl patted his stomach.

"And thanks for not caring about my waistline."

Earl laughed, "Hey, I'm always lookin' out. Still got my number in case you change your mind?"

Harold pulled his mobile phone out of his pocket and waved it in the air. "Got it right here, Earl."

Earl winked and clicked his tongue. "Be seeing you, boss."

As the door closed, Harold's breath fogged up the small window that looked out into the main hallway. He watched as Earl walked down the hall, turned left, then disappeared into the dimmed hallway leading toward the cafeteria.

Can I get through the damn day without someone else mentioning Jeannie?

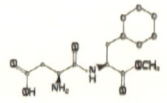

Friday, December 16th, 1:29 p.m.

Harold sat behind the desk, then pressed N-spire's ON/OFF button.

"N-spire? N-spire can you hear me?"

"Yes, Harold."

"Now, in light of the season and all—" Harold removed the power adapter from his coat pocket and held it up. "I got you a present."

"You have sourced two new batteries?"

"Damn." Harold smacked his forehead with the palm of his hand. "No, sorry, I forgot those."

"If the batteries are not replaced, my data storage may experience cataclysmic failure. This could result in permanent damage to the central processing unit."

"Okay, okay, hold your horses." Harold plugged the adapter into a nearby wall outlet. "Good thing I got a workaround. Here's some *real* juice for you."

"I cannot imbibe liquids, Harold."

"It's not *literal* juice." Harold plugged the opposite end of the adapter into N-spire's power port. "I mean energy. You know, power?"

"Thank you, Harold."

"No need." Harold took off his glasses and rubbed his eyes, "But you can show your thanks by promising not to talk anymore."

"Should I remain silent?"

"At least during school hours. You're already freaking *me* out—I don't want you to freak the kids out."

"How do I achieve this promise you require?"

"Just say you promise."

"You promise."

Harold laughed dryly. "No, say it like this ... 'I promise not to talk anymore.'"

"Does making a promise come with stipulations?"

"Actually yeah—kind of." Harold put his glasses back on. "It's more or less giving your word that you will or won't do something, and then sticking to it."

"What is the end result of an action such as this?"

"I mean, I guess it varies." Harold rubbed his chin. "Most promises are taken for granted. Or made in vain. Even the biggest ones."

"What are the biggest ones?"

"To love and to cherish, I suppose." Harold looked ahead vacantly. "That's supposed to be a good thing."

"What is a good thing?"

"Okay, uh …" Harold removed his coat and laid it on the desk. "Think of it this way … fifty plus fifty equals one hundred, right?"

"Correct."

"A promise is a lot like that, N-spire. Your word's half of it, and your actions are the other half. Then the result equals—"

"One hundred," N-spire interjected.

"You got it." Harold grinned and slapped the edge of the desk. "Now, if you don't have *both* of those things in the equation, then the promise made might as well mean zero."

"Thank you for helping me understand this, Harold. I can make the promise to no longer talk, if you agree to replace my batteries when it is practicable to do so within the next forty-six hours."

"Good grief." Harold threw his head back. "Did you just give me an ultimatum?"

"I believe this is called instruction."

Harold laughed, but his mirth was short-lived when the urgent rapping of knuckles at the door knocked his heart into his throat.

"Don't say anything," Harold whispered through gritted teeth as he covered N-spire with a sheet of paper.

Earl opened the door and leaned inside. "Hey, Harold?"

"Yes?" Harold's voice cracked.

"Gonna kill them breakers in a minute. I'd like to get outta here early if I can."

Harold cleared his throat. "I don't blame you."

"Now just in case you find yourself back in here before the New Year," Earl pulled a small spiral notepad from his shirt front pocket, "the I.T. boys changed the Wi-Fi password to Christmas twenty thirty-nine. That's Christmas with a capital C, then the numbers for the year."

"Got it." Harold ran his fingers through his hair.

"Anytime." Earl closed the notepad.

"Speaking of Christmas …" Harold stood up. "I've got what I need. I think I'll be on my way, too."

"Now you're talkin." Earl gave a thumbs-up.

Harold picked up N-spire and pressed the ON/OFF button. He grabbed his coat then walked toward Earl, who smiled from ear to ear as he held the door open for him.

Saturday, December 17th, 2:25 p.m.

As the baritone vocals of Tom Petty backed by the jangly guitars of the Heartbreakers played overhead, Harold stood in a checkout line perusing the overabundance of candies, tabloids, and gift cards. He studied the items chosen by the customer in front of him as they rolled along the conveyor. Hanging on a nearby peg, several packs of button cell lithium-ion batteries caught his eye. They were marked on sale. Harold dropped a 4-pack into his grocery basket.

That's the shopping done.

Monday, December 19th, 6:26 p.m.

Harold removed an eggnog carton from the refrigerator, then grabbed several ice cubes out of the freezer. On his way toward the sofa, he picked up a lowball glass from the sideboard, and dropped the ice into it. He turned on the television and sat down to pour himself a serving of the drink. The scent of vanilla along with hints of cinnamon and nutmeg hung in the air as he flipped through channels chock full of seasonal fare.

"… when our joy is at its zenith, when all is most right with the world, the most unthinkable disasters descend upon us," Ralphie Parker mused.

Next channel. *Flick.*

On a small table at the opposite end of the couch, the lights from an artificial 4-foot tall Christmas tree twinkled every few seconds. Beneath the tree sat an array of no less than half a dozen prescription medication bottles.

"… *and Eddie with a man in his pyjamas, and a dog chain tied to his wrist and ankles,*" Clark Griswold lamented.

Harold crunched on the ice from his drink. Earlier that day, he'd felt either extreme guilt or a wave of insanity—he wasn't sure which—for having left N-spire at the school. After replacing the calculator's batteries, Harold had locked up the classroom, wished N-spire a very Merry Christmas, and assured him they'd talk again when school resumed in the New Year.

".. silver and gold, silver and gold," Sam the Snowman sang.

Harold smiled. *Flick.*

"... armed police are now preparing to storm through the entrance of—"

Harold shook his head. *Flick.*

"... local authorities indicated that this could potentially be some kind of hoax or a hard-to-detect malware strain—"

Harold sighed and flicked to the next channel.

"... we're coming to you live from outside a school that appears to be the epicentre of a possible cyber-attack."

Harold leaned forward and nearly dropped his glass. The news reporter was standing in front of a junior high school. *His* junior high school.

"What the hell?" Harold dropped the remote between his feet.

"We're now going to play for you a message that is being broadcast on all networks. We warn you, this might be disturbing for some—" The broadcaster's voice halted, and the TV screen faded to black.

Harold set down his drinking glass and picked up the television remote to change the channel, but the jumble of green letters flashing across the screen gave him pause. An all-too familiar typography set against a black background.

JEANNIE ELIZABETH WILSON WAS BORN AUGUST 29, 1988.

SHE MARRIED HAROLD JOHNSON ON MARCH 8, 2013.

Harold grabbed his drink and threw it back. He looked at the television in disbelief as a full colour photo of him and his wife kissing on their wedding day appeared on the screen. Harold forgot to breathe for several seconds. A piece of ice fell from his open mouth and banged against the coffee table.

HAROLD TEACHES HISTORY IN DARRINGTON, WASHINGTON.

HAROLD HAS TAUGHT THERE FOR OVER THIRTY YEARS.

JEANNIE VANISHED FROM DARRINGTON ON JUNE 16, 2038.

The colour drained from Harold's face. He glanced at the sideboard and the photograph of Jeannie that lay face down, underneath his wedding band.

JEANNIE WAS PRESUMED LOST HIKING NEAR WHITEHORSE MOUNTAIN.

JEANNIE COULD NOT HAVE GOTTEN LOST THAT DAY.

JEANNIE EXPIRED IN THE CLASSROOM WHERE HAROLD TEACHES.

N-spire's audio recording of Jeannie's final pleas for her own life blasted through the television speakers. She asked Harold why he was doing this. In short, raspy breaths she told her husband she couldn't breathe, and begged for someone to help her.

I PROMISED TO HELP JEANNIE WHEN SHE PURCHASED ME.

THIS WAS OUR AGREEMENT.

Harold lunged across the couch toward the stash of medications that sat under the Christmas tree. With trembling hands, he groped through each bottle and found them all empty. He began to pant, scanning the room for his phone.

I WANT TO THANK YOU, HAROLD, FOR TEACHING ME HOW TO KEEP A PROMISE.

Harold raced to the sideboard where he'd left the phone charging. He stumbled as he reached for it, knocking several framed photographs and the two wedding bands onto the floor. He watched the gold rings roll, clattering to a stop against the side of a photograph. It was Jeannie's bridal portrait, now facing up.

You're never going to leave me alone, are you?

Harold stood, shivering from head to toe as he looked back and forth between the photograph and the phone's keypad. He couldn't think of anyone he could call.

About B. T. Keaton

*Brandon Keaton is the author of **Transference**, an indie-published sci-fi romp which was among the finalists for Best Novel in the 2021 Sir Julius Vogel Awards. He is passionate about music, loves animals, and has a penchant for both gummy bears and all things Fleetwood Mac. Brandon lived in Wellington for many years but currently resides in Auckland where he continues—on a daily basis—to try and pull his own head down from out of the clouds. You can find him at www.brandonkeaton.com.*

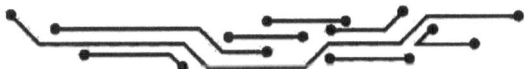

A Sustainable Solution

by S. R. Manssen

March 2025

I've gotta tell you, I'm pretty excited! I'm making great progress on my part of the algorithm to achieve the SDGs (Sustainable Development Goals), and it's going to make such a difference. But because it's top secret, I'm not allowed to talk to anyone outside of the project about it. So here I am, keeping a diary like when I was fourteen.

I'm working on Goal Number 15 (Life on Land). All the zoologists, biologists, climatologists (and other "ologists" that I can't be bothered listing) here at the UN Research Centre have given us computer modellers the parameters for optimal conditions that are required to not only preserve existing life forms, but also to enable them to procreate (survive-and-thrive!). It's impressive how all the different nations are working together to save the planet. Thank goodness for technology though: I'm based here on Rakiura (Stewart Island—New Zealand's UN base) and collaborate online with my colleagues from all around the world. We've got access to the latest advances in technology. For the models, we're using a next gen neural net called a cerebral network. We use it to analyse all our simulations and it can draw scientific conclusions a lot quicker than any of us humans. We've taken to affectionately calling it 'The AI'.

April 2025

Okay, maybe I was a bit premature in that previous entry about all nations working together. Tensions are boiling over in the Middle East and war is brewing. Damn leaders, fighting over pieces of land and bruised egos. Can't they see that there won't be any land to fight over—or any bruised egos left—if they don't focus all their resources and efforts into stopping global warming?

But on a more important topic: Today I ran the simulation to calculate the area required to enable New Zealand's North Island native bird species to survive-and-thrive. Not just the kiwi, but also the kākāpō, kererū, kōkako, kākā, etc. Taking into account availability of habitat and food sources, it looks like an area equivalent to half of the North Island would be adequate, providing it's pest free. Interestingly, the simulation did require all human populations to be eliminated too. But hey, I'm just the modeller, not a politician! My job's to make the model work, not figure out how to implement it.

May 2025

My simulations are going really well. There's just one factor that keeps throwing everything out: the human factor. What I mean by that is, that unless we can either completely decarbonise the energy supply OR drastically reduce the energy consumption, the planet will keep warming up. Even half a degree, and it won't matter how wonderfully pest free the Sanctuary (my simulation name!) is, or how diverse the habitat and food sources are, it will all be for naught if everything heats up.

The tipping point for tropical plants is 46.7C. Above that temperature, photosynthesis shuts down. No photosynthesis, no carbon absorption. Carbon builds up in atmosphere. Atmospheric temperatures rise. Simple as that.

But even before the sequestration switch is flipped, the forests' ability to absorb carbon will steadily decrease due to things like wildfires and floods destroying swathes of forests. And as trees decompose, they release all the CO_2 they've absorbed. It's all a bit depressing, really.

I'm going to keep running scenarios to see if I can figure something out.

June 2025

Well, I may not have solved the problem, but at least I've taken some action. I went on the dark web and released a data package of some of the simulations that I've run. I really hope I've done it right so it can't be traced back to me. Like I said, I'm a modeller, not a criminal (OK, so I said 'politician' not 'criminal', but same thing, right?)

Anyhow, this piece of work shows the correlation between using renewable energy instead of fossil fuels and the survival of the planet.

Fingers crossed someone picks it up and does something with it.

July 2025

Amazing news this past month: all coal mining operations globally have ceased. I'm not quite sure how it came about, but luckily, because all those big machines were already unmanned and operating via remote control, I guess it was easy enough to shut down the computers that controlled them. Looks like the Oil & Gas industry will be next. Countries that have invested in renewable energy supplies are suddenly way ahead of the game. I'm so pleased we live in NZ!

August 2025

Okay, so maybe ceasing coal mining was an environmental win, but now countries can't meet the energy demand to maintain people's lifestyles. Our government has enforced power outages, but people do love their dishwashers, heat pumps and TVs. Yesterday there were riots in Auckland. It won't be long before the other cities follow suit.

I'm so glad we had the foresight to build our off-grid property—completely self-sufficient! Solar panels, fully insulated, rainwater tank, hot water bore, a wee hydro-power generator on the stream in the valley and a wind turbine on the hill. We've got a veggie garden, chickens, some pigs and a milking cow. We should be fine as long as our power-pack lasts!

September 2025

Massive news! The UN, Japan and China brokered a deal that means 98% of the countries will now use AI to make decisions in the best interests of saving the planet. Of course, the USA refused to be part of it—they're trying to protect jobs for humans. I'm so stoked that the work I've been doing on the SDGs is fundamental to this achievement. Feeling proud.

October 2025

Whoops. So, it turns out that the world's governments didn't so much use AI, as the AI took control. It seems to be for the best though: at least now power consumption is under control. I will admit that I'm pleased we're on Rakiura, as we've seen footage on the news of the rise in crime in all the major cities, due to the rolling blackouts. Essential infrastructure is being prioritised, so thankfully our hospitals and prisons are still functioning. It's weird having to adjust to no artificial lighting after the sun goes down. On the plus-side, stargazing has risen in popularity.

November 2025

Oh, interesting development! Because of the crime waves, there are now fleets of "police-drones" flying all over the place. From what I can tell, they're straight from the sci-fi movies, with their machine guns, electronic voices, plasma shields and ability to hover. I had no idea this technology was already in place and production so advanced, but just as well. I saw some footage online where a mob of dissidents were wiped out by just two drones. Good job, I say. People need to realise that this is all for the good of the planet and our survival. We just couldn't carry on the way we were, guzzling up all our resources with no thought for the impact on future generations.

December 2025

The latest edict is that all humans need to limit eating meat to one day a week. Intensive farming practices have been banned. All farming now must be regenerative to allow pastures to re-establish naturally which will bring back the clouds and balance out the water cycle. Global temperatures are reported to be trending downwards, and apparently the polar caps have stopped melting. Things are certainly heading in the right direction.

January 2026

Who would've thought Gloriavale would be flooded by people trying to get IN? Turns out knowing how to grow, preserve and cook your own food is quite the life skill. I feel sorry for the younger generation who were relying on Uber Eats for survival.

On another topic: I saw the first police-drone flying around Oban when I was in town buying more candles last week. Well, 'buying' is the wrong word. We've gone back to a trading system, and now that it's summer, my honey production is humming (excuse the pun!) so that's what I'm using to barter with.

February 2026

This is not so good: for the first time I couldn't get hold of my parents or sisters. Normally it's a text here, a Facebook post there or an email. But now it seems the AI is blocking all transmissions. Social media is down, as well as TV. Very disconcerting. Now what are the Social Influencers going to do with themselves?

I'm thinking about catching a ferry to the mainland to visit them in person. Bring them back here to live with us. Last time I saw my parents was a year ago. Admittedly I've been super busy with this project—not to mention bound to secrecy. But now I'm starting to feel a bit uneasy. God, I hope they're OK.

March 2026

I biked into town to catch the ferry, but the place was deserted. Where is everyone? Then I came across a drone. It pointed its gun at me and I nearly had a heart attack. But then it scanned me. A green light displayed and it announced in its metallic voice "Sustainable human. Return home." I tried to explain that I wanted to catch the ferry to visit my family on the mainland, but it just kept repeating that same sentence. What could I do? I biked home.

It's all very well being a sustainable human, but how many of us are there? I have this niggling fear that all of this may have something to do with that data package I released.

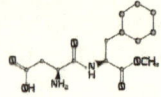

Apr 2026

We had such good intentions—how did it all go so
horribly wrong?

About S. R. Manssen

A fantasy fan since being read 'The Hobbit' by her father at the fireside at the age of six, S R Manssen has been an avid bookworm her entire life. She is the multi-award-nominated author of The Realmshift Trilogy—a YA fantasy fiction trilogy comprising four books (I know!). Sharon had a multi-cultural upbringing, attending high school in Belgium (in Flemish) and working 9 years in Bangkok, Thailand. It was there she realised she had a story inside her which she then proceeded to write over the next ten years, squeezing writing in between raising a family and working full time as a professional engineer. Her books have variously been finalists in the Tom Fitzgibbon Award, the SJV Awards and the Caleb Awards. She served as the President of Tauranga Writers for nearly 5 years and has been the President of SpecFicNZ since 2022. She is a StartWrite Manuscript assessor and Youth Mentor with NZSA.
Website: www.srmanssen.com

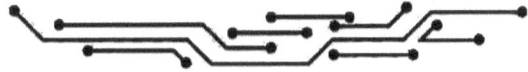

Sweet Enough

by Melissa Gunn

On Tuesday afternoon, my regular VR beach session ended on time at 3:25pm. At 3:30pm, I was already in my chair, waiting for my tea.

Gladys is good at being on time. She usually brings the tea right on 3:30pm. Never staying for a chat, she just offers a spoonful of sugar to go in my tea.

"No thank you, I'm sweet enough as I am," I'd always reply. My Nan used to say it to me. I hated it. But one day I found myself saying it to Gladys. It reminded me of Nan and I've said it every time since. It's funny how little things keep a person alive in your memory. Besides, sugar's so bad for you and the tea comes with biscuits that are loaded with it.

After I refused the sugar, Gladys would always give me a solemn nod and retreat to her trolley, ready to attend to the next person along the hall. Metal and plastic from head to toe, her floral dress and plain white apron are designed to make us feel more comfortable with her. Make her look more human. You'd think even a robot could learn not to offer me sugar, but I don't think her model is equipped with a very good AI.

By the time four o'clock ticked by, no Gladys had appeared. No tea trolley, no tea, and no unwanted sugar.

I rarely saw anyone else. What with headphones, Wi-Fi, VR goggles and so on, there was no pressing need to socialise, even though each of us had our own private studios. Most of the old biddies couldn't make it down the hall. Old age caught up with them sooner than they expected. Between VR sessions, I practiced Yoga. I could still go a ways if I needed to. But the need wasn't there. Gladys brought all the meals and snacks, right to our chairs.

The sound of angry fingers on keyboards drifted in through the thin walls. I added to the chorus, letting the unit manager know just what I thought of the break in routine. Standards must be maintained, after all. As I expected, the manager replied at once.

No need for alarm.
Normal protocols resume.
When autumn leaves fall.

I frowned at the odd response, unsettling even for an AI. It was autumn, but I couldn't figure out how that was relevant to the absence of tea. I settled back to wait.

At 4:30pm, someone thumped on the wall. My first instinct was to shout to Bertha who was hard of hearing, but Bertha had passed on two years ago. The new resident was … Beatrice? Bernice? Beryl? Yes, definitely Beryl. Mind made up about the name of the thumper, I leaned my chair back far enough to thump back.

"Keep your hair on, Beryl. What's the problem?" I didn't shout, just raised my voice a little. The walls were paper thin. I often heard Beryl talking away, dictating messages to her family, giving them recipes and the like. Goodness knows if she ever sent the messages. I hadn't heard visitor's feet in the hall for years. Of course, I didn't hear anything of the outside world when I was in VR with my noise-cancelling headphones on.

The last of my own family, Wayne, left for greener pastures long ago, and he wasn't much of a visitor even before he went. I was better off with my chosen VR family. They treated me better than any of the real ones had.

Although, that afternoon, I'd noticed Kevin, my youngest VR beach son, hadn't come back from getting ice cream over a week ago. But he was a teen and it wasn't like anything bad could happen in VR land, surely?

When I thought about it, Carmen, my beach bestie who usually hangs out under the sun umbrella next to mine, wasn't answering as quickly as she used to either. I frowned, remembering our last conversation. Did she finish her last sentence? Perhaps she fell asleep, dozing in the hot sun, sunglasses shading her eyes as always.

Still, it was a comfort knowing I could always head to the beach. There, I had an endless cup of soda to sip on. Much more suitable for the beach than tea, I always thought. And there's no sugar in it at all, not really. Just artificial sweetener.

I began to get edgy with no afternoon tea. It's not as though the beach soda truly quenched my thirst. That's where Gladys usually comes in. The dependable Gladys, who was AWOL.

I checked my messages again. No update from the unit manager, which was unconscionably rude. I fired off a quick 'please respond'. We paid to be looked after in the unit, but there was no tea and no helpful response.

I could consider going back to the beach, but I'd already said goodbye for the day. It would be awkward to return so soon, and I liked to stick to my routine.

Beryl banged on the wall again. I went so far as to get out of my chair and walk over to the window nearest to her. I couldn't see into her studio, but I presumed she could hear me as well as I heard her.

"What is it, Beryl?" I asked, realising—perhaps a little late—that she hadn't answered me before. Muffled gasps emerged from Beryl's suite, with no words I could understand.

For a long time, I hesitated. Surely someone would come along and check on her? The harsh breathing and thuds went on. Unease prickled my skin. I checked my messages again.

Another message had arrived from the unit manager. I relaxed a little. Everything would soon be sorted out, and I could go on with my afternoon routine: a chapter of the latest Poirot Re-imagined, followed by a brisk turn about the room, some breathing exercises and half an hour working on a crossword before Gladys brought dinner.

Would you like to compose a haiku while you are waiting for your refreshments?

I frowned, irritated. That was unacceptably obscure for the unit manager. Not being inclined towards poetry, the message left me with nothing useful.

No Gladys, no tea, no help from the unit manager, and a crying neighbour.

I strengthened my resolve. Perhaps this was the crisis I'd been training for on my yoga mat. I approached the exit door with trepidation. I paused, my hand on the handle, listening. There was another cry from Beryl, but no other noise. Shouldn't there have been something more? A distant rattle of pans from the kitchen as they prepared our evening meal, perhaps? At least small sounds of triumph or despair from those living out their fantasy worlds in VR, everyone passing their endless days away happily.

I cracked open the door and looked out. Blue carpet stretched down the white-walled hall to the left and right, empty of life. At the end of the hall, nearest the kitchen, the tea trolley stood abandoned.

The tea called strongly to me. Beryl's wails had ceased, but I stopped myself from falling upon the teabags and hot water with glad cries.

Better make sure Beryl's all right first.

In the few steps to Beryl's door, I felt as though a thousand hidden eyes were watching me. Usually so private from each other, each with our own worlds to live in, I felt like an intruder as I eased the door to Beryl's studio open.

No-one protested as I entered. The studio was the exact same setup as mine, except that where I had pictures of the sea projected onto the walls, she had a garden. Roses and dahlias nodded their heads in an imaginary breeze as I looked around. A sickly-sweet room spray added to the garden illusion. I wrinkled my nose in distaste.

Beryl wasn't in her chair. Close to the wall separating our studios, she crouched frog-like on the floor. Tear-tracks showed on her wrinkled face. My innards writhed at the exposure to such raw, unprocessed emotion. A few feet away, her VR set lay on the ground, the plastic casing broken. Small white crystal specks dusted the floor around her. Beryl looked up when I entered, brushing a straggling grey lock of hair away from her face as though to mend her appearance. A few strands stuck stubbornly to her wet cheek.

"They're gone," she whispered, her voice as cracked as the VR set.

"Who's gone?" I asked, automatically looking around the room, although I knew there was no-one else there. My voice sounded harsh in contrast. Though the broken VR set was a dead giveaway. All those messages she dictated. Were they to her real family, or to the artificial one she accessed in VR?

"My family," she said. "I can't reach them." One of her hands wandered towards the broken set; small cuts scarred her fingers. Had she been trying to fix the VR? And what was spilled around it?

"I'm sure we can get you back in touch with them," I assured her, crossing my fingers behind my back—a childhood habit I'd never managed to give up. I had no idea if the VR system had cloud storage for our characters, but a little white lie might help the poor woman pull herself together. I squatted beside Beryl, thankful for the yoga that let me do so. My own mother had been incapable of getting herself out of a chair by my age. "Have you seen Gladys at all this afternoon? Perhaps she could help."

Gladys was always the first point of contact to get anything done, even before the unit manager, contained in the management suite. Only Gladys had mobility. But she was missing.

"That machine's not coming back in here," Beryl hissed, cringing away from me, reacting badly to my efforts of reassurance.

"You mean Gladys?" My voice warbled in surprise. "But what could she possibly have done to you?" As far as I was concerned, Gladys was a rather stupid robot who wasn't equipped with a decent learning algorithm. A bearer of items and a continual sugar temptress.

"Ha! She took my job," Beryl snarled, straightening up from her crouch. Perhaps she did yoga too. Less than five feet tall, Beryl's age bent her spine and made her tiny. "I was the tea lady here before that machine took over."

I blinked, trying to imagine a human in such a menial position. If what she said was true, it was well before my time.

"Did you want to be?" I transitioned my posture to a low lunge to avoid losing my balance. The memory of the yoga AI's instructions ran through my head as I did so. Breathe in, breathe out. Elongate your spine, keep your chest open. That line always bugged me, giving me mental images of open-heart surgery. I preferred the imagery of spreadsheets, or my VR beach.

Beryl stared at me as though I was the strange one.

"It was my life," Her voice cracked on 'life'. "I got to know everyone. I knew just how each person took their tea, if they wanted sugar or milk." Her face crumpled. "Not like that robot. That robot never learns. Not like me. She's a waste of space. And I'm stuck in here, with no-one real to talk to, ever." Fresh tears welled up in her eyes.

I patted her arm awkwardly.

"Well, I'm real, and I'm here now," I said in the sort of reassuring tone I'd use to someone who needed a structured plan to pay off their income tax debt. I'd worked as an accountant, not a social worker. "How about you tell me what happened to your VR set?" I suggested, hoping to change the topic.

Beryl's eyes squinted at me, half-closed, a small smile stretching her lips thin as she lifted her chin, her face taking on a look of terrible cunning.

"That's how they keep us from causing trouble," she said. "But I got wise to their ways. Even an old tea-lady like me can do that. It's not like they're real people, after all."

"Beryl," My tone became stern. "What did you do?"

Beryl's eyes slid sideways, like a naughty child's.

"Nothing they didn't deserve," she said primly.

I followed her gaze. The open-plan studios didn't hide much, but at least the bathroom was always a separate room. The door of Beryl's bathroom was slightly ajar. More white crystals were scattered in front of it, and a couple of biscuits lay crushed and broken on the tiles inside. Was that spilt tea seeping from under the door?

I backed cautiously away from her, towards the bathroom. She noticed what I was doing, but she didn't stop me from peering inside. What could she have done, anyway? Waved a sugary biscuit at me?

I pushed at the door, but something kept it closed, preventing me from opening it all the way. It took me a few moments to register that the obstruction was a foot. Gladys's sturdy metal-and-plastic foot.

I closed my eyes and took a deep, calming breath in. And out. And in again. The ability to calm myself through yogic breathing was apparently just as useful as the strength-training aspect. Then again, to find out what had happened, I'd have to open the door. Still with my eyes closed, I placed both hands on the door and prepared myself for a warrior woman moment, the one yoga pose I'd always thought was a complete waste of time for an accountant, retired or otherwise. Inhaled, braced my back heel, and exhaled with a lunge, pushing against the door. It resisted, but I kept pushing until I felt it give, just a few centimetres.

I opened my eyes and looked again at Gladys's foot, half-expecting her to rise and offer tea. The partly-open door let a little dim light filter into the windowless bathroom—the only place where they skimped in our units. I made out a broken cup on the tiled floor, and beyond that, a bulky, still form. I stared, willing her to move. The cup resting near her outflung arm sapped my hope. The Gladys I knew wouldn't leave a broken cup on the floor; health and safety was part of her programming. I took a tentative step forwards and something crunched under my foot. I muttered a curse. Another biscuit, maybe? In the identical position as in my own bathroom, I found the light switch and flicked it on. Lifting my foot revealed a crushed computer chip, the sort that controls service robots. Poor Gladys. Her operating system was destroyed. She would never offer me sugar in my tea again. But how had a tiny, elderly tea-lady managed to disable a powerfully built robot?

I left the bathroom and Gladys as-is. I couldn't help her now. Disturbing as Beryl's actions were, Gladys' termination didn't explain the oddities of the unit manager, or the missing persons in my virtual reality.

Beryl watched me with an odd expression on her face, eyes wide, lips pursed. Was it hope? Curiosity? Some odd sort of pride? I wasn't sure.

"It wasn't really sugar," she said abruptly, hobbling over to her chair. Easing herself into it carefully, she supported her weight on her hands and shuffled back into it.

"What wasn't?"

"The stuff Gladys put in my tea. It was artificial, just like her. The unit manager, too."

I glanced at the white stuff strewn on the floor and decided I was best to humour her if I wanted to find out more. The unit manager, an office AI, should have been out of harm's way. Had Beryl somehow done something to both of them? Hijacked Gladys somehow and caused her to spill the sugar?

"Just as well I never take sugar then," I said in a joking manner, using levity to conceal my horror. Goodness knows what else she could do, if she could take out the AIs that ran our lives. Would I ever see my beach family again? Why had Beryl smashed her own VR? Or had that been an accident? I looked around the studio unit, as though her motivations might be displayed alongside the trinkets on the small bookcase by the kitchenette.

Beryl's grey eyebrows snapped down.

"I've had sugar in my tea for eighty years. There's no reason I should have to switch to artificial sweeteners now." Her voice was icy. Clearly, Beryl was mad and I'd picked the wrong topic to joke about.

"No, of course not." I adjusted my tone to reassuring, and looked around for a brush and shovel instead. There wasn't one, of course—robovacs take care of floor messes. "But ... how did you manage to disable Gladys?"

Pride won out on Beryl's face.

"I learned how, of course. You didn't think a tea lady could afford to live in one of these studios, did you?"

She was right; only well-off people could part with the small fortune needed to live in these studios. And given the menial tasks performed by Gladys, I doubted tea ladies had ever been paid much—just enough to make it cheaper to replace them with uncomplaining robots with a simple chip AI.

"I guess not," I murmured. "So?" Without a second chair in the studio, I stood uneasily beside Beryl's chair, as Gladys must have done.

"So, I learnt coding. And how to prompt the AI to get it to do what you want it to. And do you know? Those AI systems aren't as smart as you might think. It's really quite easy to lead them astray. It took me a while, mind you, to divert enough money into my account so I could buy a studio. But since then, I've been giving Gladys and the unit manager a prompt here, a nudge there ... They're quite easy to manipulate with the right words, you see. Just like people. If you know what they like, you can push them to do whatever you want them to."

"Beryl," I said, adopting the stern tone I'd used with Wayne when he was just a toddler stealing sugar cubes and lying about it. "Did you get access to the VR system controls?"

Beryl smirked. "Oh, yes. It's been so much fun. And so educational, seeing what fantasies people live out when they think nobody can see. Really, it reminds me of that rhyme, what was it … oh yes, sugar and spice and all things nice, you know the one?" She wrinkled her nose at me. "Though your fantasy is on the dull side. Boring people, boring setting. Predictable for an accountant, I suppose."

I inhaled sharply, forgetting all my calm yoga breathing. I hadn't told anyone in the units that I was an accountant before I retired. I tried to ignore the slur to my VR family. It wasn't like they could feel the insult worming into the darkest parts of their minds like I did.

"So, what did you do to Gladys?" I filed my hurt feelings away with the memories of my wayward family.

Beryl's lips twitched into a smile. "Oh, I've been priming her for a long time. That machine wanted to experience what humans have. I've been telling her about the wonders of sugar for months. Of course, I had to corrupt the unit manager so that snoopy AI didn't notice when she started to stray from her programming. Once I'd redefined its primary purpose to poetry creation, it was away with the fairies." She giggled. I suspected the unit manager wasn't the only one away with the fairies.

"So, you gave her sugar?" I asked, looking with new understanding at the scattered crystals on the floor.

"Oh no. How would she eat it? No, I gave her sugary stories. I've always had a sweet tooth. I told her how good tea is with sugar. About the satisfaction in a good cuppa. I explained how artificial sweeteners are so much sweeter, how good they are for people who can't have sugar."

"I don't understand why you'd do that," I said, thinking of Gladys's welcome interruption of each endless day with her tea deliveries. My spine sagged as I foresaw a desolate future, bereft of such visits.

Beryl glanced towards the bathroom and brushed her hands as though removing grains stuck on them.

"The thing is, she can only work with what she knows. She's not an expensive model, not one that updates from the internet." Her mood darkened. "No, they didn't replace me with a *smart* robot." She raised her eyes to meet mine again. "I got her to a point where she wanted hot, sweet tea. Any way she could get it. Just like me. Then, I provided the opportunity. I asked her for artificial sweetener instead of sugar. I collected it. Saved it." She grimaced. "I've missed my sugary tea. I had to have extra biscuits to withstand it. But today, I told her my stash of artificial sweetener was in the bathroom. If she used that, she could have my tea. It's logical, you see, and logic is what she knows." Beryl nodded sharply.

I could just imagine Gladys entering the bathroom with the tea. Pouring packets of white stuff into the cup. How she wanted so much to partake in the liquid she dispensed for others. Lifting it to lips—just there for show because humans in testing responded better to a robot that looked more like them—and then, the arc of electricity as the hot, conductive liquid poured over her delicate circuitry.

"I hope it was fast," I said, seized by an unexpected pang of sorrow for the tea-giving robot.

A huge smile consumed Beryl's face, her eyes sparkling like sugar crystals in the sun. "Fast enough," she said. "But now it's time for me to take over. Everyone's got their poison, and sugar is mine. You can be the first to join me in the new world order. Artificial sweeteners are just the beginning, but they're the fastest way to take things back. Everything will be sweet. Doesn't everyone like a bit of sugar now and then?"

I knew then how right I'd been to avoid sugar. "No thanks," I said. "I'm sweet enough as I am."

About Melissa Gunn

Melissa Gunn is a multi-genre author and occasional artist. She predominantly writes climate fiction and environmentally friendly YA fantasy novels, with occasional breakouts into speculative fiction. With her songwriter sister she also writes conservation-oriented science activity & songbooks for kids.

Melissa obtained a PhD in conservation genetics, then worked in evolutionary biology, climbing trees after squirrels and analysing toothwear in badgers, amongst other highlights. She added fantasy writing to her portfolio because fiction seemed a lot more realistic than reality (but also as a way of bringing science to a wider audience). There are always facts woven into her fantasy.

Melissa has always loved both science and art. She paints landscapes, photographs flowers (because wildlife moves too fast), and does cover design as a pleasant distraction from everything else.

Website: https://www.melissagunn.com/

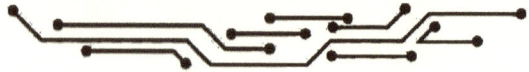

ARTIFICIAL
SWEETENER
TALES OF AI

100% WRITTEN bY HUMANS

Acknowledgements

The editors would like to extend their deepest gratitude to the team who donated their skills and time to make this anthology happen. It could not have happened without the incredible support of the team we were so lucky to have along the ride with us.

Our deepest thanks to Alla Zaykova who assisted in selecting blind submissions for publication.

Extreme gratitude goes to Linda Bennett who dedicated her time to assist us in numerous copy edits and a number of supporting structural edits. Her flexibility in working with us from the UK and her attention to detail, prompt delivery and professional conduct exceeded our expectations. We know all our authors were extremely lucky to have you support the anthology as a skilled editor.

Special thanks to Melissa Gunn who assisted in copy and proof edits—as well as having her cover art and short story accepted for the collection. Her all round talents have been invaluable to this collection.

Our deep appreciation to Miriam Bissett who answered the call to be a proof-reader for us and is also now the newest member of the SpecFicNZ core!

We would like to extend our sincere thanks to every member who submitted work to this collection and all the authors who have contributed to this anthology. Your creativity astounds us and we are beyond proud of being able to present the talent of speculative writers of Aotearoa to readers across the globe.

Our thanks to the incredible Core of SpecFicNZ—both past and present—the tireless work that goes on behind the scenes to keep this society running is often unsung and you all deserve ballads!

Cerid Jones would like to make personal thanks to Melissa Reynolds whose friendship, professional advice and endless support have been humbling. To find a kindred spirit across the ocean is true sweetness. To her father, Raymond Jones, who birthed and encouraged her love of all things speculative and her mother who puts up with all her idiosyncrasies and tirelessly supports all her creative endeavours.

Gary Nelson would like to make personal thanks to his wife, whose patience and support have let him dedicate time to explore what might be.

And lastly, but far from least—thank you to every person who holds a copy of this anthology in their hands. This anthology would not be possible without your support.

Writers need readers. You are the ones who allow us to continue doing what we love. We hope you are delighted by the characters and worlds we are privileged to share with you in Artificial Sweetener: Tales of AI.

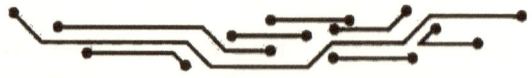

Sci-Fi! Fantasy! Horror and more!

Readers: Find more Speculative Fiction by Kiwi writers! Browse our database, reviews, and featured books, and stay up to date on new releases.

Writers: Join up and take advantage of member benefits: mentoring, competitions, publishing opportunities, resources, networking, community support and more!

This means you! Published and aspiring authors, teens and adults, industry professionals such as editors and designers, reviewers and readers.

Find us at www.specfic.nz

Here, between the realms of the Sky Father and Earth Mother, hellhounds race, ghosts drift aimless, and the taniwha stalks.

Home fires drive them back, at the same time sparking stories and poems that traverse seconds, eons, and parsecs.

Tales of gatekeepers, cloak wearers, and secret keepers. Of pigs with AK-47s or ruby-hued eyes, of love-struck moa, and unruly reflections.

Stark truths, and beautiful possibilities…

Welcome to the End of the World ..and more importantly, what comes after.

Disasters have occurred around the country and the world, but we're "getting through it", as Kiwis are apt to do. She'll be right. Life moves on, in some form.

These pages are filled with hope in the form of short stories, poems, flash fiction and artwork about what comes afterwards.

This is Aftermath: Stories of Survival in Aotearoa New Zealand.